Hutari

Scion of Prophet and Crown Book 1

Donovan M. Neal

TornVeil

Contents

Hutari

Scion of Prophet and Crown

Book 1

By

Donovan M. Neal

Dedication

I dedicate this book to those who dare to dream and see it through to completion. May your imagination ever lead you to new realms.

Acknowledgments

To the Lord Jesus Christ, who loves me.

To my children Candace, Christopher, and Alexander—you can do great things!

To the authors, comic books, artists, and writers who have come before, and who unknowingly have breathed on the embers of my imagination.

To all my beta readers and friends who shared both critiques and encouragement.

To my beloved wife Nettie, you are the color of my world.

May God truly bless you all.

Prologue

The Provenance of Gods and Men

M'Msee sat in the storyteller's chair as he had every spring equinox for nearly ten centuries. At this spot within the city's center, he would tell the story of the creation and of the four clans. As has been the custom for many years, the clans would bring their youth to him to initiate their schooling. An education that would begin by hearing the story that underpinned all Bussar culture and thought: the Provenance of Gods and men.

Parents slowly gathered around him and set their children in a semi-circle, and many sat with their young ones to listen as well. And the crowds filled the sitting rocks and trees with people who quieted themselves to hear the eldest of them all speak.

And M'Msee, seeing all had gathered, opened his mouth to begin the tale. "Akuma...," he said. "... did not know that his son would one day seek to kill him. For which parent among you... no, which father would ever conceive love lost between himself and his son? But let me not rush to tell of such troubles before the time. Much transpired before Enkai and Hesphus grew at odds with one another. For, there was a time children even before the creation of men, that the Kifu did not roam Tanara and was not always as he is now. Even the walking dead was once loved by another, even loved by the father of all---Akuma. And why would not Akuma love his beloved son?"

The grouping of children sat around their teacher and looked at him with their gazes locked on M'Msee's face. Their attention fixed on his every word, while little ones sat wide-eyed, and some held their mouths open and fidgeting, while a few propped their chins with their hands, waiting for the clan's greatest storyteller to continue.

"But why, Wisdom? Why did the son want to destroy his father?" said a boy.

One child in attendance, near to M'Msee, held his head tucked down and his arms folded across his chest, and muttered, "I would kill my father if I could." And M'Msee heard the boy's murmur and his face became downcast as he overheard the words and spoke.

"What is your name, child?"

The young boy looked up. His eyes bore the hurt of a child withered from a drought of love. And his face gave no hint of a smile but only a stoic seriousness untoward for a child who could not be over ten years of age.

"I am Kemet, son of Saifet."

"From which clan do you come, my son?" said M'Msee.

"I am from the northern watch, Wisdom."

M'Msee nodded and motioned for the boy to come and sit next to him in the storyteller's chair.

The other children immediately wailed and vocalized their disapproval. "I want to sit next to you!" Some raised their hands and waved them wildly to draw the old man's attention. But M'Msee held his peace and looked at the boy, who reluctantly made his way through several disappointed and envious children to sit next to the elder.

M'Msee placed his hands lovingly on the boy's small cheeks and felt their warmth. He noted the bruising around his neck and spoke. "Did your father do this to you?"

Kemet sheepishly turned his eyes away from M'Msee and replied, "Yes, wisdom."

M'Msee inhaled knowingly and then sighed aloud. "Know that I will see that he will not hit you again and though the bruising will heal. You must be careful to not let your heart become poisoned or Enkai would have you, and that cannot be. Listen to my story, Kemet, and learn. Learn why you cannot allow the heart poison inside of you to take root and fester. Take heed, child, and mark my words."

Kemet said nothing, but looked at the old man sheepishly and gave an affirming nod. M'Msee then turned to all that sat before him and said. "All of you hear me. What is the first lesson all must learn?"

Various children whisked their hands wildly into the air for M'Msee to call on them. The old sage pointed to a young girl. And she stood upon his acknowledgment and spoke. "Wisdom is the principal thing; therefore get wisdom: and with all thy getting, get understanding."

"That is very good young lady. Well said indeed. Now, all of you; listen to wisdom and get understanding. And hear the tale of creation from the Book of Provenance. For, it is written that in the beginning, when Akuma had finished his making of the sky, and the sky above the sky. He made one sky dark and set lesser lights to watch us while we slept. He then made the greater light of the day and released it to run its course through the lower sky. But of all that he made, he was most proud of the two children he made. Twin boys to which he would teach his wisdom so that in time they too might make lights and skies above skies. And he named them Hesphus and Enkai."

Some children hissed when they heard the name Enkai, and M'Msee lifted his hands to quiet them.

"Did Akuma have a mommy and daddy wisdom?" asked one of the seated children.

More adults gathered to hear the four clans' oldest member recall the story of the Book of Provenance. Many took their seats, and the seated crowd grew even larger. M'Msee waited for the new arrivals to be settled, and he continued.

"No, child. Akuma was the first, and it is from him that all things were made. And without him, nothing could be made. But Akuma wanted to share who he was and, in the making of his sons, sought to create a family that would one day fill the night sky and the blue sky. And he charged his two sons to learn, even as you learn now, to sit at his feet and be tutored. To be taught how to handle the most precious of gifts, he could ever give them, and they were to share what they had learned with those that would follow: the gift of everlasting life. But to do this, the boys needed to also understand death. So, making sure that they schooled themselves, Akuma created a book that contained the sum of all his wisdom and gave it to both of them to study."

"And he left them for a season to prepare them for their lessons that upon his return, each might make his first living thing."

"But time passed, and Akuma did not return right when the boys thought and so alone and without their father; Hesphus determined to continue in his studies as his father had charged them. But Enkai did not do so. He set aside his studies, believing he had learned enough, and took it upon himself to create before the time. Enkai was determined to create a realm and life apart from his father. Enkai then left Hesphus to his studies and walked a distance into the great void and there created land in between light and darkness: a realm of eternal twilight. And Enkai named the place the Duat. And he placed the realm next to his fathers, and thinking to impress him, he took dust from his skin and from it fashioned a people as countless as the snow in the Whitelands and he breathed into them and gave them his life and he named them the Nephthys."

"And they were indeed beautiful to behold and powerful beyond the measure of any mortal man, and each was as different to one another as you are to me. And they towered and walked through the Duat and brought a semblance of light to its dimness, and for a time, all was good for Enkai and his newly created children."

"But Enkai was not skilled in creating life and it was soon revealed that the children lacked food to sustain themselves. And though the light of life within them burned bright, it burned so quickly from within that they became disfigured, and in time, their bodies grew deformed. And some hungered so that they even turned on themselves to consume each other's flesh. But once filled with new life, they returned to their former beauty and power. But when famished, they were like the beasts of the field and would lose all sense of control. And Enkai did all that he could to keep them fed, but it was beyond even him to satisfy their incessant hunger for life. And they all became mad such that they even turned on him to consume him alive and take the power that the father Akuma had placed within him. Enkai was then forced to fight with his children to stay alive and became trapped in the Duat and he could not leave lest the Nephthys escape and consume his brother."

"Hesphus, who had continued in his study of wisdom, had finished his lesson and, when checking on his brother's progress, noted his sibling was nowhere to be found within the celestial realm that Akuma had created. And so, he looked into the distance of the Void, and he saw that a new plane existed but one not made by his father. Hesphus then called out to Enkai and noted a door to this new realm and as he went to open it, he heard his brother call out to him from within and warn him away and to not open the door. And Hesphus, seeking to save his brother and knowing that his father worked behind the veil of existence, summoned him so that he might save his brother from the creatures he had made. And Akuma heard his son's prayer and returned as bidden and when he had crossed from one existence to this one, he knew what his son Enkai had done. Akuma then entered the Duat and rescued Enkai from the dark realm and fended off the Nephthys and saved his son alive. And he sealed the Nephthys within the Duat so that they could not escape."

M'Msee paused to see if his audience was paying attention. And the crowd of hundreds was silent as many adults and children sat at his feet, while some leaned or sat upon rocks, and others sat in tree branches to get a view, and his story enchanted all.

"Why did Enkai create the Duat, Wisdom?" said a young mother seated with her daughter and son.

"That is a good question, but the books are silent and leave us to our thoughts on the matter. But though he was a Demigod, Enkai seemed to have fallen to the most common of faults that besiege us men: pride. For he thought more highly of himself than he should. And this led to his thinking that he could do what Akuma could do. But tell me... have *you* ever wanted to impress... have *you* ever wanted to make others think more favorably of you?"

One young girl remarked, "One time when the children of my village went to play kicker, I wanted them to pick me so badly that I tried showing them how good I could kick that when I tried to kick the ball, I missed it and ended up falling and breaking my foot."

"Ah, said M'Msee. And did you feel foolish afterward?"

"I did. But mammae told me I do not have to be picked for everything and that I must be careful to be influenced by the good and never to show off."

"Your mammae has taught you well and has passed on to you wisdom from Akuma. For Akuma would not seek for you to impress. No, Akuma would have you be who he made you to be. Do you think you can do this, child?"

The girl smiled widely and nodded.

"Good," said M'Msee. The old man then looked down at Kemet to see how he fared and noted that the boy's eyes drew to someone in the distance. And M'Msee followed his gaze to a man who leaned against a tree.

M'Msee whispers to him, "Is that your father?"

Kemet nodded.

M'Msee smiled, "Have no fear, child. For Wisdom will see him soon." Kemet smiled slightly, and he scooted closer to M'Msee.

"Now, where was I?" said M'Msee.

"Akuma rescued Enkai!" said a girl.

"Ah yes! Thank you! Yes, so Akuma rescued Enkai from his creations and sealed the Nephthys in the Duat so that they could not escape. Now, some have, over the years, asked why Akuma did not destroy Enkai's creation. But the past fathers tell us from Ambilikie that Akuma prefers not to destroy. So, he devised a plan to heal the creation his son had made in his hubris. Akuma then turned to Hesphus, who had obeyed his father and who completed his father's teachings as instructed and he took his obedient son, and together they crafted the physical realm, and our world and Akuma allowed his son Hesphus to name it. And Hesphus named it Tanara."

"Enkai watched his father and brother make Tanara and it was even more beautiful than the realm he had created alone. And Akuma allowed Hesphus to fill Tanara with all manner of birds, fish, plants, and animals. And Akuma was pleased, for Hesphus was wise in how he crafted, and he made Tanara thrive with life so that it could sustain all that he created. Thus, Hesphus set all living things in place as his father and his brother watched. And Hesphus fashioned his designs with wisdom so that all things held purpose and the whole of nature was in balance and harmony prevailed. And the magic of Tanara was strong, and it held."

"Akuma, then seeing all that his son had made, took from the ground dirt and with it fashioned a creature he called a man. And with this vessel, Akuma gave life from his own breath, and he became a living soul. And no creation of Hesphus or Enkai, save the two brothers, had held the life force of Akuma himself."

"Akuma then assured Enkai that the man he had created held the key to removing the pollution from the realm Enkai had made. And that when men's studies were complete, men would ascend and take their place next to him and his brother, and together they would heal the Nephthys and free them from the Duat that all of creation might be whole and one, and there be no more division between the realms."

"Did Hesphus love Enkai, Wisdom?" said a child.

"Oh yes, yes he did, little one. In fact, it was Hesphus' love for his brother that made him search for him when he realized he was absent from his studies, and it was the love of Akuma that caused Enkai's father to rescue him from the Duat. Hesphus loved Enkai very much. But alas, Enkai did not return his brother's affection. For when Akuma made Tanara and placed the man to live in it; he gave Hesphus dominion over the entire material realm of men and to steward all of Tanara. And for this act, Enkai's eye became evil toward his brother and his father."

"So, Akuma, gave Hesphus *the entire world* of Tanara teacher?"

"All of it, child; from the great ocean depths to the flowers that sprinkle the prairie grass. Hesphus was meant to walk among us and to teach us the wisdom of Akuma and the laws of life and death: all that we too might one day create, even as Akuma, Hesphus, and Enkai. You see, little ones...." M'Msee then waved his hand to the entire crowd. "You were destined to create stars."

Faces of many in the audience grew wide with wonder and oohs and aahs ushered from those in earshot.

"But how were men supposed to cleanse the Duat?" said a teenager who was in the group and listened.

"Well, child, the tales and books do not share all things. What we know is that Akuma planned to sleep and allow himself to be seeded in Tanara and to marinate every blade of grass with his life. And that in time, when men were ready, Akuma's power would saturate all of Tanara, and when his power concentrated enough in one man he would ascend, and that man then would one day be able to help lead others so that all might one day ascend to even be like him and to bridge Akuma's home, the Duat, and Tanara. So Akuma shared his plan with his sons and commanded them to watch over their respective realms until his return. Thus, Akuma charged Enkai to watch over the seal Akuma had placed over the Duat lest Enkai's children flood their home and Tanara. Akuma also charged Hesphus to nurture and keep watch over Tanara so that in time, men might ascend without fear of the children of the Duat."

"Thus, Akuma adjured his sons to pledge their loyalty to his plan, as he would be gone much longer than before. And because Hesphus loved his father and wanted to see the Duat people freed of their hunger for life and desired to see his brother's plan to create life realized. He pledged to continue his studies while his father was away and watch over Tanara and shepherd men to learn of his father's ways and to ascend."

"But Enkai became angered over his father's plan. A plan that would have him wait when he believed that there was another way... a faster way to save his creation. Thinking he knew best; he turned his back on his father and brother and left Akuma and Hesphus to their plans and broke the seal of the Duat and returned to the home of his children."

"Akuma, realizing what Enkai had done, warned Hesphus that with the seal broken he must leave to seed Tanara immediately, for the Nephthys would not be contained within the Duat, and their unchecked hunger would consume all of existence. Akuma then created a barrier between the celestial realm and the material of Tanara so that bridging the two planes became impassable; save by Hesphus or a work of his hands. He then gave one last command to his son to create a being of eternal life and to send him to Tanara. This being would be the match to ignite men's power to ascend. He then gave his son a hammer that he might forge such a being from the celestial rock of Aaru: the floor of existence."

"Hesphus did as his father commanded and went to the forge of his father and fashioned a man unlike all others from the mantle of Aaru and anointed his creation's head with spittle from his mouth and breathed into him and the man became a living soul unlike any that came before him. And Hesphus named him Hutari, meaning the eternal one. And he took the man and taught him as much as he could about the history of his father, him and his brother, and of the knowledge of life and death."

"Akuma, meanwhile, prepared himself a chamber to sleep so that he might disperse his essence throughout the material plane. And he set himself within and allowed himself to sleep so that his body might dissolve into the world of Tanara. And Hesphus brought his son Hutari to see Akuma before the father of all life departed and fell into his great sleep for a season. Akuma smiled at his son's son, even as he transferred his life force into Tanara and he fell asleep, only to disappear as he smiled at Hutari."

"And while Hesphus and his son hovered over the coffin-like chamber of Akuma. Enkai returned alive from the Duat, and it soused him in dark magic, which Hesphus recognized from his studies as the power of Death."

"Now children, Ambilikie recorded the words told to him by the Hutari and he shared what the brothers spoke between them, and Ambilikie wrote all that Hutari told him."

M'Msee then opened a leather pouch that held a long, well-preserved parchment and, upon seeing the ancient book, all bowed their heads in reverence at its opening and even as he read aloud from a scroll. And the words from the scroll were on this wise.

The Book of Provenance
Book One: Scroll of the Beginning
Written by my hand, Ambilikie Armor bearer to his
Lord Hutari

"Father already begins his journey to walk in the lands between. I have come from the Nether realm of Duat and come with lessons attained outside the schooling of our father. Did I not tell you he held back from us, held back from me? He has lied Hesphus, for there is indeed another way to rescue my children from the plague of hunger that ravishes my house."

"What way would this be, brother? What way would you take other than that which Father leads? Know ye not that departing from wisdom is to embrace foolishness? Be wary, we cannot break the commands of wisdom or wisdom will break us."

Enkai replied, "Nay, brother, I have learned the knowledge of death and life. And have gleaned from the study of my children that there is indeed another way: a way to transfer the life of another. Now join me, and we can take the life of Father even now as he embarks on his sleep and before all of his magic dispels away to the realm of men and let us transplant it within the Duat and give life evermore to my seed. Then when he is gone, we can rule and create for ourselves heavens and earth beyond measure, and nothing that we imagine shall be restrained from us."

Enkai then set himself between the coffin of his father and the Hutari who hid behind it, watching and listening. "You are mad Enkai. The abortion of one life does not allow life..."

Enkai then noticed movement from behind his brother and the father's tomb and spoke. "What moves behind you? I sense a presence that emanates the life spark of celestial life... life like us. What have you done? Let me see!" And Enkai went to move past Hesphus, but Hesphus stood against him to bar his path and replied.

"No, brother... even as you have created, so to have I."

Enkai frowned and scowled at the man-child that gleamed with light from the eternal life of the forge of Akuma and his face glowered in contempt even as he spoke. "But this creature contains the life given us by our father... how..." And Enkai saw the hammer of his father in Hesphus' hand and knew at that moment that his father had shown his brother the secret of forging eternal life and he became wroth and fueled by jealousy for the love that Akuma showed his brother and covetous to take the newly formed eternal that he might feed him to his children that they might live.

"It does not matter," said Enkai. He lifted his eyes as he watched the golden embers of Akuma's magic float into the Tanaric realm below. "I need but one life to enact my plan. Give this creature to me, this child, you have produced and create another if you must but give it to me or move aside and I will take the last of Father's virtue."

Hesphus balked and replied. "I will do no such thing. Nor will your plan to take father's life bear fruit. I love you. But will not allow this thing. You have already, by your traffics brought the shadow of death from Duat into the celestial realm. Leave these schemes within the Duat and do not pollute the Aaru further by bringing death here."

Enkai nodded. "Then it is decided... you must die."

Enkai then attacked his brother, and the two fought whilst the Hutari looked on, and Hesphus did all he could to prevent his brother from approaching Akuma and the Hutari. And the titans clashed and Hesphus beat his brother back with the Hammer of Akuma such that the originator of death could not prevail. And when Enkai knew he could not defeat his brother, and as he watched the remnant of Akuma's life force slip away, escaping to seed the world of men. He opened the door to the Duat.

"No!" screamed Hesphus. "Do not do this!"

But Enkai would not heed and replied, "There can only be one realm... my realm."

And he unleashed the Nephthys from the Duat, and the scourge of his children flooded the gate into the celestial realm of Aaru like a rushing tide. And the creatures ran to consume Hesphus and the Hutari for they hungered for all life save Enkai's, who was their master.

And Hesphus valiantly battled to keep the flood of the Nephthys at bay. But their numbers were as the sand on the shore and he could not prevail. And seeing his cause lost, he raced to the Hutari before the Nephthys could consume him alive and took the man into the palm of his hand, and cast him down into Tanara. And the man fell like lightning into the earth.

"Nooo!" Enkai screamed.

And as the Hutari descended to the earth, and the celestial skies above closed behind him, he watched as his creator and father Hesphus, was swarmed alive by the Nephthys, and the son of Akuma fell to his knees and the hammer of Akuma dropped from his hand and fell to the celestial floor. And the stars slowly concealed his fate from Hutari behind the expanse of night. But not before he bore witness to the ultimate betrayal of Enkai.

Enkai waved his hand, and the swarm of Nephthys released him, and the newly titled God of Death stood over this brother who had earlier saved him from his creation and spoke these words.

"Father has robbed me of my children's restoration; you also have robbed me by denying me the life of thy son. But know that I will not rest until I have stolen eternity from his breast and with it give eternal life and rest to my children. But first I will take from you life itself, and though father has sought to confine me and my kind to the realm celestial. Know that his plan will not stop or stymie me. For you, dear brother will be my key to unlocking the realm of men. You, their creator, will be their scourge, and through you will they know the fear of death and thus, the fear of me."

"And Enkai then took the hammer of Akuma that was dropped by his brother and with it smote him that he died. And the life force of Hesphus seeped from his heart and joined to Enkai's and the power of Hesphus made the demigod even more powerful than Akuma himself had ever planned."

And Enkai's newfound power allowed him to tether the life of Hesphus that the body of Hesphus moved at the thought of Enkai and he controlled it. And with the shell of his brother now empty of life. He took one of the Nephthys and placed it inside the corpse of his brother and then took the body and flung it down into the realm of men. And it was the last thing the Hutari ever saw of the home he escaped before he smote the earth of Tanara.

And because Akuma's magic allowed his son Hesphus to breach the barrier between the celestial and the physical; Hesphus' descending body passed unharmed, shielding the Nephthys within and the leech-like creature entered the world of men and plummeted into the navel of the world. And Enkai animated it from afar and when the demigod's corpse arose from the crater of its descent, the body of Hesphus walked the earth at the command of Enkai; and because the Nephthys lived within; it drained all life around it. And in time men called the corpse of Hesphus the Kifu, meaning walking death. And all bowed to the command of Enkai, who spoke through the Kifu.

And lo in the first age of men, Enkai promised men power and life eternal if they worked to bring him the Hutari, and many in their folly also desired the power of death, and the promise of eternal life, and rallied to his cause to find the Hutari for Enkai. And in time, the Kifu marched across Tanara unstopped, dragging behind him a million corpses of beasts and men to find the Hutari. It was said that the Kifu could even walk on the ocean floor. Entire kingdoms fell under the darkness of death and were decimated in its wake. And men suffered because Enkai used the Kifu to hunt the Hutari. But Akuma-be-praised, the Hutari son of Hesphus had also survived his fall from the realm of Aaru and he rallied brave men and kings to his side, and they met the Kifu and his armies on the field of battle beneath the great mount of Moshek. And the two armies fought and for forty days and nights their battle cleaved the land into great continents such that they pushed away from one another so that they are now established in their bounds.

But alas, on the cusp of victory and for reasons unknown to those that observed the battle; the Hutari did not destroy the Kifu but sealed him deep within the dark places of the earth away from the living.

And Ambilikie, his armor-bearer, saw the Hutari shutter the Kifu away from men, hoping it would forever remain hidden from the eyes of the curious who might, in their foolishness, ever rouse again such a power and release the dead celestial once more. Many wondered about the defeat of the Kifu and some left Hutari not understanding why he did not destroy the Kifu.

Many have supposed that he could not stand the thought of destroying his father. And that he hoped men would one day ascend and realize Akuma's dream and save even the Kifu from the grip of eternal death. But none knows for sure, save the Hutari himself.

The Hutari then left men to themselves with the promise that if the Kifu would rise again, he too would rise to meet the threat. For the power to stop the Kifu drained even him, so he took his leave of armies and kings to recoup and to teach men so that they might one day realize the dream of Akuma and ascend. And men, over time, forgot who the Hutari was, and his identity has become lost to the annals of time, and his whereabouts no longer known.

But one man—Ambilikie seeing the Hutari had not destroyed the Kifu and that the capture of Akuma's life force was still possible saw a weakness of the Kifu during the battle between his master and the walking death and wrote the words in a book: the Book of Kings. And though we know he wrote the book; none have ever read it as it has been lost through time. But fear not my children, for Akuma's plan even now has borne fruit, for magic has seeped into the land that some of our kind have done wonders. The marvels of the deep life of Akuma echo throughout the land, and be diligent younglings, for one must study hard to capture it. And who knows if perhaps *you* will help us all one day to ascend and bring Akuma's hope to life!

"For, the voice of Akuma speaks to those with ears to hear and know that the Father Akuma will even give visions to you if you will not harden your heart and seek to hear his voice. And what do we call these men?"

"Seers!" many yelled.

"Yes, Seers. Perhaps you can be a Seer and help preserve the knowledge given by Ambilikie. And one day find the Hutari and destroy the Kifu or even restore him alive again as our creator. Strive to listen to wisdom children. Listen to your parents and gather knowledge as you would gather wood for a fire or stones to build. Gather knowledge that one day we might ascend and for the Hutari and the Ascendant One to save us all and release men to be what Akuma has desired."

"For it is said that in the third age of humankind, the Kifu will escape and lay waste to the kingdoms of men, but the Hutari and the Ascendant One will stand against him and bring the cycle of cataclysms to an end."

"So, as I charge you before all the elders of the center city. Will you seek wisdom, children?"

"Yes, Wisdom!" many yelled in unison.

M'Msee smiled and nodded. "I have found you to be hearers. Now, go from this place and practice to always show that you are quick to hear and slow to speak, that Akuma's word might live in you. Go, and may the grace of Akuma go with you."

The entire seated congregation of children and adults rose from the grass and many parents clapped at the hearing of the tale by the chief elder of the four clans. M'Msee smiled as parents hugged their children, and some came to thank him for taking his time to teach them the histories of their people.

Kemet then also turned to shuffle away when M'Msee grabbed him and stopped him. "You, lad, will take me to meet your father."

Kemet nodded and helped M'Msee down from his seating place and allowed the old man to lean upon him as he balanced himself with his cane, and the two walked slowly towards Kemet's father who eyed that the elder of the four clans was coming with his son towards him. He quickly straightened himself and stood up tall as his son and M'Msee approached him.

"Wisdom," said Saifet. "Thank you for taking the time to teach my son."

M'Msee nodded. "It would seem that I must also teach his father."

Saifet looked flummoxed and appeared unsure of how to respond, but tried nonetheless. "I am sorry, but I do not understand wisdom."

"No," said M'Msee, it is clear you do not. Did you hear the lesson today? "

"I did, teacher. And I have remembered it even from my youth."

"Why then, did you strike your son and not discipline him so as to keep him in the way? To strike him as to leave such bruises... this is not the way of someone who has learned the wisdom of this story."

"The boy is stubborn Wisdom. He will not heed..."

"No, Saifet, that is not the way of Akuma to accost the lesser. Have you ever considered that perhaps with your actions you have bruised the Ascended One? Has it been lost on you that we are all created from the loving mind of Akuma, even this young one here? Would you dare strike Akuma this way?"

"No, of course not teacher, never!"

"No, Akuma would cause your life to cease." M'Msee then stood up straight as if he had no gait and he took Saifet by the arm and squeezed it so that Saifet winced. "Do not touch the boy in such a manner again. If you do, I will come for you. Do you understand me?"

Saifet nodded, and M'Msee released him. "You will come once a week to see the King and several of the men who have already raised men. There, you will learn the skills needed to deal with the lad's stubbornness... and your own. If you do not appear, I will summon the Ufami to drag you to their court. Do you understand?"

Saifet nodded and replied hesitatingly, "But Wisdom the Ufami do not deal in the affairs of men." M'Msee turned to him and replied. "No, no, they do not. But I am Wisdom and am unlike other men. Therefore, if I call upon them and they come. Would you not be wise to fear and take heed? I ask again. Do you understand?"

Saifet nodded. "Good," said M'Msee. He then turned to Kemet and spoke firmly to him. "Do not think that because wisdom has disciplined your father that he is to be mocked. He is not. He has much to teach you, that is good and, with further training, will teach you even more. You will heed his word without disrespect or willfulness. You must one day face the wilderness, and while your father might leave a bruise, the wilderness will take your life. Obey him. Do you understand?"

Kemet nodded. "Good. Now the two of you be off with you, for I am tired, but know Saifet that I will come to visit you in four days' time. I will know if my words have been heeded."

Saifet bowed in acknowledgment and placed his arm around his son, and the two walked quietly away.

M'Msee watched them depart, angry over what the father had done to his son, but angrier at himself that he allowed his ire to reveal his true strength. The old man sighed as he watched many of the townspeople depart. He could not recount how many centuries now he had told that story. How repeatedly, each year, people gathered to hear it, and with each telling it saddened him the more. It was an unpleasant experience to re-live. Unpleasant indeed save the children. They always brought a smile to his face, and their innocence was a bright reminder of home.

He missed Aaru.

Missed the words of his father and hated Enkai for robbing him of so much. Nonalive, nor those that existed before, could ever fully know his grief in living in a world made by his father Hesphus, but the same, having fallen so short of what his father and Akuma intended. M'Msee knew that many of the clan's people thought his tales were just fables to give lessons to children. But such was the way of men to forget the ways of old.

He missed Ambilikie, missed the faithfulness of his servant and their friendship. A mortal man who stood by him even as he fought against Tanara's creator and who never wavered in his loving faithfulness; even when he could not bring himself to smite the final blow that would have ended Hesphus' damnable immortal life: a life puppeteered by Enkai from afar. For, despite the destruction and death that his father's blighted body wrought. He simply could not bring himself to kill him.

Not after he learned the truth.

Thought upon thought plagued him as he replayed his actions all those centuries ago. His mind wearied and tortured with questions on if he had done the right thing to allow the Kifu to live. M'Msee reflected on his ancient past and remembered raising his sword to cut the celestial tether that would kill the Nephthys within the chest of Hesphus and end his father's life only at the end to have Hesphus speak to him in his voice... not Enkai's, pleading with his son to kill him.

M'Msee heard his father's voice, and he paused from destroying him, for at that moment he was not the walking dead but his beloved father. A father who was still alive despite what he had seen as he plummeted from Aaru. Hesphus was still alive and yet able to wrestle against Enkai's control, somehow battling against the schemes and magics of his brother. And in that moment of revelation, it was then that he lowered his sword and vowed to find a solution to release Hesphus' from the prison of his own body: to rescue his father from the evil curse Enkai had laid upon him and restore the celestial realm of Aaru to the glory it held before the Nephthys. His hope now restored by the hearing of his father's voice, he vowed he would see Akuma's and his father's dreams come true.

But to do so he needed to study, to remove himself from the petty aspirations of men who would have him lead nations or wage war or covet land and wealth. For such things were meaningless to a being that could live forever and had come from the celestial realm only to be stranded on Tanara. Only wisdom mattered; only wisdom could undo the work of Enkai. All else was dross in comparison.

But men were not meant to live alone. Not even one such as him. So, in time, this storyteller chose to love and chose once again engage with men. But he did not foresee the loss of those he loved, and their passing into death affect him so. And the years of seeing those that he loved, age and die, stretched him: stretched him as a thinning parchment ready to tear. For such grief was never in the design of Akuma. And the death of each loved one only hardened his resolve to see death itself undone.

Akuma's plan required patience, but even he grudgingly admitted to himself that the years of waiting for Akuma's plan to reveal itself wore on him... not from physical exhaustion; for he held within his breast the forged immortal heart given by Hesphus. But with each passing year, the Kifu's imprisonment took virtue from him.

He was old beyond the years of men and the power to contain the Kifu siphoned his strength ever so slowly. He was immortal but to keep the Kifu at bay aged him like a normal man. A price he willingly paid for choosing to find a solution other than the complete annihilation of his father. He didn't mind. Aging allowed him to blend in; allowed men to forget who he was. And before any grew wise to his true nature, they passed the way of all men on the earth: to the grave. But this was a dangerous game, M'Msee realized. For Enkai still hunted him, and he could feel something was changing: something both in him and something in men... even something in the Kifu. M'Msee felt the weight on his shoulders. A burden he bore alone to be the sole celestial, keeping the end of all things at bay. A weight none in the world could know save the Hutari: a name and title he had abandoned lifetimes ago.

M'Msee felt a tug on his robes that broke him from his ruminations, and he looked down to see a young girl with bronze skin and ivory-colored teeth smiling up at him with her arms raised high and beckoning him to lift her.

"Mudiwa!" he spoke happily, and he picked the child up into his bosom and hugged her. And he allowed her hair to brush against his aged cheek, and her smell was like jasmine.

"You know you are my favorite child, young lady. It is always a pleasure to see you."

She tilted her head and smirked. "M'Msee, you say that every child is your favorite child."

M'Msee thought for a moment about how sharp her wit was for such a girl her age and replied. "Well, that is true, but today, you are my favorite."

She laughed and replied. "M'Msee, you said you would take me to see your butterfly sanctuary. Will you take me now?"

M'Msee set the girl back down and extended his hand. "How could I ever deny such a wonderful smile? It would be my honor, little one. Come, butterflies would be a welcome reprieve from the thoughts of this old man."

M'Msee then leaned upon his staff and the young girl and the aged one men once called the Hutari gingerly walked hand in hand to see the wonders of caterpillars break from their cocoons.

End of Prologue

Chapter One

Heralds of The Coming Storm

B utterflies are never thought to be the harbinger of the end of the world. But M'Msee remembered the words of a now-dead seer that when the wings of the K'olohis's were once more seen in the land, the end would soon follow. Their migration followed the magic that Akuma left in Tanara. So M'Msee tended to his butterfly sanctuary, as was his task from the days of old. and carefully trimmed the white flower petals that one day would give the K'olohi butterflies rest for their yellow and black wings. A rare butterfly that would reproduce and pollinate the Ahkasi flowers that bloom every five hundred years. And for three hundred years M'Msee had tended the sanctuary waiting for the K'olohis to once more grace the Bussar people and to prepare him for what he knew would inevitably come. The return of his father the Kifu.

The butterflies' migratory pattern took them all over the world, but it is said that they originated in the World's Navel, a crater on an isle in the center of the great sea.

And though they traveled across the world, the ancestors said that it was only their arrival in the land of Bussar that would signal a portent of things to come; of events destined to shape nations and mankind itself. M'Msee sighed within himself as he cut the stems of the flowers. For the K'olohi butterfly had not been seen on the continent in over four hundred years and M'Msee was the only one long-lived enough to know what they looked like. And so, he waited for their arrival that with their return perhaps his time upon Tanara would someday end and he would be released to die and his spirit allowed to return to his home in Aaru.

And yet this day began as any other day. Uneventful, and quiet until he went to prune a white Emberbloom branch, and the beautiful wings of a single K'olohi settled upon a flower petal in front of him. His eyes widened, and he reached to touch the insect, and it lifted itself into the air and M'Msee followed the creature with his eyes as it left the flower and floated higher and his eyes followed and widened in amazement as a flock of the butterflies graced the domed ceiling of the sanctuary. Hundreds fluttered in a circular fashion above his hoary head, and he lifted his hand to his mouth and gasped as he marveled at the sight.

His gawking was only interrupted by the panting voice of Nina: sister to the queen Mudiwa.

"Wisdom, you are needed in the king's chamber. Mudiwa has given birth.'

M'Msee did not immediately acknowledge the ancient title of respect the Bussar gave the Seers of their people. Nor did he face her, but continued his wide-eyed gaze upon the rare butterflies whose migration had led them after five hundred years to Bussar...and to him.

But Nina did not move but waited respectfully and patiently for M'Msee to acknowledge her presence. The hoary man sighed, and his face tightened in a disapproving frown, and spoke. "Away from me, child, do you not see me attending to the gardens? Why do you bother this old man with work that has for generations been done by the midwives of the land? For if she has given birth, what need is there for a Seer?"

Nina was not slow to answer the sage and replied. "Because, Seer, the child's mshahara will not allow itself to be cut from its mother. And King Haidar himself has requested your presence."

M'Msee nodded in understanding the lifeline between a baby and its mother must be severed in a healthy birth. For the blood cord to resist cutting was not a good sign for the child. M'Msee reached for his walking stick and gestured to the young woman to support him. She dutifully grabbed his arm to help him walk and he leaned upon her as they hastily made their way out of the butterfly sanctuary and as fast as his thousand-year-old legs would allow. M'Msee noticed Nina looking up at the circle of yellow and black butterflies that flew overhead as they departed, and she spoke. "M'Msee, I have never seen this butterfly. Is this normal?"

"No, child, it has not been seen in many a lifetime. Take note, for before you fly the K'olohi and with their arrival, a great season of change for our people. For when they are gone...no one alive will ever see them again."

He turned once more as he exited the sanctuary and frowned at the fluttering butterflies, for upon their last sighting much of what was originally Bussar was destroyed in his battle with the Kifu and had fallen into the sea.

They hurried to the center of the village. Many smiled and even more bowed upon seeing M'Msee; a sign of their respect for the living ancestor that lived within their midst. He tilted his head to acknowledge the courtesy shown him and he and Nina arrived at the residence of King Haidar, the King's Hall. A large wooden building designed like an enclosed pavilion, a structure surrounded by homes made of sun-baked mud and straw. Umfami soldiers stood outside the entrance and gave way to the old man and the king's sister as they walked through the doorway and traversed the king's hall past the tables of meetings strewn throughout the great hall. Nina helped him ascend the wooden and stone platform upon which the twin thrones of the king and queen who ruled Bussar passed judgment. Set behind the thrones was a wall that separated the private chambers of the king and his family. M'Msee walked behind the barrier and shook his staff upon which dried beads rattled within a circular dried-out cone of pine. The sound announced his presence, and he spoke. "Wisdom has arrived."

Haidar, the King of the Bussar, turned from his exhausted but smiling wife and a now sleeping newborn son and replied, as was the way of the people of the plains. "Wisdom is welcome. Look M'Msee, look at my beautiful son! I am a proud father. But he still holds to his mother's womb. The midwives cannot cut the blood cord. We seek your wisdom."

M'Msee bowed, as was the custom, in the king and queen's presence. "My queen, may I approach and examine the child?"

The queen smiled at her old friend. A man she had known since her youth. "Wisdom is welcome... please come."

Mudiwa, queen of the Bussar people, then turned to her side and lifted the swaddling child to the Seer of the Bussar tribe and watched as he took her young son into his arms. M'Msee stared into the eyes of the babe. "Shaba" he said to Mudiwa. "His eyes and skin are bronze. A good metal. A good omen," he said. Mudiwa smiled in pride.

The child was asleep, exhausted by his journey through the birth canal into the land of the living. He touched the baby's hand with his pinky, and the babe closed its hand around M'Msee's small finger.

"The boy's spirit is strong." He remarked. "He is indeed the son of Haidar."

King Haidar's face widened plastered with the biggest of grins, a newly minted father who now beamed with pride.

Mudiwa noted her husband's loving gaze and the gloating smirk he gave her.

"Now let us see if we can cut the cord. Nina, give me your knife."

"But Seer, I have tried, and it will not cut."

"I believe you, child. And my request is not to dishonor your word. But this is something these old eyes must see for themselves."

Nina obeyed and lifted her knife from a bowl of warm water on a nearby stand and gave it to the village elder.

M'Msee attempted to cut the mshahara and, as was relayed, the blade would not penetrate the blood cord. M'Msee noted that the knife itself seemed to dull against the tissue even as he applied pressure.

His eyes widened, and he spoke. "My King, I must ask everyone to leave. I will need to use the old magic to cut the cord. But fear not, all will be well. But I can only protect one from the power that must be drawn from Aaru."

Nina immediately received her knife from M'Msee and left. King Haidar walked to the side of his wife and kissed her on her forehead. "Beloved, star of my youth. Let not your light go out and know flower of my heart that I will be outside."

Mudiwa and Haidar nuzzled noses then pressed their foreheads to one another, and then the king and his sister-in-law left the building, leaving M'Msee and Mudiwa alone with the child.

"I remember when you were but a child. insisting for me to show you the birth of butterflies, and now you are a woman who herself has borne a man. As I age, I find that time quickly darts from my presence. Have you a name for the child, my queen?"

Mudiwa gazed at her newborn son, her fingers tracing the smooth curve of his cheek, her voice steady with a certainty that echoed through the chamber. "He is strong," she murmured, the words carrying the weight of prophecy. "Even the Seer will journey to lay eyes upon him. This is no child of our time but of a season yet to come. He sleeps in *ama*, the stillness of calm, and *ni*, the essence of being. Balance flows through him as naturally as breath. Yes, Amani is the name for a king. Amani, my son of harmony and balance. The son of Haidar, the Lion."

M'Msee stood nearby, his head bowed, yet his eyes glimmered with understanding. He stepped closer, the air around him heavy with reverence. "Amani," he repeated, his voice soft but firm as if weaving the name into the fabric of destiny. "It is a name that will endure, my queen, and a legacy the ancestors will watch over. Now, if it pleases you, I will pray Akuma to sever this blood cord and release him into the world that awaits."

"Wisdom is welcome," said Mudiwa.

The old man then knelt next to the bedside of his queen as he had done many years before her mother, and her mother before her. M'Msee laid his hands upon the forehead of the babe, closed his eyes, and prayed to the god of creation and life, Akuma: maker of all things.

"In wisdom, he placed them together. In wisdom, he placed them apart. Hear mighty One the plea of your servant and let your hand rest upon mine. Let your light reveal the truth of this boy and grant me your strength that my task may succeed."

M'Msee's face ignited with a brilliance so fierce it seemed as though he had swallowed the sun and now bore its light. Mudi-wa gasped, lifting her hands to shield her eyes as the radiance threatened to sear her sight. She turned her head, unable to endure the overwhelming glow, yet the power of it still pressed against her skin like fire. Beams of light escaped the hut as though it could no longer contain the divine energy within. Those outside paused in awe as shafts of light pierced the windows, the cracks in the walls, and even the seams beneath the doors of the King's Hall, casting the surrounding land in an otherworldly glow.

M'Msee then pulled from beneath his robes a knife given to him from long ago. An Aarunite blade, made from cut stone deep within the Navel: the legendary crater made when Hutari fell to Tanara. The knife glowed as M'Msee unsheathed it and he took the blade and with it cut the umbilical cord. And as it sliced through the blood-chord, amniotic fluid and blood leaked as expected. The village sage then took the cord and tied it so that the midwife might tend to both the baby and mother upon her return.

The baby woke from his slumber and wailed his displeasure. His wails were like a mighty rushing wind, and M'Msee was confused, for the child should not have felt pain from the cutting, but try as he might; the babe would not be comforted. Winds howled and beat against the King's Hall as if nature herself was discomforted and with each cry of the child, the wind also screamed. And M'Msee looked up, and he saw the roof of the king's hall begin to rise as if it would tear open and fly away. And in those moments, Haidar ran in. "There is a storm above the village and Akuma's finger has been seen!"

A shriek split the air, sharp and unrelenting, as though the sky itself had torn open. Outside, the winds howled their fury, and the wooden, thatched roof above them wrenched itself free, peeling away into the roiling heavens. All eyes turned upward, terror etched into their faces, as the dark tendrils of a funnel cloud descended, spiraling with vengeful purpose.

The hall groaned, its foundations trembling beneath the weight of the storm's fury. Haidar's instincts surged like fire in his veins. He dashed to Mudiwa, his arms encircling her in a desperate shield of flesh and resolve. With his body, he covered her and the infant, his voice a raw command against the chaos. The winds clawed at them with a ferocity that sought to tear them from the earth, but Haidar held firm, his strength a bulwark against the storm's wrath.

Still wreathed in radiant light, M'Msee moved swiftly, cradling the infant in his arms. As he held the child close, his gaze locked onto its tiny face, and his breath caught. The child's features shimmered, reflecting the glow of his countenance and the ethereal gleam of the Aarunite blade. Awe tempered his movements as he bent to whisper into the child's ear, his voice an inaudible murmur of ancient words.

The child's cries softened, the tantrum dissolved into a quiet calm, and with it, the wailing winds fell silent. The storm's fury ebbed, leaving the air heavy with a fragile peace. Slowly, the brilliance faded from M'Msee's face, and when he looked again, the child's face had returned to its natural hue.

With a solemn expression, the sage placed the infant back in Mudiwa's arms, his voice steady yet reverent as he spoke. "Amani is but one part of his destiny," he said, his words heavy with meaning. "His name, too, is D'horuba—the storm."

Haidar's jaw tightened, his mind racing as M'Msee's words settled over him like a storm cloud on the horizon. His gaze lingered on the infant, who now lay nestled in Mudiwa's arms, so small, yet already brimming with a quiet power that seemed far too vast for one so young.

M'Msee, leaning on his weathered walking stick, paused at the threshold of the hall. His voice, heavy with the weight of prophecy, drifted back to the king. "Prepare yourself, Haidar. The K'olohi do not come for mere storms. They come for what lies beyond the wind, what shapes it. Your son carries the weight of a mantle long forgotten, but it will not remain hidden much longer. Watch the skies, my king. They will tell you what is to come."

With those words, the old sage departed, his figure dissolving into the twilight beyond the doorway.

Haidar turned back to Mudiwa, who now sang softly to the child, her voice a fragile melody against the silence that had settled in the hall. The king's thoughts swirled like the very winds M'Msee had spoken of, tethered only by the name that lingered in his mind: K'olohi. The butterflies of legend.

Haidar's fists clenched as the truth unspooled in his mind. The K'olohi were no simple omen—they were harbingers of transformation, of cycles broken and reforged. If they had returned, it meant his son was not merely tied to the storm; he was its fulcrum, its will.

The child stirred, his tiny fist reaching out as though grasping for something unseen. Haidar exhaled, his voice a murmur carried only to himself. "Not just the storm. No... he is its master. The storm will serve him, as will the winds, the rain, and the skies themselves."

Mudiwa then spoke. "With Haidar's will. I will that you be Amunzu to Amani. A second father to teach him the way he should go. Will you be godfather to my child M'Msee?"

He looked at Mudiwa, whose eyes shone with a mother's love and an unspoken knowing. The storm's shepherd, they would call him. But Haidar knew better. His son was no mere shepherd—he was the storm reborn, the harbinger of winds that would reshape the very foundations of their world.

"I would be honored, my queen," M'Msee replied.

And somewhere within the shadows of the village butterfly sanctuary, the K'olohi danced, heralds of what was to come.

***

The sun rose and fell countless times since Amani first breathed life into the world. A sacred moment that echoed through the four clans of the Bussar. His cries pierced the dawn, a symphony of hope that sent ripples of joy throughout the village. On that day, the earth seemed to hum with promise, the spirits of their ancestors celebrating the arrival of a prince destined to bear the weight of a legacy.

As the seasons turned, Amani grew, embraced by the warmth of his people and the teachings that wove through their lives like the vibrant threads of a tapestry. He took his first steps, guided by the sturdy hands of his father, King Haidar, and learned to navigate the bustling markets where merchants shouted their wares and children laughed, weaving tales of adventure and mischief. The stories of their ancestors whispered in the wind, grounding him in the rich history that flowed through his veins, reminding him of the duty that awaited him.

Every evening, under the watchful gaze of the stars, Amani's mother spun tales of Akuma, the Master Builder, whose hands shaped the world. She taught him that within the light of the moon and the dance of the flames, the essence of their people pulsed with life, the mysteries of existence beckoning him to understand both the beauty and fragility of their journey.

As seasons turned and the sun danced across the sky, Amani grew, his small hands reaching out to grasp the world around him. In the early days, he was a bundle of energy, crawling through the grass, reaching for the vibrant colors of wildflowers that dot the landscape. His laughter echoed like the tinkling of bells, drawing the attention of those nearby. Each moment felt like a gift, a precious bead strung onto the necklace of time.

With each passing year, Amani transformed, his spirit intertwined with the rhythm of the village. He learned to walk and then to run, his feet pounding against the earth as he joined the other children in their games. He danced beneath the sun, twirled through the rain, and felt the pulse of the land beneath his bare feet. It was a land rich with tradition, where stories of ancestors flowed like water from the elders' lips.

At five, he first discovered his connection to the elements. The weather swirled around him, responding to his emotions. A storm would brew if he felt anger or frustration; sunlight would break through the clouds when he laughed. The villagers whispered of his potential, their eyes filled with a mixture of awe and trepidation.

As the years unfolded, Amani's curiosity deepened. He spent afternoons with his godfather M'Msee, the village seer, who shared tales of the ancients, the balance of life, and the wisdom of the elements. "The world is alive, Amani," M'Msee said, his voice gravelly yet melodic. "You are a part of it, and it is a part of you. Learn to listen, and you will understand."

By the age of ten, Amani had grown into a boy of the village, his name spoken with a mix of admiration and unease among his peers. In the dusty courts where the children gathered, he trained relentlessly in the art of kashari. His feet danced over the earth as though guided by an unseen rhythm, his movements swift and unerring as he dribbled the tightly woven hay ball. Laughter echoed around him, a melody of innocence and camaraderie. Yet, beneath Amani's laughter, a quiet realization stirred.

With every game he won, every cheer that rose in his name, he felt the growing divide between himself and the others. His strikes were too precise, his speed unmatched. He leaped higher, ran faster, and struck harder. At first, he thought it was the mere practice that set him apart. But as time passed, Amani understood: that his strength was not like theirs. It was not a boy's strength.

There were moments, fleeting yet sharp when he felt the weight of this truth. When he tackled another boy, sending him sprawling, and saw fear flicker in his friend's eyes before it was masked by laughter. When he ran and others struggled to keep up, their admiration tinged with something he could not name.

What he carried within him was more than talent; it was something other, something that hummed beneath his skin, always waiting. It was a power that whispered of responsibility, of burdens yet to come. And though Amani did not yet understand its full meaning, he could feel it pressing against the edges of his childhood, reshaping him in ways he was not yet ready to s ee.

The laughter of children echoed in the air as Amani, now twelve, stood tall, the sun glinting off his dark skin. He felt the energy of the world coursing through him, a powerful force that both thrilled and frightened him. The village had become a tapestry of memories woven with threads of joy and sorrow, lessons learned, and battles fought.

As the village tournament approached, he sensed a change in the air. The whispers of the past mingled with hopes for the future, and the storm brewing within him echoed the tumult of the world outside. Amani was no longer just the king's son; he was a boy on the brink of understanding the depths of his power and the expectations of his legacy.

And on that fateful day, the lines between joy and rage would blur, shaping him into the leader he was destined to become, the storm within him finally unleashed.

The sun blazed overhead, casting a warm glow over the village, where the air crackled with excitement and the scent of wildflowers danced in the breeze. Children gathered in a dusty clearing, the ground marked by rough patches of grass and dirt, creating the perfect arena for their tribal game of kashari. Made from woven hay, the ball gleamed like gold in the sun, and the shouts of eager players echoed across the landscape.

Amani stood at the edge of the makeshift field, his heart racing with anticipation. Today was the last match of the annual tournament, a cherished tradition that brought the entire village together. He tightened his grip on the wooden spear he used as a makeshift goalpost, determination burning in his chest. His opponent, Tarek, flashed a confident grin, and Amani could feel the competitive fire igniting between them.

"Last one standing wins!" Tarek shouted, his voice cutting through the chatter of the crowd. The other children cheered; their excitement palpable as they prepared for the game to begin.

As the whistle blew, Amani sprang into action. The ball sailed through the air, and he sprinted after it, weaving through his friends with agility. The sun glinted off his dark skin, and his laughter mingled with the shouts of his teammates. With each kick and pass, the energy of the game surged, fueling Amani's spirit.

But then Tarek, playing a cunning defense, intercepted the ball. Amani's heart sank as he watched Tarek dart away, a blur of movement as he raced towards the goal. Anger flared within Amani—how dare Tarek think he could take this victory from him?

"Get it back, Amani!" someone called, but the words seemed to dissolve in the heat of the moment.

Amani chased after Tarek, his breath coming in sharp bursts. As he closed in, frustration boiled over, and with a surge of power he couldn't quite control, he felt the air shift around him. The sky above darkened ominously, the breeze whipping into a gust that sent chills down the spines of the onlookers.

"Stop!" Tarek shouted, turning back just as Amani lunged. With a fierce punch, Amani connected with Tarek's face, the impact sending shockwaves through the crowd. Blood burst from Tarek's nose, staining the ground as he stumbled back, surprise etched across his features.

Gasps echoed through the clearing, laughter fading into a heavy silence. The wind howled around Amani; the once joyful atmosphere was now charged with tension. He stood over Tarek, fury coursing through him, as clouds swirled above, reflecting the storm within his heart.

"What have you done?" someone whispered, but Amani could not hear them over the pounding of his pulse.

"Stop him!" another voice cried; the command lost in the chaos.

Just then, a powerful voice cut through the uproar. "Amani!"

King Haidar stepped forward; his presence commanded the attention of every child. The authority in his voice silenced the whispers, grounding Amani in the moment. "What have you done?"

Amani's defiance crumbled as he looked at his father, confusion, and shame mingling in his chest. "I—he—" Amani stammers; the thrill of the game was now overshadowed by the weight of his actions. "I just wanted to win!"

Haidar's eyes blazed with concern. "Winning does not give you the right to hurt others, Amani. You are more than a boy—you are the future of our people. Your powers are not toys to be used in anger."

The wind died down, the storm within Amani fading as reality sank in. Tarek sat on the ground, his hands pressed to his face, tears spilling from his eyes.

"I didn't mean to—" Amani whispers, guilt flooding his heart as he glanced back at the boy he had hurt.

As Amani's anger melted away, replaced by a deep sense of regret, he nodded, his heart heavy with the realization of his actions. The murmurs of the onlookers faded into the background as he turned back to Tarek, remorse etched on his face.

"I'm sorry, Tarek," Amani said softly, but the boy merely turned away, nursing his wound, the joy of the game lost amidst the weight of their confrontation.

Haidar placed a hand on Amani's shoulder, grounding him further as they walked away from the gathering. The once-vibrant energy of the game had transformed into a grim lesson of growth and understanding, a journey of self-discovery stretching out before him like the open sky.

Amani strode beside his father through the village, where every bow and nod from the passersby felt like a blessing but also a watchful trepidation filled the village's gaze, a tenuous thread connecting him to the heart of his people. Their respect wrapped around him like a cloak, grounding him in the weight of expectation while filling him with a fierce sense of pride. But while all bowed to the prince of Bussar there was also a sense he had learned also was present. Fear.

"I am sorry father," said Amani.

The King of Bussar gazed down at his sorrowful son and replied, 'I understand your heart. Go and inform your mother of our departure. Gather your belongings; we embark on a three-day journey. It is time for us to Kikurudumu and strengthen our bond through a shared adventure."

"Where are we going, father?" Amani asked, his voice bright with curiosity, a spark igniting in his chest.

Haidar looked down, his beard touched with strands of silver, eyes still fierce and full of life. "We go to Moshek, my son... once there, we will pay homage to Akuma."

Amani's heart quickened. "The Master Builder?" His dreams of adventure swirled like the vibrant colors of the sky at dusk, the journey ahead promised revelations and deeper connections to his ancestry.

As they stepped into the sun-kissed plains, the land breathed beneath their feet, vibrant and alive. Each blade of grass shimmered with stories waiting to be uncovered, and Amani felt the pulse of his heritage thrumming in time with the rhythm of his father's voice.

"Akuma has scattered his life in all things," Haidar explained, pointing to the soaring condors gliding above them, a testament to freedom and spirit. "His essence lives within you."

"Will we one day live in the sky, father?" Amani's eyes shone with wonder, innocence mingling with the weight of destiny.

His father chuckled, a sound like distant thunder. "Perhaps when we arrive at the mountain, you can lift a prayer to Akuma and ask him yourself. For such truths belong to Seers and not to Kings."

Amani's laughter mingled with the wind, but deep inside, questions danced like fireflies fluttering in the night. The world stretched before him, a canvas of possibilities, each step taken knowing that he was being shaped for greatness, woven into the fabric of a story yet to unfold.

Haidar had yet to take him outside the nation's borders to see what lay beyond. It was the duty of every father to school his children in the ways of survival and of the world. And it was tradition to show one's child the way of life and death. To understand purpose. The hope was that when the child grew old, it would not depart from the ways of the people.

"Father, why can I not see Akuma? And what is so special about Moshek that we would journey there?

Haidar laughs aloud. "You are like your mother—full of questions. What has M'Msee told you?"

"M'Msee's words are like riddles—except no one's ever solved them."

Haidar laughed out loud. "M'Msee does have a way of wrapping truths in mysteries. But you have untangled some of what he has taught. Share it with me."

"He has said that Akuma is still alive yet sleeps within Tanara, that he waits to be awakened."

"And what is he waiting for, my son?" said Haidar.

"M'Msee said he is waiting for us to...he used the word *ascend*. For men to rise in his power to the realm of the sky watchers. He said the place was named Aaru. And in time, we and the sky watchers might live together as one."

Haidar nodded as they exited the village and entered the plains of Bussar. "You have heard well. What M'Msee has said to you is true."

"But father I do not understand. What does it mean to *ascend*?"

Haidar stopped and beckoned his son to look upon the plains, "Akuma has scattered his life in all things." Haidar pointed to the condors overhead. "In the birds..." He then bent down and allowed an ant that carried a leaf in its mandibles to crawl over his hand and he lifted it to show his son. "His life is in the ant." He then placed the insect down to continue its journey and pointed his finger into the chest of his son. "He even lives within you."

"His life is a gift, but as with all life on Tanara... it is passing. All life is fleeting, and we all must one day die, my son. We will one day all return to the dust and the magic of our lives, all that we are returns to Akuma. But when Hutari comes... he will bridge the gap between the living and the dead, and on that day, we might ascend to be something more.... something that never dies... then and only then will we be like the sky people."

Amani looked up into the blue sky. "Will we live in the sky?"

Once again, Haidar smiled. Amani was smart. He was a bright child from his youth and the King of the Bussar people nurtured his love of knowledge. For one day, his boy would be king of the Bussar, and a keen mind would help him rule well. "I am not sure... perhaps when we arrive at the mountain and present our gifts at the altar, you can lift a prayer to Akuma and ask him yourself. For such things are the knowledge of Seers and not of Kings. Yes, ask M'Msee... and when you do, tell me what the old man would say to you."

Amani frowned, "M'Msee is grouchy father. I do not think he likes my questions."

Haidar burst out in laughter. "Well then, I will most definitely have to have a talk with him to be less grouchy then, won't I?" He laughed again.

They waded through the sun-scorched grass and fields. Each holding a spear and shield. They headed south towards the range of mountains and the three-day journey to Moshek. "Father?"

"Yes, son?"

"What is M'Msee?"

"He is the village seer and an Orsee of Akuma. You know this." He is your godfather. You know all this."

Amani ran to grab his father's arm and pulled him to stop. "No, father... what is he?"

Haidar stopped and looked at his son. He stared at him and realized that at twelve years of age; he had come to understand that M'Msee was far more than a normal human. He looked down at his son and replied. "He is a flickering light in this dark world, son. An emissary of the sky people. He is from a time long ago when people were still freshly bathed with Akuma's presence and power before the battle with the Kifu created the Sunder. Long-lived he is... so long that he remembers the Hutari."

"But the scrolls say that the Hutari lived over four hundred years ago?"

Haidar nodded in reply.

Amani, undaunted, pressed his father further. "Can M'Msee die?"

Haidar drew back, surprised at this son's question. "M'Msee is over five hundred years old. He is older than your grandfather's father. He has survived the heat plague, famine, and our people's war with the Hogarth. I doubt anything can kill him unless he wills it. Why do you ask me such things?"

Amani turned to look back at the village. "I have dreamed dreams... and in my dreams... M'Msee's heart was given to dogs to eat."

Haidar's eyes narrowed, and the two stood in the grassy plains in silence. And M'Msee, who saw through the eyes of a condor that flew overhead as they walked, heard the words spoken. And as he sat in his hut in the spirit trance and pondered the words of the young prince in his heart.

Chapter Two

The Measure of a Man

*I*t is said that when Hutari comes, there shall be peace. But the people will have grown weary of waiting and the Kings of Old will be no longer remembered. Yet the daughters of our people shall say, Peace! Peace! When there is no peace.

Ambilikie 6:14

The Book of Kings

Amani stood at the edge of the grasslands, his eyes tracing the undulating horizon, a sea of gold beneath the fading light. He wondered if this would be the place of his end—the ground that would cradle his bones if he failed. Here, in the vast expanse, his manhood would be tested, and if he proved inadequate, it would be the very soil that would swallow him whole.

The breeze, warm and fragrant with the scent of long grass and wildflowers, stirred the tall blades around him, their petals swaying like silent hands, waving their farewells. The air held a softness, rich with earth and life—sweet yet earthy, like the deep, untamed soul of the land itself. The familiar smell of the grasses, with their faint notes of hay and honey, filled his nostrils, bringing a strange comfort amid the tension. His lips curled into a wry smile; the sun's retreat would mark his final hours of safety. Only a fool ventured into Akoolah territory after nightfall.

The cat was near now, its presence unsettling as it drew closer, a shadow stalking the quiet edges of his thoughts.

The Akoolah's tracks were still fresh, the pungent stench of its urine clinging to the earth like a warning. Amani's eyes dropped to the ground, where the deep indentations of its paws marked the soil—a heavy print, adult in size, suggesting a lone scout hunting away from the pack, perhaps seeking food, or worse, an opportunity.

The breeze carried east to west, running in his favor. He was upwind. The beast could not smell him yet, but the tension in the air told him their confrontation was inevitable. One of them would not leave this place alive.

Amani's gaze lifted, eyes trailing southward, following the path of the stars that led back to his village. Never had he ventured so far from home. The tracks curved toward the Untu River, its waters the cat's obvious goal. The beast sought a drink, and Amani knew he had little time left.

He lifted his zarún, its heft designed to cover his body from attack, and feeling the weight of his Aaru knife settle into his grip, he readied himself for the moment that was sure to come. His rite of passage had begun three suns ago, and with this kill, he would secure his place in the clan, and assume his role as High Prince. By this time, his father would not believe him dead—not yet. No one would look for him before the fourth sun. His task was simple: complete the rite in seven suns or not return at all.

He would either return home with his prize or fall beneath the shadow of the rumbling Moshek, the river's current his grave.

Amani knew from his training that no man could be expected to rule the tribe if he was not willing to face his fears. For to lead was to protect the people. And he remembered his father's words, "Fear only that which would keep you from protecting your people," the king said, his voice unyielding. "A leader must cast off fear when deciding, for the weight of those choices shapes the lives of his people. And you, young one, must learn to shed your fear if you are to lead."

The Akoolah could smell fear as surely as they could scent blood. A single shift in pheromones betrayed a person's terror, and at the slightest hint, the great cats would strike, swift and unrelenting. To face them required a warrior to master their fear entirely, for even a flicker of hesitation could mean death. Among the people, it was tradition—an unbreakable law—that all kings must first prove themselves as warriors. Only through blood and trial could a ruler earn the right to lead. And the king's son was no exception. The weight of legacy pressed heavily on his shoulders, as unyielding as the gaze of the beast that stalked him and he, it.

Amani reached into his shaman's bag, his fingers brushing against the soft powder within. He drew out a pinch of quill dust and smeared it over his brown skin once more, the earthy granules clinging to his sweat-dampened flesh. The concealment wouldn't last forever—M'Msee had promised it would mask his scent from the Akoolah, and so far, he was alive. Perhaps the old shaman had been right. But nightfall loomed, and the dark was the beast's domain. If he faced it then, he would die.

His eyes turned to the looming shadow of Moshek, its jagged peaks piercing the dusk. At the mountain's base, within a cleft of stone, he would set his trap. There, the cat would be forced to attack head-on, where his flanks and back would be shielded by the rock. It was a solid plan. It could work.

Amani's lips quirked into a faint smile as he recalled his father's words: "Everyone has a plan for a fight—until they're struck in the face." He let out a low chuckle, quiet and grim. Whatever blow the Akoolah dealt, he would have to endure it. Or, at the very least, lessen its sting long enough to strike back.

He climbed down a hill and the great river Untu sang as the mists from its churned waters crashed against the rocky shore and filled the air. Amani watched the grassy path before him observing for any indentation in the ground, any broken tall grass; hypersensitive to any indication that the cat might be near and careful not to mistakenly run into the invisible claws of the creature if so, all would be lost. Akoolahs were some of the most fearsome creatures on the plains. Their fur was prized by warriors as it made the wearer virtually invisible. To wear an Akoolah's hide was a mark of great courage. The cats hunted alone when scouting a territory and once prey was found, they would bring the pack back to track and kill their quarry. One of the cats was a challenge, but a pack of the beasts could destroy a village. Amani's father had set up hunting parties to protect the outer settlements. The challenge was to kill the scout before he was able to escape and bring back the pack. A warrior would seek to kill the scout because if they were wounded, they would retreat and return in force. They were highly intelligent animals, only respecting the strength to repel their numbers, and had no hesitation in attacking larger beasts. They were wary of the village and usually stayed away. But if a member of the clan left the territory of the four clans and went into the wild, it was certain death. Everyone knew that to follow at night was to eventually run into the cats. If a clansman was shamed or convicted of crimes against the clans; honor demanded that the condemned be exiled to the outskirts of the nation. For in the wilderness, men would go to die. And Amani's father ever reminded him that the wilderness was skilled in the killing of me n.

He found a cleft on a large hill, looked up, and noted that it covered him from attacks above. He entered the fissure of the low-rising hill and took his knife by his side.

I will make my stand here.

He knelt and quickly took the tacks he had made in the village forge. It had taken weeks to make dozens of the small six-bladed jacks. He arranged them far enough from the entrance so that the cat could not simply jump over them to evade them. Once the cat traveled into the den, Amani had made it so the cat could not help but impale its feet, giving him a needed advantage. He would not be able to see the cat at first, and it would be important to remove the beast's advantage.

Amani's head turned as the sound of twigs breaking could be heard several yards in front of the entrance of his position.

It tracked me. The cat is closer than I've realized.

Amani then took those remaining jacks there were in his hand and flung them to the ground. They scattered before him and he crouched, moving backward deeper into the hill's crevice until his back was firmly against the crevice wall.

He looked up at the stars, and each twinkled in the black as a host of watchmen. His chest rose and plunged, and the thumping of his heart felt like it would burst against his breast cavity. He recited the mantra M'Msee told him. *"A leader must be free of fear,"* he said. Adrenalin heightened his already keen senses, yet he reminded himself to remain calm. Tonight, he would skin the Akoolah's pelt and bring it back as proof of his kill, or he would shine like the stars in the night sky with his ancestors and walk among the same with the sky-people.

The crackling of dried grass and dirt interrupted his thoughts and the menacing snarl of an Akoolah floated in the air.

He then crouched lower with zarún in both hands, ready to thrust its blade through the hide of the creature.

The breaking of sticks was followed by a low roar that pierced the cleft's opening, and a brownish cat with black stripes materialized. Blood oozed slightly from its paw, and it stared incredulously at Amani hissing as it approached with fangs bared.

"A leader must be free of fear," Amani repeated to himself.

He breathed deeply to calm himself as the cat again stepped on a tack and then belted out an indignant roar.

"RAAAAAHHHHH! COME ON, YOU BEAST! COME AT ME!" Amani yells in the tongue of his people.

The cat confidently lunged; its claws extended to kill the teen warrior.

Amani thrust his zarún forward with all his strength, the long-shafted pole finding its mark as the blade buried deep into the Akoolah's shoulder. The beast let out a guttural wail, its roar a mix of fury and pain as it stumbled back, withdrawing its bloodied paw. Pressing itself against the cleft wall, the creature's eyes burned with primal rage.

It lunged, jaws snapping around the shaft of Amani's spear, splintering the wood with a savage crunch. The broken halves clattered to the ground, useless. Yet the blade remained, embedded deep in the cat's flesh, a cruel thorn that refused to be shaken loose.

The cat limped, favoring its wounded shoulder, yet its predatory gaze locked onto Amani, unyielding. It bared its fangs, the glint of sharp ivory catching the dying light, and lowered its massive body to the ground. Its muscles coiled, rear legs hiking, ready to pounce—to crush him beneath its weight and sink its teeth deep into his flesh.

But Amani refused to see himself as prey. He would not cower, not falter. Instead, he did the unthinkable—he attacked.

With a roar that tore from his chest, raw and unrestrained, Amani gripped his knife and leaped toward the beast. The distance closed in an instant, and in that moment, as the shadow of death loomed over him, clarity struck like lightning.

He heard the words of M'Msee as if the sage stood beside him. "The thing which represents your fear must be killed, or it will destroy you. Kill it, Amani, or be hollowed out, left a ghost—a shell of a man. Kill your fear, my child, or forever wear its chains."

And so, with his blade raised high, Amani chose. Fear would not claim him.

Only now did Amani grasp the full weight of the lessons M'Msee had woven into him—a lifetime of preparation for this moment, for facing death itself. What he had once dismissed as harsh, even cruel, was revealed now as a vital tutelage, a relentless shaping of his will and body for the trial he now faced.

The memories surged within him, M'Msee's words a torrent that ignited his resolve. Every strike, every grueling test had led to this. Amani's grip on his blade tightened, and his eyes burned with newfound clarity.

The Akoolah would learn, as he had, the most unrelenting of truths. Amani would teach the beast the lesson he now embodied—that in his presence, it was no predator.

It was prey.

***

The room was heavy with the stillness of dread as Amani sat with his arm outstretched, the black scorpion crawling across his skin. Its claws ticked softly against his flesh, each step deliberate, its stinger poised and glistening under the flickering torchlight. Sweat dripped down his temple, but his arm remained still, rigid with the effort of self-control.

"Do not move, youngling," M'Msee said, his voice calm as the morning wind. "The scorpion will not strike you unless it perceives you as a threat. You must understand that it, too, is not a threat to you. Like all creatures, it moves according to its nature. The scorpion strikes to defend itself and to survive. Tell me, my prince, are you, it's food?"

Amani's voice wavered his arm still and sweat beaded down his head as the black scorpion crawled over his arm, but he managed to answer. "No, I am not M'Msee"

M'Msee inclined his head in approval. "No, you are not food for the scorpion. Therefore, youngling, if you are not food, then you must be a threat. So, are you a threat to the scorpion, young prince?"

Every fiber of Amani's being screamed at him to yank his arm away, to flee from the creature that carried poison in its tail. Amani bit his lip as the entirety of his senses told him to withdraw his arm and to place as much distance between himself and the scorpion as possible. "No teacher. I am not a threat."

M'Msee's eyes narrowed. "Incorrect, young prince. You do not consider yourself a threat, but that is different child than being a threat. Your wish alone does not determine your standing in the eyes of the scorpion. Understand, boy, that there will be men... one day even kingdoms, who like the scorpion will see you as a threat, though in your mind and intent, you do not deem yourself so. Your mere existence is a disturbance to the order of their world. And thus, they, like the scorpion, will have the propensity to strike out in fear."

Amani swallowed hard, the weight of M'Msee's words settling over him like a shroud.

M'Msee continued. "So, if you are not its food, neither predator that it should fear, then act... do not react, control your actions and allow your fear to take its rightful place beneath your feet. You child must simply decide if you will be still until stillness is no longer the action to pursue. Do you understand this, young prince?"

"I, I think so," Amani whispered, though his voice betrayed his doubt.

M'Msee nodded. "Good, now allow the scorpion to sting you."

"What?" Amani's eyes widened in disbelief, his arm trembling despite himself.

"You must experience that which you fear, M'Msee said, his voice unyielding. "So that you may know the limits of its ability to harm you. Fear, young one, is a state of mind. The product of your imagination is based on your perception of danger. But the scorpion's sting will not harm you."

"But won't the poison be painful unto death?" said Amani.

"No, not to death... not for you, but it will be painful. You must experience pain. So that you understand that pain should be respected but not feared. You must intimately learn the lessons from pain, make it your own, and how to use it to your advantage. Or you will never be king."

"I believe I respect it enough now, M'Msee. In fact, I am certain that I hold the utmost respect." Amani said, desperation edging his tone.

"No," said M'Msee. "You do not. To respect the scorpion, and ultimately your foe is to understand that despite its size, it can still inflict pain and discomfort. These things cannot be fearful for a King. For they are parts of life and cannot be avoided. Therefore, your fear of avoiding pain and discomfort must be purged. Experience your fear. Understand its nature until you realize that fear is nothing but the imagination of your mind."

M'Msee then struck the table where Amani's arm was extended and the scorpion, startled, reacted on instinct. Its tail arched and struck, its stinger piercing Amani's arm.

Amani cried out, the pain sharp and immediate, like fire spreading under his skin. His arm recoiled, and the scorpion fell to the ground. and M'Msee calmly took a net, captured it, and placed the creature in a cloth bag.

Amani let out a yelp. His breathing sped up, and he could feel a tightness in his chest. "Teacher... I can't breathe..."

M'Msee said nothing, his dark eyes fixated on the boy. The flap of the tent rustled, and King Haidar entered and saw his son writhing on the floor gasping for air. He eyed his son and then looked at his spiritual adviser. "Will he die M'Msee?" Haidar asked, his tone steady as the mountains.

"Yes, my king, but only to that which he fears."

Haidar's face was impassive. "Good," said King Haidar. "Then continue his training so that his fear may be purged and nothing, but a man remains." Without another word, the king turned and left the tent.

M'Msee returned his attention to Amani, his expression calm yet resolute.

The pain throbbed in Amani's arm, radiating up to his chest, each breath harder than the last. Darkness crept at the edges of his vision as he gasped, his body fighting to hold on. But before unconsciousness claimed him, he caught one last glimpse of M'Msee—watching him, unshaken, a faint, approving smile on his face.

And then, the darkness took him.

***

Amani's sudden attack had startled the cat—a predator unaccustomed to becoming prey. Its hesitation cost it dearly as his dagger plunged into its eye with brutal precision. The beast howled in agony, thrashing wildly as Amani ripped the blade free. A spray of warm blood streaked his face, and the knife gleamed crimson, dripping with the feline's life force.

The cat recoiled, its movements frantic and uncoordinated. Desperation drove it to retreat, but its escape led directly into the entrance lined with tacks Amani had scattered earlier. A guttural roar erupted from its throat as the metal spikes pierced its tender paws. It stumbled, each step betrayed by sharp pain, and raised its paws instinctively, only to find no relief.

Amani stood motionless, his chest heaving as he watched the trap perform its grim work. The beast wounded and cornered, writhed in futility, its powerful frame betrayed by the unforgiving ground.

Then, slowly, the cat turned its mangled face toward him. Blood streaked its fur, and its single remaining eye burned with a mix of pain and primal rage. But beneath that fury was something else—something M'Msee had taught Amani to recognize long ago.

Fear.

As Amani locked eyes with the beast, clarity settled over him, the creature now understood.

The lesson Amani himself had learned so many years ago was now dawning upon the cat's predatory mind, though far too late to save it. It saw, in that fleeting moment of awareness, the truth that could no longer be denied: Amani, not the Akoolah, was the predator here.

With that knowledge burning within him, Amani surged forward, his body alive with purpose. He was no longer the hunted; he was the hunter. His voice erupted into the wild, a thunderous roar in the language of the Bussar people, echoing through the wild lands and the shadowed grottos of Moshek.

The roar carried with it a defiant proclamation, one that every creature would hear and understand: "I am not prey!"

The Akoolah lashed out, its claws raking across Amani's chest, drawing blood. The sting burned, but Amani had already endured the venom of the scorpion—he was no stranger to pain. Instead of succumbing, he embraced it. The searing slash was a vivid reminder that he was alive, and with that awareness came resolve.

He surged forward, headlong, into the embodiment of his clan's deepest fear. The blood seeping from the beast's ruined eye testified that fear could bleed, that it could be challenged and forced to pay a price.

The Akoolah retaliated, flinging Amani hard against the jagged wall of the cave. Pain radiated through his back, but the boy's focus did not falter. Sensing weakness, the cat pounced, its massive body sailing through the air, intent on finishing its prey.

But Amani was ready. He raised his knife high, bracing for the collision. As the beast descended, he drove the blade upward with all his strength; the tip piercing the tender underside of its jaw. The resistance of bone met his steel, but he pressed harder, twisting the blade even as the Akoolah's jaws snapped perilously close to his face.

The struggle was primal, man against beast, and Amani's determination burned brighter than the pain coursing through him.

The cat collapsed in stillness and Amani breathed a sigh of relief and allowed himself between pants to savor his victory. His pulse slowed and he could feel the weight of the cat press against his sternum. He shimmied himself out from underneath the great cat and stood over his kill. He reached underneath the lower jaw of the cat and withdrew his knife, and wiped it over his cloth. He also took the blade from the shank of the cat's shoulder and, with the same, cut several teeth out of the mouth of the Akoolah and placed the proof of his prize within his satchel.

The coolness of the evening breeze announced that nightfall was soon approaching, and he started a fire stripped pieces of the cat's flesh, and placed them over the fire to cook. The smell of the Akoolah's cooking flesh and the light of the fire would keep other predators at bay. A signal to the creatures of the wilderness that something far more deadly was in the plains.

A man.

Eventually, he would have to make his way home, and it was a three-day journey back to his village. He would skin the cat now and allow its pelt to dry out overnight near the fire. He would later add the herbs that would interact with the skin of the corpse to release the cat's pheromones. Pheromones that would trigger his new cloak's ability to render him partially invisible.

He sliced into his prize and allowed the night sky and the sky watchers to keep him company. And he reflected on his tutor growing up and wondered if M'Msee was near and if he had watched his kill through the eyes of the crow that stood within a tree staring down at him.

***

Tell me teacher... why do the people call you "Wisdom?"

M'Msee scaled the fish caught by the tribesmen who had gone to the coast and continued cleaning the duo's dinner without response. Amani fidgeted with M'Msee's lack of an immediate reply and silence.

"I am sorry teacher, if I offend. It is not..."

M'Msee raised his hand to cut him off. "You do not offend me, young one. I merely consider how to answer. I was not always called wisdom. It might surprise you that like you, I also was once a boy and foolish before I ever was a warrior, let alone 'wisdom', but that was another lifetime. A time when I was even lover and husband..." Amani watched as M'Msee's face softened as he seemingly reflected on his memories. He sighed and continued.

"I was in the before time all those things. However, time, loss, and the humility to learn, how much there is to learn, has made me 'wisdom'. The people of the plains know me by this name and my many lifetimes have given me a perspective and knowledge that has helped the Bussar people prosper. But know youngling I am nothing compared to the wisdom of Akuma. I am but a droplet in the ocean of he that has made this world and the worlds beyond. Remember always that we are but dust and he the mountain. And it is because of this that when I am called 'wisdom' I do not correct the people out of respect for their tradition youngling. But never think to yourself that I think myself so full of pride that I consider myself the embodiment of wisdom. I too, despite long life, am ever a student of that which Akuma would teach me. And he is ever ready to impart his lessons if we are open to hear. Do you understand?"

"Yes, M'Msee," said Amani.

M'Msee nodded his head in approval. "Good, then let his words fill your heart, child. For Ambilikie has written in the scrolls and asks us all, '*Where then cometh wisdom? And where is the place of understanding?*' My many days have taught me that the answer can only come from Akuma. For only he is truly wisdom and the fear of Him is the beginning of knowledge. Listen Amani, and learn this lesson well. Wisdom is the principal thing. Therefore, get wisdom and, in all your effort, get an understanding."

Amani's lip curled, and his face scrunched. M'Msee watched as his young pupil turned the words he had spoken over in his mind.

"So, since you are called Wisdom," said Amani. "Am I getting understanding? Am I getting wisdom?"

M'Msee spoke softly as he continued scaling his fish. "Only time will tell if you recognize my words as such."

Amani raised his eyebrow and looked curiously at his teacher. "But despite all that you have said, I still do not understand why YOU are called wisdom, teacher."

M'Msee grinned as he continued to remove the skin from another fish. "I will tell you a secret." He leaned close to his godson's ear and whispered. "I know neither. It was an honor bestowed upon me long ago and seemed to have stuck with me through the years and with the people of the plains. As I said. I do not correct them. The Bussarim are as fixed as the stars in their circuit: bound by their traditions. But you, my son, are not so. You are a flexible wineskin that can receive new things. So, to you, child, I would not steer you to me who is but a man. A long-lived one, but nonetheless a man. I would instead steer you to he who is wisdom itself."

"Akuma?" Amani asked.

M'Msee nodded, then replied. "Akuma." M'Msee then put his knife down and looked at Amani. "I have dreamed a dream. And have foreseen for many a year that one day the *barrier breaker* would come. You, Amani, are that breaker. Though I know not how, I believe you, my boy, will help the people to one day ascend and break the curse of death upon this world. You possess the power of air, the power of Aaru, to control the very currents of the storm in the sky. You are strong and I suspect will grow stronger still, and when you reach the height of your strength, you must remember the reason for these gifts. To one day use them to save the people from a great evil." M'Msee massaged his wrist as if he were removing tension or pain. He smiled as he looked at Amani. "The Kifu will inevitably awake and when he does, you and the entire world must be ready to f ace him."

Amani turned the words of his godfather over in his mind. His eyes betrayed his inquisitive nature.

"Has he not been asleep for centuries, what would cause him to rise again?"

M'Msee sighed, weighing his words carefully. Even now, he wondered how much of the truth the boy was ready to bear. He straightened himself, his voice low and measured.

"What you say, my son, is true. The Kifu is drawn to the power of Aaru, like a moth to a flame. While all of Tanara carries this power, some things... and some people... possess it in such a way that it calls to the Kifu. Even in his slumber, if the power stirs enough in Tanara, he can sense it, and should it erupt in use, it may even cause him to awake. Already he stirs, aware that his ancient nemesis walks the earth. A beacon in his mind. He waits for anger to fuel death, and when that moment comes, he wi ll rise."

A solemn silence followed as M'Msee's gaze lingered on Amani. His words grew sharper, laden with urgency.

"So be careful, my child. Never strike to kill, for with each life you take, you feed his awakening. You loosen the seals that bind him. The two of you are linked. I do not know how, but I know it to be true. The Kifu smells the stench of death we invoke over each other, but this alone will not awaken him. No, you, my son, are not like other men."

M'Msee's eyes bored into Amani's, the gravity of his words deepening. "You must be careful. Never take a life in anger, for in doing so, you will feed the Kifu's return. The blood of your enemies is not just blood; it is a lifeline for him. A force that strengthens his power. And when the time comes, and you take that life—be sure, my child, that you are prepared. For with each life you take, thousands more may die. Do you understand?"

Amani's mind raced as M'Msee's words settled deep within him, a sense of foreboding growing.

"You are bound to the Kifu, Amani, by more than fate. You are bound by your emotions. If you kill in hatred, in anger, in fear—each act will speed his awakening. He thrives on such dark emotions. But if you strike in mercy, in justice, or out of protection for others, the effect will be slower. Still, you must remain vigilant, for his stirrings will grow stronger."

M'Msee's expression softened as he continued. "You must learn to control your emotions, Amani. The fight you will face is not only in the world outside but within. You must learn to wield your power without succumbing to the darkness within yourself. To use your strength to protect, not to destroy. For you, my son, have a terrible gift. A power that can cither save or doom us all."

Amani stood still, his mind whirling with the weight of M'Msee's counsel. A bond with the Kifu? A bond of death? His hands clenched into fists, and for a moment, he struggled to contain his emotions. His mentor's warning echoed in his ears—anger would awaken the Kifu. Fear would strengthen it.

M'Msee's voice broke through his thoughts once more. "Learn, Amani. Grow. You must cultivate peace within your heart, and only then can you truly control the storm within you. Never forget, that you are not only fighting for yourself. The world waits for you to find the strength to defeat not just the Kifu, but the darkness that is within you, too."

Amani's lips parted, but the words of his teacher had already taken root. The realization was dawning on him as if the true weight of his powers had finally been revealed. And so, he nodded, vowing to carry the burden his teacher had placed on him.

The future was uncertain, but one thing was clear—he would never strike without considering the cost.

Amani pulled himself free from the weight of M'Msee's words, his breath catching in his chest. He turned toward his mentor, and for the first time, he saw him—really saw him. His gaze locked onto M'Msee's face, searching the lines of his features, the depth in his eyes, the faint wrinkles that creased his skin. It was as though a veil had been lifted from his eyes, and at that moment, he saw something he had never noticed before.

Age.

M'Msee looked... older.

M'Msee felt the weight of his godson's gaze, sharp as a spear. Amani's piercing eyes studied him with quiet intensity as if seeking to uncover a truth that hung between them. Though no words passed between them, the air thickened with unspoken understanding. M'Msee, aware of the scrutiny, moved with deliberate care, drawing a scarf over his face, as though shielding himself from the revelation Amani had begun to see. The gesture was subtle but a silent acknowledgment of the bond they shared and the truth now rising between them.

Amani held his silence, allowing the moment to pass, choosing not to press further. Instead, he turned his mind to the question that had lingered in his thoughts since the people of the plains first posed it. Ambilikie's writings had failed to answer it, leaving an empty void where understanding should have been.

"M'Msee," Amani's voice was calm but heavy with the weight of his inquiry. "You were there when the Hutari and the Kifu clashed. You saw when he defeated the Kifu and sealed him away from the world of men. But why did he not finish what he started? Why leave the Kifu entombed, only for us to suffer its lingering shadow? Why, M'Msee, did the Hutari leave men to such a fate?"

M'Msee paused, his hands still over the fish, the blade momentarily forgotten. He looked down, the weight of his thoughts pulling him deeper into the silence. A heavy sigh escaped him, the kind that seemed to carry the burden of ages. Slowly, he turned to face the young boy, the one the king had entrusted to him—a boy meant to learn, to grow, and perhaps one day rule the Bussar people. But M'Msee's purpose ran deeper than mere governance. He had his own vision for the boy's future, one that stretched far beyond the throne. A future where this boy would one day stand against gods themselves.

M'Msee studied the sixteen-year-old's face, searching his eyes for the spark of understanding that he needed to see. With a steady gaze, he shared the thoughts that had been circling in his mind, offering the answer to his godson's question.

"Because, like all men, my son," M'Msee's voice was rich with the weight of experience, "the Hutari was but a man. And like all men, he feared. He feared the loss of what he loved, just as we all do. Love and fear... these are the forces that bind us. And sometimes, these forces—these frailties—fuel a future of hope. Or, worse still, a future of false hope."

Amani studied his mentor, his gaze sharp and direct, as if trying to peel away the layers of history that clung to M'Msee's every word. His voice was quiet but full of intent. "Is this why you teach me not to fear?"

M'Msee paused, the question landing like a weight he had long avoided. The eyes of youth, untainted by the years of regret and self-deception, seemed to strip away the defenses M'Msee had built over a lifetime. He felt the years, the shame, the scars of his past pressing in, and in that moment, it was as if the boy's gaze saw straight through him. His eyes glistened with unshed tears as he looked at Amani, the words heavy in his chest.

"Fear... and hope," M'Msee said, his voice thick with emotion, "can destroy nations. They can make a man stumble through the darkest depths of the Duat. I teach you this, my son, so that you may be better than me. When the time comes for you to face the creations of gods—and even the gods of men—you might redeem what was lost long ago. Perhaps undo what I…"

His voice faltered. He placed a hand over his partially scarred face, as if to hide the rawness of his grief, and hunched his shoulders. The weight of his past, too much to bear, finally overtook him, and he wept.

Amani watched quietly, his gaze lingering on the man who had imparted the life lessons of his clan, preparing him for a future that may one day see him crowned king. He had witnessed M'Msee's anger, shared in his laughter, and seen him deep in thought, but never had he seen him so broken, tears marking a sorrow that ran deeper than any lesson. Amani wondered what could wound his teacher so. What grief had burdened M'Msee to this point?

Without a word, Amani reached out, his hand gently taking M'Msee's. The old man's eyes met his, and for the briefest moment, a smile flickered on his lips.

"Take the fish to your mother," M'Msee said softly, his voice tinged with weariness. "Leave this old man to his thoughts."

Amani nodded and, with a final glance, backed away, carefully lifting the basket containing the fish they had caught from the waters of Ambilikie's mouth. His heart, heavy with unspoken questions, remained with M'Msee as he walked towards the path leading home.

M'Msee watched the young prince, his steps sure yet burdened with the weight of his destiny. As Amani disappeared,

M'Msee's gaze turned upward, and his words escaped into the air, prayers whispered to the heavens.

"Grandfather, you who, in your wisdom, deposit the power of being into the earth... How can this child be your chosen? Since when does one who carries fish bear the burden of fighting death itself?"

The silence stretched, and M'Msee knew the answer would not come from the heavens above. Akuma was not there. He sighed, his voice breaking the quiet with a whisper filled with regret.

"I am sorry, child. Sorry that you must carry the burden I failed to complete ages ago. I hope one day you will forgive my selfishness."

Tears continued to fall as M'Msee watched the boy, the prince he had raised, as his own. And in that moment, the full weight of what lay ahead crushed him—the knowledge that, to defeat the Kifu, this boy, this godson, might one day have to die.

Chapter Three

The Meeting of Princes

The sun's rays and the warmth of its heat caressed Amani and woke him from his slumber. He turned to see that his camp had been undisturbed. The smell of Akoolah's was enough to keep other animals at bay. The rope he placed on the ground in a circle around him was enough to keep the venomous grass snakes from curling up to him to seize his body's warmth while he slept. He stretched and eyed the cloak he had fashioned from the carcass of his kill. He had fashioned wristbands and leggings as well. He stood to his feet and rubbed oil into his creations to keep the leather soft. Later, when he reached the camp, he would make a pouch and slit the bands to hold protective weapons. He slipped his created wear over his wrists and his new boots over his feet. The teeth of the Akoolah would make good jewelry and excellent darts. He tore down his camp lifted his kill over a travois he had constructed and began the slow trek back home. It was three suns to get home and after four, they would declare him dead. He breathed in the summer air and, with the additional weight of his prize, began the journey home.

Pulling the travois behind him for a day and night, he finally reached the ocean inlet of the Kishanaw. It was crucial to get home soon, as the Hogarth traveled the plains and the waters of the Kishanaw were near to the Dark Mouth: the path that led through the burning sands to the land of Hogarth. Amani knew the Hogarth people also sent their young men to the plains to complete their rites of passage, and slave caravans traveled back and forth from the capital city of Hogarth to the Medja city of Aphis. An alleged city of magic users who, it was said, had powers over seas and winds and who held back the great dune sea from spreading and overrunning the plains of Bussar. Magic users who built the Dark Mouth so that travel from the coastal sea to the inland could occur. His father had warned him to never go near their domain and where he was located was neutral territory and susceptible to Hogarth slavers. The treaty between Bussar and Hogarth depended on the magic of the Medja, who were not kind to passersby on their territory.

Amani leaned down to a stream and filled his water pouch, then took some of the water and splashed it on his face. And cupped his hands into the stream to drink.

A male voice then spoke gruffly behind him and caught the young man by surprise.

"It would seem that what my father said is true. The Bussar drink water like Hogarthen dogs. I wonder if I kill you. Will your hide serve as tribute to my people instead of the hide of this whelp of an Akoolah who you have somehow managed to slay? Because no dog needs such a pelt."

Amani looked up and saw a ruddy youth of a man. Similar in shape and build to himself. His skin was *Nyati,* clearly darkened from the desert sun like all Hogarth. His eyes were golden brown, but his hair was red and white war paint marked his face to outline a skull. He stood with a spear in his right hand and a dagger tucked into a cloth belt and wore a bola that was draped over his shoulders. Amani stood, placed his right hand over the palm of his dagger, and replied.

"You are far from home Hogarni desert child. And you should know that if you think to kill me, be warned, as the Akoolah once thought likewise."

The Hogarth boy then spit on the ground and replied. "A Hogarthen claims what he sees... that is the way."

Amani meditated on his words and nodded his head in understanding, then sauntered towards the young man. He weighed his odds of combat with the stranger and concluded that they were doubtless evenly matched. He stopped two arms' length from the sworn enemy of his people and looked him in the eye. "If you think yourself able to claim whatever you see.

Perhaps you lack clarity of sight and require change. But be it known that I, nor my people, nor our lands: are yours to claim."

The Hogarni snarled in return, his fists poised to back up his threat to harm him. "Do you challenge me, Bussar dog? I hope so." He smiled. "Because if your skills in fighting are like your skills in covering your tracks, then I will return not just your prized Akoolah pelt, but your corpse to my father."

Amani moved slightly closer to the young man; his eyes narrowed as he watched his opponent. "*I* am the predator of the plains, *not* the Akoolah; and anything; creature, man or otherwise; would find that tracking a predator is not a task to be taken lightly. As the Akoolah whose hide I now wear can attest. Anything or anyone that cannot realize this truth of nature and seeks my death. Will nothing but death by my hand."

The Hogarth boy looked at Amani and weighed his words. He sized him up and realized that the teen like him did not walk in fear. A coward would not wear the Akoolah as a shawl over oneself. He smiled in respect at the bravery of his people's enemy.

"Well said, I will respect your kill and the hands that bear it. I also pledge not to kill you. But you have drawn the attention of a pack, and they are not far behind me. I have passed them with fire in the night to find what they hunt: you. But they are not far behind me and will for certain find us. Your camp spot has your back against the water, and neither of us can kill an Akoolah pack alone. I have deemed you worthy to die with me by my side. If it were not so, I would have already killed you.

Today, you will have the honor of dying with me. Do you accept this honor?"

Amani was taken aback by the brashness of the boy. Chuckled to himself and replied. "And what is the name of he who would grant me this honor?"

The boy then placed his spear on the ground, took his dagger, cut into his palm, and extended his hand for Amani to take.

"I am Jo'than prince of Hogarth and son of the Sandking. Today I would know if you will die with me?"

Amani looked at the boy's hand and weighed his options. Refusing would simply cause them to go into battle with one another and the pack would devour the victor. There was no honor for his people in that death. But if a Bussar warrior fought with a Hogarthen prince. When and if their bodies were found, perhaps the tale of two enemies fighting side by side against a larger threat would inspire either or both peoples to find a way to peace other than that brokered by the Medja; in that there would be honor. And at that moment, Amani knew what he had to do.

Amani then took his dagger grasped the hand of his people's foe and spoke as he noted that the cats Jo'than had spoken of had now found them.

"No, Jo'than I will not die with you today. But I will give *you* the honor of living with me to tell the tale."

It was in that moment of alliance four Akoolahs peered their heads from behind a protrusion of rocks and slouched towards the boy's position.

The two young men: enemies, now turned allies: turned to face the pack, each drew their weapons and waited for the attack from the beasts that would in moments surely come.

***

M'Msee had been thinking about his godchild for days. Amani had now been gone for five.

King Haidar, though a man of formidable composure, was clearly distressed by his son's prolonged absence. As king, he dared not show fear openly—his people required strength. Yet M'Msee, having lived over five centuries, knew the subtleties of human nature. In his long pilgrimage across the earth, he had observed countless parents. Kings and paupers alike shared one immutable truth: all worry for their children.

Haidar was no exception. Despite his crown, he was a father first. And M'Msee sorrowed for him. He understood too well the ache of love's absence, the void it left when extinguished by death.

M'Msee had loved once. A woman with eyes like stars and hair as pale as moonlight. Love had been a torment, a luxury too costly for one such as he. It had broken him, driving him to a century of self-imposed exile. Once a leader of armies who had sealed great darkness beneath the earth, he had become a shadow of himself—a wanderer, nameless to all but ghosts and legend.

Yet even he, with all his power and age, needed companionship. After the Sunder, he emerged from seclusion, entering Bussar as a stranger. There, he found a home among its people, allowing himself to love again. He loved Amani—the son of the king—as if the boy were his own.

But as the Wisdom of the people, M'Msee could not show his grief. He retreated to the solitude of his hut to mourn in silence. His thoughts swirled around the boy's fate, and he wept quietly until a knock interrupted his reflection.

"Come in, my king," he said, his voice steady.

Haidar stepped into the hut, lowering his head as he crossed the threshold. "How is it that you knew it was me?"

M'Msee offered a faint smile. "Who else would it be? I've known you, your father, and his father before him. It surprises me more that you waited this long to visit."

Haidar chuckled. "You do know me well. And you know I've come seeking wisdom."

"Wisdom is here," M'Msee replied. "What would you ask of it?"

The king hesitated before speaking. "Is my son dead or alive?"

M'Msee frowned, leaning forward on his staff. "That is what you ask. But it is not what you wish to know. Speak plainly."

Haidar nodded reluctantly. "You would make me say it, then?"

M'Msee rose, steadying himself with his staff as he approached his old friend. "No, my king. I share your worry for the boy. But I would remind you—once, you too were gone for days without a word."

"True," Haidar admitted. "But don't pretend you don't wonder after him. Mudiwa and I both know you love him as we do. That's why I made you, his godfather. He needs someone like you—someone who understands his powers. If he is what you believe... the Hutari... he will need more than a father and mother. He will need a guide."

M'Msee nodded solemnly. "What greater strength is there than a parent's love? But I will grant your request. I will use the true sight to see if he lives. Walk with me to the raven's cage."

Haidar stepped forward, offering his arm to steady the aged Wisdom. Together, they moved to a birdcage in the corner of the hut. Inside sat a raven, its feathers gleaming like polished onyx.

M'Msee seated himself before the cage, scattering herbs that filled the air with their pungent aroma. Crossing his legs in a lotus position, he chanted, his voice rising in a low, rhythmic cadence.

The raven stirred, flapping its wings in response to the growing energy in the room. Its cries matched the tempo of M'Msee's chant, rising and falling in perfect harmony. As the chant reached its crescendo, the raven silenced itself, pecking at the cage's latch.

Haidar stepped forward and opened the cage. The bird soared out, cutting through the air before circling back. It returned to its perch, cawing softly.

M'Msee stood, securing the latch as the raven settled. Without a word, he motioned for Haidar to follow him outside. Together, they stepped into the open air and looked toward the distant horizon.

Far off, two cyclones twisted violently, their fury untouched by the surrounding clear skies. Lightning cracked the earth, illuminating the distant plains.

Haidar's expression hardened, but M'Msee smiled faintly. "Two cyclones dance where there are no clouds," he said, his voice calm. "The wrath of the Stormcaller has been stirred. It would seem, my friend, that our boy still lives."

**

Amani had been told that he was special. Informed that he possessed the power of the storm and the wind. That in time, he would harness this power to bring relief to his people. M'Msee had attempted on several occasions to help him control this power. And his tutelage taught him that he could summon the wind and, with an outstretched hand, push objects from their place. And occasionally he would look up when he was in distress and see that clouds churned in the sky above him and the rumblings of thunder would drumbeat across the sky. And in those moments, he was conscious of controlling his emotions to not unleash the power of the sky upon his people. Trained incessantly by M'Msee to maintain control lest he unleash fire from above or, worse, bring destruction upon the land.

"M'Msee, will there be a time when I can control the lightning and the storm?"

"Yes, but when you do, you must understand that such power is meant to keep back the walking death. You are a shepherd of storms. A great power given to but a few in my lifetime."

"And exactly how old is that?" Amani asked with a smirk, attempting to bait him.

M'Msee chuckled at the boy's boldness. "Old enough to know I am grateful I never had a son. Now, focus again. See if you can ignite the straw dummy over there."

M'Msee had brought Amani away from the village and near the sea. To help him control his power, thinking that the ocean's tide with its ebb and flow would instill serenity. And for the waves' motion to teach him peace. Amani had learned much in their sessions, but now, as his rite of passage loomed just a year away, M'Msee introduced a more dangerous lesson: the art of destruction.

Amani gritted his teeth, his brow furrowed with concentration, but nothing happened.

M'Msee stepped closer, his tone deliberate. "Tell me, boy, do you never feel anger? Does life never frustrate you? I've seen the way the other boys look at you. And I've seen the way the men in the village look at your mother. She is fair, is she not?"

Amani's eyes snapped toward his mentor, a flare of indignation sparking. "I do not appreciate your words, teacher. My mother's name, let alone her form, should not grace any man's lips except in respect or praise as our queen."

The sage's expression remained unflinching. "She is fair. And men—weak as they are—see your father and wish to be him. I have heard whispers, my prince, whispers carried to me through the deep sight. Some would even dare depose him."

"Who are these traitors? Who speaks such things in our village?"

M'Msee's voice hardened, pressing the boy. "Many do, child. They speak of taking your father's head, and when he lies slain, and you are gone, they would steal your mother to their beds."

Amani's fists clenched, the first sparks of lightning crackling along his fingers. "You speak of rebellion. Treason," he growled, stepping toward the elder.

M'Msee stood firm, his voice unwavering. "Your mother... she is a fruit many would desire to taste, a flower that men would kill to pollinate and the waters from her, well, an elixir kings would wage wars to drink."

"Arrghh!" Amani roared, spinning away from the elder. Twin streaks of lightning erupted from his hands, arcing through the air and striking the straw effigy. The dummy ignited instantly, flames consuming it as Amani stood, chest heaving, the glow of his power still crackling faintly.

Amani turned back, his voice low with anger. "I do not appreciate this lesson, teacher. Nor appreciate how you sought to tutor."

M'Msee placed a steady hand on the boy's shoulder. "Your appreciation will come when you must use this power to protect those you love. You possess the storm Amani, and the storm is driven by emotion. Your feelings are the key to its churning—but you must master them, lest they master you. Others may rage and strike out, their anger harmless. Yours, however, brings fire from the heavens and death to the earth. Learn this now, before the time comes when the stakes are real.

Above all, conceal this power. Should those beyond our borders discover it, they will come. Medja, who would seek to control you and hurt those you love to use all that they might use you as a weapon. Do you understand this, my prince?"

Amani's eyes lowered, the weight of his mentor's words pressing upon him. "I understand," he murmured reluctantly.

***

Now, a year later, Amani watched as an Akoolah had pounced on Jo'than, the prince of Hogarth. The cat was atop him and with his spear; he struggled to keep the weapon lodged in the beast's mouth, holding its snapping rows of incisors at bay. But the cat was large and with a swipe of its claws ripped into the chest of Jo'than and the boy let out a scream. Amani's heart raced within him, his chest hurt, and he could feel the power of the storm course through him. It was a fire that was painful. He never told M'Msee that releasing the power of the sky caused him pain. But now surrounded and to preserve the life of his ally, he had no choice but to unleash the fire, like an involuntary reflex that could not be controlled, he would once more allow the fire within to run across the veins of his arms and be unleashed through his hands.

Amani then raised his hands and reached out as if he were to throw a projectile toward the great cat. And though nothing was in his hand, the air itself understood his whims, and a gust of air pushed the beast hard from atop Jo'than and into a jagged boulder, impaling the creature. It let out a roar, then its head went limp, and the cat was still.

Two cats they had already killed between them with their knives and spears, and now two yet remained. The animals encircled them, and Amani backed towards Jo'than and stood as a wall between the beasts and his injured ally.

"How hurt are you? Can you fight?" Amani asked.

Jo'than took his hand and placed it over his chest and lifted it up for Amani to see. And it was covered in blood. He shook his head and replied. "No."

Amani looked down to get a view of the injury and he grimaced at what he saw. Part of the pectoral muscle had been sliced open as if it could be lifted as a flap from his chest. He would require sutures to close the wound and medicine to heal. He must get him back to the village.

Growls behind him turned into a snarl and he realized that by turning his back to the cats they instinctively saw an opportunity to attack. And attack they did as the predators lunged at their prey.

Amani turned with hands raised. The anxiety of their battle, the stakes of lives lost, and thoughts of home churned the source of magical power within him, and the emotion ignited the latent power of lightning that coursed through his frame. His eyes turned white, and where once he had felt pain as the energy ran through him, he gave himself over to the power, and bolts of lightning rained down in front of him, and an impenetrable wall of lightning stood between he and they. And the cats acrobatically swiveled their bodies so that they landed away from the bolts that fell from the sky. But it was not enough to frighten the beasts to leave, for though the cats feared, they merely dashed away from the dancing arcs that would sear them alive. Amani sensed that though he and Jo'than were safe for the moment, he perceived that the cats also considered them trapped behind the curtain of lightning that crackled before them, and they sought to go around the electrified screen.

Amani harrumphed that the display of power was not enough to scatter them and became angered. The sky responded to his emotion and grew dark, clouds circled in swaths of putrid green and the wind raced as two funnels reached down from the now raging sky and they skipped and darted with a thunderous roar whilst Amani stood over Jo'than within an eye of calm. Roundabout them the winds raged, and the cats attempted to flee the moving winds, but they were swept up and Amani motioned the funnels out to sea, and in obedience to the Stormcaller, the cyclones carried aloft the Akoolah's out and into the deep waters far beyond the shore and released the cats into the ocean waves that overtook them. The cats struggled to stay aloft and swim against the pulling tide and the pounding wind and soon drowned under the deluge. And when Amani saw that the danger had passed, the skies themselves cleared and the sun once more shone and its radiance beamed in crepuscular rays between parting clouds.

Amani turned to see that Jo'than struggled to remain conscious and was slipping away from the loss of blood. And as Jo'than closed his eyes, his hand was raised and with his index finger, he pointed at Amani and uttered a word in his savior's hearing. A word Amani was not aware the Hogarth people knew. A word he had heard M'Msee use towards him in private when he did not think he was in earshot.

"Hutari..."

The word struck Amani like a thunderclap. Amani knelt beside Jo'than, his mind racing. The word, the responsibility it implied, and the weight of what had just transpired all pressed upon him. But for now, there was only one goal: to get Jo'than back to the village alive.

Chapter Four

A Mother's Worry

M udiwa, queen mother of the Bussar people and wife of King Haidar, loved her son from the day of his strange birth to his rites of passage to become a contributing member of the clan; she had always been proud of him. But knowing what his destiny entailed. To hear that M'Msee thought he would be the one to save the world from the Kifu always weighed on her. How could a child that nursed at her breast be the hope of stopping the walking death?

Mudiwa left the bedside of her sleeping husband and went outside to look at the stars as she leaned upon the wooden trellis outside the great hall that was the center of the Bussar Kingdom. A quartet of four cities spread around the center city of the kingdom. Each generation: the head of a clan, was chosen to lead the Kingdom of the Plains. Haidar was chosen and has led his people well. Mudiwa was proud of her husband and happy to be married to such an honorable man.

The night wind is gentle.

The full moon lit the evening sky and illuminated the city. She loved the night, loved the way the stars winked at her as they traveled to unknown parts. Each constellation was a traveling band of her departed ancestors who had settled in the heaven above. And one day when she left this earth, she too would travel the astral winds and dwell above as one of the sky people. One day, men and women would look up and take comfort knowing that her presence beamed down upon them. She smiled at the thought and looked forward to the journey that would carry her beyond this mortal life.

A journey that would originate with her death, but tonight... tonight she would wait, for tonight she was alive. Alive and still young enough to bear another child if Haidar desired. But now old enough to have watched her son go off into the plains to affirm his manhood and acceptance as a leader in the clan. And now Mudiwa wondered if her son had fallen prey to an Akoolah and had already made his journey to the sky. She wondered if even now he looked down upon them all and contributed to the light of the moon. Mudiwa gazed at the night sky and then to the plains and wondered about the wellbeing of her son.

Many boys left the village that year. Over twenty had made the annual pilgrimage to show themselves worthy to sit on the

council. A forum to discuss the clan's needs and submit pe-
titions to the king. Twenty-two had left to find manhood in
the wilderness. And of those that entered the plains, only nine
had come home. Nine, sunburnt or branded by the scars of
beasts: nine judged by the wilderness worthy to live...and to
lead. Nine to guide and protect the Kingdom from harm as
warriors or one day be elected by the people to be king. But
yet there were thirteen of Bussar's progeny that would never
be seen again. Mudiwa's heart grew heavy for the mothers of
the clans whose sons had been lost. The wilderness was ruth-
less in its ability to erase the existence of the dead from the
vultures that circled over those soon to die. To the Akoolahs
that were the most feared land predators. Many a past mother
was grief-stricken and prevented from seeking the remains of
their sons. The wilderness was a callous thing and withdrew
such hopes for discovery. Even the spider grass was carnivorous
and would consume any human remains with their digestive
juices, removing even the bones. But such was the way of the
wilderness, and such was the way of the plainsmen of the Bussar
Kingdom. Such a large number to not return would hurt the
kingdom. For thirteen, to go missing was no small matter and
was the most lost in Mudiwa's memory. Thirteen of Bussar's
sons were swallowed up by the wilderness or perhaps kidnapped
by the brutal Hogarth or by Aphis to be used as experiments
by the Medja. Mudiwa frowned at the thought as she gazed
towards the moonlit horizon.

The Medja had always been a shadow over their land until her husband put a stop to their efforts. In his youth, King Haidar, then the fearless chief war-master of the kingdom, dared to wage war against the Medja. Their crimes were many—none more grievous than the abductions of men and women from the southern clans. When evidence surfaced of their transgressions, including the capture of a young hunter who had ventured too near their borders, Haidar's fury ignited, and he roused a hundred warriors. And marched upon the Medja's pyramid tower city of Aphis nestled between the Dark Mouth and Bussar. All to rescue a young man who hunted too close to Medja territory. Thus, the four clans made war upon the Medja, fueled by rage to avenge those kidnapped and made chattel to traffic. Mudiwa looked to the southern sky and remembered the balls of fire that rained down upon the men. Blooms of orange that could be seen even from the center city. But though fire rained upon them, they scaled the Medja's tower, battered down its doors, and stormed into the ancient magic fortress. And when it was done, the lad was returned, but fifty men perished in the boys' saving: fifty to save one, but even more of the sorcerers died by the sword than the Bussar. Haidar and the three men he most trusted entered the mage's Veilkeep Sanctum, and she learned Haidar had held the chief mage's throat in his hands but relented and allowed the mage and his people to live. All she knew was that M'Msee had somehow brokered a peace. And they made a pact with the Medja, and they swore to never take the people of Bussar ever again. But Haidar never spoke of its terms, nor its cost. But since that day the Medja have left the people of Bussar alone.

And for a while, it was clear that the fear of an army of marching Bussar had kept them in check. But that was thirty years ago, and Mudiwa wondered if the memory of the treaty had succumbed to the passage of time and was lost as rumors of abductions from scouts and travelers seemed to question if the truce still held. Some on the council questioned if the Medja still feared the Bussar and had rebuilt their forces such that they felt emboldened to continue the demonic practices of old. Some men of the council even raised the prospect that they should gather the four clans once more and burn the tower of mages down for good.

But Haidar and M'Msee dissuaded them and assured them all that the Medja could not be the cause. And though Mudiwa was queen, even she never knew why her husband had spared the Medja. And while some would eventually question the wisdom of Haidar. No one dared openly question M'Msee, and despite the rumors, nothing ever materialized that the Medja had gone back on the treaty of peace between the powers of the area. And though Haidar did not fear them. Mudiwa noted within herself that her husband was changed after he came back from their pyramid city of Aphis. She had asked him, and others had as well, what he saw in the innermost chamber when he went to confront the High Mage of Aphis for his crimes. But despite her prodding, Haidar nor the two who entered with him into the chambers ever spoke of what they saw. Haidar himself would quickly change the subject when discussed. As if even mentioning the Medja's name was dangerous somehow. Mudiwa resisted pressing him on the matter but carried the thing in her heart.

Nevertheless, she wondered about the Medja; it was said that they trained storm shepherds. Medja, who were powerful enough to keep the fingers of the gods from destroying the plains. Allegedly, their school focused on controlling the power of the wind and sky. And trained in the summoning of clouds and rain. Haidar had told her that they possessed a tower amid the great sea. A monolith they called the Tower of Sight. A tower where the mages work to control the Z'otho Linithe. A world storm that per legend rotates above and around the Kifu and that keeps all others away. A storm that does not move.

Amani could summon storms. Mudiwa knew this and had seen it with her own eyes. Her son would surely be prized by the Medja. She wondered if his abilities if known, would cause them to breach the peace with Bussar just to claim her son. If he had not already been claimed by the wilderness. Her mind raced with anxiety and her breath quickened at the thought.

The breeze against her cheek felt stronger now.

Is Amani powerful enough to summon a world storm? She wondered

She chuckled to herself. *How could such a boy who tripped over his own feet contain the power of Akuma to stop the rotating eye of the World Storm?*

But her son had surprised her before. She smiled as she re-called him running through brush and falling into a small lake. He was submerged only briefly, but the experience of water forcibly going into his lungs scarred him. He rose from the lake, wailing. His cries were not from injury but from being immersed underwater and rising, soaked from head to toe. For the longest, he would never go near the lake again. Only using enough water to bathe himself, and of course to drink. Mudiwa knew her son. Knew that this fear would rot and fester to one day spring to life: perhaps unexpectedly in his rite of passage. She determined within herself to equip her son to survive the wilderness's hand, for fear in a Bussar child could not be tol-erated. Fear was a weakness that exposed one to death in the wilderness. So, the mother of the prince sought to purge him of this fear of water, this fear of drowning.

Her training began with the solace that water was nothing to be feared. But instead, was to be respected, savored when parched, and could quicken death in the desert in its absence. She taught him everything she knew about water, and when her own knowledge was exhausted, she acquired tutors from the clan to teach him even more. All that he might confront his fear with truth. For knowledge was known to diminish fear of the unknown and no warrior could be paralyzed by inaction due to fear: such was the way of Bussar.

For two years, she took him to watering holes and then one day to see the great waters of the coastal shore. Waters that no one could swim, and occasionally she and her son watched as great vessels sailed in the distance, presumably from Hogarth or to the southern lands of Aksum.

Now, after ten seasons, he watched in the distance as great fish leaped from the water. In his excitement, he turned to his mother to capture her attention. Mudiwa already saw that the waves had shifted and while she had coaxed her son into the ocean shore, she did not expect a rip current to claim her son. She watched his smiling face move further from her. A smile that soon turned to terror. While rare, she had seen others die in an attempt to provide rescue, as a loved one was carried out to sea. Watched as others were caught in the waters, only to drown and their bodies drift as flotsam atop the great waters. But she was Bussar, and she held no such fear. If her fate was to die in the waters with her son, she of a surety knew one thing. He would not die alone.

But Amani did not die. M'Msee said that her son was known by the Medja as an Enari. he preferred the word D'horuba, or Storm Caller. But for many seasons, Mudiwa noted no powers of significance from her son. Only fear of water, fear that would get him killed in the wilderness. Fear that would disqualify him from leading his people. She entered the breaking of the waters, prepared to drown if it meant saving her son. But her fears were not realized, and the day would not see his death by drowning in the Great Sea. Her eyes widened and her mouth fell open. For the winds shifted and before she entered waters that came to the waist, she saw the clouds churning overhead and her son, her beloved son, rose above the waves and walked on the water towards her and the shore. Confident, and strong, he had summoned the strength of the wind to lift himself atop that which he once feared. He walked to his mother until his foot hit the sandy shore.

She recalled the words he spoke. "I am fine, Yiyi." She touched the cheek of her son and replied. "I think my son that one day.... one day you will fly with the birds!" She exclaimed excitedly.

Mudiwa sighed as she remembered her son's powers and her admonition to never disclose his ability unless absolutely necessary. "Promise me!" she urged.

"I promise Yiyi."

The evening's cool breeze carried with it fond memories of her time with her son. She smiled as she thought about her boy and chuckled as she heard Haidar's snoring, even from outside. *He is truly a lion. Even in his sleep*, she chuckled.

She motioned to return to her husband's bed when she saw a figure in the sky descending towards her home. It was a man. A flying man! A man who held another in his arms. Her mouth instinctively widened into a grin and her hand lifted upwards to cover the same. She gasped as the dark figure came closer into view and tears welled up in her eyes as he spoke in the familiar tenor voice of her son.

"I am sorry, Yiyi, but this man needs a healer. Do not be angry, but he is a prince of Hogarth."

***

Haidar's voice fumed with rage. "You have brought the son of our nation's enemy into my house? Has the sun-bleached your mind? Did I raise a boy who took no thought for the wellbeing of his homeland? Do you know what you have done with this act? You were supposed to kill him where he stood!"

Amani was silent, his head bowed as his father raged at him. Several attendants surrounded the boy from Hogarth and worked to stop his bleeding, and Mudiwa spoke up in her son's defense.

"Haidar... hear him out, my love. The wilderness has allowed them both to live. He is now an elder of the gate and would not any elder be allowed to speak?"

Haidar looked incredulously at his wife, the queen of his people, and replied, "You would remind me of the laws of our people when the boy we have raised has endangered the very law and people it was meant to govern?" Haidar waved his hand and lifted his voice to give command. "All of you leave me with the Hogarth boy. Out."

Immediately, the healers that attended Jo'than hurriedly exited the room. Mudiwa herself sighed and placed her hands on her son's shoulder and motioned for him to walk with her. The two royals of the four clans then stepped into the judgment hall of their home and Mudiwa sat at a table. Amani paced back and forth as his mother watched him and then the son spoke to his mother. "The wilderness has shown me to be a man. I am allowed by right to speak to the king."

Mudiwa nodded, "What you say is true. But it is not wise to speak to him when his mind is cluttered with emotion and filled with fear."

Amani recoiled. "Fear?"

Mudiwa nodded. "Yes, child...fear. He is a king. Kings are allowed but one thing to fear. And that is the well-being of their people. Your bringing the enemy into our home has stirred fear in your father. For who can know what outcome would come from such a thing? The young man who lies injured in our chamber is the prince of the man who killed your father's father. And whether it be fate, Akuma, or happenstance. You have brought the blood of he who has struck at our family to the door of Haidar. I have known your father for many years, but even I do not know what churns within him to have a prince of our enemy in our camp. I only know that as of this moment, the boy's life and war between Hogarth and Bussar is in your father's hands."

The sound of a sword being unsheathed from its scabbard came from the bedroom chamber. Amani immediately ran back into the back chamber, while Mudiwa stayed and lowered her head in prayer. Her soft voice muttered her petition to Akuma for her son, husband, and the young man who lay injured in their home.

Amani entered his parents' bedchamber to see his father standing near the side of his bed, sword raised, and Jo'than still fast asleep.

"Father, King of the Bussar, and Lion of the Plains. You cannot strike an enemy with whom we are not at war. No aggression can be made to an enemy of the clans, save by the consent of the elder men's vote to commit their sons to do the same. I stand on their behalf and of the sons of those you serve and adjure you to sheath your sword. Do not do this... father, do not take Bussar to war over hurts done in the past."

Haidar said nothing, but his sword was raised over the young man's chest. His arm trembled as he held the weapon aloft over Jo'than. Slowly he retracted his arm and sheathed his sword, and it returned to its scabbard, bloodless. He stared at the boy in his bed and spoke to his son.

"This boy you have saved. His father killed your grandfather. You have not just rescued the enemy of our people. But one from the very line who has struck to the hurt of our family. Because I am king before I am Haidar. I must as king submit to the rule of our laws. And I will do this thing as king. But as Haidar, father of Amani..."

Haidar then turned his eyes from the prince that lay on his bed to the prince that stood as a new elder man before him. "I must now wonder will the man who stands before me protect our family. Does the fire to revenge our line's dishonor burn within you? Know that as your father... your actions force me to question this."

Haidar then walked from Jo'than's bedside shoved past Amani and exited the room.

Chapter Five

Interrogations

J o'than awoke and immediately noticed soreness in his abdomen. He turned to his right and water, dried fruit and venison were on a plate on a nightstand where he slept. He grimaced as he sat up and let out a small groan. His body was sore from his fight with the Akoolah. He reached over to grab some water when he noticed an old man covering the pummel of his walking stick with both hands sitting in a chair, staring at him.

The man wore the ceremonial garb of a Seer. His skin was like brass, and his hair was white as wool. He wore the sigil of Akuma and the crest of both the Umfami, the Orsee, and the Medja. ancient sects of warriors, priests, and mages known to destroy spirit shards that created passages from the celestial world of

Aaru to Tanara. Slightly startled by the staring old man who watched him, Jo'than opened his mouth to speak.

"I am Prince Jo'than..."

"I know who you are, young prince." Interrupted the old man. "The question you must answer before you allow pride to make you haughty in a land that is not your own; is, do you know who *I* am?"

Jo'than paused, studying the elder. The man's musculature was incongruous with his apparent age—strong, unyielding. Then the symbols adorning his garb jogged a memory from his royal education. Lowering his gaze, Jo'than adjusted his tone. "My apologies, Ancient One. I did not recognize you. I ask your forgiveness... Hutari."

The old man rose from his chair, and a faint blue glow emanated from his frame.

"Your people were young when I cleaved their mountains. And infantile when the Kifu last walked the world. You are forgiven. Know that I have taken residence among the plains people, and you will not speak of me to them. Nor will you tell your own people whom you have seen today. If you do, I will stir Moshek, and all that you know and love will drown under the fires of its wrath, and I will build a new Hogarth atop the bones of the old. Do you understand me, young prince?"

Jo'than swallowed hard and nodded. "Yes, Ancient One."

The elder's expression softened. "In this land, I am known by the name M'Msee and have been entitled Wisdom. You will address me as Wisdom while you dwell in this land. If I come again to yours, you may call me by the titles *your* people have chosen, but you will not use them here. Now that it has been established who we both are. Tell me, what happened in the wilderness?"

Jo'than thought for a moment and realized he did not even know how long he had been out; let alone what day it was. He strained to recall the events that led him to be in what he presumed was a Bussar bed chamber.

"I was out scouting for Akoolah. I caught the trail of a pack on the move. hunting. I knew that if I hunted them while they hunted, it would be the ideal time to kill one. Akoolah, as you know, are one-track-minded when it comes to the pursuit of the kill. They would not think about looking behind them. I followed them, I realized they hunted a man. And so, I turned my attention to what manner of man would cause a pack of Akoolah to pursue him. The animals are known to be vengeful in tracking and attacking the specific humans who kill their kind, and I discovered that who I followed wore an Akoolah's pelt. I maneuvered past them as quickly as I could and met up with the man who they stalked."

"And this man was Amani?"

"Yes, Hutari...I mean wisdom."

"And how did you two escape a pack of Akoolah?"

Jo'than looked down and his eyes darted as if determining if he should speak about what he remembered. M'Msee noted his reservation and spoke. "Speak freely, child. What you say here will not leave this room."

"He is Hutari, wisdom. But how can that be? My father says that *you* are Hutari. But I cannot deny what my eyes have seen. He moved the waters and the wind, and he bore me in his arms in the air, even as the crow flies. How can such a thing be unless *he* is the Hutari?"

M'Msee sat up from his chair and walked with a slow gait and sat upon Jo'than's bed and spoke. "Your eyes did not deceive you, child. Nor do they deceive you now. But know this. You cannot tell anyone else what you have seen. If you do, your people will think you are contagious with desert madness. No one will believe you. But I give you command to never mention what you have seen to your people. If I find that they are aware, and their knowledge comes from you. I will cleave the life of the king's youngest son. As for me, and these here, they will not share what you have told me. Nor will I speak of it to another. You are alive, and a prince of Hogarth. You must get well so that you may return to your people. Now tell me, has the custom of Hogarth changed, that the body of hunters must be brought home either dead or alive?"

"The tradition has not changed wisdom."

"Then we must be quick to see you to your home, child. For the Sandking cannot come here and find his son in the hands of his enemies. Now rest, that a party may be assembled to return you home."

Jo'than looked at M'Msee, concerned. "But wisdom, I cannot return home empty. I would be dishonored, and if I am not dead, my family...the king, would be dishonored. How can I return without the pelt of my prey?"

"M'Msee nodded, I understand. We will think of something, child. We will sort it out together."

Jo'than nodded and laid himself back down to sleep. His mind troubled over what the days ahead would bring to him.

Chapter Six

L'ihondo'Murwa

An emergency meeting of the city's elders had been called. The sharp, mournful sound of the horn echoed across the quiet city, rousing its clans from sleep. In the watchtowers, flame keepers lit the sacred blue fires of the L'ihondo'murwa—a beacon signaling that the matter at hand was grave and demanded immediate attention and decision.

Messengers, swift and purposeful, carried the summons through the winding streets and out to the far-reaching enclaves of the clans. One by one, the clan elders, draped in their ceremonial garb, made their way to the city's central meeting place: the Culsha, a grand circular forum carved into the living stone of the earth.

The Culsha had long been the seat of judgment, the cradle of alliances, and the place where decisions that shaped their people's fate were made. Now, beneath the flickering light of the blue flames, the elders gathered, their expressions shadowed with concern.

Whispers filled the air as speculation spread about what danger or crisis might have prompted such a rare and urgent assembly. Whatever it was, they knew it could shake the foundation of their city—and their way of life.

Amani had passed his trial and, as was tradition, was now a defender of the assembled clans of Bussar. For this honor, he now possessed a seat among the men of the council who judged the direction of the nation. M'Msee had urged Haidar to awaken the council, and at the advice of his nation's seer, the King of Bussar did so. And after several hours of messengers sprinting across the plains and waking sleeping elders from their beds. The assembly of the four clans was gathered and M'Msee as chief Seer spoke to explain their gathering.

Amani noted that many of the men who had listened to M'Msee had yawned, still undoubtedly fatigued from being awakened in the middle of the night. But no more; any that might have had a semblance of weariness were now focused on M'Msee's words.

"I greet you in the name of Akuma, Bussar. I greet you protectors of the plains and defenders of the ancient way. You who were the first to give a son to the Umfami and to the Orsee. You, fathers of Bussar, are here tonight because we must decide, and decide quickly, of a matter that has been thrust upon our people. And while the matter should have been brought to the council's attention sooner..." M'Msee glanced at Haidar, who sat quietly and stared straight ahead. "What we decide tonight will either send our sons to war or avert one."

Murmurs echoed throughout the assembly, and all that may have been fatigued were now alert, their ears and eyes now sharpened by the word *war*.

"What threatens the peace of Bussar?" asked an elder.

M'Msee looked again at Haidar, and the king returned his glance, sighed, and stood to his feet. "We have in our midst a Prince of Hogarth; he has been injured and his wounds are being tended to and he is currently recovering in my chambers."

Gasps and looks of confusion permeated the crowd, various ones turned to one another in disbelief and one elder raised his voice in query.

"How has a son of our enemy come to be in our camp? No Hogarth has trod the plains of our lands for a generation. The Treaty of Glass still exists between us and the Hogarth nation and has held, preventing violence between our peoples for over fifty years."

Amani swallowed hard and stood to speak. He would not allow his father to explain the actions of his son. As he was officially accepted as a man of the clans. He realized he must now give an account of how his deeds had now endangered the clans.

"It was I. I am the man that brought the prince of Hogarth to our land."

Many gasped. Some muttered words of dismay and Amani heard a few mutter words of contempt.

"Young Prince, your father's father, by his own life, gave us peace through the sacrifice he made for Bussar. Explain how you would undo and perhaps even dishonor the work of your grandfather?"

Amani was taken aback by the words of the elder but took a deep breath and proceeded to give an explanation. "We were attacked by Akoolah, I fended the beast off, but the prince was gravely injured...it was leave him to the wilderness to die or give aid. I chose the latter."

An elderman raised his hands in a display of disbelief. "Then you have robbed the wilderness of its life and have interfered in the order of the plains and salvaged that which the land would claim for its own. It is no small thing to rob the plains of its kill. His blood will bring the wrath of the plains upon us if not his own people."

"We cannot keep the prince!" said another.

"Kill him and return him to the land," said one.

Mumblings and debate broke out among the quorum of men, and Haidar looked at M'Msee, who knew his king's mind. Haidar then stood and when he did, all the men of the assembly grew quiet. For when the king stood, his mouth was soon to utter judgment.

"We will not kill the boy. He was brought here under the intent of sanctuary. And sanctuary he will receive."

"But Haidar...he has crossed into Bussar. Our treaty stipulates on the day that this is done, any Hogarthen who crosses the desert into the plains of our land will have declared war."

Amani gasps at the statement. "Forgiveness, please. I was not aware that my actions would endanger the clans."

An elder spoke up and replied, "Your ignorance is no excuse. You were required to learn the treaties between Bussar and the other nations of the coast of the western tharun. Your history of the plains and those of the desert should have made you aware that the Hogarth follow their men into the desert and will not cease their pursuit until their man is found." The elder then looked at Haidar and spoke to him in the hearing of all.

"Haidar, this cannot stand. Though he is your son, he cannot sit with the elders. Feats of strength alone and the ability to escape the wilderness are not enough to lead the people. This very act demands for a review I invoke Haith."

Haidar grimaced at the proposal while Amani looked at his father. His eyes glistened with tears that all his years of preparation to be seated with the men of the four clans could be undone in an instant. A commotion rose among the elders. It had been over ten years since a member of the clan had been dishonored and stripped of his title to sit with the Culsha. Historically, men who were stripped were anathema to the women of the clan, as they could not own property and were bound to their house of birth, nor could they establish their own. They would bear no children, and their name would die out with them and eventually all those that spoke their name. Amani wanted to scream, enraged that his act of mercy would warrant what he deemed such an unfair judgment. But because an elder had made this proposal, the king was now duty-bound to discuss the issue and bring it formally before the Culsha to decide.

"An elderman brings a cause of Haith before this Culsha. Is there another that will echo the thing?" Haidar proclaimed.

Another elder immediately spoke up in reply. "I echo his words." A third then rose. "I echo."

Haidar frowned, torn between his duty as king of his people and his love as a father. His mind raced to find a solution to the dilemma before him and he spoke in reply. "A call for Haith has come from the Culsha. We will convene at the height of the sun tomorrow and will decide on the fate of Amani's house."

"And what of the Hogarth?" said an elder.

A gruff voice then spoke from the misty twilight and slowly walked towards the gathering. "Neither the fate of my son or if Hogarth will war with Bussar are yours to decide, but mine."

All the men of the council turned to their rear, and the ground vibrated and pebbles moved across the ground of their own accord, leaving trails in their wake as they congregated at the foot of gilded leather soles. And the feet that filled them were attached to muscular legs to reveal a bronzed-skinned man clad in leather armor. An encrusted crest of two crossed axes of gold adorned his chest. And to his left and his right were an entourage of Hogarth soldiers that flanked him. His face was wrinkled, and he wore a black eye patch, and his arms were braced with leather straps that made his biceps bulge. His hair was white as wool and styled in long braids, and a golden wreath-like crown was upon his head.

Amani knew that he viewed none other than the legendary Sandking of Hogarth. King N'Kosi. The father of Jo'than, and the man who murdered his grandfather.

Chapter Seven

Choices and Terms

The Sandking walked towards the men and all parted to make way for the King of Hogarth and sworn enemy of the Bussar: N'Kosi the Sandking. The King stepped toward Haidar and stood ten feet away from him and spoke.

"I do not come for battle, Haidar, son of Bogani. Nor do I desire war with your people. But though I come in peace. Also know that I am prepared to shred that peace and lay waste to the plains and extend the desert sea over your kingdom if you do not return, my son."

M'Msee quickly shawl'd himself and backed into the shadows so as to go unnoticed and walked slowly to not draw attention and quickly left the scene to find Amani.

Haidar stared his father's killer in the eyes and slowly reached for the hilt of his knife. His heart quickened to reach out and slit the throat of the murderer of the man who sired him.

"You come into my land with soldiers, and claim to desire peace? But all I see is a king who is the murderer who killed my father in ritual combat. I behold an armed spy who has the audacity to come into my camp and threaten my land. But I will forgive the insolence to not show honor where honor is due."

N'Kosi guffawed and replied. "I *have* done you honor son of Bussar by not immersing you and all that you love under the sand. The only thing that stops me is the pact I made with your father Bogani. Because if it were not so, believe me when I say that all that you know, and love would already be entombed beneath my feet."

Immediately, Umfami warriors came from behind the wall to Haidar's rear and stood flanking their king.

Haidar then spoke to the men of the clans. "All of you return to your homes and comfort your wives and little ones. Bussar will not go to war tonight. I will take the king to see his son."

Immediately the people disbursed as commanded and when they all left, none were in the square that faced the king's home, save the guard of Haidar and those that had accompanied the Sandking. "My Umfami, you have been faithful. Watch these and let none pass as the Hogarthen king and I see to his son."

The soldiers brought their fists to their chests in salute, then immediately ran and formed a line in front of the Hogarthen soldiers.

"Come Hogarth and see to the well-being of your son."

Haidar turned his back on the visiting king and entered his royal home and the Sandking followed.

The two entered a bedchamber. Upon the bed was Jo'than asleep and a woman who sat in a chair to nurse his health. Haidar moved to the side to allow the king to attend to his son and spoke.

"While he is not a friend of Bussar, he came to us injured and he has been treated with respect and care with the intent that he might return home."

N'Kosi said nothing but sat on the bed and looked at his son. He stroked his head and spoke to the woman who nursed him.

"His injuries?"

"He battled an Akoolah and has survived the beast's claws to his chest and abdomen. He was brought to us in time that we may tend to him and his wounds are healing, the herbs and balms have helped. He is strong and we expect him to recover."

N'Kosi emitted a slight smile. He then nodded and looked once more at his son then stood to face Haidar.

"You have shown kindness to my son. This is a thing I will not forget. But how did my son come to be in your house?"

"Come," said Haidar. "Let us talk alone in my private chamber."

Haidar motioned for the Sandking to once again follow, and he did so. The two men walked to an adjoining chamber with a desk and chairs and Haidar bolted the door and the men of the two nations sat one across from another.

"It is pleasing to a father to see his boy alive. Thank you for the service you have done to him. I would have understood if you had shown me a corpse. Especially considering the injury your family has sustained at my hand."

"Do not thank me. The thought had crossed my mind to take the boy's life."

"Yet you did not?" said N'Kosi. "Why?"

"My son prevented me."

N'Kosi retracted his neck in surprise. "Your son? Your own blood stopped you from killing *my* son?"

"Yes, and he is the reason your boy still lives. Based on the tale he shared. They were together when attacked by a pack of Akoolah. They somehow survived, but not without your son being gravely injured. My son did not leave him to the wilderness to claim him. But upon his own back brought him to be tended that he might live. *He* is the reason the wilderness did not have your boy and the hand that stayed my own from taking his blood. Your boy did not wander into Bussar. He was brought here."

The Sandking breathed heavily. His hands covered his mouth and his eyes. N'Kosi then let out a long sigh and spoke.

"It was perhaps best that he had been left in the wilderness to die."

Haidar replied. "I echoed the selfsame words to my son, and I recognize them as my own: words that only a king would dare speak concerning his son."

N'Kosi nodded. "Then we both see the dilemma to the is-sue?"

Haidar nodded sadly and spoke somberly. "I know that nei-ther of our peoples benefit from war. The only ones who profit would be the sorcerers of the tower. For with their magics, they might even animate the dead to give offerings to Enkai and sustain the storm."

N'Kosi nodded. "Then we are in agreement. We must protect our people from war until Hutari comes."

Haidar once more nodded in agreement.

"My armies have orders to overrun the plains and destroy every living thing they encounter if I am not back in two days' time. I have created a sandstorm at the edge of Bussar territory and I hold the storm at bay. If I fall, the storm will overrun the plains until it centers upon my corpse and dies out. My army knows to follow if it moves, for it means I am dead. A natural precaution that I have taken to protect my people from yours. I would not have you do to Hogarth what you did to the Medja. But neither can we be in a stalemate. We must resolve this breaking of the treaty. For this knowledge will escape both of us and some among our people will certainly desire war. But despite their ill will, I will not be so foolish to give strength to the Kifu to escape his bonds and overrun my people. My son has brought dishonor to my house by living; now even more so by being taken captive to your land. Your son has brought dishonor to his house for not letting the wilderness take him, and more for bringing the offspring of his people's enemy into your home.

Neither of our houses, our kingdoms, and the archaic culture and rules of dead men will settle for anything less than each boy's death."

N'Kosi stood up and paced, frustrated at the situation. "Both of our people are still stuck in the old ways and do not know what you and I know. The land cannot be given as a blood offering to the Kifu lest it rise and destroy those that remain after war. We are indeed in a quandary, you and I. Two kings bound by the laws and traditions of our people. How ironic to command armies between our two nations that could ravage our kingdoms yet be powerless against the traditions of the dead."

Haidar replied. "What you say is true, but do not mistake agreement with my desire to not see you dead. I still very much want to kill you."

N'Kosi smiles. "As you should. But we are kings, and what we want must be set aside for the good of our people. Your father knew this and gave himself to my blade to bring peace that has lasted a generation between our two people. I knew your father, and he was not a fool. I perceive that neither is his son."

Haidar gritted his teeth and replied. "No, the needs of my people outweigh my desire to avenge my father's death. The brokered deal still holds. But my council has come into the knowledge of your son's presence. And desire that my son should be given to the wilderness and take no wife from the families of the clans. Your son, according to your fathers is captive in the house of your enemy. Yet lies before you mending, safe and free to go home. However, to do so dishonors both him and you, and threatens your image in the eyes of your people. Perhaps even your rule? My son, out of compassion, saved your son's life, because your son fought by his side, and he would not see such honorable blood taken by the beasts of the field. But I know your trials of manhood to be as our own and it is clear that the king's son has failed his trial of manhood, and allowed himself to receive comfort from his enemy. Consequences that would be shameful to your people. All that is true before us now is that there are two honorable boys, bound within a web of old men's laws, traditions, and pressure from the dead. As fathers, such a quandary does not seem fair. Yet we are kings, and we must look to that which goes beyond the welfare of even our own flesh. It is for this reason that I will not unleash the Bussar against the Hogarth for vengeance done to my house and will honor the will of the Hutari's peace."

N'Kosi stood and stood at arm's length from Haidar and spoke to him as one father to another, and from king to king.

"I also will not go to war with your people. Nor will the desert storm overtake your lands. But we must also address the dishonor to our houses. Both of our sons must be given the opportunity to redeem themselves from their shame. You and I already know how we can resolve this, though I imagine we are loath to say it."

Haidar nodded. "In the morning, Amani will fight Jo'than to the death. If either chooses to forgo. Your son will be my slave, or my son shall be yours. Do you agree?"

N'Kosi sighed, closed his eyes put his hand over his mouth, and shook his head so that he acknowledged what had been said.

"Then it is settled. Rest in my house and sleep with your son. For if Akuma wills it. Tomorrow your son will die at the hands of my own."

Haidar then turned and exited the room.

N'Kosi watched him leave and looked to the window to see a raven lift from the sill and fly into the darkness.

Chapter Eight

A King's Decision

M 'Msee sat in his hut, his eyes glazed and his pupils unseen. A raven flew into his open window and settled on a chair. The bird squawked and lifted off to return as it came.

M'Msee awoke from his trance, and his face hardened. He stood to his feet grabbed his shawl and headed to the king's home.

The old man approached the entrance, his steady gait drawing the attention of the guards stationed at the door. They recognized him and, with a respectful nod, stepped aside to grant him entry. Inside the dining hall, Queen Mudiwa sat in quiet reflection. When she noticed his presence, her brows lifted in surprise, and she addressed him.

"Wisdom? What brings you to come at this hour to the king?"

"My apologies, my queen. But I come not to see the king but to check on my Amunzu. Is he still up?"

Mudiwa shrugged her shoulders and replied. "If your godson is not in his room, I am sure with all that has happened, he sits by the Elder Tree. Is everything alright?"

M'Msee sighs, "Ask me this time tomorrow, and then we shall both know."

M'Msee then left the king's abode and walked to the rear of the king's house and down a path that led to a grove of trees that lined a small creek. He noted in the distance a figure sitting on a log against the largest tree near the rear of the grove and walked toward whom he knew was Amani.

The boy noticed M'Msee as he emerged from the dark into the light of the night sky and spoke. "I wish to be alone, M'Msee."

M'Msee sat down next to his godson and replied. "Good, then we shall be alone together."

Amani let out a loud sigh in irritation and scooted over as M'Msee sat next to him.

"You, young man, are my pride and joy. If I had a son. I would have very much wanted him to be like you. I also know that though you question your father's love. He loves you so that he would give his own life as an offering for your own. And though your father might appear hard, he is the king, and kings cannot show favoritism if they wish to remain king in the plains. You must understand that his love for you as a father does not now bode him well as king. As king, he must abase his desires to those of the people he rules...even to his own hurt. And know that your father is about to endure a most grievous wound. An injury akin to the cutting off of even one's arm."Amani sat silent and stared off into the night.

"It is for this reason that you must understand why tomorrow is so important and why you must leave all that you know and love behind. Why tonight you must remember the words that I say. Because in the future they will sustain you when times are hard and because I may never have another chance to speak with you ever again."

Amani now turned his head and looked at the old man. He noted the wrinkles on his brow and that he appeared older, and weathered. And though it was clear M'Msee still possessed much vigor, Amani knew he was tired, and he turned to give ear to the man he loved even as his father and replied.

"I know it is possible that I might be banished to the wilderness, or if allowed to remain, I would take no wife of the clan. Is it this of which you speak?"

M'Msee shook his head. "No Amunzu. Tomorrow, you will be given the choice to take life to restore your name and your father's name. And if you succeed, you will bring great honor to the Bussar, great honor to your house and I doubt there would be no woman, young or old, who will deny you their bed. And I know your honor and that of your own house weighs upon you now. The wilderness itself has shown you a man, and you have proved you deserve to stand at the gate and judge your people. I see you, Amani, son of Haidar, son of Bogani. I see how you have worked and striven to see all that you have desired, be lost by the decision of the Culsha. And know that on the morrow, opportunity will be given to you to restore all that you desire... but know that it must come at the expense of Jo'than's life."

Amani cocked his head to the side and stared incredulously at his godfather. "You lie! How do you know this? Surely the council will not permit his slaying."

"It is not the Culsha that wills this to be done. But your father is in agreement with the Sandking. For in the morning, you and Jo'than will be set within the city square. And there you will both be given the option to take the life of the other. By doing so, the kings prevent tradition from forcing their countries from going to war and, in return, they save many lives. If you kill Jo'than, both houses will be honored. If Jo'than kills you. Both houses will be honored. And peace will still exist between the two nations. Even now the Sandking holds at bay the desert sands that, if unleashed, will cover the plains and extend his realm, perhaps even to the great sea. His wrath was only checked on his last push into our land by the death of your grandfather. And it is a certainty that the plains will vanish if his wrath is once more unleashed. This cannot be allowed to occur. Nor can Haidar be allowed to unleash the might of Bussar and the Umfami against the Hogarth. The Kifu lives off the blood of the land. Such horror cannot be allowed to walk once again to overrun the world."

"But I also have power, M'Msee. You have seen what I can do. You have trained me I can wrestle from the sky itself. I will kill the Sandking and his people if he dares unleash the sand against us."

"You must resist the temptation to use your power, my son. Your actions only serve the Kifu and would ignite a war from those who also possess the powers of Akuma, but who use them to advance the cause of Enkai. The Medja cannot be allowed to think of you as an object to control. You do not yet understand the limits of your power and your ability to awaken the Kifu. Nor yet understand your importance."

Amani rose from his seat, his movements sharp and his hands clenched into fists. His chest heaved with each breath as years of unspoken resentment surged to the surface, his voice trembling with barely contained fury.

"Then tell me, M'Msee!" he shouted, his eyes burning with unshed tears. "You've been in my ear since I was a child, filling my head with this destiny you say I was born for! Do you know what it's like? To be told every waking moment that I carry a storm inside me—a storm that could tear apart everything I love if I'm not constantly on guard? That I must train, restrain, and discipline myself every second of my life because if I slip, even for a moment, I could awaken a force that would devour the world?"

Amani paced like a restless lion; his voice raw with anguish as the weight of his words crashed against the darkness of the night. "And then you have the audacity—the audacity—to demand I take responsibility for everyone else's failures? For the choices you and your generation didn't have the courage to make? Maybe—just maybe—if you had done what needed to be done with your father, my father wouldn't be fighting now to salvage his honor!"

Amani stopped, and slammed his fist against the elder tree with a force that made the air around him feel heavier. A flash of lightning brightened the night sky, and its rumble could be heard in the distance. "I could've had a normal life, M'Msee. A life where I didn't have to carry the weight of every mistake, every regret, every expectation that isn't even mine to bear. But no. Instead, I get this. This endless prison of duty and sacrifice!"

His breath came in ragged gasps as the silence that followed swallowed his outburst, leaving the night heavy with the echoes of his pain. In the distance

M'Msee stood silent, his eyes drifting to the horizon, where the sound of approaching rain grew louder. Amani's words struck like a spear to the heart, piercing through the armor of wisdom he had worn for generations. Each syllable carried the venom of truth, the kind that seeped deep and reminded him of every failure, every misstep, every life lost in the shadow of his choices.

The irony cut him sharper than any blade. He, who had sacrificed nations and oceans of lives—not to destroy the Kifu, but to cling to a fragile hope that one day, somehow, he might redeem the father he had failed. The weight of that contradiction bore down on him now, and for the first time in centuries, M'Msee felt... small.

His voice, when it came, trembled with an unfamiliar fragility, like the edges of a cracked pot holding back a deluge. "You wound me, Amunzu. But perhaps... it is right that you should. Perhaps you speak truths I have hidden, even from myself." He swallowed, his gaze falling to the floor as if it held the answers he had long sought. "I have lived long enough to see the cost of my choices, to know that the pain I carry will demand a reckoning. And perhaps, when that day comes, I will pay a price I cannot bear. A price owed in a coin I do not yet understand."

He lifted his head, his aged eyes meeting Amani's fiery gaze. For a moment, the storm between them stilled, replaced by a raw and unspoken ache. "But this moment, Amunzu is not about my regrets or my past. The sand in an hourglass cannot be returned." He drew a shuddering breath, his voice deepening with the weight of inevitability. "This moment is about you. And a choice you will soon be forced to make. One that will demand far more than you think you have to give."

M'Msee stepped closer, his presence was as heavy as the gathering storm outside. "You saved the boy in the wilderness. But to save your honor to obtain the life the Culsha would strip from you, you must kill him."

Amani looked at M'Msee and he realized his words were bereft of kindness owed a man who, with his own hands, brought him into the world. And he came to himself. "I am sorry M'Msee." M'Msee broached a smile and nodded in acknowledgment.

The tension fractured like brittle stone as Amani grasped the weight of the choice laid before him. Slowly, he spoke, his voice steady but edged with a dawning clarity. "You believe I have a choice in this, M'Msee," he said, the words heavy with both uncertainty and resolve. "Let me make sure I understand. If I kill Jo'than, the Sandking will not go to war?"

"Correct, my son, for he and your father have agreed that there shall remain peace between our lands. And only the sons of kings will be placed in harm's way. Each nation's prince to stand in the stead of armies. It is the way of old to give one's life that many might be saved."

"And if I kill Jo'than, N'Kosi will leave our land, and my honor will be restored?"

"What you say is true," said M'Msee.

"How is it that in saving *his* life from the wilderness I have unleashed such potential death towards my people?"

"Your act of mercy has dishonored the Sandking and would make him look weak in the eyes of his people. Jo'than has been dishonored as well. Hogarthen tradition demands that he have died in the wilderness or return alive with his prize. He has done neither. By your actions, you have robbed the wilderness of its kill and have placed yourself above the wisdom of the traditions of both Hogarth and Bussar. Your father and N'Kosi are kings and think like kings. But I have shown you the way of Aaru, and to think as gods would think. Remember this lesson, Amunzu. That the ways of a godling are not the ways of men. Your act of mercy, to see beyond tradition, has spit in the face of generations of ritual. And though you were following your heart to save an ally. Your heart has led us to this path, and tomorrow...it shall be seen what path your life must now take."

"But Jo'than is not my enemy, M'Msee. He saved my life. How can I repay him by taking his?"

"It is a king's decision, and tomorrow you must show yourself a king to two peoples. And the decision you make will be told by the storytellers of two nations. Therefore, choose wisely what you do, my prince."

"You make it sound as if I have a choice. To kill my newfound ally who has saved my life or to let him take mine."

M'Msee stood up and leaned himself upon his walking stick. "There are always three choices, my son. You may take his life, or spare it, but there is a third choice that is even harder to walk. To choose *not* to fight. You and I know you are the standard to the Kifu. You have seen him slumber and know he is not a myth. Your father would have only burdened you with this knowledge if he knew that as king you were ready to bear it. It is for this reason you cannot shed a man's blood in passion. Why, *you* above all cannot walk like other men. For I reveal to you now what few alive know. It is I who holds the Kifu in its slumber. Allowing him to live off the life that I possess. For this reason and this reason alone do I grow old. I have given my life to feed the undead god. But you could undo all that five centuries has wrought. You have the power of youth coupled with Akuma's power from Aaru within you. I believe that when the dream of Akuma takes hold, and men ascend, you will be among the first. I am not as strong as I once was. It would take centuries to recoup my strength to fend off Hesphus from destroying Tanara and breaching the cover Akuma has placed around Tanara to keep Enkai at bay. For if I fall, all that stands between certain doom and life is you, young man. Because if Hesphus discovers your life, he will rise to feed upon it and will walk the ends of the earth to find you and consume it, and this we cannot allow. For you and I possess the power of Aaru. And while I was once known and am Hutari. I foresee that you too will be Hutari. And the power that I bear. I can give it to any I seek. But I believe that you also possess this life, the seed of Akuma is strong in you. but if *you* are not careful, you have within you to weaken my hold on the creature and empower the Kifu and give it rise and know that upon its awakening it will seek you out, and everything that you know, and love will die. Not just you, nor your parents, or Bussar itself, but all the peoples of Tanara, even those that exist beyond the great sea. Nor will there be a place that you could go that the Kifu would not follow. There would be no place you could run. He would pursue the life of a godling. One day, you may be forced to confront him without me. And on that day, the true decision must be made. But neither you nor I can contend with him now. So, I adjure you, young prince, leave Jo'than his life. As far as your power to move the wind and sky, you will know of the need to use your power when Tanara itself is at stake. Then your power may be unleashed unrestrained. But know that on that day you release your power to kill in passion, you will open the tomb of the Kifu and start a future where you must face this god. Until then, promise this old man to restrain yourself. And train in silence to hone your skills and away from the eyes of them that would speak whispers to agents of the dark one. Those that would harness your power to allow Enkai entrance into this world. Be wary of the rogue sorcerers. Medja of Enkai, who would come and take you if they knew such power, lived in their midst. Remember, my son, that you must fight for the living and not the dead. For who is Jo'than against the tide of death that would follow in the wake of the Kifu? So, know that yes, if you kill the boy, you will keep your honor, but all that you gain will one day still come to ruin. You have spared the boy's life once. I ask for the sake of the living and those not yet born that you spare him once again. Choose the path to be the scion of both prophet and crown and restrain your great powers and flee the simple path to be a mere king."

Amani pondered M'Msee's words and replied. "And if I spare him. What happens then?"

The old sage then lifted from his rock and replied. "All things are as dung compared to the waking of the walking death. Know that I realize what I ask of you is a hard thing. But I ask you to choose hardness as a loyal soldier, not for Bussar but for all those who stand on the side of life. And though all may not know the why of your choice. Your choice is a godling's burden. A burden that only you are strong enough to bear Amunzu. Consider my words and know that I love you, and your father, though he would place you in harm's way, also loves you. But he refuses to fully believe what I know is true about you. And is still bound to tradition, but you...there is hope for the world in a boy that would save his enemy to one day fight a common foe. For no nation can stand against the Kifu, but only a world united were it to rise."

M'Msee placed his hand on Amani's shoulder and smiled. "Fear not tomorrow but gird up your loins as a man and be strong. Choose neither the path of a prince or King but that of a Godling, one who might one day ascend, and know that if you do, you will suffer abasement for a season. But will reap in due time if you faint not."

M'Msee sighed. "It is late, and I have so many things that I desire to say to you, but you cannot bear them now. But in time, you will know the words that I speak are truth and a light for you. I have said all I can say. I must go to my bed. And you must do the same as you will need your strength. But before you go, make sure to hug and kiss your mother tonight, boy."

M'Msee then stood to his feet and turned to walk away, and Amani stood silently as the old man melded into the black of night and pondered the words of his godfather in his heart.

Chapter Nine

The Kasset

Amani woke from his slumber and washed himself. He noted food was set at his bedside and he took eat. But when he tried to exit his room, the door would not budge. He could see through the wooden slates that a guard stood and prevented his leaving and the prince of Bussar spoke his irritation. "Guard, why do you prevent my exit? I command to be released at once!"

A voice bellowed back in a moderate but decisive tone. "I know who you are, my prince. But I am commanded by your father, and when he gives the command to withdraw, I will do so."

Amani sighs, "Does your command prevent you from telling me what is happening?"

A Kasset has been called. You and the Hogarthen boy are to engage one another in combat. For the honor of Bussar and of your house, you will fight to atone for bringing the Hogarth boy into our land and for not allowing the wilderness to have its flesh.

Amani withdrew from the door. *What M'Msee said was true. A Kasset a fight to the death.*

The boy prince slumped back into his bed and thought upon his situation.

I am to kill Jo'than. He has done nothing wrong but aid me. I would not have survived in the wilderness if not for his help. And this is how our fathers would have us repay a debt of life? Blood for blood? He placed his hand over his mouth and rubbed his face into the palm of his hands, then sighed.

Breath Amani...breath.

The door then opened and an Umfami guard stood at attention with a spear in hand, and the traditional Akoolah knife tucked in his waist. He spoke with authority and his directive was clear. "Rise, young prince, it is time to face the Kasset."

Amani did as ordered and he tightened his sash around his waist and held his head up high. and he walked out of his quarters and entered the great hall of his father, King Haidar. A line of men assembled from the four clans created a path, and to the left and right of him were the eldermen of the clans, and as he walked past each one, some sneered, while others nodded as if to wish him luck. He followed the procession until he exited outside.

The sun was aloft with not a cloud in the sky to hinder its heat. Across the city sea was the population of Bussar and across from them was the Sandking on horseback and several of his men to his rear and side. Haidar stood to the side with Mudiwa, and M'Msee, staff in hand, solemnly looked on, his eyes locked on Amani's.

Amani then saw Jo'than and smiled at him, but the boy did not return his gaze. But he looked down and made pleading glances at his father, who did not acknowledge him.

An elderman of Bussar then stepped into the middle of the throng and spoke. "Our two peoples have been at war for many years. We now live in a time of peace, purchased in blood by the father of Haidar, son of Bogani. This blood right has now been broken, and to prevent a war that would consume our two peoples and bring loss of life. These two great kings now stand to deliver their sons as a sacrifice to the Kasset that war might be averted. But moreover, that the way of the wilderness be respected. For Amani, the son of Haidar stands accused of foregoing the ways of our fathers that have purchased this peace and dishonored his own house by sparing the life of an enemy that the wilderness would have. Moreover, the accused has brought the son of the man who has killed his own grandfather into these lands' contrary to the way of the Bussar..."

Loud jeering echoed across the crowd and gasps were heard among the throng, but the elderman continued. "But the ways of Bussar and Hogarth are they not shared? For the Sandking of Hogarth brings claim from his house that Jo'than has failed his people to secure life from the wilderness or die in the attempt. In his failure to secure this life, he has failed even to secure his own death. But not just a failure to die, but to receive life from the hand of an enemy and the son of a former enemy who stood in defiance to his rule over these lands. Hogarth will see this remedied and death to the Bussar boy and son of the son of the last rival who dared challenge him. Two kings, two combatants. One life for the sake of many. Live or die, let the Kasset decide. This is the way of our two kings, and this is the way of the sands."

A guard then shoved Jo'than into a circle of stones and tossed him an Akoolah knife. Amani then was also shoved into the same circle and given the same and soldiers then surrounded them and voiced a roar. And when they did, they lowered their spears such that if any of the two young men were to get too close, they would be impaled upon the spears of the Bussari or Hogarthen warriors.

Amani picked up the knife felt its heft and checked to see that the blade was firmly tucked and secured into the shaft.

"Begin!" cried the elderman.

Both young men locked eyes, their gazes sharp and unyielding. Amani adopted the fluid, lethal stance of the Akoolah, his knees slightly bent, his movements measured and deliberate as he began to circle. Jo'than, in contrast, took the imposing stance of the bear, his upper body swaying with a hypnotic rhythm, his form turned diagonally to minimize his profile. Jo'than's hands were open, ready to grapple with his rescuer.

The onlookers stood at the edge of the circle, watching with bated breath. Mothers clutched their children, and fathers stood with tense shoulders, all aware that only one warrior would leave this circle alive.

The oppressive silence of the arena was a weight that bore down on every soul gathered. From opposite sides of the circle, two families stood, their fates intertwined with the deadly clash about to unfold.

Queen Mudiwa's face was a mask of calm, but her trembling hands betrayed the tempest of emotions roiling within. She clutched the folds of her shawl as though it could shield her heart from what she might soon witness. Amani, her firstborn, her pride, stood poised to kill or be killed, and she could only pray the gods would see fit to spare him. But prayer felt hollow now, as though the heavens had turned their faces away from the blood about to be spilled. Her husband, King Haidar, was rigid beside her, his jaw set, and his fists clenched. Yet even in his stoicism, she could feel his pain, the agony of a father forced to let his son prove himself in a way no parent should ever have to bear.

Across the circle, King N'Kosi loomed, his expression inscrutable. But those who knew him well would have seen the shadow of doubt flicker in his eyes. His son, Jo'than, had inherited his strength, his ferocity, but had the boy truly understood the gravity of this trial? N'Kosi's thoughts churned with memories of Jo'than's childhood—his laughter, his stubborn resolve, his eagerness to prove himself worthy of his lineage. Now, as his son squared off against the prince of Bussar, N'Kosi questioned the price of that worthiness.

M'Msee stood apart, his fingers digging into his palms until they left crescent-shaped marks. His lips moved silently, murmuring prayers that wavered between defiance and despair. His godson had been raised to fight, to dominate, to carry the pride of their people—but here, under the unforgiving gaze of the sun and Bussar's enemies, the prospect of losing him was unbearable.

The families avoided each other's eyes, the invisible chasm of grief and hope separating them like the gulf between life and death. They were bound by the unspoken truth: when this trial ended, one family would walk away victorious but broken, while the other would be left in ruins, clutching only memories.

The tension in the air grew thicker as the two young warriors moved, circling like predators, their every step watched by those who had raised them loved them, and now stood powerless to save them.

The two combatants took a moment to size each other up. Amani's eyes flickered over Jo'than's stance, noting the positioning of his feet, the tension in his muscles, and the way his eyes narrowed with concentration. He could almost hear Jo'than's heart pounding, matching the rhythm of his own. Jo'than's broad shoulders and powerful arms spoke of raw strength, but Amani knew that brute force could be outmatched by speed precision, and cunning.

Jo'than, for his part, watched Amani with the gaze of a predator. He saw the fluid grace in Amani's movements, the way he shifted his weight with the agility of a cat. Jo'than recognized the confidence in Amani's eyes, a confidence that spoke of countless battles fought and won. He remembered Amani's ferocity from their battle with the Akoolah and knew this would not be an easy fight. Would he use his powers? How could he stand against an opponent that could control the wind? But this was a Kasset. And he judged his opponent would be bound by its ancient rules.

They slowly circled each other, each waiting for the other to make the first move, the air between them thick with tension. Every step was a calculated measure, a silent conversation between warriors who understood the stakes of the battle to come.

Jo'than, seeing that Amani would give him no opening to strike determined he would create his own and with a guttural yell that seemed to resonate with the very ground beneath their feet, surged forward, his knife glinting like a shard of sunlight. His battle cry sliced through the air, a verbal harbinger of imminent violence. He moved with the brute force of a charging bear, every step pounding against the earth with intent.

He brought his knife down upon Amani and the Amani expertly caught his blow.

The clash of knives rang out, sharp and clear, like a chorus of deadly intent. Amani moved with the fluid grace of a predator, his blade a mere extension of his will. He deftly parried Jo'than's initial strike, his counter thrust a blur of precision. Jo'than twisted away, narrowly avoiding the lethal edge.

They repositioned themselves and once more circled one another in a deadly dance, the air around them crackling with tension. Once more, Jo'than extended his arm to strike and Amani ducked beneath a wide slash, rolling smoothly to his feet and delivering a swift kick to Jo'than's midsection. The impact landed solidly, but Jo'than absorbed the blow, his eyes never leaving Amani's. And with a savage backhand swipe, he grazed Amani's arm, a thin line of crimson appearing on his dark skin.

Amani winced, but ignored the pain, and pressed a counterattack, his movements a study in controlled ferocity. Their blades continued to clash, each strike and parry a testament to their skill and determination. Sweat mingled with blood as they pushed each other to the brink, their breaths coming in ragged gasps. The watchers gasped and murmured, every movement on the battlefield reflected in their tense expressions. Amani closed in to attack and landed a blow with the back of his fist to the square of Jo'than's jaw. Jo'than stumbled, his eyes flashing with fury as he quickly regained his footing. He countered with a swift slash aimed at Amani's midsection, but Amani twisted away, narrowly avoiding the blade.

Seeing an opening, Amani pressed his advantage, launching a flurry of rapid strikes. Jo'than parried and dodged, his movements fueled by a mix of desperation and determination. Their knives clashed in a rapid, metallic rhythm, each strike and counterstrike a testament to their honed skills and fierce resolve.

The combatants circled each other, their breathing ragged, eyes locked in a deadly stare. The shouts and gasps of their families barely registered in their minds. With each passing second, the intensity of their battle grew, both warriors pushing themselves to their limits.

In a sudden, synchronized movement, both fighters surged forward. Blades flashed and clashed, the impact resonating through the ground. Amani's knife sliced through the air, narrowly missing Jo'than's arm as Jo'than retaliated with a wild swing aimed at Amani's head. Amani ducked just in time, feeling the rush of air as the blade passed inches above him.

As their movements became more frantic, the precision of their strikes began to falter. Amani aimed a powerful thrust at Jo'than's chest, but Jo'than deflected the blow, their knives locking in a brief, intense moment. Muscles strained and sweat dripped as they struggled for dominance, their faces mere inches apart, each feeling the other's breath.

Finally, with a powerful twist and a burst of energy, they broke apart. Amani stumbled back, his grip loosening on his knife, while Jo'than reeled from the exertion. In the heat of the moment, the fierce exchange of blows disarmed them both as their knives flew from their hands and skittered across the ground. Without hesitation, they launched into a brutal hand-to-hand fight. Fists pummeled flesh with sickening thuds, each impact resonating with visceral intensity. Amani ducked a wild swing from Jo'than, stepping in to land a crushing blow to his ribs. He felt the bones give way slightly under his fist; the sensation sending a jolt through his arm.

Jo'than retaliated with a powerful uppercut, catching Amani under the jaw and snapping his head back. The taste of copper filled Amani's mouth as he staggered, but he quickly regained his footing, his vision sharpening with renewed determination. They grappled fiercely, muscles straining, gasping for air. The scent of sweat and blood filled the air, a pungent reminder of their primal struggle.

Jo'than managed to lock his arms around Amani's torso, lifting him off the ground with a guttural roar. Amani wriggled and twisted, driving his elbow repeatedly into Jo'than's side until he was dropped. The moment his feet touched the ground, Amani spun and delivered a knee to Jo'than's midsection, forcing the air from his lungs in a wheezing gasp.

Both fighters, now visibly fatigued, scrambled to retrieve their knives. They warily eyed each other, knowing the next phase of their battle would be decisive.

Locked in a brutal grapple, the two warriors fought for dominance, their strength waning but their resolve unbroken. Sensing a fleeting moment of vulnerability in his opponent, Amani executed a masterful strike, disarming Jo'than with a swift, precise movement. The knife spun out of the circle, a distant echo of their struggle.

With a cry of triumph, Amani pivoted and delivered a devastating elbow strike to Jo'than's temple. The blow landed with a sickening thud, the force of it driving Jo'than to the ground, unconscious.

Amani stood over his fallen opponent, his chest heaving with the exertion of the battle. The victory was his, yet it carried the weight of inevitability, a stark reminder of the unending struggle for survival and honor. The sands of their battleground whispered around them, the echoes of their fight fading into the vast, silent desert that extended beyond the land of Bussar.

Soreness made its presence known and the taste of Amani's blood was as salt as the cut above his eye stung as the open wound dripped blood onto his face that ran down his cheek into his mouth.

He looked up from his unconscious quarry and noted the faces of those that encircled him. The Sandking's eyes locked on Amani waiting for him to administer the death blow that would surely come for his son. In the end, it was a fight for more than just honor—it was a fight for the future of each king's family, and Amani had emerged as the bearer of that fragile, blood-soaked promise. And yet despite his best efforts King N'Kosi could not conceal the pride that he had for his beaten son, and he nodded his head, then inhaled, waiting for his son's throat to be cut by the hand of people's enemy. To deliver the final blow that would send Jo'than's spirit into the land of the Sky-people.

Mudiwa wept, tears of both joy and sorrow streaming down her face, while happy that her son would live. The scene she had just witnessed also horrified her. To behold the ferocity that dwelled in her son. In her eyes, she saw that whatever innocence she had imputed to him had now been removed. He was a warrior and a trained killer of men, even if it was justifiably the life of an enemy.

Haidar's face was easy to read. His body was taunt, and his fists were clenched as if he watched a wrestling match between the top warriors of the clan. Yes, his father's face was easy to read. He wanted the Hogarth boy dead and cared nothing for his young life. It was disposable the moment he entered the territory of the clans. Haidar cared nothing for cost save honor for his house and perhaps recompense to the man who killed his father similarly so many years ago. Vengeance rooted for Amani and desired him to slice his victim's throat. Haidar's position was indeed known. But it was M'Msee's reaction that caught Amani off guard.

For when Amani looked at his Godfather he saw that M'Msee rocked silently and his hands trembled and he held his stomach as if pained at what he saw, and he shook his head at Amani to dissuade him from his course, and a look of dread covered his face and Amani paused to consider what he was about to do and M'Msee's words from the night before echoed in his mind. *"All things are as dung compared to the waking of the walking death."* And when he recalled the conversation from the night prior, he loosened his grip from Jo'than's throat and let the lad go. He then took the Akoolah knife, raised it for all to see, and then tossed it into the dirt and spoke that all might hear. "I have bested my rival in combat, but he is not at his full strength, and

I challenge the rightness of this cause. And though he might best me if he were at full strength, know that I will not kill a man who has saved my life. And if I must forfeit my life that he might live Then know warring kings of desert and the plains that I renounce my life."

Haidar immediately cried out in anger and disbelief. "Amani kill him! I command it as your father...as your king!"

Amani looked at the Sandking to see if the King of Hogarth would reply but the regent stood mute as he watched aloof upon his horse in silence. Amani then turned to his father.

"You cannot command in the Kasset. By right I hold the man's life in my hand, and I have chosen to spare it. What must be done to me now is of no consequence."

Haidar and all of Bussar and the assembled Hogarthen entourage stared fixated on Amani. Some were perplexed that he would spare an enemy, others spit in the dirt that he did not follow the customs of the ancestors and did not shed Jo'than's blood. The murmurs from all who witnessed were clear in their judgment: disapproval.

King Haidar felt the weight of the realization settle heavily upon him. Amani had chosen the unthinkable—the third path, the one Haidar had hoped his son would never choose to tread. His boy had spared his enemy, forsaken vengeance, and chosen peace at the cost of his freedom. It was the decision of a king, one born of wisdom and sacrifice. Pride stirred within Haidar, yet it was smothered by the anger that also burned within his chest.

His jaw tightened, and his teeth ground together as his fists curled at his sides, trembling with suppressed wrath. The veins on his neck stood out like rivers under strain, betraying the storm within. This was not the path Haidar would have chosen; this was not the way of kings he had sought to teach his son.

Mudiwa observed him, her keen eyes catching the restrained fury in her husband's posture. She stepped closer, her hand finding his clenched fist. Her touch was light, yet firm, her presence an anchor against the tempest in his soul.

With quiet strength, she whispered to him, her voice steady, yet brimming with conviction. "He is no longer a boy, Haidar. The father in you has raised him well—into a man of honor and wisdom. You may not agree with his choice, but as his king, you must respect it."

Her words were a balm and a blade, soothing yet cutting through both his pride and anger over what his son had done. Haidar closed his eyes for a moment, wrestling with the truth in her words. Amani's choice was not the act of a rebellious son; it was the action of a sovereign in the making. And though the father in Haidar seethed, the king in him could not deny the courage and wisdom in what his son had done.

Haidar held back tears, and his body shook to keep himself from crying aloud for what he knew he must do to keep the peace of his people. And knowing he could not act other than what he was bound to as ruler of his people, spoke the words that would seal his son's fate.

King Haidar's voice rang out, steady and unyielding, though laced with the sorrow of what must be done. "Amani, Prince of Bussar: son of my flesh and bone of my bone. You have fought in the Kasset, the circle of combat according to the laws of our people. And have by your actions renounced your house by choosing to preserve the life of your enemy. You have done this in defiance of the laws of Bussar." Haidar paused, the weight of his next words bearing down upon him. His gaze bore into Amani's, fierce as the desert sun. "You are therefore handed over to the enemy of your people, no more will you be called prince of Bussar and are now cast out from her clans, stripped of your name and lineage. From this day forward, you are marked for death; should any Bussar find you, they are bound by honor to kill you where you stand. I banish you into exile and spew you from the plains into the sands of Hogarth to do with you as they will. I bind you over to the Hogarthen king to serve at our enemies' whim." Haidar's words fell heavy like stones, echoing in the air, unshakable and final. Amani stood silent, his shoulders square, his gaze unwavering, though the weight of his father's decree bore down upon him like a mountain. The judgment had been passed. There was now no turning back.

The Umfami then immediately moved to bind Amani placed a rope around his wrists and gave the end of the rope to the Sandking. And when the Umfami bound him over to King N'Kosi, he took one last look upon his son and a tear finally shed from his eye and he bit his lip and turned his back to his only son. Mudiwa saw the pain in her husband's eyes and also looked upon her child, grief overtook her, and she collapsed to the ground in wails of tears. And when King Haidar turned, all of the Bussar people present also turned their backs to Amani. And Amani stood resolute and wanted to reach out for his mother, who sobbed with sorrowful groanings for her son. But the Bussarim guards stood to bar his path.

Amani, knowing the weight of his fate, straightened his shoulders and inhaled deeply. Without a word, he mirrored his father's action, turning his back on his people. King N'Kosi locked his gaze on the boy and waved his hand to his guard to take Amani into custody. Hogarthen soldiers then held Amani fast bound his wrists and tied the end of his rope to the saddle of the Sandking. The ruler of the Hogarthen people then looked at his son, who groggily rose from the dirt, blood marking his form. And eyed both men. He sighed, then turned his horse to depart to his own land. Amani stumbled, the coarse rope digging into his skin as he struggled to keep pace. He tripped and fell to the ground as the unyielding pull of the Sandking's mount dragged him through the dirt for all his people to see,

The once-proud prince of Bussar, his name now stripped of its honor, was paraded as a symbol of Hogarth's triumph. Amani lowered his head. But it was not the jeers of his people or the weight of shame that pierced his heart—it was the sound of his mother's uncontrollable weeping. Her cries carried over the plains like a ghost's lamentation heard and the anguish of his heart fell at the uncontrollable weeping of his mother, whom he knew he would likely never, ever, see again.

Chapter Ten

The Birth of a Slave

The entourage of the Sandking marched across the plains in four columns of twenty-five men. And at the lead was the monarch who commanded all: N'Kosi, King of Hogarth. To his right was a man Amani noted was a general in the king's army.

Amani lumbered behind the king's horse; stumbling as he was pulled in a forced march behind his captor, sharp pains wracked his wrists from the ropes that bound him as his eyes beheld he was leaving the plains of the four clans. The greens and browns of the hills slowly gave way to rock and desert.

Amani turned to look to his rear and Jo'than, second son of the king, rode horseback behind his father: a man whose life he had now saved twice. The bruises from his combat with Amani were still clear on his face. Occasionally during their trek, Amani would look at the eyes of the man who once fought by his side to kill Akoolah, only now to see him avert his gaze, presumably in shame. The former prince of Bussar could only imagine the thoughts running through Jo'than's mind. His bowed head and the slumped posture on his horse communicated one thing: disgrace. Amani turned his eyes away from the man he had bested in combat to once more take in his surroundings. And he observed that the elevation grew steeper as they moved up a hill. His quadriceps ached as he climbed the protrusion of grass and rock. He could feel his ankles constantly adjust to the shifting ground beneath him as his wrists chaffed against the ropes that held his bound hands. And despite the change in elevation of the terrain, the Sandking's pace never slowed for his captor, nor did he look to his rear to see to his need. It was clear to Amani that if he died while on the journey to Hogarth, it would mean nothing to the man who led the nation that killed his grandfather. Amani wondered what barbarism awaited him in Hogarth. What manner of man must the Sandking be to allow his son to be sacrificed all for the sake of honor? The king's horse grunted as it climbed the hill, and its rider jabbed his heels into the animal's sides to prod it ever forward. The rope around his wrist once more grew taunt and Amani lost his footing and was dragged across the barren ground. Pain reverberated throughout his body as his skin scrapped against the protruding rock underneath him and tore flesh from his arms, abdomen, and legs. Amani grimaced in pain, but his cries of pain only echoed laughter and snickering jeers across the Hogarthen men.

Ten soldiers quick-stepped alongside the Sandking to meet a waiting Jiyadra of one thousand men that camped on the outskirts of clan territory. A roar grew as a thunderclap across the sky as men pumped their fists into the air upon the acknowledgment of their leader's return. The sound of trumpets blared throughout the camp and cheers, and the sound of spears beaten against metal shields clanged and made the ground rumble. And at the head of the throng was a man with a sword who came out to meet the king of Hogarth; first son of the Sandking and commander of the armies encamped and awaiting their nation's lord, J'abari, high prince of Hogarth.

The prince saluted his lord with his fist to his chest, then spoke. "Greetings, father. Is my brother alive? What word do you bring?"

"Jo'than is alive. Bested in combat by this boy here."

The Sandking dismounted from his horse and pointed beyond the rear of the horse to a man bound by his wrists and moaning lying on the ground.

J'abari looked in disgust at his father's captive and replied. "A Bussar? A dog? Why does he even live?"

The Sandking looked at Amani, and Amani stood to his feet and gazed into the eyes of the king. The king then spoke, "J'abari, High Prince of Hogarth. I present to you the former High Prince of Bussar. Amani, son of King Haidar. Defeater of

Jo'than in the Kasset. Now captive to your father, and prince of nothing. He is a gift from our enemies, a payment I have accepted in place of unleashing the burning sands to overrun their land. He will be trained to be my new ward."

J'abari looked at his father's captive and sized him up. He thought of what type of man he must be to defeat his brother in combat. He looked into Amani's eyes and Amani did not turn from the gaze and stood staring at the prince; steel-jawed in silence.

"I dislike his eyes," said J'abari. "He lacks the proper demeanor of a servant."

The Sandking smirked, "Then untie him, and familiarize him with the tasks suited to a prisoner of your father. An initial lesson would be best given to break him into his new life of service. Cleaning the camp's latrine should suffice."

Jo'than had now dismounted from his horse and walked towards his brother, and the two embraced. "You are well?" asked J'abari.

"I live. But this one here held my life in my hands and gave it back to me," said Jo'than.

J'abari looked again at Amani, who no longer looked at him, and inquired. "Why would a Bussar return the life of a Hogarthen?" He slapped the back of Amani's head. "What is wrong with you, Bussar? Do you have no stomach for blood?"

Amani remained silent.

J'abari then backhanded Amani and spoke. "You will speak when spoken to. It would seem that there is much we must break you of."

He was about to strike Amani again when Jo'than grabbed his hand. "He is Father's trophy, not yours to abuse."

J'abari then lowered his hand and gave the rope to untie his father's captive to Jo'than. "Then take your Bussar savior to the latrine and have him clean it. I trust that this is a task you can manage without getting once more beat by this dog?"

Jo'than scowled, bowed his head, and untied Amani from the king's horse, then whispered to him. "You would do well to not provoke my brother. He will not hesitate to kill you even though you are now Father's ward."

Amani replied. "I have no fear of death. It is but the change necessary to ascend to the land of the sky people."

Jo'than led Amani tied as the two walked through the camp. Various men hailed and cheered Jo'than as he pulled Amani along as an animal on a leash. "You truly believe in the sky people? That there is a land beyond this life?"

"I do," said Amani. "And if Akuma wills it. We shall all one day stand on its shores and build the world Akuma dreamed of on Aaru."

"You are a strange one," said Jo'than. Aaru is the land of Enkai and the Nephthys. There is nothing but a land of shadow after death. This is what the Oracle of Hogarth teaches us. This is the truth of the Hogarth: weakness is death and only strength can keep the Kifu at bay. This is why Hogarth prospers and why you are now a slave."

Amani then stopped and turned to his jailer and replied. "Then why are *you* alive? Was it weakness that kept my blade from your throat? Was it weakness to give myself to slavery and to leave my people to prevent a war between our two nations? There is more to life than domination and many forms of strength, Jo'than. And far more to Aaru than Enkai."

The elevation dipped and the smell of feces and urine filled the air and Amani had to place his hand over his nose to prevent himself from vomiting. Before them was the latrine for the Hogarth encampment. Amani saw various male slaves that had traveled with the king's army, a rag-tag combination of both strong and haggard men who dug ditches to cover up the excrement from the encamped soldiers.

Jo'than stopped at a tree and Amani with him. He untied him, gave him a shovel, shoved him towards a watchman, and replied. "Behold the weakness of the Hogarth Amani prince of Bussar. Now go and bury it."

Amani turned from Jo'than and towards the small river of piss and shit and spoke aloud his woe. "God of my fathers...help me."

Chapter Eleven

The Stare of the Medja

A mani awoke to the sound of a trumpet. His eyes saw the twilight sky giving way to blue and the embrace of the morning sun. Its golden hues were a welcome sight. His nose, however, reminded him he dwelt in the presence of Hogarthen shit and piss.

He stood to his feet as Hogarth guards made their rounds and roused the other slaves to assure everyone was up. He lifted his arms to smell himself and realized he was the one who smelled like dung and urine. He called an approaching guard and spoke.

"Is the camp on..." He was slapped and blood spewed from his mouth. Angered, he looked at the guard, who smote him.

"You will speak when spoken to. A slave does not ask, a slave responds to the orders given to it. Do you understand, *slave*?"

Amani's breathing quickened, and he sized the soldier up and knew that if he were of the mind, he could snap his neck or with the gesture of his hands summon the very wind to steal his breath from his lungs, but he stood still and eyed the guard and nodded that he understood.

"We are breaking camp. We are moving through the desert to the Darkmouth. The king does not wish us to be long traveling through the land of the mages. You will follow Kaffe and stay by his side. He has traveled the corridor for many seasons and knows how you should walk so as to lessen notice. I would not have the king's new toy lost to the Medja of the trench. Do you understand me?"

Once more, Amani nodded and with those words understood the danger the king's army was about to embark upon. Nestled to the south of Bussar was the territory of the Medja and they claimed all land from their tower to the Darkmouth. The cost of unauthorized passage through their lands was nothing less than blood sacrifice. It was said that they sought those who were ripe for ascension. People called *Enari*. Amani knew his father believed they used those caught to empower their magics for a cause no one knew save Haidar. A cause he would not speak of. Not even to his son. Amani surmised that M'Msee possibly knew. With his being as long-lived as he was, he could not believe that M'Msee would not know otherwise.

Amani was aware of the treaty that the Medja had made with the Bussar through his father, but he could only surmise what alliance existed between the Sandking and the Medja that lived in the pyramids. He noted that the soldier's demeanor made it clear that fear was in the air. Amani wondered how Jo'than had managed to travel so far to be near the Bussar trial grounds and Medja lands. Perhaps it was part of Hogarth's rites to brave the Medja's territory? He surmised he would have many days to ponder such things. A swarthy man of about forty years approached. He wore tattered clothing, slightly better than that of the other slaves. Upon his shirt was a chain that draped the golden emblem of the Sandking.

"My name is Kaffe, and I serve the royal family. I was informed that you are to be the king's ward." Kaffe looked Amani over and his neck snapped back, and he scrunched his face in repugnance. "You stink. But you must never stink in the king's presence. If you stink, it means you hold disfavor in his eyes or are punished at his hand. When I was captured, I too cleaned latrines. He has stated that you are to be trained. So do not be afraid. His actions are his way to humble you. To make you ready for service. Do your job well and your station will rise. Honestly, I do not know whether to envy you or to pity you. To work close to the king of Hogarth invites both reward and danger. Nonetheless, I am now your guide. You will obey me and will not give me trouble. Know, Bussar, that I do not care if you are the ward of the king or not. I will not be taken by the Medja because of your foolishness. Do you understand?"

Amani noted the man's fear and nodded. Kaffe motioned for him to follow. They walked through the camp and Amani beheld horses and men clad in leather that carried sword and shield. Everyone rushed to assemble in ranks and the two slaves of the King's house also quickstepped and assembled themselves to the rear of the throng and they stood side by side as did the rest of the king's entourage, and after a moment, all were still and then two blasts from a trumpet blew into the air and to the rear two trumpets' blasts were returned by the rear guard of soldiers. One long blast then blared over the troops, and upon its ending, all moved as one man and marched into the valley of the Medja.

Men on horseback were the first to move forward. The Sandking, his sons and generals, and those of the royal guard proceeded into the gulch. Followed by the king's soldiers on foot. Amani and the band of slaves and support servants, and finally more foot soldiers and two men on horseback who watched the rearguard.

The column of men stretched across the descending plain. The sand was more pronounced, and Amani knew it was only a matter of time until they entered the Darkmouth and the land of the Sandking.

"You, Bussar. What did you do to become both slave to the king and his steward?" said Kaffe.

Amani was quiet for a moment, sighed realizing that making himself more of an enemy than he was would not endear him to anyone, and replied. "I spared the king's son's life on two occasions."

Kaffe looked at Amani and laughed. "You lie! Our people have been killing each other for centuries. And YOU would defy this way of life, not once, but twice? Are you soft in the head, Bussar? Now it all makes sense, why Jo'than hangs his head in shame and does not wear the pelt of the Akoolah. Tell me, soft head, what prompted you to spare your enemy's life?"

"There is a saying among my people, *'Do not give what is holy unto the dogs, nor cast your gold before swine, lest they trample them under their feet, and turn and tear you into pieces.'*"

Kaffe turned and scowled at Amani. "Do you mock me, boy? I am Sherpa to lead you through the gorge, and you would insult me? Your very life depends on my guidance. You would do well to remember that."

Amani was not slow to reply, "My life is in the hands of Akuma. And if he wills it, then the Medja will take it, or I will die at the hands of my enemy or one day ascend. Of the three, I do not know. But I will never bow to fear. For fear is the precursor to the Kifu. And the Kifu, the precursor to Enkai. Akuma is good, and he is king of all creation. I will trust in him."

Kaffe laughs, "So you believe in that old religion? No wonder you spared the prince. Let me tell you the truth, boy. There is no Akuma, and there is no Enkai, both are myths told by seers to keep the population in check. Religion is, but a tool created by men to control other men. Hogarth is strong because of fear, boy. She is a nation whose center is a man who controls the sand itself. One touched with the alleged god taint and was able to travel into Medja territory and pluck the enemy's son from his own land and return to his land unscathed. *That* boy is power. And a power you are now a slave to. You would do well to remember that." Kaffe turned and continued as before, but quickened his pace to catch up with the soldier ahead of him.

Amani was silent in response. His thoughts hovered about him as vultures circled the dying.

If Kaffe is anything like the rest, then the Hogarthen are a godless people. Akuma hear me. And watch over your servant. Let not evil triumph over me, nor allow me to succumb to evil..."

"DEATH CLOUD!!" shouted a soldier.

Amani then looked ahead as soldiers pointed to a gloom that rose from the ground, and he watched as a wall cloud descended and began to overtake the army. Screams and the sound of swords unsheathing could be heard as the cloud approached. And Kaffe spoke firmly to him. "Do not move, boy. The Medja approach, so when the gloom comes and the earth moves, do not move. Or what you fear will kill you. Do you understand?"

Amani nodded.

The fog drew closer and with each passing moment, Amani saw men disappear into the desert dust and the sounds of hacking could be heard and the blood-curdling cries of men dying as if by drowning. Amani watched Kaffe who now stopped and stood perfectly still, and Amani duplicated his posture and as the dreaded fog drew near, Amani saw hands extend from the ground and hold fast the legs of both men and all steeds and any who resisted were immediately dragged into the earth screaming. The cloud then descended over Amani and Kaffe and as it passed over them bleached skeletons of the undead trod within the gloom several approached with swords in hand, and as they drew closer two hands reached up and grabbed Amani by the ankles and he resisted the urge to panic and to break free and a skeleton walked towards him sword drawn and the fascination of seeing animated bones walking towards him was more powerful than the fear that should have compelled him to run. And the creature stopped and stared into the eyes of Amani, and the clanking sounds as it moved rattled in his ears. Its head moved as it studied Amani, and it hissed with whatever flesh still existed in its mouth and let out a cry like a woman's scream. Immediately, several skeletons converged on Amani's position, and they all joined in the screeching cry that pierced the ears of all present. And for a moment Amani thought to summon the wind and disperse the gloom and call fire from the sky to destroy the walking dead before him, and as he did he noted that a crow flew overhead, and he paused in his thoughts to defend himself and whispered to himself... "M'Msee?"

***

N'Kosi was familiar with the way of the Medja Trench. In his youth, he had seen the Medja take men and women from his company before. All taken, and all...never seen again. It was rumored that those taken were made to serve the Medja. Others spoke that the sorcerers were as old as time and fed upon the god taint, sometimes resident in lesser men. N'Kosi initially met them as a child and he feared them when he was brought before them. "Godling" they called him. And in his fear, N'Kosi summoned power from within himself and made the earth move to protect him and his company. He was thirteen when his power was first displayed. A power that moved the earth and made the sands rise like ocean waves across the earth. Upon seeing his power, the Medja studied him and decided to let him and his men live and as his company prepared to depart the sorcerers spoke to him of a prophecy, a prophecy that foretold that one day he would die in the same earth that he sought to wield against them. N'Kosi grimaced as he recalled how they examined his thoughts and winced in remembrance as he heard them speak in his mind. And he recalled their discourse as they weighed if he should live or die. *"He is too "unstable" to power Lynnette's Eye. Too dangerous to be given to Hesphus."* He heard them say. He did not know what Lynnette's Eye was, and in his curiosity, he dispatched men far and wide across the land to spy out any knowledge of this *eye* the Medja concerned themselves with. But he remembered his journeys through Medja's Trench to know that so many times before if the Medja appeared, some-one would be taken as others had been in the past. Others who possessed the budding power of Akuma: a *godling*. A person they called Enari.

It was a painful truth to know that despite all his power, the Medja held a power, nay a connection to death itself that frightened the king. There were few things that moved the King of Hogarth to fear, but the Medja were beings who were like him; empowered beyond normal men. He would have to once more hold this fear in abeyance and show strength to his men. "Do not resist the Medja," he ordered. "Calm yourselves and all will be well. Fear... and you will surely die."

Many men nodded their heads in acknowledgment and J'abari and Jo'than looked to their left and right as skeletal hands reached to take hold of the ankles of both men and mount.

And as the fog parted, three men floating above the ground made their way toward the king, and with a wave of a hand, the fog dissipated from him and the Sandking's horse was also released and the king rode toward the sorcerers.

"Hail Medja. We travel peacefully through your lands and mean your order no harm. Allow us to pass."

The three floated above the king's horse and replied. "The guardians have detected God-taint. An Enari exists within your midst. The godling will submit to testing as is the way of our order and all who seek to pass from the coast to the Darkmouth. You command this company and are responsible for those under your command. Do you consent for the man to be sighted?"

"I respect the Medja order but will not be spoken to in such a manner. I have not been this way for several circles. You know who I am. I would have you mindful to whom you speak," said the Sandking.

The three floating mages replied as one and looked off in the distance to the cries of their skeletal minions that surrounded a young man and replied, "We know who you are N'Kosi, Son of Kempec and we do not care. We have seen your life and its end. Be wary of threatening those who commune with death. Nor meddle with forces that you do not understand."

"You are not a threat to us, for have we not told you that even one of your own will one day bury you in the very sand you command? We serve a greater power than he who commands earth and sand. We serve the scion of life and death. But do not incite us to wrath, for the dead do not take kindly to the living. We have allowed you to travel through the gorge unmolested and have allowed your army through our land to Bussar's coast. Why, then, upon your return, do you defy our treaty by bringing back one in your number who possesses the God-taint? You will surrender the Enari to us, or we will test all within your company to find him."

The Sandking replied, "I do not know of who you speak. My entire regiment has traveled from Hogarth days before, all save two: my son and a boy slave from Bussar."

The three Medja spoke as one. "Bring them before us that they may be seen for who they are. We would know all who possess the god-taint. We would know if Enkai would breach our world."

***

Amani noted that the company had come to a halt and whispered to Kaffe.

"Why have we stopped?"

Kaffe quietly replied, "We were allowed to pass unmolested on the way to Bussar. Something is different and has alerted the Medja...something new." Kaffe then turned to stare at Amani and slowly backed away. "It can only be you."

Kaffe and Amani then watched as the Sandking pointed their way and immediately a soldier on horseback galloped towards the end of the line and stopped in front of them and spoke. "You there...Bussar!"

Amani raised his eyes, and the soldier spoke to Kaffe. "Help him up to my horse! Now!"

Kaffe nodded, bowed then unshackled Amani and grabbed him by the arm. The soldier reached out with his hand and Amani grabbed it and the soldier pulled him atop his horse and the duo galloped at full sprint to the front of the company to the king.

"What is the matter?" asked Amani.

"Mine is not to ask, boy. But to obey the king. And the king commands your presence."

Amani looked at the passing soldiers as he rode horseback and observed that many of the soldiers held both looks of wonder and fear. Amani then turned his eyes to the front and noted three floating men in robes. One was arrayed in red, the other in black, and one in blue. And as he noted his surroundings, the Sandking spoke. "Amani, come to me, boy, and do not be afraid."

Amani lowered himself from the soldier's horse and walked towards the Sandking, and the three Medja stared at him. Amani then stood before the king and slightly bowed never taking his eyes off the monarch.

"I am summoned, king?"

"Stand boy and show yourself to the Medja."

Amani did as bidden and turned to face the three floating men. Their robes flowed in the wind like silken banners, and golden-colored runes of Zar'atal were stitched within their garments. One's face was afflicted with the skin disease of albinism and had brown eyes, the other two were darker and all three of their eyes shimmered with a blueish hue.

"Do you know who we are, child?" spoke the Medja in blue.

Amani simply shook his head.

"We are watchers of the god taint. Seekers of Enari. Those who possess the germ of ascendancy or those who possess the powers of Aaru to use it for destruction. You and this one here will submit to our trial. We have detected the God taint, and our order compels us to investigate its source."

The Medja in black spoke, "I recognize this one. He has the look of Haidar of Bussar. Who are you, boy, and who are your people?"

Amani stood tall, squared his shoulders, and replied. "I am Amani, son of Haidar, King of Bussar."

All three slightly floated back at his words, and the mage in red robes spoke to the other two. "He is the Medja killer's boy."

The Medja narrowed his eyes and spoke. "Why are you in the company of the King of Hogarth?"

Amani was quick to reply, "My business is my own. You have stopped the company in the midst of the burning sands. The horses, and the men, all are provisioned for the journey home to Hogarth. Let us proceed. I pray that the men are not burdened."

All three spoke as one, "None shall proceed until confirmation is made of who carries the taint."

"And then?" The Sandking asked.

The Medja in black looked upon King N'Kosi and replied. "Then — we shall see."

"Know Medja that I have traveled now twice over your land all to see to the wellbeing of my son. If I would brave your land and enter my sworn enemy's home and bring him back alive. Do not think I will tolerate my son being taken from me by you."

Amani immediately chimed in to raise the stakes for the Medja, hoping to improve what were apparent negotiations, and spoke. "I am here upon the exchange of kings between two nations. Do you think my father will stand idle once he hears that his son was taken captive by the very people he once raised arms against? No, he will descend upon Aphis and your disciples as before with a wrath never seen. Do not be deceived. You may indeed kill many, but the order of Medja will cease to exist if both Bussar and Hogarth go to war with you. You are powerful. But you are not all-powerful. Do you wish to test me? Then test me. But in conclusion, know that I will not come with you. This company and I will continue our peaceful journey and proceed unharmed."

The Medja were silent for a moment, then turned to the Sandking. "We agree to this thing. No matter what the outcome, we will leave you in peace. But we would know if germination of ascension exists on this side of the great sea."

The Sandking nodded, "Proceed, my son Jo'than also stands before you."

Jo'than stood before the Medja and the three sorcerers linked and two took their hands and laid hands on the forehead of the boy, and Jo'than tensed up and his eyes became white.

The eyes of the three magi also glowed and all save Amani and the Sandking stepped back for wind gusted around the prince of Hogarth and the Medja.

Jo'than's face contorted, and he grimaced and cried out in pain. He lifted his hands as if to keep something invisible from crushing him and screamed.

Amani reached out to touch him and the Sandking unsheathed his sword and with the flat of his blade smacked his new slave's arm and Amani winced and retracted his hand.

"Do not interfere with the Medja again or there will exist no need for them to test you, for you will be dead. Do you understand?"

Amani massaged his wrist and quickly nodded he understood.

Jo'than's eyes then returned to normal, and he collapsed to the ground. Soldiers and his brother rushed to his aid and the young man lifted his hand to wave them off. "I am fine.... I just need a moment...a moment...to recover." He then slowly lifted himself, looked at Amani, and gingerly walked towards him.

He then leaned himself on Amani's shoulder and whispered into his ear. "They know." Then he hobbled towards his horse.

The Medja then spoke as one. "He is tainted...but he is but a leaf. We will watch him. Know King of the Sands that if he turns to Enkai, treaty or no...we will come to Hogarth and destroy him, and all those that would stand in our way."

The Sandking stood defiantly mute.

The three then looked at Amani and motioned for him to come forward.

Amani stood before the men and spoke, "Proceed."

The three linked arms once more with the middle sage, and the sorcerer on each end reached towards Amani to lay their hands on him. His eyes turned white, and he trembled as the feeling of the sky fire coursed through his veins and unlocked something within and he gritted his teeth and rose several feet into the air.

Electrical current then rippled through him and was visible to all and bolts of lightning crackled around Amani into the ground and reached out to enshroud the Medja but did not harm them and all looked in wonder at the boy from Bussar who for a moment shown like a star, and the Sandking himself and all those that were with him backed away in fear.

***

"We see you, Amani, son of Haidar slayer of Medja."

Amani struggled to keep his mind closed from the mental scrutiny that the Medja unleashed against him, and he attempted to focus his thoughts on his family back home but a brain-splitting migraine assaulted his forehead as if his mind was being ripped in two by hands that reached within his scalp to lift his brain from his skull and pry apart his thoughts. Amani grimaced as the Medja were relentless and forced themselves into the hidden compartments of his thoughts. Peering behind the locked and unconscious doors of emotion, memory, desire, and decision. Each memory was accosted and reviewed as if tables were being overturned.

"He rescued the Hogarth boy...curious," said one.

"He wields the lightning!" said another.

"The winds hearken to him, and he rides them!" said the third.

And they reviewed the past of Amani until they saw Haidar and his son enter a cave and when they saw the portals to other lands, they also saw the crypt of the being that all men throughout history have feared. For the Kifu was at rest deep in the recesses of the earth. Lain quietly within a crypt, away from the prying eyes of men. And as the three walked in the mind of Amani towards the crypt to see if he whom men feared still slept, they beheld the eyes of the Kifu were shut, but his eyelids darted left and right, moving as if the creature dreamed. And as the three wandered through the crypt to examine the tomb of the Kifu. The black Medja bent over to examine the scourge from

Enkai and the monster of creation opened its eyes and stared at the Medja and all three then screamed out in collective terror and pain and the three were flung backward and their hold on Amani was released.

The boy fell to his knees and heard the cries that now echoed from the Medja, who pointed at him wagging their fingers. "Enari!" they cried out as one.

Amani rose to his feet and stared at the three sorcerers who hailed from the Pyramid city of the Medja and who kept the way of the trench to detect those who possessed any vestige of Akuma's power and spoke to the three. "You have seen my thoughts and viewed my memories. You know what I have seen, and now...it has seen you. Will you now compel me to serve in your tower where, if I remain, you know what will follow? Or will you release me into the hands of this king?"

The Medja in blue composed himself and floated towards Amani. and lowered himself to whisper into his ear. "It is not us who the Kifu eyes, boy... it is you." The blue Medja then lifted himself away from Amani and settled with his brethren and spoke to N'Kosi.

"King of Hogarth. Know that you travel with one who bears the God taint. We will not come for him. But beware, for there is one that will follow, one that will one day come for your kingdom and all who live within. The death that will come for us all. Go your way and depart from our land. We will not restrain your company nor seek your destruction."

The Sandking looked curiously at the Medja and then at Amani. "What if I leave him here in the desert to die?"

"No," said the Medja. "Take your son and the Bussar prince with you and do not bring him this way again. And know that if he crosses our sands, we will not tolerate this beacon of death on our land. Now away with you and do not travel this way with the boy ever again or know that our treaty is forfeit."

The Sandking looked at Amani who turned his eyes away from the staring king. "Who are you, boy, that the Medja cower?"

Amani then turned to the king and replied. "You know who I am, great king, I am your servant."

N'Kosi Sandking of the Hogarth people chuckled. "You are a subtle one, boy. Very well then. Come, Amani, son of Haidar, now servant to me. Come, he whom the Medja fear. Ride with me. I would talk with you and know what secrets would compel sorcerers to leave you be." N'Kosi then turned to the three keepers of the Medja Trench and spoke. "We leave your land Medja and to the Darkmouth we now go."

The three sorcerers looked at the king and nodded in acknowledgment at the monarch's word.

Amani then turned from the king and raced to the departing Medja and whispered to the three floating men that they might hear. "Know that one day I *will* traverse this way again. And let Heaven and Earth bear witness to my words that upon my return, if you bar me from my home, you will have more to fear than the Kifu."

The three sorcerers looked at him in silence and then turned from the Bussar and vanished behind a wall of fog, and the gloom that floated above the ground as a grayish river that courses through a canyon also evaporated into nothing, and the skeletal hands that held both horses and men released the ankles of the company and withdrew into the earth. The Sandking then reached for Amani and offered him a hand unto his horse and the men whispered among themselves.

"Who is this boy that Medja fear him and that the king would honor him so?" murmured some of the men.

General Saith whispered to Prince J'abari. "I have known you all your life. Never has the king ever, even as a boy, allowed *you* to ride with him on his prized horse."

J'abari did not respond, for both men already knew the statement was true.

"Forward!" commanded J'abari. He then snapped the reins of his horse and followed his father at the head of the army.

And when all saw that the boy that had cleaned the company's latrine was now on horseback with the Sandking; all in attendance marveled that the king would ride with a slave and wondered who the young man was. And J'abari eyed with disdain the favor showed to Amani and from that moment on conspired on how he might destroy him.

***

M'Msee's head jerked from side to side.

Sweat streamed down his brow as he mumbled in his sleep. His body twitched, limbs straining against unseen forces in his dream. With a sudden gasp, he thrust his hands forward, pushing himself upright from the bed, and a single name escaped his lips: "Amani."

He bolted upright, his chest heaving, the bedding beneath him damp with sweat. The humid air clung to his skin, thick with the chirping of crickets and the songs of night fowl that filled the plains.

M'Msee closed his eyes, inhaled deeply, and exhaled, grounding himself. Amani was alive. He could feel it, as sure as he felt his own heartbeat. Akuma's power coursed through the boy—a presence so familiar, so potent, it resonated with his own. It was a tether he could not sever, a light he could not ignore.

Rising from his bed, M'Msee pulled a thin cloth over his shoulders and stepped outside. The night sky stretched before him; a canopy of stars interspersed with the silhouettes of clouds drifting across the moon's glow. His gaze lingered on the clouds, and he wondered if they moved at Amani's command. Was his godson summoning the wind, shaping the sky in a moment of resolve—or was he in distress?

The visions from M'Msee's dream surged back, vivid and unrelenting. Something had been probing the boy, an entity pressing against the barriers of Amani's mind, seeking to pry open secrets that should remain hidden.

He tightened his grip on the cloth draped around him, staring into the distance. "Akuma," he whispered into the night, "watch over him."

Chapter Twelve

To Cross the Burning Sands

Amani rode astride the Sandking's steed, his youthful frame dwarfed by the immense figure seated behind him. Though still a boy, he carried the bearing of a prince. The Sandking, however, was a man whose presence commanded the respect of time itself—his broad shoulders and dark, muscular frame were as unyielding as the walls of a fortress. Amani leaned against him as they rode, and from time to time, the great man's deep voice broke the rhythm of their journey.

"You are a most astonishing boy," the Sandking rumbled. "Twice, you have spared my son, even with the blood feud between our houses, even amidst the strife of our nations. I understand your father stood against you in these acts, and yet you defied him. Why? What compels a boy to believe he knows better than his father and elders, to disobey the traditions of his forebears?"

Amani sat in silence for a moment, the question weighing on him like a stone. At last, he answered, his voice steady. "I know nothing, save that which is of Akuma. He is the life and light of men."

The Sandking's thick neck recoiled as he turned to glance at the boy. "Do you fancy yourself a prophet of Akuma, then? Have I taken a seer as my prisoner?"

Amani let out a soft snicker. "I am neither prophet nor seer, great king. But I have seen a vision. My purpose lies beyond the traditions of my people—and yours."

The Sandking arched a skeptical brow, his voice edged with curiosity. "Then speak, boy. What purpose emboldens you to address the master of the sands in such a way?"

Amani turned his head just enough to meet the Sandking's gaze, his expression calm yet grave. "I have seen a vision—not in dreams but waking. I have beheld death, yet not decay. The Kifu sleeps, for now. But one day, the living death will rise. And when it does, it will come for me. Where I am, it must follow."

The Sandking's laughter rolled like distant thunder. "You speak of myths and legends. The Kifu has not walked the earth for over five great circles. The Hutari defeated that creature long ago, and men have lived free of the living dead's torment ever since. Who whispered this tale to you? Who confirms this vision you claim to have seen while your eyes were open? Your father?"

Amani exhaled; his tone was quiet but firm. "No, great king. Not my father."

"Then who?" the Sandking demanded, his voice sharp as steel.

Amani's answer came without hesitation. "The Hutari."

The name struck the Sandking like a hammer blow. His eyes widened, and for a moment, he could only gape at the boy. The Hutari—names from childhood stories and whispered legends. Could it be that such a being had truly spoken to this young Bussar captive?

For a time, N'Kosi, the Sandking of Hogarth, fell silent. The boy's words lingered in the air between them, heavy with portent. The king pondered them deeply yet chose not to question Amani further—for now.

***

Jo'than nudged his horse forward until he was riding beside his elder brother. "I see the weight of your thoughts, brother," he said, his tone cautious. "Think nothing of what Father has done. He only seeks to question the boy, to understand why the Medja hesitated to take him. That is all. It is in Father's nature, is it not, to interrogate away from the ears of others?"

J'abari scowled, his expression dark. "Why do you speak to me like this? Have I given you cause for concern?"

Jo'than smiles faintly. "I am your brother. We played as boys in the castle together, tormenting our sister and mother alike. I know that pensive look you wear. It has always been a portent of trouble."

J'abari's gaze narrowed, and his voice grew colder. "Then let me ask you something, now that we are out of earshot of the others. This boy that Father dotes on—who is he, that the King of Hogarth would place him on his own horse, a privilege denied to his own sons? And is it true? Father said this boy bested you in combat?"

Jo'than fell silent for a moment but did not falter. "I was bested, yes."

J'abari scoffs. "If my brother—famed among our people as a fierce warrior, trained by the king's own guard—could be defeated by this boy, how is he not a threat to Father?"

Jo'than hesitated, his eyes fixed on the path ahead. "He is what the Medja call a godling. A Bussar, yes, and young, but Akuma is with him. You may not understand this, but it is difficult to kill a man who has saved your life. I owed him a debt—a life debt—and I consider it paid, even at the cost of my stature among our people and, it seems, in your eyes as well."

J'abari smirked, his tone mocking. "Do not trouble yourself, little brother. Your stature was already small. You are, after all, second born. When Father ascends to the sky, I will be king, and your name will be covered by mine. You might yet possess some honor. For under my reign, Hogarth will stretch from the Medja's trench to the coasts of Bussar itself. Take heart; your disgrace will not stain you when I am king, only while Father l ives."

Jo'than's jaw tightened, his eyes narrowing as he looked at his brother. "I wish Father nothing but long life. Under his rule, we have prospered, and I would see Hogarth continue to prosper—peacefully, if possible. Has not the King of Bussar made peace with the Medja? It's said that Bussar was on the brink of destruction, yet their king's wrath was turned away. What gain could you seek by stirring up what two nations have sought to avoid?"

J'abari's gaze turned toward their father, riding ahead with the boy astride his horse. His voice was low and deliberate. "Fear, brother. In the end, Hogarth cannot be great if she is not feared. If our father fears the Medja, and the Bussar king kept his hand from destroying them, it can only be because of fear. But I am not afraid. One day, I will end this fear. I will do what Father and the Bussar King could not. I will destroy the Medja and bring both them and the Bussar to heel. When I ride to the coast, it will be with the sand at my back, erasing the people of huts. Hogarth will prosper, even if I must compel it myself."

Jo'than said nothing, his eyes fixed on their father ahead. His brother's words hung heavy in the air, a foreboding that whispered of ruin under J'abari's reign.

The horizon began to glow with the approach of dawn, the sun's brilliance spilling across the land. Both brothers watched as their father dismounted his horse before a massive dune. N'Kosi, King of Hogarth, raised his arms to the sky, palms open. The earth groaned and trembled in response, and a dark, tubular stone began to rise from the ground. Sand poured from its peak like a waterfall, and for a moment, J'abari's chest swelled with pride.

Before them stood a towering cylindrical monument of stone, dwarfing the gathered army of Hogarth. With a motion of his hands, N'Kosi commanded the rock to split. A craggy, oval entrance parted like the jaws of a great beast, the colossal slabs of stone sliding aside to reveal a tunnel descending into the earth.

"Behold the Darkmouth," J'abari said to Amani, his voice edged with a strange satisfaction. "See the doorway to your new home."

Amani remained silent; his expression unreadable as he followed the marching army into the darkness.

Chapter Thirteen

The Darkmouth

The harsh sun cast its long shadows over the dunes as the army descended into the depths of the Darkmouth, a tunnel hidden beneath the endless expanse of desert, an old passageway once used by the armies of men to engage the forces of the Kifu. The tunnel meandered through the heart of the rock, its walls adorned with intricate carvings and hieroglyphs, telling tales of the city's founding, its rise, and its eventual fall. The language was archaic Zar'atali the source of Zaratu, the meaning cryptic, but any onlooker could feel the weight of a history stretching back millennia. The tunnel was carved through the rock with a precision known only to those who had mastered the desert's secrets. A defensive pathway made centuries ago to protect the denizens of the continent from the march of the

Kifu and the undead armies that trailed in his wake. A way of retreat that led to the great ancient city of Hogarth.

The fabled city was indeed a place of legend, shrouded in mystery and riddled with wonders and terrors known to only a few. But one thing was clear among all the old tales of Tanara from the Endwar; it was from Hogarth that saw the armies of men launch their last desperate attack against the Kifu, and from Hogarth, the combined armies of men marched to Mt. Moshek to confront the pestilent undead god from Aaru. Hogarth was a defensive citadel whose back stood against the shores of the sea and offered a way of escape for the people if ever the land became hopelessly overrun by the undead. M'Msee once said that where the desert now stands between the plains of Bussar and Hogarth a great lake once existed but after the battle between the Hutari and the Kifu the waters wasted away in fire, and nothing remained save the blistering wound of vast scorching sands. Amani found it difficult to imagine that water once existed where the desert now dwells.

The scenery was alien to him, for he had never ventured this far towards the lower coast nor traveled this far from home. As he entered the ancient, constructed wonder from the first age, he thought how much more would be alien from all that he knew. The army's march through the Darkmouth was a baptism into the dark and sand. Torchbearers lit the army's way as the entire company drifted further from all that was familiar to Amani: away from anything that gave the semblance of what he once called home.

The tunnel meandered through the heart of the rock, and slowly the army ventured deeper. The first wonder to greet them was the play of light and shadow on the rocky walls. The torches each man carried cast flickering; dancing patterns that seemed to come alive. Shadows stretched and twisted, sometimes forming phantasmal shapes of ancient beings and creatures. The walls of the Darkmouth were adorned with intricate carvings and hieroglyphs, The language was archaic, its meaning cryptic, but Amani could feel the weight of history stretching back millennia. It was as if the very walls whispered the secrets of the past. Amani studied the runes carved within ancient stone beams and wondered aloud to his captor.

"Great king, has the Darkmouth always been buried under the sand? There is writing and images on the walls."

N'Kosi returned his inquiry and said, "The writing is from the first age. Herein the dark the tales of the past are written in stone. Many wrote and testified of the power of the Kifu and the Hutari. These are they which bear witness. Their stories buried by the desert sands only to be revealed by those that control the same who may raise the great tunnel to pass from the interior of the desert into Hogarth and the sea."

"Do your people understand the writing on the walls?"

"No, only the royal line possesses the knowledge to read the ancient words. But the seer knows the words. They would know the images." His tone turned sharp. "Why does a child of Bussar concern himself with the stones of my ancestors?"

Amani hesitated before he replied, "I know a seer in my village, one who follows the teachings of Akuma. I wonder what he would make of these walls." N'Kosi did not answer, and Amani chose to ask no further questions, wary of irritating his captor.

The air in the tunnel was cool and dry, a stark contrast to the unforgiving heat of the desert above. It carried with it a faint scent of age and history, the dank of untold stories waiting to be unraveled. In the silence of the subterranean passage, soldiers' footsteps marched with a haunting resonance, creating an eerie symphony and cadence that echoed throughout the desert underpass.

As they moved deeper, the torchlight revealed more wonders. Stalactites and stalagmites hung like grotesque sculptures from both the ceiling and floor of the tunnel. Some appeared to merge, creating monstrous, otherworldly forms, while others glistened with the promise of forgotten treasures hidden within their jagged embrace.

Yet, amid the wonders, terrors lurked. The tunnel bore the marks of time and decay. Cracks in the stone seemed to widen with each step, eerie sounds hinted at the possibility of unseen dangers. Legends spoke of ancient guardians, spirits bound to protect the secrets of Hogarth, and the soldiers could not dismiss the sensation of being watched by invisible eyes.

The air within the tunnel was cool and dry, carrying the faint scent of time and forgotten stories. The soldiers' footsteps echoed ominously, creating a symphony of sound that made

Amani's skin prickle. Shadows loomed and twisted, and the oppressive feeling of being watched grew stronger.

"There are shadows in the dark. Curses dwell within the walls themselves, waiting when the time is right."

Amani answers, puzzled, "What time is that?"

"When the Kifu walks the earth," came the somber reply.

Amani grew quiet as the passage continued to twist and wind its way through the bowels of the earth, and with every step, the air grew colder, and the atmosphere became more oppressive. It was as if they were descending into the very heart of the desert's mysteries, where ancient powers and forgotten horrors awaited.

The Sandking halted his horse, raising his hand in a fist. Instantly, the entire army stilled, their march ceasing as one. Amani peered into the blackness ahead, realizing they had reached the tunnel's end. The Sandking extended his hands, his fingers curling as if to pry open an unseen barrier. The earth groaned in response. Dust and debris rained from the ceiling as the rumble of stone grinding against stone filled the air.

Suddenly, light pierced the darkness. A narrow beam widened as great doors embedded into the cavern walls moved. Powered by the Sandking's will, the immense stone slabs slid back, retreating into the sides of the chamber. As they folded flush against the walls, brilliant light flooded the tunnel. Amani shielded his eyes, blinking rapidly as his vision adjusted to the radiance.

Before him stretched a grand causeway lined with people, their cheers reverberating through the air. Palm branches waved in unison, and flags of crimson fluttered above the crowd. The triumphant melodies of flutes and cornets filled his ears, harmonizing with the rhythmic clapping of celebratory hands.

Beyond the causeway, the cityscape emerged—an expanse of monumental buildings fashioned from sand and mud, their forms both ancient and majestic. Yet, amidst the splendor of Hogarth, Amani's gaze was drawn to a singular figure.

A woman approached the Sandking's horse, her stride commanding yet graceful. Her attire set her apart from the crowd; she was draped in flowing robes of deep blues, purples, and golds, her appearance a striking contrast to the simpler garments of those who lined the causeway. Her hair, as black as the night sky, was intricately braided, and adorned with seashells that glinted in the sunlight. Her skin was a rich, sun-kissed brown, and her eyes, sharp and enigmatic, seemed to hold a depth that defied description.

Amani noted her sword a gleaming weapon with a hilt embedded with a brilliant red ruby, a mirror to the blade carried by the Sandking himself. The symmetry was undeniable, and its significance struck him as he watched her approach.

She continued her stride to their horse as the Sandking looked upon her and smiled as the young woman bowed. "Osumare, my color and my light. My heart is pleased to see you rainbow."

"It is good to see you returned to us, Father. I am glad that Akuma smiles upon Hogarth once more with your presence. She noticed Amani's eyes stare at her and frowned at him then spoke once more, "What is this that rides upon my father's horse? I dislike the way it looks at me. Will you give me its eyes?"

The king furrowed his brow at her hit Amani on the head and whispered, "Lower your eyes, boy, in the presence of my daughter."

Amani immediately realized that his glancing looks were perhaps too obvious and did as commanded. "My apologies, great king."

"He is to be trained as my new ward, a former prince of Bussar, son of Haidar the Lion. You will teach him our ways and ensure that he is well-versed to serve me. So, no daughter, you may not have its eyes."

The Sandking then looked at Amani, who was now dislodged from the horse of Hogarth's ruler, and continued. "However, if his actions displease me or see my daughter disrespected. His eyes will be the least of his concerns." And N'Kosi took his sword and pointed it towards the young man's groin.

Amani swallowed hard and nodded in understanding, but the flushing of his cheeks and the rush within him for the beauty that stood before him was such that even he was aware that it was too late. He might die in Hogarth. Though it would not be in battle. It would be because he failed to train himself to keep his composure in the presence of the king's daughter. He sighed, knowing that this test was not one he had taken in Bussar. He breathed worryingly, knowing that he indeed might die at the hands of the woman before whom he was undeniably smitten.

Chapter Fourteen

The Bathmaster

Escorted by two Hogarth guards, Amani followed the princess of Hogarth. He had heard the Sandking refer to his daughter as Osumare. He eyed her form as she walked before him and his thoughts were revealed as he spoke the meaning of her name aloud enough that she could hear.

"Rainbow indeed."

The princess stopped and turned to her captive, "Does the pup from Bussar speak? You eye me as all men have done. But your imagination exceeds your reach. And just so that we understand one another. I want to make this clear. You are a dog. I am your trainer. Your master is my father. Because you are a dog, you will learn to fetch at my command. You will learn the proper etiquette when in the presence of my father. Now, because my father has spoken, I will teach you our ways and like an obedient dog you *will* learn them. And who knows, perhaps you will live long enough to even be of some use to him." She looked him up and down to inspect the man and shrugged her shoulders. "Or perhaps you will die. This is, of course, yet to be seen. My wager is that you will die by winter's end. But before your death, you reek from your journey across the sand and so you will be taken by my men to the servant's kennels to remove the stench from you that I might begin your training. Do we understand each other...dog?" She glared at him, awaiting his reply.

Amani looked at her. Her inner strength was clear. She was royalty, confident, beautiful, and she knew it. To her, he was nothing but a nuisance in the path of whatever plan she had made for her day. Yet Amani did not know fear. Trained to not even fear death. His smile of admiration and amusement stretched across his face. For despite her attempts to humiliate him, he was too secure in who he was. He had killed the Akoolah and had even bested her brother one of Hogarth's best warriors in combat. He knew he controlled the very fire of the sky and could call the wind to carry him aloft. He was careful not to allow his internal jesting at her display to reveal itself. He did not want to be seen as disrespectful. Nevertheless, her words were as the yipping of a small dog to him, and seeing her desire for a response from him that she might feel comfortable about who was in control of this relationship, he said in the most subtle yet alluring manner possible to show his infatuation with her, smiled and eyed her and said, "woof."

The two guardsmen snickered, and she leered at them both disapprovingly. Then she turned her gaze back to Amani. "You enjoy jests, we will see pup if your yelp is as amusing as your ' *woof*.'"

The air crackled with tension as the two children of royalty eyed one another. Amani's unwavering resolve clashed against the perceived superiority of his counterpart, creating a palpable energy between them.

"Guards, I am done with this pup for the day. Take him to the servant's kennel. See that Kaffe has him bathed and fed. I would not let my father's prize be gaunt before him..." she eyed him up and down. "He is much...smaller than expected."

Amani smiled at her sarcasm while the guards laughed and tugged at the arm of Amani who pulled against his captors and walked past the Sand King's home as the daughter of this land left to parts unknown.

Amani noted that all the major arteries of the city led to the center of the city. And that Hogarth was built like a horseshoe, with the king's palace set to the rear and above the rest of the living quarters and areas of exchange. A city built around an arena. He eyed what could best be described as a communal fortress-like existence of residential homes layered atop one another. He noted the stares from the populace that eyed him as they walked. The press of gawking stares and the whispered questions of who this outsider was evident on every face. The guards walked him around the outside of a sunken circular arena. An arena fenced with bones and protruding metal that pointed inward and designed to keep whoever occupied it from climbing upward and out to safety.

"What is this place?" He asked the guards.

"It is the Feud Grave. Here, challenges are made, and men show their worth. The worthy leave alive. The unworthy are discarded and their bones added to the Feud Grave's wall of remembrance. A reminder that one should not enter if they are not willing to be added to the wall.

"So, if I have an offense against another, I may call him to task by publicly challenging him to combat within the feud grave?"

"Yes, but since the combat is to death. Few choose to make a challenge and fewer still accept. Once accepted, it cannot be reversed."

"Can any make a challenge?"

"All who live before the Darkmouth and under the rule of Hogarth may challenge."

Amani pondered the words of his captors as they walked closer to the home of the king. "And what of Hogarth's great king? Can he be challenged? And can he refuse to accept?"

Both guards stopped and looked at the young man before them. And the senior of the two replied. "The King is Hogarth, and Hogarth is the king. To challenge the King is to challenge Hogarth. And Hogarth does not retreat from a challenge. All may challenge the king to his throne. But be warned if such foolishness ever crosses your mind. He has never lost a challenge in combat. But if you ever seek to be the ruler of Hogarth. If you kill a king within the teeth of the Feud Grave, then on that day know that you will be king. Until someone seeks to challenge you."

"Seems barbaric," Amani spoke aloud.

"I would not expect a Bussar to understand our ways. The Feud Grave is a solemn place of memorial dedicated to ending cycles of vengeance and allowing Hogarth society to move forward from our most divisive conflicts. Before combat, each party must state their grievance publicly. The victor must perform a ritual acknowledging the end of the feud. And the weapons used in killing blows are ceremonially buried, symbolizing the feud's death."

"And what about these men? They do not seem to be memorialized in honor." Amani pointed to translucent obelisks that glittered in the sunlight, and which surrounded the Feud Grave. Within each, a man was encased, his mouth open agape in terror.

"These are monuments to those who dared oppose the king. Encased within these pillars are the bodies of criminals, forever preserved as warnings to all who might defy the Sand King's rule. Know that this will be your fate, Bussar, if you were to cross him." Amani nodded in understanding, ruminated on those words, and eyed the macabre reflection of the consequences for treason or insubordination. The two guards continued their march towards the palace servants' quarters, which Osumare had called the "kennel." And Amani followed.

Amani looked up as they approached the palace. It was a simple structure. Two towers were built into the base of the

mountain, with a large rectangular span of a bridge that connected them. Imposing in height, it was made out of the black
lava rock of the mountain and mud bricks, and chiseled rock
gave each tower its rounded form. The exterior was garnished
with gems and polished shards of glass were embedded along its
exterior. It gleamed in the gleaming sun and the light bounced
off the decorated walls and cast long beams of light across the
city.

"Look upon your new home, Bussar. You will now remain in
service to the king for the rest of your life."

They entered a corridor built within one of the towers until
they came to a wooden door and a guard who stood in front of
it.

"We bring a new servant to the king. We are to escort him to
the hot springs so that he might be bathed."

The guard took a key and unlocked the door, and the three
men entered. The guard closed the door behind them and
Amani could hear the clank of what was most likely a lock of
some sort that shut them in.

The air was humid, and the moister gave off a scent akin to
wet fur. They passed men and women who tasked themselves
with cleaning, baking, and preparing food. The men passed
rooms where women were sitting and made blankets from furs.
The smells of stews and roasted chicken filled the air. And
they all looked upon the newcomer that walked with the king's
guards but only for a moment and then continued in their
duties.

Amani followed one guard while the other walked watch-
fully behind him. The three men descended deeper into the
palace and the dimming light reflected from the sweltering stone
black walls. Torches lined the walls, and the steps grew slick,
and the air became more humid as they entered an open room
with pools of water. From the mist emerged a man—tall, lanky,
and commanding. His hair was streaked with silver, his face
held sharp features framed by a long unkempt beard. His robes
were grungy, but also flowing and embroidered with intricate
patterns of gold and black that glimmered in the dim light.
His eyes, piercing and unnervingly observant, seemed to strip
Amani bare of pretense or deceit.

"Who do we have here?"

"A Bussar dog that needs a Bathmaster. By command of the
princess, see he is bathed. He is to be trained to attend to the
needs of the king."

The gray-haired man replied. "The king, you say. Then he is
special indeed."

He turned to a sand clock on a desk to his side and flipped
it over. Then flipped a smaller one and handed it to the guard.
"Return when the sand has expired. And when you return, he
will be properly bathed for whatever the king desires."

The guards nodded. "We will see to your food, Bussar. Then
you will see the princess per her command."

Amani did not reply but turned to the old man and spoke. "I
will give you no trouble. What would you have me do?"

"Of course you will not. You would die. But you do not strike me as a man that would enter death lightly. No, you are a subtle one. Stand on the stone over there against the wall near the wellspring and remove your clothes."

Amani did as bidden as the Bathmaster poured oil into bottles, and spices into decanters. Amani could smell the aroma of jasmine, and the smell reminded him of home.

"What is your name, old man, and why do the guards call you Bathmaster?"

The old, grizzled man rubbed a concoction into his hands, smelled them, and then replied. "Now step into the spring. It will initially be hot to the touch, and you will be tempted to draw back, but you will adjust in time."

Amani stepped off the block of stone and dipped his foot and then his entire leg into the spring. He gritted his teeth, and his check muscles clenched. The old man was prophetic of his description as he watched Amani sink into the spring.

He emptied two glass beakers of reddish-brown fluid into the spring and when the contents touched the water, an aroma of cinnamon filled the air.

"That smell," said Amani. "It is intoxicating."

The old man smiled. It should be the smell that lifts from the king's favored servant at all times. The ingredients are from an old sage from the days after the Kifu walked the earth. Once they touch with water, it brings out the aroma of its wearer. Most are unique, yet familiar. But you...your smell is something

I must admit I have never encountered. You have asked me my name.

But the way of Bussar is to only give one's name when one has been offered first. Although, the princess will teach you our ways. You will find as Bathmaster that here in the palace there are also many lessons. Consider this your first."

Amani nodded. "My name is Amani, Son of Haidar, King of Bussar. Slayer of Akoolah."

The old man nodded in return and lowered his eyes in understanding. "I see it now. You are a prince. Royalty. And a stranger to Hogarth. But accomplished. This would explain your rudeness and demeanor. You think of yourself above other men. Your speech and manner to ask interrogatively betray you."

Amani lowered his head and replied. "I mean no disrespect, Bathmaster."

The old man chuckles, "You are a dog. Why would you think I would feel disrespected by a pet?"

Amani frowned and started to reply, but held his peace.

"Good, you do possess the ability to restrain your impulses. There might just be hope for you after all. But your face still betrays you. You must learn to center your inner and outer man. Or you may find yourself dead before the spring."

Amani scowled at the man and furrowed his brow. "I am not a dog."

The old man took some tongs and a lump of hot coal from the kiln behind him and tossed the black shard into the water between Amani's legs. Amani yelped and scooted backward to avoid being burned. He looked up angrily at the old man, who simply sat on a block staring at him.

The Bathmaster could see that Amani wanted to object to his actions and spoke before he could speak. "You call yourself Amani. Thus far, the King has allowed you to retain this name. He sees you... sees something special about you. But if you are moved by merely a coal. You would not be worthy to serve him. Do you think that you will not do things or experience things that may turn your stomach? Anger you? No boy who thinks he is royalty in a nation that sees him as the enemy. Here in Hogarth, you are a dog until you can demonstrate otherwise. In Hogarth, you are a servant. A follower. NOT a leader of men, let alone a leader of a nation like Bussar. Your being here proves that. You young man are a stranger in a strange land. The sooner you come to grips with that, the better off you will be. You must show yourself of value in Hogarth. Of value to King N'Kosi. Do this and you may yet prosper in this land so far away from your own. Do not, and Haidar, king of Bussar, will never know what happened to his son."

Amani stood naked in the wellspring, water sliding down his muscular but thin frame. He smiled. "You remind me of my old teacher. He and I did not always see eye to eye. But I loved him. He was more than my teacher...he was my godfather. I miss him."

"Come from the water and lay face down upon the table."

Once more, Amani did as instructed and placed a towel over him and lay on the table. He had traveled ten days across the land with the Sandking's army. He had not slept on cloth, or anything padded since the night before the Kasset. His body ached and tension now made its home within every muscle from his long journey. After many days, he could feel his muscles shout with relief from the waters of the wellspring. His hunger became more apparent as his stomach growled its displeasure.

The Bathmaster made his way to the table and laid and took several hot stones and placed them on several points on his back. Amani winced at the heat, but his body adjusted, and he felt the relief already in his back beginning to partially subside. The Bathmaster placed oil in his hand and began to massage oil over his arms and legs.

"How did a prince become a slave to our king?" asked the old man. "I have not heard that we are at war with Bussar and that we would have prisoners. Let alone those that we bathe. How has the king of our enemy's son become his servant?"

Amani looked at the sundial on the table to his left and saw the glass was half empty. He sighed and turned his head face down once more and spoke towards the floor. "I made a choice. A choice to kill the Sandking's son or let him live. I chose to spare his life."

The Bathmaster stopped and looked at the young man he was attending. "Our Lord King has two sons. Of whom do you speak?"

"Jo'than," said Amani.

"Truly, this is a tale. Jo'than is a known fighter among our people," said the Bathmaster as he began to wash Amani's hair and massage his scalp.

"He is a warrior indeed. He is also honorable, and in the wilderness, he saved my life when we battled a pack of Akoolahs. I will not slay what Akuma has spared. And though kings and fathers of nations would command me to do otherwise. Am I greater than the father of creation? No, I will not slay what Akuma has spared. Nor kill a man who has risked his own life to save mine. I would rather die." The Bathmaster then dried Amani's head with a towel, took shears, and began to shave the face of Amani and cut his hair.

"Was this choice given to you? To die?" said the Bathmaster.

Amani could feel the irritation rise within him, and at that moment, the Bathmaster placed his elbow hard into his shoulder blade. Amani let out a grunt of pain.

"Yes, this choice was given to you. Your body, as I said before, betrays you. Your decisions have knotted themselves within the muscles of your being. I can relieve some of the tension. But only you can release this sickness from within. Or it will be stored within your body until it hardens and paralyzes you. This burden is something that you must let go."

Once more, the Bathmaster kneaded into his back and massaged muscles that Amani had forgotten existed.

Amani grunted once more and spoke. "I have had to make many choices...choices that will hopefully save many people alive. May I ask you a question, Bathmaster?"

"Say on," the old man replied.

"Why are you called the Bathmaster?"

The old man chuckled. "A bath, young man, is not simply the washing of the body with water. But when performed by a Bathmaster, it is a means to extract the deep things that live within the body. Truth, healing, lies, pain. It is the art of releasing the chains that bind one from their past. Even from the recesses of the flesh. To be bathed by a Bathmaster is a privilege and an art known only to a few."

"I have never heard of such a skill before. We have no such craft in Bussar."

The Bathmaster took Amani by his arm and helped him up. He pointed to the wall upon which hung some blue robes. "Go put those on. Never leave your room without wearing these. These robes show you are the property of the king. They will keep you safe from those who think that as a dog you should be put down."

Amani nodded his head in a gesture of thanks and did as commanded.

"I have one last question for you before you depart. Do you mean the King of Hogarth harm?"

He noted the hourglass had now emptied, and the two guards had returned just in time. He looked at the two guards knowingly and then at the old man called the Bathmaster. "Harm Hogarth?" Amani chuckles. "No. I am not Hogarth's enemy. And though she knows it, not. I am probably her greatest ally.

No old man. I mean the king no harm. There are things in Tanara that men should indeed fear. But I am not one of them."

Amani then turned himself over to the guards, who proceeded to escort him out.

"Young man," yelled the Bathmaster.

Amani turned from his guard detail to see the thin, frail figure who had tutored him in the palace bathhouse. He eyed the old man, expecting to receive something.

"My name is Islu. If you are ever in need of a bath...you know where to find me."

Islu bowed.

Amani smirked and bowed in return.

Chapter Fifteen

Secrets and Observations

O sumare looked through a hole in the bathhouse. She
eyed Amani's muscular form, then bit her lip. He was a
strong man — handsome and as Islu had him sit on the table
and administer the poisons into his body; she listened as the
family Bathmaster interrogated their new prisoner. The truth
serum toxins that Islu massaged into his skin would be quick
to take effect. Quick to force the truth from this Bussar's lips.
Islu was wise in the arts of bath-making. His years of study with
the Medja honed his craft. And no one could resist speaking
the truth after the toxins from his potions seeped into the skin.
And Amani, under the skilled spy craft of Islu, spoke his truth.
A truth that revealed that her father took the son of Hogarth's

enemy. But this man was a strange enemy. A man who would rather surrender himself than kill her brother. A man who had slain an Akoolah and was destined to one day be king of his people. And yet left his own land and kin in the belief that he knew more than the traditions of his people. She had watched him earlier. Noted how he walked. He was not timid in other men's presence. Even the guards seemed to defer to the man. She discerned that he was like her. Proud, and an heir, and as she watched him leave with the guards, she found that she admired him the more. She covered the opening into the bath chamber and pressed a stone on the wall. It receded, and the wall pivoted so that she could enter to the other side. Islu sat on his chair behind his desk and he looked up from his studies.

"Did you hear?" He asked.

"I did," said Osumare. "I have never heard of such a thing. The guards told me that my father let him ride with him. They must have spoken along the way. I would know what words the king would say to this man. I will see that he is bathed again, that you might question him further."

Islu smiled, "Does the princess fancy this new slave?"

Osumare scrunched her forehead and spoke in reply. "My reasons are my own Bathmaster, Yet I will not deny my eyes pleasure, nor the truth of your words. He is pleasant to look upon."

Islu smirked. "The predilections of the princess are not my concern. But I would caution you that conversations with the king and those he would speak to are not to be idly inquired of.

If your father wanted you to know his words, he would inform you. It would be wise to ask him than wrest them unknowingly from the boy's lips. I value my position as the king's spymaster. There are forces in Hogarth that would see him undone. I would not want such actions to be traced back to me and he surmise to think I am his enemy."

"Your concern is noted Islu. I will do as you suggest and take the matter up with my father. I would not want your trust compromised nor Father's wrath to be turned unnecessarily towards you. But tell me Islu, why do you think the Bussar would leave his people?"

Islu stroked his gray beard and spoke, "I have questioned many men in my life, killed even more for their lies. This man is ... different somehow. Different in a way the waters do not tell. But I do not believe he means Hogarth harm. From what I can tell from the waters, he believes he is...protecting us."

"Protecting *us*?" said Osumare. "From what?"

"The waters do not show me this thing, princess. But the boy *believes* that we are in danger. He *is* hiding something. The waters on the matter are not clear and show while he is not false. He *is* closed even under the control of the potions administered to him through the bath. There is something about him that burns the truth toxins from him. I would have to go to the archives of the Medja to see if such a thing has ever been recorded before. I have never encountered such a thing in my lifetime."

"Curious," said Osumare. "Since when has a slave ever thought he was *our* protector?"

Islu turned from studying the bowls of water on his desk and turned to look at the princess. "He is in captivity, yes. He may even be shackled by your men. But, know this princess. The waters tell me he is no man's slave."

Osumare looked at her Bathmaster and eyed him, "You, admire this man?"

Islu smirked and replied, "He is a breath of fresh air to these old eyes. Now, if I may give leave to the princess, I will learn more about what the waters might tell me and will report my findings when there is more to speak."

Osumare nodded in respect to the king's spymaster and said. "He may *think* he is not a slave. But he *is* the property of the king, and his life is in my father's hands. And my father has ordered me to see that he is trained to serve. I will go and begin his instruction and will learn for myself why a Bussar slave would think he needs to shield the Hogarth people."

Osumare then exited the room and Islu sat at his desk and heard movement from the wall behind him. "We may speak freely, my prince. Your sister is gone."

A stone door opened behind the desk of the old man and from it exited J'abari. "It would seem my sister fancies this Bussar. But I would have him put to his paces. There are far more deserving Hogarthen that deserves to be ward...and of course, whom I can trust. See that Guam makes his training rigorous. I would know from each of you why my father has taken to this foreigner."

"I do not believe he poses a threat to the kingdom, my prince."

J'abari's lips curled into a sneer as he turned to Islu. "A foreigner has turned the king's ear," he hissed, his voice brimming with disdain. "My father has placed him upon his own horse—a privilege no son of his has ever been granted." His gaze darkened, and he stepped closer, his tone sharp and cutting. "What has he whispered to the King of the Sand? What power does he wield to command such favor? I would know what magic bends a king to his will when his blood cannot."

"I will not tolerate such influence towards my father. Such power can change a nation's course. Therefore, the Bussar boy must be watched. When my father left, he was set to destroy Bussar, and now returns with one of its people upon his horse, and my brother is alleged to have been bested in combat by the enemy. *This* is unacceptable power Islu. And if I had my way, the Bussar dog would already be dead. But I am patient. I will see him and his people all dead in time. I plan to do what my fathers have not done. To one day destroy Bussar. So, we will use this man's presence to learn of their people, culture, and defense. My father has stayed his hand from overrunning Bussar and extending our territory. I would know why."

Islu turned to the prince and replied, "Perhaps he has grown tired of war and the price it exacts. Perhaps he seeks prosperity for his people through peace. Sheer might, my prince, is not always the tool to use on all occasions. Your father has ruled long enough to know this."

J'abari's fingers brushed against a beaker resting on Islu's desk. He lifted it briefly, the glass catching the dim light, before setting it back down with deliberate care. Each step he took drew him closer to the aged spymaster of Hogarth, his presence commanding the room as he turned to face the man. "My father is old. New leadership is required. We are Hogarthen, a mighty people who housed the army of men and from which the Hutari fought the Endwar to defeat the Kifu. We are warriors and the first on this side of the great sea to yield the God-taint. We are destined for more, and if my father will not see or grasp the legacy, that is ours. Then, I, as his heir, will. I will learn this secret that stays his hands against the Medja and the Bussar. I would know what hold they have on a king who controls the sands of Tanara."

Islu frowned and replied, "And when you have learned what you need to know. What then?"

"Then I will be king Islu. And Hogarth will once more stretch out her hand to conquer."

Prince J'abari turned from his father's spymaster and entered the way he came and Islu eyed the prince, worried Hogarth would see her sons once more thrust into the throes of war. And spoke aloud his innermost thoughts. "And what of your father? He will not just stand idle and see himself overthrown. Only his death or abdication would allow you to rise to the throne."

Prince J'abari halted mid-step, his piercing gaze cutting back toward Islu. Slowly, he raised a hand, and the air stirred in response. The ground beneath them trembled as grains of sand swirled into motion, coiling together in a fluid dance. The formation slithered across the stone floor, rising higher until it stood before Islu, a snake of sand shaped like a cobra poised to strike. Its head flared wide, casting an ominous shadow over Islu, whose breath quickened. Panic seized him as he stumbled backward, his eyes locked on the animated creation looming over him.

"As you can see Islu, my father is not the only one who controls the sands. And is it not the destiny of all sons to replace their fathers? But lest you forget your place to be the secret bearer of the house of N'Kosi, then be reminded of the secrets that I hold on Hogarth's spymaster. How you have eyed my mother's naked flesh while bathing and pleasured yourself from your viewing. I am sure my father would be enraged and have your stones removed. I would not kill you myself. I would be too entertained to see how imaginative my father would be in your torture to rob myself by your quick death at my hand. But if a demonstration is in order of if I *were* to have to say, personally dispose of you..."

The sand snake coiled around the beaker J'abari had placed on Islu's desk, its body tightening with menacing grace. At a mere squeeze of the prince's hand, the animated creature responded, its constriction slicing cleanly through the fragile glass. The beaker shattered with a sharp crack, sending shards flying. Tiny flecks embedded themselves into Islu's cheeks, while larger fragments scattered across the desk.

Islu cried out, clutching his face as small crimson beads dotted his skin. The snake dissolved into a cascading spill of sand, spreading haphazardly over the desk's surface. Islu shielded his eyes, his trembling hands stained with blood from the shallow cuts that marked his face.

"I trust the lesson today has been learned?"

Islu vigorously nodded in understanding as he struggled to remove shards of glass from his face.

"Good," said the prince. "I would hate to repeat this instruction." The prince then turned and exited the room.

Chapter Sixteen

Responses and Reactions

O sumare approached the guards stationed on either side of Amani as he dined. She paused, her keen ears catching snippets of the palace servants' conversation. One leaned forward with a deferential smile.

"Do you find the dish to your liking, my lord?" the servant asked. "Have you tasted such delicacies in Bussar?"

Amani nodded politely; his response drowned out by the growing hum of admiration. Several young women—and a few older ones—lingered nearby, their gazes fixed on him with poorly veiled interest. Their fluttering laughter and sidelong glances betrayed their obvious intentions, each vying subtly for the attention of the foreign prince.

Osumare cringed and made her irritation known. "He is not a lord. He is a dog. All of you, I will speak to the Bussar slave alone. Leave us."

The servants bowed, and the guards stood and saluted. "We will be outside the door, princess, if we are needed." Osumare nodded in acknowledgment and everyone exited the room.

She sat down across from Amani and stuck her finger in the mashed potatoes on his plate and scooped some into her mouth. "They are good," she said.

Amani's scowl deepened; his displeasure was evident as the princess's hand intruded into his meal. Though every shift of his body bristled with irritation, he held his tongue. Instead, with measured calm, he reached for an empty plate at the table's center. Scooping a portion of mashed potatoes and a generous cut of meat from his plate, he slid the offering toward her.

"I can't possibly finish all of this, Princess," he said, his voice composed despite the tension in his gaze. "Please, do me the honor."

She picked up a fork and knife and cut into the meat on her plate and as she did; she spoke her mind. "I must admit you are a strange one, Bussar. However, I would expect a dog to clean his plate."

Amani frowned at the remark but again said nothing.

Osumare noted his face and spoke. "Have I insulted you? Are you offended? Do my words cause injury to my father's new pet?"

Amani put his food down finished chewing his meat and replied. "Princess, I am yours to command. I committed myself to your father when I left my own. If his daughter would elevate herself by debasing her servant, then so be it. But you should know that I am compelled to ask, If I have done wrong, bear witness of my wrong. But if not, why do you insult me?"

Osumare was taken aback by his words, and her face grew red. "You dare speak to me as a commoner? She rose to her feet, glowering at the impudence of her trainee, and Amani stood to his feet as well and replied.

"I think we both know that neither of us is common princess. We are children of kings and, as with all children, whose fathers rule nations and command armies. We know what it means to sacrifice. And because I see that you know that I speak the truth, is it too much to ask that you might show some honor even as your father has done to a man who has spared the life of your flesh? Or does the honor of the Sandking only extend to the King himself and not to his children?"

Osumare was flush in anger. Her mind reeled with retort, and she recoiled from the words that cut her heart and convicted her. Here was a man who exposed her. And for a moment she experienced emotions she did not recall before as a princess of Hogarth: shame and guilt. And she recognized that the man who stood in front of her was more honorable than she. And she despised the feeling.

"You are a stranger in my land, and even more so in my house, and yet you dare speak to me so? Who are you to question me?

Do you think of yourself as my equal? Does a slave think himself higher than a child of the king? Who in the sands do you think you are?" Her face was rouge, and Amani noted the tensing of her facial muscles and that she clenched her fist, and he knelt before her and spoke.

"Know, my princess, that I am yours to command. You mentioned earlier that the king had given me over to you. What would you have me do? Forgive your servant if his words bring offense. I trust you will teach me the ways of Hogarth, for in Bussar we see and speak the truth, in our land to do otherwise is considered dishonorable. My apologies for my impudence. I am not accustomed to withholding my words."

Osumare quickly caught herself and her anger fled as she looked down at the man, who was bowed at her feet. This man who had reminded her of her duty to her father, the king. A duty she was bound to obey. She wanted to slap him. He spoke with an authority that she was not accustomed to hearing save from her father or perhaps her brothers. It was not often she was reprimanded for her behavior, and the experience did not sit well with her.

"Know, Bussar, that we will continue these discussions. Know this of a surety. But despite my anger, my father's will must take precedence, and I cannot allow you to appear before my father as you are now. I hope to see that my father is pleased. Which means you must do well if you are to be of any service to him. Since it falls on me to see that you are tutored in our ways, your training, for good or ill will reflect on me."

Amani looked up from his position and spoke playfully to the princess. "So, your fate is in my hands? Intriguing, does this mean that I am in...the dominant position?"

Osumare frowned, then smirked. "It means, Bussar, that you cannot fail. As far as your untoward attempt to assume that I am held hostage to your actions, let us end what you perceive as your superior position. Because if you fail, know that at most I will, but incur my father's disappointment and perhaps some embarrassment that despite my best attempts, I was unable to train what my people consider a stray dog. But you, well, you will surrender your life. But do not fear Bussar. I will help you. I am curious to learn what will become of you. Consider yourself my entertainment for the season. So, I will impart to you the lessons of those who must serve the king. Learn them well and we shall both receive honor. I have been told that you have killed an Akoolah, and whispers from Father's troops say you have even bested my brother, one of Hogarth's finest warriors. But to be a ward to the king. To be his servant. You must learn more than how to carry a sword and kill beasts. You must learn the decorum of the Hogarthen. Learn the protocols of the King's palace. And as your headmaster, I will impart your first lesson. Rise."

Amani did as bidden and stood before the princess.

She entered his personal space, smiled, raised her hand, and slapped him squarely across the cheek.

Amani was flushed, and he gritted his teeth, his face contorting with anger.

She noted his reaction pointed at his face and spoke to him. "*That* right there is what will get you killed. Your body language betrays you. This is the first lesson you must learn if you are to survive in Hogarth. This expression...the innermost thoughts displayed in your face and body must be controlled. You can never reveal your feelings to those that you serve. Never show that you are a human with emotions. You must show that the cares of others, their thoughts, do not move you. You must become dead to offense. If you are moved by the words and the actions of those in the palace and those who my father commands. You will die. For with one hand, they will laugh at you and with the other move to slice your throat. Your offense will cloud your vision, and you will never see the knife poised to end your life." She glowered at him and pressed her finger into his nose. "Do you understand this?"

Amani stood still and replied, "Yes."

Osumare struck him again, her palm landing on the same spot as before. Amani flinched slightly from the sting of her blow, but his expression remained an unyielding mask, betraying no more than the faintest flicker of discomfort.

"Good dog," she said with a mocking grin. "You learn quickly. Perhaps you might survive after all. What I've taught you is the pinnacle of knowledge—learn it well, and you will witness the true language of Hogarth in action. Now you're ready for Guam. Follow me; he will take over your instruction in service and protocol."

With a sharp pivot, the princess strode away, her bearing exuding authority. Amani hesitated for only a moment before falling into step behind her, steeling himself to meet the man she had called Guam.

Chapter Seventeen

The Etiquette of Service

I n the royal halls of the palace, shadows whispered secrets, and the air bore the weight of expectations, Amani stood in a line along with three others ready to undergo the rigorous training that would shape him into an impeccable servant to the Sandking. A man examined them and eyed them from top to bottom. The royal tutor known as a Guam. He held the distinguished position of chief servant, also known as the Chief of the Palace. He stood before the four men and spoke while each pupil stood silently in line before him.

"The Sandking N'Kosi has ruled Hogarth since the death of his father. His will is law. If he is displeased with how you serve with your life, then know that your life will be forfeit. Guam's voice dipped into a hushed, conspiratorial tone, his sharp eyes locking onto Amani as though peering into his very thoughts. "If he chooses to act out of spite because of your service—" he paused, letting the words linger like a blade hovering above its mark, "—let's just say the consequences could twist your life into something far removed from the future you might dare to imagine."

He then leaned closer to another and paced around him, his expression darkening, as if the faint flicker of torchlight cast harsh shadows across his face. "To serve the royal family is an honor. But know this a member with wounded pride has the power to shape your destiny, not with reason or justice, but with malice. Service is not just duty—it's survival. One misstep, one perceived insult, and you could find yourself stripped of your station, toiling in the bowels of this palace, or cast into the Targus Mines, forgotten by all."

His words carried the weight of grim certainty, and the warning was as much a threat as it was a lesson. "Think carefully, as you serve them," Guam said, his voice only just above a whisper. "When dealing with royalty, the cost of their whims can far outweigh your own choices."

Therefore, I have been assigned to help you do two things. One: to care for the Sandking and the royal family with full devotion and with the highest level of service."

"And the second?" asked a pupil.

Guam looked at them all and spoke with gravity. "To survive. For if you fail to do the first, you will not live to know the second. Is this understood by all?"

All present nodded. And the Chief of the Palace spoke once more. "You will undergo several tests to determine which of you will be Zhara-Telak to the King. Pass these tests and you may gain this illustrious title of service and honor. Perhaps if you live long enough, you may even one day live to be the Chief of the Palace. Those of you who do not pass will be relegated to lower duties either in the palace or be given over as slaves to the Umdhala. Where your skills may be of use to the commanders of the city or an officer of the lower ranks. In the end, it will be the king himself who will select which of you will serve him as Zhara-Telak."

Amani raised his hand.

"Speak boy," said Guam.

Amani lowered his hand then bowed his head in respect and spoke his peace. "What is the meaning of this word, teacher?"

Guam and the others laughed at Amani's ignorance. "In Hogarth, boy, to live is to serve, and to serve is to live. The Zhara-Telak is ancient Zaratu. It carries the meaning of someone who is a devoted servant but also a guardian. The Zhara-Telak embodies both these things and is a most honored role among our people. An honor you and these here must show yourself worthy to hold."

Amani replied. "I thought the king personally wanted me trained to be the King's ward. Has this been changed?"

Guam laughed again, and several of the other students guffawed as well. "I was made aware of who you are, Bussar dog. I also believe that the King holds you in such regard that he has given you over to training to serve him as his possible Zhara-Telak. Since you are new to our ways, I will enlighten you as to the King's meaning. He has called those things that are not as though they were. To be clear, you are not the ward of the King yet. And, likely, you will never be. He merely proclaims your path. It is you who must take hold of this promise and make it real. The princess has given me understanding regarding your person. Therefore, you stand before me because our princess commands it and will train you because of this command. But you should know that I of my own would never release you to serve our king."

Amani's eyes furrowed, and he grew more tense as resentment crept from his inner man and began to reflect on his face. His mouth turned downward into a frown and Guam smiled at seeing Amani's change in body language.

"Are you surprised by my words? Offended even?" Guam then laughed. "You see, Bussar, the Sandking's word simply allowed you the opportunity to serve. Service is an honor in Bussar, a privilege.... not a right. Service is earned. It cannot be given away. I understand that your people have a saying. *"Faith without works is dead?"* This too is the way of Hogarth. Our king has expressed his desire to have you, while true. YOU must demonstrate the work needed to be worthy of his desire, and this dog. *I* will determine, NOT the king."

Guam then moved closer and stood over Amani and bent down within inches of his face. His warm breath was noxious, and Amani strained not to heave from the stench that wafted from Guam's pungent mouth.

"You should know that I will not be at all burdened if you were to be found killed. In fact, it would be expected. Know also that your failure is also to be expected. So, remember this Bussar. You will only enter the king's presence if Akuma himself speaks to the King and gives command. I consider your being here a formality to show your inability to rise to this honor. You should be so lucky as to be selected to be numbered of these here, for they have studied their whole lives to rise to the level to be of personal service to the king."

Guam then leaned close to Amani and whispered so that only he and Amani knew his words and spoke. "Do not think that these next to you will stand idle to see an outsider take the spot they have trained their whole lives to get. Watch your back, Bussar."

Guam then withdrew from Amani's immediate presence and Amani smiled after Guam retreated from his personal space, bowed, and replied. "Then may the will of Akuma be done. All I ask is that you teach me even as you would teach the others. And if I die, then I die. But if I prosper and live, then do not kick against the goads."

Guam smirked at the boy as an attendant came, whispered something into his ear, then turned and left the room.

"The king and his family are seated for dinner. You each will take a tray to a member of the royal family. I will be watching you to see that you place each dish as instructed earlier. Your assignments are as follows.... Ashar, you will have the privilege of serving the king. Hoseth, you shall serve high Prince J'abari. Phatut, you are assigned to Jo'than. And you, Bussar. You will serve the lowest in station at the royal table: the princess. Your first lesson now begins.

"Remember, I don't want to hear your breath," Guam's voice echoed through the chamber. Amani took a measured breath, suppressing any sound, as if melding with the air around him. The group then left the prep area to the king's dining chambers to serve him and the royal family.

The room was a large hall with a stone table of quartz and was decorated with flatware made from crystal and gold. Silks draped the room and covered the windows to flatten the sun's heat into the chamber. A minstrel played music in a corner and Guam spoke to the family that the meal was ready for them and proceeded to escort Ashar to the king's seat and oversaw the placement of his food to the king.

After that, the king was served by Ashar. Hoseth followed and came to serve Prince J'abari, who was then followed by Phatut, who served Prince Jo'than. Amani looked out into the dining room and watched when each left with their prepared dish to serve their assigned member of the royal family. When he saw Jo'than was served, he timed his entry as the others before him and entered the chamber. Circling the table, he was eyed by all, and he proceeded to place his tray in front of the princess and meticulously cleaned her utensils with the cloth given to him. He placed her water jug in front of her and removed her tray so that she might eat and then stepped backward against the wall and stood like the others in silence.

The Sandking then took a bite of his food, and the rest of the royal family followed. Music filled the room, and the smell of the food wafted into the air. A day had passed since he last ate.

As others indulged in their meals, Amani stood like a stone sentinel, his stomach protesting in hunger. Guam's lesson unfolded—*a servant to the king must endure discomfort without complaint, serving others before self.*

His daydream and recitation of rules came to a swift halt when he heard a bronze tray hit the floor that had slipped from Hoseth's hands.

Prince J'abari slammed his fist on the table, his voice slicing through the air like a blade., "Guam, who do you have serving me? A bumbling idiot?" Without waiting for a reply, he unsheathed his sword with a metallic hiss. The room froze as J'abari's weapon glinted under the light.

Hoseth, the trembling servant, barely had time to flinch before the prince swung down with precise, unyielding brutality. The blade severed Hoseth's right hand, sending it thumping to the floor. A scream of raw agony tore from Hoseth's throat as he clutched his bleeding stump and stumbled out of the room, leaving a dark red trail in his wake.

J'abari smirked, pulling a white tablecloth from the nearest setting. He wiped his sword clean with deliberate ease before sliding it back into its sheath. "Pathetic," he muttered, tossing the bloodied cloth to the floor like discarded refuse.

Amani's gaze flicked to the king, anticipation tightening his chest. Surely, there would be outrage, a reprimand—something. Yet the Lord of Hogarth remained an unmovable monolith of indifference. He continued eating, his jaw working with the same steady rhythm as before. The scent of roasted lamb mingled with the metallic tang of blood, thickening the already oppressive air of the dining hall.

Jo'than, the younger prince, sat frozen, his wide eyes locked on the bloody trail left by the fleeing servant. His hands gripped the edge of the table, the tension in his fingers so fierce that his knuckles stood stark white against his tan skin. Across from him, Princess Osumare's usual poise wavered. Her lips pressed into a rigid line, her vibrant expression dulled and shadowed by a mix of suppressed fury and disgust. Her narrowed gaze darted between her father and J'abari, a storm of emotion boiling behind her eyes.

Amani noted the dissonance in her demeanor. Her teachings of emotional restraint—calm over chaos—seemed distant now, overshadowed by this visceral reaction. Yet, at this moment, the value of her lessons crystallized in his mind: emotions, when unguarded, were vulnerabilities.

"Forgive your servant, High Prince," came Guam's steady, measured voice, cutting through the tension like a blade. "And my apologies, my king, for the disruption to your meal."

The king waved a dismissive hand, his focus unwavering from the meal before him. His silence was not agreement, but neither was it rebuke.

"The rest of you—out!" Guam commanded; his sharp tone snapped the room into motion.

Phatut and Ashar rose quickly, bowing toward the table with practiced precision before retreating toward the exit. Amani followed, his footsteps heavy with thought.

As he passed Guam, the teacher leaned in close, his breath sharp with menace. His lips curled into a sneer, and his whispered words carried the weight of a dark omen.

"And then there were three."

Chapter Eighteen

To Serve the Council

G uam stood in the Thulum-Rah, the ancient hall council of the palace, and before him stood the three remaining candidates who would serve the Sandking.

"Here begins your second lesson. In this room, the Sandking and his council conduct state affairs. In this room, the economy of our nation is decided. Laws are decreed and wars begin and end. In this room, you will hear names of import within Hogarth and the going ons of those whose eyes the king and his spies have their sight upon. If you serve the king, you will hear matters of state that can never be uttered outside this room. Therefore, you will never listen or react to conversation, and you will forget all that you hear. If the king or I or any of those in residence hear you gossip about the matters spoken in this room. You should expect that on my command of those that hear you speak to give you over to execution. If the King is merciful, only your tongue will be cut out and you might either live the remainder of your life in bonds working in the Targus Mines or as entertainment to the city as a warrior in the pit. I say this to you before I send you into the council chamber. Understand that you will be a target of spies, of families disloyal to the king. So, before I allow you to serve the king in a meeting that he and his advisers are in. You must be allowed to decline. However, know that if you do, you will lose your right to continue in the training for service to the king. Who then among you will consent to continue?"

Amani immediately stepped forward. Guam raised his eye and questioned the boy.

"These here have waited their whole lives to serve the king. And not even they have been so quick to step forward knowing the seriousness of what they are about to do. But you, Bussar, you are swift to assume such a dangerous burden. Before this respond to me...no tell us why an enemy of our king would be quick to hold in confidence his words?"

Amani looked at the peers beside him, then turned to look at Guam. "I am not in the position teacher to question the training, or the willingness of these to keep the King's secrets. I can only speak of myself. I am Amani, son of Haidar, King of Bussar. I am a prince. And because I was raised from a boy to one day, take my father's stead, I am aware of when to speak, and when not to speak secrets. I know secrets that kings have, secrets that, if known, would endanger the lives of their people. I also know the burden of keeping these secrets..." Amani turned away and thought of what he knew about the Kifu and the location of the door that led to other lands and to the chamber of the undead God Hesphus. The thoughts weighed heavily on him that he held the power to bring fire from the sky, but to do so would draw attention to his enemies and empower the Kifu. He carefully weighed his next words as he continued to answer Guam. "All men of import bear burdens, teacher. Some affect the bearer alone...others the lands of men. To keep the secrets of a king is not a new thing for me."

Amani bowed and stood silently as Guam and the three young men watched him.

Phatut then stepped forward, followed by Ashar. And at that moment, Guam had his answer and turned to the three who had followed Amani.

"Very good." He said. He then turned to Phatut and Ashar. "Do not let the Bussar make a mockery of you. Who can serve our king better than his own people?"

Amani stood in silence while the other three boys smirked and nodded.

Guam motioned to each to take a serving tray and spoke. "The meeting of the Umdhala is already in progress. By this time, they will be hungry. Each of you will be responsible for the four men. Do you have any questions?"

Ashar raised his hand and spoke, "Teacher, there are but three of us. How shall we see to four?"

Guam looked at Ashar with a sly grin, his eyes filled with a hint of mischief. "Ah, young Ashar, I see you possess a mind for numbers. Good! Now, let this be a lesson in the art of resourcefulness. The answer lies not in the number of trays you carry but in the grace with which you balance them. A challenge, you see, is but an opportunity disguised. Now, go forth, and let the Umdhala witness the seamless coordination of your service. Oh, and be careful not to die."

With that, Guam gestured for them to proceed, and the three young men paused, then left the room, trays in hand, ready to navigate the intricacies of their newfound responsibilities.

The young men retrieved and walked down a corridor towards the council chambers. Amani walked between the two men and spoke. "Ashar, you have already served the king. Continue to do so. Allow Phatut and I to serve the other three. Phatut when I walk in the chamber serve him who is opposite of me, and I will serve whoever is on the side I walk. Are we in agreement?"

Ashar nodded, and Phatut retorted, "What if I get the two?"

"I will take the two if it pleases you."

The door to the chamber came closer and voices could be heard speaking on the other side.

"Are we in agreement, Phatut?"

"Alright!" said Phatut. "But this had better not be a trick. Or I will have your stones."

Ashar's hand touched the golden doorknob to the chamber and opened it wide and he, Amani, and Phatut entered and took their respective positions. Phatut saw that one adviser sat to the right of the king and set his tray, table dressings, and placed his food to the side of his charge, and then backed away to his rear. Ashar also served the king as before. While Amani took his tray and prepared two dressings for each man and gave each their eating ware at the same time. He then prepared their drinks and saw that they were served at the same time. He continued this until they were both served food and then stood at their rear in between them, ready to attend to their needs.

"Ashar, is it?" said the king.

Ashar nodded to his lord.

"In these chambers, upon my command, you may speak when spoken to. To speak of the goings on within the chamber outside of these walls is death. So, tell me, Ashar, how long have you been training that you might be Zhara-Telak to me?"

Ashar stood upright and looked straight ahead. "For twenty years, my lord."

The other men looked at the boy, who stood at attention and trembled slightly.

"You see that young man there against the wall? He is a prince of Bussar. Now a slave in service to his countrymen's sworn enemy. Do you think he should be in the same room as you? Should he be given the chance to serve me when he has done nothing for this country throughout his whole life, save disparage our people?"

Ashar smirked, and his response dripped with contempt. "The Bussar are dogs and should be treated as such. His ancestors killed mine. No, my Lord. I would use his skin as a hide for the king's saddle. If you commanded."

King N'Kosi laughed. "Spoken like a true Hogarthen. I respect your lust to see our enemies vanquished at our feet."

General Zaraku Dumani sat at the council table like a thundercloud looming over a barren plain, his presence commanding every corner of the chamber. Broad-shouldered and statuesque, he carried himself with the discipline of a warrior who had weathered countless battles and the authority of a leader accustomed to absolute obedience. His armor gleamed under the flickering torchlight, its intricate carvings of snarling beasts and storm motifs hinting at both his ferocity and his cunning. A scar ran from his temple to his jaw, a stark reminder of the battles he had survived, though his piercing, unrelenting gaze seemed more capable of wounding than any blade. When he spoke, his voice rumbled with the weight of unshakable conviction, a tone that silenced whispers and froze the hearts of those who dared oppose him. The council table, laden with maps and symbols of strategy, seemed dwarfed by the sheer force of his presence as if the room itself braced against his will.

Then the walking thundercloud spoke to Phatut. "And what of you, citizen? What does my countryman think of the Bussar who now serves me and the king's Dreamweaver?"

"He is an outsider. He is an enemy of Hogarth," replied Phatut.

General Dumani nodded. "And interesting choice of words."

Seated at the far end of the table was Amokaye, the Dreamweaver, whose quiet confidence seemed to alter the very air around him. His presence immediately commanded the attention of all those gathered. His deep indigo mantle, embroidered with gold constellations, shimmered in the candlelight as if the fabric itself held the secrets of the heavens. The shimmering beads around his neck caught the light as he sat into his seat, his eyes—dark and fathomless—surveying the room with an unsettling calm. His hands rested upon the slender ebony staff, the crystal at its top pulsing with a faint, otherworldly glow. The air around him felt thick with the weight of unspoken knowledge, as though he were not merely present in the room but linked to something far beyond it. Beside him, the king shifted slightly, acknowledging Amokaye's presence with a nod that hinted at both familiarity and respect, though even the monarch's usual poise seemed to falter in the shadow of the Dreamweaver's silent power. Those gathered at the table shifted uncomfortably, their eyes drawn to the seer with an unease that was almost palpable. He had not spoken yet, but already, it was clear—Amokaye was no ordinary councilor. He was a force unto himself, one whose words, when they came, would carry the weight of prophecy. His face covered at the table, he spoke as if whispering aloud, "Tell me children of Bussar. Who deems a boy an enemy when he serves trays? Bussar, tell us. *Are* you an enemy to our people?"

Amani looked at Amokaye. His voice seemed...familiar yet distant—like the voices of the Medja from the desert. "I am not Wisdom. I serve N'Kosi King of Hogarth."

The seer then stood to his feet and N'Kosi folded his hands and leaned back into his chair. He plucked a turkey wing from the tray before him and listened as his chief counselor questioned Amani.

The Wisdom of Hogarth walked until he stood in front of Amani. His eyes also seemed familiar. His pupils were gray, and his purple robe concealed his features. A scarf covered his face, and he had a walking staff similar to those of the Medja. His head tilted to the side, and he leaned forward to scrutinize the face of who his people would call 'adversary.'

"You say you are not an enemy of the people. And in another breath note that you serve the king of Hogarth. Answer me this question. Is not service to the people and service to the King the same?"

Amani was quick to reply. "No wisdom. It is not. Hogarth did not save me. A man did. A man who even now could have me killed but has not. By the code of my people, I owe him, and all that he loves, a life debt. Whispers in my brief time here speak that there are those in Hogarth who would see the king dead..."

Amokaye looked at N'Kosi. "You see, even a stranger has discerned the unrest within your land, my king. How much more your own people?" He then turned back to Amani and motioned him to continue.

"Hogarthen even some in this room would see me dead. But the King has honored me with life. Yet all do not unite behind this decision. By your mind would not those in this very shown divided loyalty to Hogarth and the will of the king? And when there are those in a kingdom who speak openly against the decision of any king. Then that king must be watchful of those who would seek to usurp him."

Ashar and Phatut scowled at him, and Ashar dared to speak. "I am loyal to our king!"

"Silence!" said Amokaye. "I did not address you." Ashar then lowered his gaze, and in rebuke, stood mute.

Amokaye then nodded at Amani and waved his hand at him. "Continue. I would hear the whole of your thoughts, Bussar."

Amani swallowed and continued "There are always those that would seek a king harm. I do not serve them. I serve the king. What he loves I will love, and what he hates, I will hate. And above the king, I serve Akuma, creator of all life."

All eyes were on Amani now. The Seer's hand reached up to his face, and he stroked his chin, "That is an intriguing answer, boy. But be careful. I am older than all in the room, and even I can sense pride masked in humility. So, you profess allegiance to the king and to that which he loves. To hate what he hates. Is this true?"

"I have spoken it," Amani replied.

The mysterious figure walked back to the table as he nodded and spoke, "Interesting answer...but I have one question for you, boy." He then sat down and continued, "If the king were to say hate...Bussar? What then? Would you still hate what he hates?"

Amani felt the conflict within him. The old man had weaved a web to entrap him by his own words. He carefully thought upon his answer so that he might release himself from the mental snare of the Hogarthen Seer and replied.

"I would plead with the king for the life of my people. I would honor the life debt owed to the king as is the way of my people and thus honor what it means to be Bussar. I would protect the king until death or until released from this debt. But though the king might cover the four clans beneath the sands, and Hogarth's army stretch from the dark mouth unto the sea, the king should know that he could never truly defeat Bussar."

The general stood up and Amani heard him unsheathe his sword. The King tossed his eaten bone across the table and rose up in anger. "He marched towards Amani lifted a knife from the table and put it up to Amani's neck and spoke. "You speak from a conflated soul, boy. To think that my drowning your people in the sand would not grant me victory. If such would not defeat any people, then tell me, former prince. Tell me why *I* could not defeat your people?"

Amani swallowed hard and replied, "For as long as the king keeps me in his service, the Bussar will live — they would live in me."

N'Kosi smirked and then laughed aloud. He looked at the three members of the Umdhala he had summoned and nodded, pointing at them. "Exceptional...see?" He then sheathed his knife and drew closer and whispered into Amani's ear. "I like you Bussar. I do. But never underestimate a king's need to remove those around him. You, of all people, should understand his lesson."

The two men eyed each other, and Amani for the first time in his life felt genuine hatred towards his father for burdening him to trial by combat with Jo'than. He wondered if perhaps they all would have been better off if he had not honored his life debt to Jo'than. And had simply gone to war.

The Seer then spoke. "My king, I believe the boy's words to be true. For I cannot help but notice our servers today that if these two children of Hogarth are so enamored to serve our king and the people of Hogarth. Why does the foreigner serve two? Service is an honor in Hogarth and yet they would let themselves be shamed to let a Bussar serve two of their countrymen while they each serve just one. Does this failure to limit the boy to just one perhaps show they are not as ready to serve more than this Bussar boy here?"

The king looked at Amani and smiled. "Perhaps he does love our people more than they do."

Phatut and Ashar glowered at Amani, and Amani knew that at that moment, they had become his enemies.

And as he stood against the wall. His back straight, his eyes caught the stare of the Seer Amokaye looking at him. And Amani could not help but think of all present. He was the most dangerous man in the room.

Chapter Nineteen

Two Truths and Lie

G uam sat at his desk, the late afternoon light spilling through the latticework of his quarters, painting intricate patterns across the polished wood. His gaze fixed on the heavy wooden door, waiting for the summons to be answered. A faint knock echoed, and his attendant entered, bowing deeply. "He has arrived, master."

"Send him in," said Guam.

The door opened again, revealing Amani. He entered with a measured stride, his head inclined in deference, and stopped before the desk. Bowing, he spoke. "You called for me?"

Guam's sharp eyes scanned him from head to toe, lingering as if weighing something unseen. He gestured to the chair opposite him. "Be seated, Amani."

Amani took a seat, the silence between them thrumming like a taut string about to snap. Guam didn't waste time. "Somehow you have managed to impress N'Kosi. Your name continues to rise above the other students. When a man serves, he is dangerous."

Amani furrowed his brow. and replied. "Dangerous? I am sorry teacher. I do not understand?"

Guam stood, crossing the room to a small table where a pitcher of wine gleamed in the sunlight. He poured himself a glass, offering one to Amani. The young man shook his head and waved the glass away. Guam snickered. "Do the Bussar not care for the fruit of the vine?" He asked with a raised brow, a mocking edge in his tone.

Amani shook his head. "It is not that teacher. I find that wine can be wonderful, but it can also dull the mind and cloud the spirit. I sit in the presence of the head of the Palace of the King of Hogarth. A man who has let it be known that he would not mind my being dead, nor would be heartbroken if I were to disappear. I trust you would not be angry with me if I chose to be clear in the head."

Guam chuckled darkly, swirling his wine. "I must admit Bussar. You have intrigued me. I would not have thought someone from the plains folk would be as cultured, but I see I am wrong. You have adapted well since you have arrived. And while

I recognize the princess has her own agenda to see you succeed. You should know that I have but one. To see that the best servant is paired to serve the king. I have kept this charge for over twenty years now and I would not see my record diminished by a foreigner."

Amani met Guam's gaze, unflinching. "You said I have intrigued you? How so?"

Guam returns to his seat, setting the wineglass down carefully. He ran a finger over the intricately etched rim of the silver goblet, his voice lowering. "You see Bussar. The king trusts me. To serve him is to hold power—because the king's secrets are power. Every secret he shares, every vulnerability he exposes, is a transaction. And I ensure that only the most loyal, the most deserving, are close enough to receive those secrets. Now, you find yourself in that same position. I must ensure that all my students understand this important lesson. For there is nothing hidden that shall not be revealed in time. All things come to the light of day in its season. Even the secrets of kings. My students who seek to be in the presence of the king must grasp the gravity of this exchange. You are now being given the opportunity to learn this firsthand."

Amani's eyes narrowed, and he lowered his head as if to lean into the uncharted depths of Guam's meaning. "I am listening."

"Here in Hogarth, we play a game. It trains us to spot lies and we teach it to our children and they learn as they get older not to lie to their parents. I would like to play it with you now. It is called two truths and a lie. I will tell you something about myself. Two of these things are true. One will be a lie. I will ask you to choose which is the lie."

Amani nodded, "And I suppose I will, in turn, do the same and you will guess?"

"Yes, and so you and I will exchange a vulnerability for knowledge. Do you accept?"

Amani thought upon the proposition and said, "I accept. Begin when you are ready."

Guam smiled, "I have plotted to kill the king. I am without stones. I am the king's faithful servant. Which of these is the lie?"

Amani stood and looked at the items that were in Guam's chamber and he saw the meticulous cleanliness of his surroundings. A tapestry that lined the wall, and the furnishings were ornate for a chief servant of the palace. Several flasks of wine were on shelves and flowers were in a vase. After Amani surveyed the surroundings, he turned and spoke to Guam. "The lie is that you are without stones."

Guam seemed surprised. "You are correct. But how did you know this to be a lie?"

Amani pointed to his bed and gestured that Guam see his surroundings. Your bed is imprinted with the impression of someone who has slept alongside a companion. And while all men appreciate beauty. Your flowers are not something that I have seen in Hogarth. Yours is the first I have seen. It is a woman's touch. I surmise either a memorial in remembrance of a companion now gone or the hand of a woman who seeks to soften the harsh quarters of a lover that she occasions."

Guam nodded. "You are an astute boy. If you serve the King, this trait will serve you well. Your observations are correct. My wife was taken when I plotted against the king long ago. As penance for my crime, he took her, and she lives, but only as I serve loyally to him. Thus, I am the king's faithful servant. In return, she may bring me flowers as a token of the King's word. She will not be killed as long as I am faithful. Do you better understand now the man that calls you his ward, boy? Note the severity and the subtlety of his hand towards his enemies. For even if I dare take my own life, the king promises me he will murder my wife, and sons, and even those who would remember my name. I am free to leave the Palace, even Hogarth if I were to choose. But I am his prisoner. Though I am lord of all in his home."

Amani stared at the man, and for a moment he pitied him and wondered who else politely served the king under threat of annihilation. He wondered within himself why anyone would protect a man who possessed such evil to hold hostage a family. But he reminded himself that this same man bartered with his father that their two nations might not see war, and he steeled himself and spoke aloud. "I am Amani of Bussar. I will now speak two truths and a lie.

"Say on," said Guam.

"I am protecting you. I am a prince. I am a demigod," said Amani.

Guam snorted, amusement flashing across his face. "And for a moment I thought the Bussar were such an intelligent people. The lie is easy, as you are clearly not a demigod. How ridiculous to even suggest it as an option. Of course, the reason remains why you would protect me. My life is in the king's hands and he ensures that I would not even take my own life. Let alone allow someone else to do it, knowing that to do so would transfer my punishment to them. I must admit Bussar. I am disappointed, as I was hoping to discover more. No matter. You have honored me. Perhaps we shall talk more, but for now, return to your quarters. More testing awaits you and the others on the morrow."

Amani bowed and turned to walk away, allowing himself the briefest of smiles, knowing that he had not played Guam's game fairly. For he had told him three truths. Hoping that those in Hogarth would continue to underestimate him.

Chapter Twenty

The Grief of Kings

H aidar, King of Bussar, sat as the Bussar clans conducted business, as was the norm. The King looked to his left and right, and within the circle of men who upon command would muster the might of Bussar to battle, he heard nothing but garbled voices as his mind was distracted from the assembly. For one hundred and eighty suns his son had been away from home and the king wondered if he would ever see his son again. Ruminated on if there were other ways that he could have determined the outcome. Mudiwa had not spoken to him since that time. A queen now estranged from her king. And though she lay in his bed, her body was not the inviting place that he had enjoyed these many years. She was cold. Distant. And deep in a place within her heart, he knew in his soul of souls that she hated him for letting their only son be taken by the Hogarth.

But Haidar did not blame her. How else was a mother to be when she could not know the state of her offspring? She had turned inward and had sunk into her loss. A mother who grieved for her only son.

Damn you, my son! Why did you not kill the Hogarth boy? Why did you not listen?

The berate continued until his inner voice became his outer voice and was heard by all.

"Damn you Amani!"

The men of the clans all stopped to observe their elected king. And one dared speak. "Haidar." And in that moment each man of the Culsha rose from his seated position and walked towards their leader and placed their outstretched hands on Haidar's shoulders. Others extended their hands and bowed their heads in silence. Silence was all that was spoken, and the king bowed his head and then wept. And nestled within the group of thirty men that encircled him, the King of Bussar allowed himself comfort from his people.

And set apart from the group was M'Msee. The Wisdom of Bussar. The Hutari, who watched a group of mortal men seek to give solace over the loss of one. The robed man of over five hundred years watched the scene from afar, and his heart was filled with compassion. It was a pitiful scene to see a father weep and long for his only child. Even more so, to see men in unity move as one to console a father who, in the keeping of his duty as their king, sacrificed his own son. M'Msee had seen men unite under a single banner before to fight the Kifu. He remembered his call to the world of men that they must fight or be left to the destiny of oblivion that Enkai had reserved for them all. He saw multitudes of men fall to the army of the dead, only to be raised again and march against those who were once called friends. He recalled his life of old. His marriage, the birth of his children, and the dying of the same. And though he prayed to Akuma, his grandfather did not reply. For none of his seed carried the spark of Aaru. None of his children were blessed like him with immortality. And as he recalled the passing of his wife now long dead and the grief he felt over the death of his children. His heart was moved with compassion towards the pitiful scene before his eyes as a great king lamented the loss of his son. And when the wails of men and king melded into one, he could no longer hold his peace and interrupted the rituals of the men of Bussar and spoke to the king.

"My king. Lion of Bussar and leader of the clans. Please rise and meet with Wisdom in your home. I would have words with the king concerning his son."

And with that, he turned away from the group, leaving the grieving ruler to cease from his howls of anguish and the men stopped their grieving and Haidar formally dismissed his clansmen and sought counsel from the one who had witnessed the ebb and flow of centuries.

Haidar walked into his kraal and found Mudiwa and M'Msee hugging one another. M'Msee then gently stroked the hair of the woman he had watched grow into a queen of her people and he turned to the king and spoke.

"It grieves me to see my king and queen in this state. I have watched you both as children, witnessed you swear your love to one another before Akuma and before me that you would bind yourself to be husband and wife. I have beheld your exploits, Haidar, and how you have served your people even above yourself. And for this reason, the people have made you and Mudiwa their king and queen. But Bussar will not weather a royal family who mourns the loss of their only son; to destroy their union and who, through grief, has abandoned the governing of the nation. I have not lived the life I have, to continue to stand and watch those that I love wither and die of grief.

Haidar produced a halfhearted smile at the words spoken by his mentor, friend, and counselor. "What is done is done. To save many lives N'Kosi and I dealt with our nations so. And though Bussar has averted war, this victory of the nation has come at the loss of my son. For I have given my only begotten son that others might live. And this mother has lost her son to Hogarth, never to see him again. We are undone and Akuma has only blessed our womb but once. And what words can you say that my queen's unspoken resentment for my actions would heal? For what wife can look her husband in the eye knowing he has sacrificed her seed to save the seed of others?"

Mudiwa sat in a chair, and her hand was over her face, and her head was bowed. She looked up to look at her husband. Her face was streaked with dried tears.

"I do not resent you, my love. I see the burden the king bears. I do not resent the man that I married. Nor his decision to save the sons of Bussar at the expense of my own. I resent the king for allowing my son to be taken. I resent the king must be the ruler of my husband. I resent my love that of all in the Westlands. I am betrothed to not one but two men and concerning my son, each is of opposing minds, one to another."

The queen of Bussar then rose to her feet walked to her husband and placed her hands on his cheeks, her eyes red with tears. Her face was taunt with the screams that she retrained to voice. She placed her head upon the gold crown that adorned her husband's head and spoke. "I hate *this*. For if it were not for the burden of the crown, my son would still be alive." She removed it from her husband's head and shoved it in his hands. "If not for *this*, my husband and the father to our only son would never have allowed our son to leave."

Mudiwa could no longer withhold the floodgates of her tears, and she ran from the room into her bed chambers, whimpering as she left.

Haidar reached out to grab her, but M'Msee bade his hand to stay from preventing her and said. "Leave her Haidar. Let sorrow have its work. But as for you, do not fear. On the morrow, I will go see to the welfare of the lad. While I cannot guarantee his release. I will have an audience with N'Kosi. And will seek report of the boy's welfare."

Haidar looked at M'Msee. And while they had never spoken openly about who M'Msee truly was, he still dared to voice his mind. "And why would N'Kosi listen to an old man? Who are you to travel the desert and over the land of the Medja to the Darkmouth and demand entry to see the son of the king's enemy?"

M'Msee smiled and looked straight into the eyes of the king. And it was a stare that for a moment made Haidar pause for tempting M'Msee to answer. A stare that held eternity behind it, and the old man replied. "We both know who I am. You have known since you stormed the pyramids of the Medja. And when N'Kosi sees me. He, too, will remember—just as you do now—exactly who I am. Now, return to your queen and tell her this: Hutari will see to the welfare of her son. And let not what I have shared ever leave the mouth of you or the queen. Wisdom has spoken."

The king inclined his head, his reply solemn. "Wisdom has spoken."

He bowed low before the elder, reverence etched into every movement.

M'Msee turned without another word, leaning heavily on his staff as he departed the king's kraal, his figure vanishing into the shadows like a ghost of the ancients.

Chapter Twenty-One

The Order of The Medjani

For three days M'Msee traveled the sands of Bussar on horseback. As all that traveled west towards the Dark-mouth, the grand temples of Aphis, the city of the Medja, stood as stone sentinels. Three pyramids towered above the horizon. It was said that the ancients had built them. But M'Msee knew the truth. He had made them when he was then known as Hutari. And with there building he sanctioned a group of men to serve as watchmen over the cyclone that centered on the Great Sea. A storm that was fueled by Hutari centuries ago. The remaining mages who survived the Endwar: the Medjani.

But Hutari drained himself of power to both contain his father and the great world storm men called Z'otho Linithe or Lynnette's Eye, as called in the Eastlands. So, he designated men who possessed Akuma's spark to assist him in keeping the storm raised and resisting the world-sphere's desire to return its seas to normal. To push against the world-sphere his father had made was taxing. And to continue the storm's unnatural and continued existence required life. And so, sacrifice was sanctioned by Hutari to keep the storm upright. So, men who were sentenced to death were given to the Medja to keep the storm raised. And the kings of Bussar and Hogarth agreed to the thing. When either nation sentenced their criminals to death. It was agreed to release them into the wilderness to die. The Medja were ordered to find them and bring them to Aphis so that their sentence might be executed and their lives given for the people of Tanara. Some were bound as servants to the Medja, while others paid their debt in blood and were surrendered to the Kifu. So that even in their death, something useful might come from their execution.

Men sentenced to the wilderness tried to escape the Medja, some succeeded but most failed. And when men were not in number enough to feed the power that kept the storm alive. The beasts of the field were trapped so that blood might be given to provide the life that the barrier needed to keep the storm alight. For while M'Msee was powerful. It took much of his life force to subdue both Hesphus and keep the world sphere from tearing down the storm he had raised.

M'Msee recalled when he was away the Medja had mistakenly taken a boy from the wilderness. A boy who wandered upon their territory lost. This error caused Haidar of the Bussar to proclaim war on the Medja and he and his army ran through the temples of the Medja until he was stopped by M'Msee himself. And Haidar learned the brutal truth that it was M'Msee who took the lives of those captured. It was M'Msee who conscripted those who and been sentenced to death by either the nation of Bussar or Hogarth and were rescued by the Medja and now fight for the Medja. And when Haidar fought after killing many Medja, he saw that at its pinnacle M'Msee take the life of a young man.

M'Msee remembered the horrified face of Haidar, and he sighed in sorrow for the discovery the king was forced to learn. He watched the King of Bussar approach the altar upon which he stood and waited for the interrogation that he knew was forthcoming.

"Why Wisdom! What is the meaning that you, YOU, would shed the life of this boy? How can the man I love be the man who has taken the life of this boy and all those rumored to have died in the past? What dark God do you worship you would do such evil?"

And as M'Msee held a knife to a boy's throat, he turned to Haidar and spoke. "Come, Lion of Bussar. Come and see why a life must be given. Know the truth of this temple and learn of these who have sworn to keep the world of men safe. Learn what your father before you knew and the burden that a king must bear when he sentences one of his own to die in the wilderness."

Haidar approached with his sword fixed on M'Msee. He walked up a stairway to where his mentor and adviser stood looking down into a portal and within it, a great well churned with the sound of the seas. Lightning flashed and when Haidar was at the edge of the altar where the sacrifice was to be made, he looked down at a maelstrom, and lightning illuminated the sky, and the crashing of thunder echoed into the chamber. And deep within its center was a sarcophagus covered in blood. And it was then that he remembered the legends of the Kifu. Recollection flooded his mind of rumors that the Hutari had hidden the Kifu away from the eyes of men and raised a storm to shield the curious from finding the tomb of Hesphus, lest the life of men give rise to the walking death once more and it wreak havoc upon the earth.

M'Msee turned to speak to his friend and king. "I do not serve a dark god, Haidar. I prevent a dark god from overrunning all life. It is I who stands between the living and the dead. I who appease the dead that the world might live. Those who die do not die in vain. They go willingly, knowing that their sacrifice keeps Hesphus in his slumber and empowers the Medja to keep the storm aloft to contain the Kifu's great power to siphon life. Each dies knowing that their family will live another day.

"Haidar, all that I am is being used to keep my father asleep. But even I am drained by his presence. I feed it to keep it from siphoning the life of Tanara. But even I must sleep, and eat, to strengthen myself. When I am weakened and require time to restore the seals, another from Tanara must sacrifice their life so that I might recoup the power of Aaru enough to once more empower the storm and seals. Hesphus will always feed even in sleep. I am not as I was many generations ago where my might is such that I can defeat it again. Nor can it be fed the life of Tanara too much, lest it be conscious of more and rise to consume all. I have found no solution for this stalemate. I am imprisoned to nurture Hesphus for all eternity to keep Tanara from Enkai. Until Akuma reveals himself or his plan made known that a mighty people might ascend to Aaru and destroy Enkai himself. So, I ask King Haidar. What would you have me do? Choose the boy's life, and you will indeed spare him for a time. But know that in a generation, all that you love, and even the one whose life we spare today, will be lost. For who can stop the Kifu? Or perhaps I should use the vestige of what remains of my power and bring anew a sundering to Tanara? Once more, should I let the world-sphere be shaken so that the Kifu might be silenced for all time? But this too cannot be done. To save my father alone was not the reason that I kept Hesphus asleep. For to destroy him, Enkai has cursed my father and I that to kill him would destroy that which he has made. And so, Enkai has set within Hesphus a trap. To destroy Hesphus is to destroy Tanara that my father's sacrificed life might feed the Nephthys and save Enkai's damned creation. I no longer have the strength I possessed on that day in battle. Therefore, another who possesses the strength of Aaru, but not from Aaru, must do what I could not. So, command me Haidar, King of Bussar. Tell he who has fallen from the seat of creation what course of action should this immortal do to this boy to save the world of men?"

Haidar dropped his sword and cried aloud in anguish and grief. "You have damned us all, M'Msee. When you spared your blood, you have done nothing but sacrifice ours that yours might live. Damn you M'Msee." Haidar then took his sword sheathed it and turned his back on the man, men called Hutari and spoke. "Kill the boy. Do what you need to do. But I want no more part of this butcherous place."

M'Msee then looked into the eyes of the man he loved. The grief that wracked him to know that all that he believed about M'Msee was a lie. Watched as the man who had commanded his soldiers to follow him now leave to look into the faces of the same. M'Msee did not know what Haidar would tell his men. But it did not matter. His choice was logical. He looked at the boy he must sacrifice to his father. The boy who had been taken by the Medja and brought to be sacrificed. He stared into the innocent lads' eyes and even paused as the pleading face and the muffled cries of his gagged mouth begged for M'Msee to release him. And for the briefest of times, M'Msee considered it. Tired of being a slave to sacrifice the creations of his father to keep Tanara's creator from destroying *his* creation. M'Msee breathed in and, with a swift motion of his knife, slit the boy's throat. With both disgust, resignation, and grief. He took the youth's blood and, with a sponge, wiped it from the corpse and wrung

the blood offering out as he had dozens of times throughout his li
fe.

The blood drained into the well of power and when the drops breached the magic portal and reached the sarcophagus of the Kifu; they disappeared from view. And M'Msee could feel the easing of the draining of his eternal life from Aaru, was relieved. He then lifted his hands and power arched into the waters and world storm strengthened and the seals grew brighter. And tears ran down the face of M'Msee, for the lad he had slain was but a man of two circles. He resented this evil work he was forced to do. Resented his uncle for usurping the divine order. Resented that he must indulge in blood sacrifice to keep all that he loved safe. He found some measure of gratitude that once more the Kifu would remain dormant and spoke aloud his appreciation to the dead. "Thank you for your blood, boy."

Reminiscing, M'Msee sat upon his horse looking into the night sky, and wiped a tear from his eye. He remembered disappointing Haidar and the horror of the practice that kept all men alive. He watched as Haidar explained to his men that their task was over and that they could return home. He listened as he explained that the forces in the temple could not be tamed lest all men die. And that their actions helped to keep the Kifu at bay. And at that moment, M'Msee determined he would pursue another solution. The many centuries had taken a toll on him. He was tired. Tired of living...tired of saving...tired of killing. And at the birth of Amani, he saw hope that perhaps the cycle of death might be broken.

The three pyramids of Aphis entered his view and the servants of the Medja were alerted to the presence of their master. And the three appointed floated towards him and greeted the founder of their Order and bowed before him. The Chief of the Medja Kaelthion the Blue spoke for them all.

"It is not time for another regeneration, Lord. What brings you to us before the time appointed?"

"My business is my own Kaelthion. I would enter the temple to know the state of my father's slumber."

The three sorcerers bowed, and M'Msee stepped down from his horse and walked into the temple of the Medja as the three Medja floated behind him.

"The Tower reports that the Kingdom of Elandria has sent mages to bring down the storm."

"Obviously they have not been successful," said M'Msee.

"Of course, not my lord. But we have seen that their probing of the magics has accelerated the cycle of life to protect the sarcophagus of Hesphus. We believe it is for this reason that we have had to speed up the shedding of blood."

M'Msee frowned at this news and replied. "What of those emissaries we have in Elandria? Do we know who is responsible for the mages of the land that is seeking to bring down the barrier?"

"There are two my lord. One is an archmage by the name of Kaphiri. The king has funded his research in the belief that to calm the storm would improve navigation of the seas."

M'Msee sighed. "His vision, while self-centered, is not wrong. The storm was my doing. My father never intended such a monstrosity in his world. Of course, he never foresaw that one day he would be entombed on the same." M'Msee sighs. Men and their desire for coin was a powerful force. Tanara's development of commerce also saw greed travel the world. Kingdoms fought over resources. Some land, others gold, some for the pleasure or terror of exploring the secrets of the First Age and those kingdoms that existed even before M'Msee himself fell to this world. Greed fueled much of what he saw. And the northern tribes of Kissum were rife with greed, their culture built on covetousness. It was for this reason that he did not remain on the eastern continent and settled in the plains of Bussar. To live simply and to help grow a people who would be able to one day help if Hesphus was to once again awake. A people who did not know fear, and who could again stand against the undead. M'Msee had not traveled to the northern kingdom of Elandria for centuries. Their kingdom was the pinnacle of commerce, trade, and knowledge. They were a great people. But few remained after the great war. He would have to one day see to their welfare, and he and the mages of Elandria must have words. He spoke aloud as he walked to one of the pyramid overseers. "This magus...does he realize he weakens the Hutari and threatens his world?"

Kaelthion, the blue Medja, spoke. "The thing is not known, my lord. Your presence has been on the western lands for over five generations. Perhaps the truths of your existence have become a legend, and your influence waned with the lack of pilgrimages to their kingdom."

M'Msee laughs. "Perhaps. But if I remember the northern people, coin and the love of such are more likely responsible. Tell our contacts in Elandria to meet with this mage and persuade him to cease. I would hate to travel to the Eastlands for a rebuke to its king and archmage. But if a demonstration is in order to relay to this magic user that his efforts are dangerous to the order, then I will leave to travel there at once."

M'Msee walked up the steps of the pyramids and entered the chamber that magically looked down upon the sarcophagus of the Kifu. He watched as the seals that separated the seas from crashing in on the tomb of the Kifu held firm. In fifty years, he would return to once more take the life of a male. To feed Hesphus enough blood to keep his father satiated and asleep.

"Several months ago, a company from Hogarth traveled home with their king. I take it you stopped them?"

"As commanded, my Lord. The boy was indeed with them. And as you relayed. His seeps with the power of Aaru. Apart from you, he is the most powerful carrier of Akuma's light we have ever seen."

"What else?"

"The boy's power is increasing, Hutari. In time, we foretell his power will rival if not surpass your own. We have no operative in Hogarth save a Bathmaster by the name of Islu. There is no one there, my lord, who can tutor him on the use of his power. Naturally, we have concerns that left untrained, he could bring upheaval to all things."

"You believe if left unchecked. He will awaken my father?"

The three Medja bowed. M'Msee then turned to face them and spoke. "But you are holding back something. What is it?"

"He possesses an unusual taint, my lord. For his taint is as not just yours alone, but also that of your father...and Enkai."

M'Msee looked visibly disturbed. "What do you mean, he is like my father?"

"We have discerned, my lord, that he can siphon and or create the very essence of life. We surmise that if he takes a life, his actions may serve as the catalyst to awaken the life drainer itself, and if he does. We cannot assure the storm prison will hold the Kifu...pardon my lord. Hesphus, for long."

"Do you mean to tell me that Amani possesses both the traits of Hesphus *and* Enkai? That it is possible that he could become like my father...or worse?"

The Medja bowed to acknowledge M'Msee's realization.

M'Msee looked at his followers of mages, who kept the storm above his father's crypt intact. "I did not create the storm for Hesphus, but to prevent the prying eyes of curious men who would meddle in powers they do not understand. To stop those men who would dare trek the undersea to explore his place of rest."

"You should know, master, that the boy has threatened to come this way and destroy us if he were to encounter us again."

M'Msee laughs. "Does this frighten you, Kaelthion? I suppose it should. If he walks in the fullness of his power and is
poisoned by the lust of Enkai, then we should all fear. I have
battled a member of my family once and by Akuma's will have
prevailed. But my father was a puppet and resisted the power
of my uncle. Amani is no puppet, and his will is his own. I too
fear what would happen if he were to ever desire to control the
world of men. In his ignorance, he could do the work of Enkai
for him and unwittingly become a more powerful emissary of
my uncle than even my father."

"Why then did you let the boy live, Master? If your own past
deeds sundered Tanara, what might the boys do?"

"It will not come to that. But if it does...know that I will
contend with my godson myself. We need him. He could very
well be our only hope. If my father rises again. Pledge this to me,
Kaelthion, that if I am ever killed. If I can no longer complete
the mission to secure Tanara until Akuma comes. You will give
the boy your support. You will teach him all that I have taught
you and on the day that my father walks the world. You and
the Order will ally yourselves with Amani and see that men are
gathered to once more stop the walking death."

The Medja bowed and replied. "The thing will be done,
Hutari. All that you have asked, we will do. I am loath to ask
but feel compelled to do so. What if, my Lord, *you* are required
to take the boy's life to preserve all life on Tanara?"

M'Msee looked down into the center of the storm clouds that
thundered and lit the ocean cyclone that encircled his father's

tomb and replied. "If my father awakens. We will need more than my power alone to stop him this time. But if the boy must be killed, I will see it done by my own hand"

Chapter Twenty-Two

The Conception
of Desire

Amani flowed through the disciplined movements of the
Bussar martial art of Buz'Nazem his body a seamless
blend of grace and power. Each strike and pivot reflected precision, and every stance was rooted in the art's ancient philosophy.
Sweat glistened on his skin under the morning sun, tracing the
contours of his muscles as they rippled with effort.

From a distance, Osumare observed him, her arms crossed
loosely, though her gaze betrayed the intrigue she tried to sup-
press. She admired his form—the coiled strength in his limbs,
the effortless precision of his technique—but it was more than
just his physicality. There was an intensity to his movements,

a devotion that spoke of someone preparing for something far greater than routine drills.

She stepped forward, her sandals barely making a sound on the stone path, yet her presence was unmistakable. "Why does a slave, a servant to the king, practice the physical arts?" she asked, her tone curious but tinged with an edge of authority.

Amani lowered his sword, his chest rising and falling from exertion. He turned to face her, bowing in deference, though his eyes met hers. "Although I serve the Sandking. How best to serve him than to strengthen both mind and body for his service? Besides princess, what dog without a bite is ever useful to its master? I practice preparing for the combat lessons General Dumani has planned for us."

Her brows arched as she stepped closer, her expression unreadable. Extending her hand, she gestured for his weapon. Amani hesitated only a moment before presenting the sword with both hands. She accepted it, testing its weight, the blade catching the sunlight as she examined it.

Osumare chuckles, "Have you love for my father so that you would shield him from harm?"

"Master Guam states we are soon to be tested by combat. I wish to make sure I am at my best. Your people are fierce warriors. Your brother taught me this firsthand. I will not underestimate the prowess of your warriors. But know your father is now my father, and he became such when my own surrendered me to my people's enemies. Your blood neither cast me out nor treated me awry. I am in his debt."

Amani moved within arm's length of the woman and gazed down upon her. He could smell the scent of jasmine and she the musk from his fresh workout. They stared deeply into each other's eyes. She knew he admired her form; in that regard, he did not differ from other men. He leaned in as if he would kiss her, but instead, his breath brushed her ear as he whispered. "I will protect all that the king loves, including his rainbow."

He leaned back, observing the subtle flush that graced Osumare's cheeks, and their shift in color. Her eyebrows arched in response to his words, yet he held his ground. The tempo of her heart quickened, unable to deny the growing attraction. Envisioning his body pressed against hers, she released a sigh, swallowing hard, then mentally composed herself before responding. "Let us hope, for Hogarth's sake and the peace my father desires, that your skills will not be required," she said. Her eyes lingered on the sword as she placed it back in Amani's hands. She then covered her hand with his, and she peered into his eyes, whispering. "It touches me that my dog would desire my safety."

Amani grinned, lifting his hand to gently tuck a stray strand of her hair behind her ear. Her brows furrowed in response, questioning the boldness of his gesture. "Why did you do that?" she asked.

Stepping back, Amani bowed and replied. "Because nothing should ever obscure the beauty of a rainbow."

Turning away, Amani resumed his drills, each thrust and parry sharper than before, leaving Osumare standing there, her thoughts a storm of admiration, confusion, and something far more dangerous.

Her mind pondered how someone from the royal house might navigate courting a foreign slave.

Chapter Twenty-Three

Friendship

Amani woke to the cold breath of dawn, his body stiff from the thin, scratchy mattress beneath him. The barracks, with their stone walls and sparse furnishings, were a far cry from the warmth of home in Bussar. Here, in Hogarth, the air seemed heavier, the silence more oppressive. The rivalry between their nations was like a shadow that lingered in every corner, reminding him he was an outsider in a land that saw his people as weak.

He glanced across the room at Ashar, who snorted in his sleep, one arm draped across his face. Phatut lay nearby, breathing evenly, the peace of sleep evident in his features. These were his companions—wards training under the same roof, yet they couldn't have come from more different worlds.

As Amani sat up, he tried to shake off the remnants of sleep. Guam, their etiquette trainer, stood at the entrance, his face stern as ever. "Rise, boys! The king's court waits for no one."

Amani moved quickly, his instincts sharp even in this foreign place. The lessons he had learned in Bussar echoed in his mind—lessons from M'Msee about patience. From his father about honor. His people believed in peace and wisdom, yet here, in the land of Hogarth, they valued strength above all. The old stories his father had told him filled his mind: Hogarthen were relentless, and quick to draw a blade. But they also valued honor, protecting Tanara and even Bussar.

As he stood, Ashar caught his eye, a sly grin tugging at the corner of his lips. When Guam turned his back, Ashar mimicked him, walking with an exaggerated stiff posture, puffing out his chest like a peacock. Amani clenched his jaw but said nothing. Phatut, already awake, shook his head, staying silent as well.

Guam began doling out assignments for the day, and Amani felt a surge of frustration. Every task felt like another test, another way to prove his worth in a kingdom that would never see him as anything more than the boy from Bussar.

Guam's many tasks were exhausting—tedious, small errands meant to teach humility, or so Guam had said. Amani moved through the day with quiet determination, his hands raw from carrying bundles of wood, his mind restless. Ashar's jests grated on him. Every snide comment felt like a reminder of where they came from rival nations, separated by generations of war. Even now, peace was fragile. Trust a scarce thing.

As the sun dipped low, Amani found himself beside Phatut, both of them scrubbing the steps leading into the great hall. The stone was cold beneath his hands, but the work grounded him—kept his mind from wandering too far.

"You're quiet, Bussar," Phatut said after a long stretch of silence. His voice was neutral as if testing the waters of conversation.

Amani wiped his brow with the back of his hand. "I'm not much for talking," he replied, keeping his tone flat.

Phatut glanced at him, and for a moment, Amani saw something unexpected in his expression—curiosity, maybe even understanding. "You think Ashar's a fool too, don't you?"

Amani hesitated, then nodded slightly. "He doesn't take this seriously. He plays too much. This isn't a game."

Phatut smiles faintly. Hogarthen are raised to fight the undead. If we must face death, humor lessens the reality that we may die. His actions are just another way of facing fear. For us, even mocking someone like Guam—" Phatut shrugged—"It's how we learn not to fear death. We're taught to challenge it, to laugh at it."

Amani narrowed his eyes. "And the rest of the world? Do you challenge that too? With swords and blood?"

Phatut sighed, the smile fading from his face. "You think we're hungry for war? Not all of us want to live by the sword or be under a constant state of war."

The honesty in Phatut's voice caught Amani off guard. He had expected Phatut to be like every other Hogarthen—proud, bloodthirsty. Instead, he found someone who understood that peace was worth fighting for, too. Jo'than had taught him the bravery of the Hogarth, but also a Hogarth's ability to work together against insurmountable odds. Amani realized he saw this also in Phatut.

"I was taught that the people of Hogarth only seek bloodshed," Amani said, his voice quieter now. "That they conquer because they know nothing else."

Phatut paused, leaning back on his heels as he considered his words. "And we're taught that the people of Bussar are weak. That they hide behind the desert and plains reciting prayers and use the Umfami to control the minds and bend the wills of others. Because they fear battle."

For a moment, the two boys sat in silence, their hands resting against the cold stone of the steps. The weight of their people's histories hung between them, a barrier neither of them had been able to cross—until now.

"It would seem that we've both been taught lies," Amani said at last. The admission tasted bitter in his mouth, but it was a truth he couldn't deny.

Phatut nodded. "I think so too."

Days passed, and Amani and Phatut sought each other out more and more. There was still competition between them—each striving to impress Guam, to prove their worth—but it wasn't the competition that bred resentment. It became something else, like camaraderie.

During one late evening, Amani sat in the barracks, his muscles aching from the day's training. Phatut entered, his expression was tired but content. Without a word, he tossed a dried fruit he had taken from the kitchens toward Amani, a simple gesture of friendship.

Amani caught it easily, biting into the sweet flesh with a quiet nod of thanks.

"You know," Phatut began, lying back on his bedroll, "if the time ever comes when we have to fight together, I'd want you by my side."

Amani looked at him, surprised by the comment. "I thought you Hogarthen thought little us Bussar."

Phatut smirked. "Maybe I'm learning there's more to Bussar than books and prayers and your fabled Umfami."

Amani chuckles softly. "And maybe I'm learning there's more to Hogarth than just war."

Their friendship wasn't something they had sought. It had grown from the small, quiet moments—the shared understanding of what it meant to serve a king, to be more than what others expected of them.

They were no longer just rivals from different lands. Through shared chores, and Guam's training, they were brothers-in-arms, bound not by blood but by the trials they endured together. Amani wondered in the days to come if that bond would be tested in ways neither could foresee. But for now, they had forged something stronger than the prejudices that once kept them apart.

As Amani lay back on his own bedroll, he glanced over at Phatut, feeling the weight of the future settle over him. They still didn't know what the next day would bring, but at least now, neither would face it alone.

Chapter Twenty-Four

The Feud Grave

Amani stirred from sleep, his mind clouded with dreams of home when the bellow of General Dumani shattered the stillness.

"Get up, you lazy maggots!" the general roars, his voice cutting through the dim, cold air like a blade. "You think you can protect my king? HA! I could have killed you all while you slept. Up! If you want to serve the king, you must prove you're worth the air you breathe. And believe me, pretenders, I want to fight you. If you amuse me, I might just give you the honor to best me. And who knows, you might live long enough to stand before the king and prove your mettle. Imagine the honor of dying for your king! Now, get up and meet me in the Feud Grave for training!"

The urgency in Dumani's voice sent Amani scrambling. Groggy but spurred by adrenaline, he threw on his tunic and raced out of his quarters. Around him, the other prospective wards moved with the same frantic energy, their footsteps echoing down the cold, stone-filled corridors. They followed Dumani out of the servants' quarters, through the labyrinthine underbelly of the castle, and into an armory that smelled of oiled leather and steel.

The general stopped at the threshold of a wide tunnel and turned to them with a solemnness upon his face. "Understand that Hogarth was built to withstand the army of the dead. To allow the last vestiges of men to garrison and if the great war was lost, to provide an escape to the sea.

Our people have trained centuries to hold this city against all foes, and every man, woman, and child are taught to defend this stronghold and schooled in the art of war against the undead. Our chief servant. A servant whose duty is to protect Hogarth's people is its king. To do this, our king must be a student of war, skilled in mind and body. It was Hogarth's king, who was tasked with providing leadership to the armies of men in the last great war of the living. And a good king will ever be a pupil of combat and war and hone his skills in battle. Thus, all Kings of Hogarth develop skills that among the Hogarth people are typically unmatched—save one. The Zhara-Telak"

Which brings us to why we are here. To be a ward of the king is to protect Hogarth's greatest military mind and leader. To serve as armor bearer to the one person in all of Hogarth who can order the ultimate command if the war against the undead was lost: flee."

Amani swallowed hard, his stomach twisting with equal parts excitement and dread. Around him, the other wards stood tense, their faces pale but resolute. The weight of Dumani's words settled on their shoulders like an invisible yoke, the enormity of their purpose becoming chillingly clear.

The General continued. "These words, if ever breathed from the Hogarth's king's mouth. Know that the world of men will have collapsed, and no known land exists where the Kifu's influence was not present to enact the will of Enkai. All kings of Hogarth take this pledge to serve. To protect the world of men from the Kifu if ever he were to march again.

So, to be a ward is to understand the king's oath. An oath that extends to the ward. Therefore, if you would serve the king, you must gain his respect in combat. For he would likely die by his side protecting him. To prove your worth, it is custom that the man chosen to serve as Zhara-Telak be equal to the king to stand against the undead. This man must show himself tempered and able to demonstrate the means to fend off all who would attempt to strike down one of Tanara's generals if the armies of men are once more called by the Hutari. You will be tested now."

Dumani unsheathed his sword with a deliberate motion, the blade catching the faint torchlight. He pointed at the group, its tip steady, as if to punctuate his next words.

"Through those doors above lies the Feud Grave. If you think this is just another training ground, you are mistaken. Now armor up and grab a weapon," he barked. "I would see what you are made of."

Amani hesitated, his eyes scanning the racks of wooden weapons. But Dumani wasn't done. His gaze settled on Amani with the intensity of a predator sizing up its prey.

"Especially you, Bussar," Dumani sneers, stepping closer. "I heard you bested Jo'than in hand-to-hand combat. Impressive. Especially since I trained him. I wonder, though, how you would fare against me. Should we find out?"

The general leaned in, forcing Amani to take an instinctive step back. His breath carried the sharp tang of bitterness.

Amani held his ground, though his heart burned with restrained power. "I would rather fight the wooden dummy if given a choice than risk killing you. Hogarth needs its general," he replied evenly, his voice laced with a faint edge of defiance.

Dumani's eyes narrowed, his lips curling into a scornful grin. "Ha! You are funny, Bussar, but be very careful. The king's favor won't shield you if we cross metal in the ring. And know it would give me great pleasure to show everyone just how useless a Zhara-Telak you would be."

Amani bit back a sharp retort, his hands twitching at the thought of unleashing his power. With a mere flick of his wrist, he could snap this man's neck or summon a tempest to hurl him skyward. But he couldn't. He wouldn't—not if he wanted his family to live, or to protect the innocents from the apocalyptic horrors of the Kifu.

With a deep breath, Amani quelled the emotional storm within, grabbed a wooden staff, and ran to join the others at the Feud Grave entrance. His grip on the weapon tightened as he lined up alongside Ashar and Phatut, each of them bracing for whatever trial awaited.

The trio exchanged uneasy glances as they stepped into the sunlight. To their surprise, a sea of onlookers had gathered, their voices rising in a cacophony of cheers and whispers.

"The citizens are watching us?" Phatut mutters, scanning the throng of Hogarthens who pressed against crude wooden barriers and who stood in balconies above.

Amani leaned closer to his companions. "I thought we were going to fight behind the palace walls," he whispered, his voice tinged with confusion and unease.

General Dumani's sharp ears caught the remark. He whirled around, his booming voice silencing the murmurs of the crowd.

"I heard that, Bussar!" Dumani spat, turning his attention to the wards. "No, boy. You will fight here, in the open, where all can witness your worth. If you seek the honor of guarding the king, your strength must be seen by his people. Here you will show before all that you are not just pretenders, but warriors capable of protecting their king's life!"

The crowd roared with its approval, their fervor adding weight to Dumani's declaration. Amani's pulse quickened as he felt the eyes of Hogarth upon him. He glanced at Ashar, who stood resolute with his shield and club, and at Phatut, whose twin wooden swords glinted in the sunlight.

The stakes were clear now—this was not just a trial of skill but a test of their very right to compete for the right to be called Zhara-Telak.

The Feud Grave loomed ominously, its jagged boundaries marked by cruel protrusions—blades, bones, and thistles. Each edge seemed to whisper promises of pain and death to any who dared too close. The arena was a place of reckoning, where pride and skill were tested against brutal finality.

General Dumani's voice boomed across the arena, carrying the weight of judgment. "Today's combat exercise is not merely a test of your skill. It is a showcase—a display of individual prowess and your ability to fight as one."

The audience grew thick along the edges of the Grave. Tribal elders stood stoic, their wizened faces betraying no hint of favoritism, while seasoned warriors crossed their arms, scrutinizing every movement. Ordinary citizens mingled with the elites, their murmurs rising into a steady hum of anticipation. Sure enough, as Dumani had promised, the entire city had gathered to witness the spectacle, their eyes fixed on the contenders who dared to seek the honor of guarding Hogarth's king.

Amani stood at the center, the weight of their expectations pressing on his shoulders. His wooden staff rested firmly in his calloused hands, his stance low and steady. His body was coiled with tension like a serpent waiting to strike. To his left, Ashar raised his shield, the morning sun glinting off its polished surface, his club resting against its rim, ready to swing. On Amani's right, Phatut twirled his twin blades in a blur, their arcs catching the light in dizzying flashes. Each movement spoke of precision honed through endless hours of training.

The jagged walls of the Feud Grave thrummed with anticipation; the assembled crowd was restless as the heat of the sun bore down upon them. The citizens of Hogarth filled every crevice of the towering amphitheater, their voices a cacophony of excitement and fervor. Banners bearing the sigil of Hogarth snapped in the dry wind, their vibrant colors casting shifting patterns across the arena floor. The air smelled of dust and sweat, of tension and history.

In the center of the arena, General Dumani stood, his imposing frame clad in dark leather armor adorned with the silver crest of Hogarth. His presence alone commanded silence as he raised a hand. The crowd fell still, the echo of their last cheer fading into a breathless hush.

The wards stood at attention, their weapons gripped tightly, their gazes locked on Dumani. Amani's heart pounded in his chest as he stole a glance at Ashar and Phatut. This was no ordinary trial; this was a test that would decide their fate.

Dumani's voice rang out, deep and resonant, carrying easily to the furthest reaches of the Feud Grave.

"Wards in training. We are here to see what prowess you possess to defend Hogarth against her enemies. On this day, you will now show our people your worth to stand by our great king's side in battle."

His gaze swept the arena, lingering on the royal balcony where the King of Hogarth stood, a pillar of unyielding authority. The king's arms were crossed, his expression carved in stone. Beside him stood Prince Jo'bari, his sneer sharpening with each passing moment. Princess Osumare remained unreadable; her gaze locked on the wards. And Jo'than, leaning forward with eager intensity, watched as if the entire spectacle were a personal wager of fate.

Dumani turned his eyes back to the wards. His voice lowered, thick with foreboding.

"If the sky turns towards evil and the march of Necrosent one day walks the earth in legions, our king will lift up a standard against them. And if you are blessed, perhaps you will die by his side in defense of our great city."

A murmur swept through the crowd. Dumani's tone grew heavier, the weight of his words pressing down like the sun above.

"But today, your foes are noble soldiers of the people. For on the day the Necrosent march again, the dead shall be comprised of both noble and peasant. Lord and prisoner. And all will seek nothing but to extinguish the light of the living."

Amani felt a chill despite the heat. He glanced at Ashar, who clenched his shield tighter, and Phatut, whose confident grin, faltered for a moment. Dumani continued his voice like the toll of a great bell.

"You who have assembled for this cause now stand before foes who own the light of life and seek to extinguish your own. For those who you face, combat will be to the death. But understand this special condition: you must all walk out alive. If one dies, you all die. If one of you is killed, you shall all be killed. But you may not kill your opponent."

A ripple of disbelief moved through the wards, but Dumani silenced it with a sharp gesture.

"This is the way of Hogarth, and this is the way of the sands."

The crowd erupted in cheers, their cries reverberating through the arena like a storm. Dumani raised his hand one last time, his voice cut through the noise like a blade.

"Let the Feud Grave decide! Begin!"

A gate at the far end of the arena creaked open, and six warriors emerged, their steps purposeful, their eyes locked on their prey. They descended from the lower levels like shadows given form. Two men broke off toward each ward, their weapons gleaming, their intent unmistakable.

Amani's pulse quickened as he eyed the oncoming storm. He glanced over his shoulder at Phatut, his voice low but urgent. "Any words of counsel for me?"

Phatut's gaze never wavered from the charging foes. He gave a smirk that was equal parts confidence and mischief. "Don't die, Bussar."

Amani rolled his eyes, gripping his staff tighter. "You are ever a bastion of wisdom."

The first wave of combatants closed in, the crowd's roar rising to a deafening crescendo. Amani shifted his stance, his senses sharpening as he prepared to meet the challenge head-on.

***

The Feud Grave fell silent as General Dumani's voice thundered across the arena, "Let the Feud Grave decide!" Amani's fingers tightened around his staff, the weight of the moment pressing down on him like the sun's unrelenting glare.

Above, the royal balcony loomed over the pit, framing the King of Hogarth like a statue carved from stone. His arms crossed; his inscrutable gaze swept over the combatants below. To his left, Prince Jo'bari stood rigid, his sneer deepening as he watched Amani step into position. Beside him, Prince Jo'than leaned forward, his boyish grin betraying both curiosity and mischief.

"I'll wager ten gold crowns the Bussar falls first," Jo'bari said, his voice dripping with disdain.

Jo'than smirked, eyes still fixed on the arena. "And I'll take those odds—for his survival."

J'abari scoffs, crossing his arms. "You're too young to see what's in front of you."

"Youth has nothing to do with it. I have both fought with and against the man." Jo'than replied, leaning back with an air of confidence. "Perhaps your pride prevents you from admitting when you're wrong."

The tension between the brothers hung thick in the air as Princess Osumare shifted her gaze from the arena to her father. The King's face remained impassive, but a subtle flicker of amusement danced in his eyes before he resumed his stoic watch.

The groaning creak of the arena gates broke the stillness. Six soldiers emerged, clad in the dark leather of Hogarth's elite, their movements precise and unrelenting. They split into pairs, each set of eyes locking onto a target.

The crowd roared as the warriors charged. General Dumani raised his hand again, his command resonating like a hammer striking an anvil: "Begin!"

***

Ashar looked at his peers in a panic. "None of us can die?"

Amani replied. "We will not die if we fight as one man. We are one. We use the advantages in our being three to strike as one creature. Remember this and we will live. Allow fear to consume you and you and we will die," said Amani.

Amani stepped forward, his staff spinning as his first opponent charged at him and swung high with a broad axe. Amani ducked and countered with a strike to the ribs. The impact landed solidly, but his attacker merely staggered, slamming into Amani with a shoulder charge that sent him sprawling. Before he could recover, a second trainer loomed over him, sword raised.

Pain lanced through Amani's side as the sword's flat struck, leaving a livid bruise. Gritting his teeth, Amani rolled away, narrowly avoiding another blow. He swung his staff low, tripping the swordsman, and scrambled to his feet, his breath coming fast.

Phatut, always the showman, darted between his two assailants, his twin blades flashing in the sun. His speed was his shield, but his opponents moved with military precision. One feinted, drawing him into a parry, while the other lunged. A blade grazed his leg, and he stumbled, biting back a cry. Blood darkened the fabric of his pants, but Phatut pressed on, weaving between their strikes like a dancer.

When one trainer lunged for Amani, Phatut made a snap decision. "Hold him!" he shouted, tossing one of his short swords with pinpoint accuracy. The blade spun through the air, striking the trainer's arm and forcing him to drop his weapon. The distraction allowed Amani to land a decisive blow, but it left Phatut exposed, his remaining blade barely keeping his second attacker at bay.

Ashar stood like a fortress, his shield absorbing strike after strike. Yet even his strength began to wane. A heavy mace smashed against his shield, the force reverberating through his arm. His grip faltered, and a spear sliced across his thigh, sending him to one knee. With a growl, Ashar swung his club upward, catching the spearman in the chest and forcing him back, but the blood dripping down his leg betrayed the cost.

The crowd's cheers turned frenzied, their cries mingling with the clash of steel and the grunts of pain echoing across the pit.

The trainers regrouped; their discipline evident as they pressed the wards relentlessly. Amani found himself cornered by two opponents, their attacks coming in a dizzying blur of strikes and thrusts. His staff blocked one blade but left his side open to a kick that knocked the wind from his lungs.

"Amani, move!" Phatut yelled, forcing his remaining opponent back with quick slashing strikes.

Amani sidestepped just as Phatut lunged forward, reclaiming his thrown blade from the ground in one fluid motion. With both swords back in hand, he launched himself at the second warrior, pinning Amani. His strikes came fast and brutal, the swords cutting a deadly rhythm that forced the man onto his heels.

Ashar, meanwhile, faced his own dire moment. His shield arm trembled under a relentless barrage of strikes, and his wounded leg gave out. He fell hard, the dust clinging to his sweat-soaked skin. One trainer raised a sword to finish him, but Ashar, with a guttural roar, swung his club in a wide arc. The blow shattered the man's kneecap, leaving him writhing in the dirt.

"You're not done yet, Ashar!" Amani's voice cut through the chaos as he deflected a blade aimed at his own throat.

The three wards regrouped, battered and bloodied. Their breaths came in ragged gasps, and their movements slowed under the weight of pain and exhaustion. Yet their eyes met in a moment of unspoken resolve.

"Phatut cut off their flank. Ashar, shield high and drive forward," Amani commanded, his voice steady despite the chaos.

Phatut nodded, his movements were more cautious now as he engaged two trainers. His blades worked tirelessly, carving shallow but effective cuts that kept his opponents on the defensive. A sudden strike from one trainer slashed across his forearm, and he hissed in pain but retaliated with a downward slice that disarmed his foe.

Ashar lumbered forward, his shield raised despite the agony in his arm. He absorbed a brutal strike that dented the metal but surged forward, slamming the shield into his opponent and pinning them against the wall.

Amani faced the last trainer, their duel a clash of speed versus precision. His staff whirled, deflecting blow after blow, but his arms burned with fatigue. A sharp jab from the trainer's blade nicked his shoulder, drawing blood. Amani gritted his teeth and feinted, drawing the man off balance before delivering a decisive strike to his temple.

The crowd erupted as the last trainer fell, their cheers deafening in the arena. Amani, Phatut, and Ashar stood victorious, but their bodies bore the marks of their struggle. Amani's ribs ached with every breath, and blood seeped from a shallow gash on his shoulder. Phatut leaned heavily on one blade, his leg trembling as crimson streaked his torn pants. Ashar's shield hung loosely from his grip, his dented armor a testament to the battle's ferocity.

From the balcony, Jo'than clapped Jo'bari on the back, his grin triumphant. "I believe I am owed ten gold crowns."

Jo'bari clenched his fists, his face dark with frustration. He pulled a satchel from his robe, withdrew ten crowns, and then threw them at this brother. He then stormed off cursing, his hatred for Amani burning brighter than ever.

Osumare lingered, her gaze meeting Amani's for a fleeting moment before attendants ushered her away. The King, arms still crossed, allowed his faint smile to linger and nodded approvingly before turning to follow.

General Dumani descended into the arena, his voice gruff. "Well done." His expression betrayed no emotion, but the weight of his approval hung heavy in the air. Amani glanced at his comrades, each bloodied and exhausted but alive. Their survival was a fragile triumph, the weight of Hogarth's expectations already pressing down like the heat of the unforgiving su n.

Chapter Twenty-Five

Sibling Understanding

J o'than practiced the Bussar martial art of Lok'Thala. Quietly, in the palace's private courtyard, he weaved and moved. Sweat dripped from his face and beaded from his body as he tensed each muscle to strike at the target in his mind's eye. He held in his hands a staff and with it swung the staff in the air and brought its tip hard upon a wooden manikin.

He moved back and lifted his leg and brought his foot square on the dummy's face and the wood gave way to the force of his blow and cracked slightly.

He moved back and then pulled the staff back into his chest. Moving as if blocking makeshift attackers. He then twisted the middle of the pole, and it split into two wooden staffs. He moved forward, striking the air with his left staff advancing then striking the air with his right. He beat the manikin's face in a flurry of pummeling strikes that if the wood were alive would scream for mercy. Splinters and small shards flew from the manikin and one small splinter pierced his skin and he withdrew his attack.

"Ow!" he said. Then gingerly looked at the object and pulled a splinter from the top of his hand. He kissed the area that smarted and looked up to see his sister staring at him, smirking, and she spoke her amusement.

"Is this how the Bussar bested my brother in combat? Did he strike you with a splinter that you withdrew from your attack?"

Osumare jumped from the balcony above and landed on the ground and a small swell of dirt displaced from her landing. She walked towards the dummy to inspect her brother's destructive work and then leaned her arm upon it.

Jo'than's face turned red. "How long were you watching me?" he asked.

"Long enough to know that you did not train these many seasons to be bested by our people's enemy. Long enough to see my brother flow in his gift. You are one of our finest warriors. It is said that you could spar father to a standstill. I have watched you in the city tournaments. Observed you be bruised and with such cunning, strike a blow to an opponent that would send him reeling. I know your strength. I've seen you kill a man. If the Necrosent were to walk once more. I know for sure you would take many before they ever overran Hogarth. And yet somehow...father's new toy bested one of Hogarth's finest warriors. I have never asked you since you arrived from Bussar how this could be. But we are brother and sister. We sit in the quietness of our family court. I would ask you to tell me. What art did he use to defeat you?"

Jo'than reassembled the two components of his staff and placed the weapon on an arms rack. He then took a wooden sword and felt its heft and the pummel in his hand. He then turned and flung the sword at the dummy. It flew through the air and landed straight into the objects would be face. The force of his throw caused the head of the manikin to splinter and shards of wood flew into the air. Osumare covered her face but did not move and looked at her brother. "Sore subject?"

"I apologize. You should know that I have been attacked and have attacked many a boy and man,"

Osumare interjected, "And from what I hear at the flesh district, a few maids as well. Rumor has it there are a number that have enjoyed your advances."

Jo'than blushed. "The Bussar boy is not just...a boy. He is a skilled warrior. His people have trained him well. The Bussar art he used is not known to me, but I have faced it firsthand through him. I have watched him wield..."

Jo'than lowered his head and turned from his sister. "Never mind."

She ran after him, placed her hand on his shoulder, and turned him to face her. "You have watched him wield what?"

Jo'than looked down upon his sister and studied her eyes. "You will not let this go, will you?"

"Oh, you have not imagined the lengths I will go to spy on you. Besides, this burdens you, and save Father, who will not say what he saw. No one will speak of it. What is this boy that he has quieted my brother and that father would take to him so?"

Jo'than looked up, closed his eyes breathed in and out, and spoke. "On my trials to kill an Akoolah. I was almost upon my prey when I saw Amani lure the beast into a crevice. It was a clever strategy. Something I too might have done. But the beast entered and when I watched to see what would become of the boy. Two entered. One exited. It was Amani dragging the cat behind him and preparing to skin it. I was indeed impressed. I followed him, knowing how the cats hunt and that they are smart and seek those who can kill them. I knew it was only a matter of time until they caught up to kill him. He could not survive a pack. He would be my bait, and when the time was right, I would isolate one of the Akoolah and have my prize."

Osumare took Jo'than by the hand and he followed her to a bench. and the two sat, and she placed her hand upon his knee. "No man can survive a pack of Akoolah."

Jo'than continued. "This is true. Eventually, as expected, they came for him, and I tracked him before they arrived. There was something about him. I do not quite know. But I did not wish to see him die at the hands of the beasts, so I approached him to see his worth. And I deemed him worthy to fight beside. The Akoolah attacked, and we fought them. Killed several. But I was bested by one of the cats and the Bussar...Amani would not let it take me. He killed the rest. With great skill, he fought them off. But then he...he..."

Osumare squeezed his hand. "It's OK...you can tell me. Whisper it if you must."

Jo'than looked at his sister and then nervously looked around as if looking for others. He leaned into her closer and whispered into her ear. "He called fire from the sky; he lifted the beasts into the air and flew to me...even lifted me into the air. He is a godling or what the Medja call Enari...he must be Hutari."

Osumare jerked herself away from him. Her hand covered her mouth. "You lie!"

Jo'than shook his head. "He spared my life that day. Took me to his home, and the Bussar nurtured me back to health. However, his father addressed his displeasure and wanted my life. A Kasset was arranged and our father commanded me to take his. We fought in the Kasset at Bussar. And to my shame and to honor our people. I attempted to kill the boy who rescued me. I struck and drew blood. But there is a strength to him. A strength that no normal man possesses. He is not a man that can easily be felled. And in honor, he bested me, and yet when he could have killed me. He refused. He chose to be a slave rather than take my life. To defy the will of his father, and his people. The will of the desert even — all to save me. He said he would not kill what he had once saved."

Jo'than placed his face in his hands and wept. "He is here...because he would not take my life. And who am I that my life should be spared twice by the same man?"

Osumare looked at her brother and began to understand the deep thoughts of introspection that weighed on his heart and mind. This burden was one that she could not bear. As she watched her brother cry, she stroked his strong shoulders, ruminating on his words. The realization setting in that the Bussar...Amani. Was not a dog. But perhaps like her father. Or even the Hutari himself. Her curiosity roiled within her. Her desire even more potent to know what it was to couple with such a man. She would have him, and she would make him hers despite his standing. For already, she had decided in her mind that a princess would love a slave.

Chapter Twenty-Six

To Defend the King

I n three days, the king would determine who of the trainees would become his Zhara-Telak. As was tradition, King N'Kosi had taken the prospective wards to the coast behind Bussar for fellowship and reflection, a time to observe them away from the weight of palace walls and prying eyes. N'Kosi had commanded that Amani and his peers ride with him to the edge of the Great Sea. For Ashar and Phatut, the prospect of spending time in the king's presence was exhilarating; their youthful excitement bubbled over in whispered speculations about what the outing might reveal. Yet not all shared their enthusiasm. General Dumani, a stoic pillar of the king's guard, had implored N'Kosi to take additional guards on the journey.

N'Kosi had waved away the suggestion with a dismissive chuckle, his voice steady with confidence.

"If I cannot abide a walk within my own land without fear. Then I am no king worthy of Hogarth. Is it not true that any may challenge me to rule? Why conceal intentions when one can just make one's desires known and take what one wants? I will not abide cowards. Besides, am I not called the Sandking for nothing? We go to a beach. I control the sand. Who can harm me when surrounded by the very element I command?" His words carried a quiet finality, silencing further protests.

Amani watched as General Dumani grudgingly conceded to his lord. Bowed and removed himself from the King's path.

N'Kosi smiled and he and his three ward prospects walked towards the stables.

The scent of horses and oiled leather filled the stables, mingling with the salt of the sea carried on the wind. Amani tightened the reins of his mount, a midnight-black steed with a mane like storm clouds. Ashar and Phatut were already mounted, their faces alight with boyish eagerness. The Sandking, however, seemed unbothered by the youthful excitement, his gaze steady, unflinching.

Amani noticed the way N'Kosi's eyes swept over the horizon as if seeing something beyond the blue expanse of the sky. The king was always in thought, always calculating, but today he seemed at ease — a dangerous thing, Amani thought, for any ruler, even one as powerful as N'Kosi.

The party rode towards the beach in songs of mirth, the hooves of their horses striking the earth in a rhythm that matched the steady beat of Amani's heart. The path to the beach was narrow, winding between cliffs that jutted into the sea like the ribs of some long-dead beast. The cliffs were jagged, ancient, and covered in a fine layer of sand that shifted with each gust of wind. Amani could feel the sands respond to N'Kosi's presence, like a whisper of recognition, a bow of allegiance.

The sea came into view, a vast, endless stretch of blue that kissed the horizon. The beach was a wide crescent of white sand, unmarred and pristine. N'Kosi dismounted first, his feet sinking slightly into the sand as if the very earth welcomed him. Ashar and Phatut followed, their laughter mingling with the crash of the waves.

N'Kosi took in the ocean's salty air and spoke to the young men as they assembled to his left and right. "All of you look in the distance. What do you see?"

Amani and the others strained to see over the horizon of the crashing waters. And off in the distance, a great black obelisk touched the sky. At its top, a light shot straight into the clouds, its brilliance a beacon to any sea-faring ship to avoid. Amani had never crossed the great sea and could not fathom how far the journey would take to sail to the structure, but it could be seen from this great distance. Up close, its immensity would be imposing. He wondered about the power and skill needed to build such a thing in the sea itself and concluded that none in

Tanara possessed such power save the Hutari and he spoke his thoughts aloud to the king.

"Who can make such a wonder save the Hutari?"

The king nodded. "It is there that if Hogarth was ever overrun, that is where we must find refuge."

Ashar looked at the king, confused, and reaffirmed that he had heard the king correctly. "So, if the undead were to walk the earth once again. If you commanded us to vacate Hogarth...*that place* is where we would flee?" said Ashar.

The king nodded and replied. "If the hope of men is lost in the west, then we must escape to the great Tower of Sight. The Medja have posts around the world. I am told even in the Kingdom of Elandria. It is said that they are the eyes of Hutari. Ready to summon him if ever he is needed again. The Medja watch across the whole of Tanara if the Necrosent were to rise again in the world. And to warn its people if the unthinkable were to occur. While I have never traveled to the tower. It is recorded that the Medja watch over the world storm Z'otho Linithe where the Kifu allegedly sleeps. They will be the first to know and signal to the world to ready herself if it returns."

"And if the creature does return my king, what then?" asked Phatut.

N'Kosi grew somber and replied. "On that day we must gather all men to withstand him. He is the agent of Enkai. And if Enkai is allowed to enter the world, he will plunge us into darkness, and we will be food for the Nephthys. And know this." N'Kosi then looked at the prospective wards and said.

"The King of Hogarth will not be the meal of either god or demigod. Am I clear?"

All three men nodded. "Our city, the Darkmouth, the Medja, even the Bussar and garrisons abroad were all established by Hutari after the great war to band together to withstand the Kifu if he were to ever walk Tanara again. This is my call. To be ever ready to defend against the incursion of the undead. To prepare Hogarth to once more garrison the armies of the west if she were ever again under siege. Hogarth is the standard to prevent the undead and, if necessary, to give men time to escape to the tower. The ships in our harbor are ever maintained to take our people across the ocean. To evacuate our home if ever I give the command. If the unthinkable were to occur and we must abandon the Westlands to the undead. This is my charge, and the change of my ward is to protect me and serve so that if all that stands between the Kifu and the world of men is Hogarth's king. My ward will be there on my right hand to face the monster with me. This is what you must prepare to give your life for and of which I demand utmost loyalty."

The men stood on the beach and looked back at the city of Hogarth. Each realized that she was not just their home, but a refuge should mankind need a place to garrison and launch to the sea if necessary. Amani looked at the great tower that stood as a sentinel in the ocean. A tower that no man could reach save the typhoon that moved near it fell. And if on that terrible day, the great world storm Hutari commands should fall and the world storm's clouds break, that ships no longer need sail to avoid the storm's edge. On that day, men must take courage. For the Kifu has arisen and the undead shall walk the earth once more.

N'Kosi drew his sword from its scabbard, the blade catching the light of the setting sun, gleaming like a promise of war. His voice was thunder, rolling over the sands. "Kneel. And prepare here on these sands to make your oaths to me. I would know which of you would stand by my side if the world storm fell — and if battle with the Kifu must once more be man's fate. Who among you will choose to fight and die at the side of your king?"

Two of the young men dropped to their knees, and the words drilled into them by Guam spilled from their lips with the ease of ritual. "We will follow you into fire and into death. We serve the world of men, and the land of Hogarth by serving our king. To fight for the living and pledge to stand against the walking dead."

N'Kosi smiled, but his eyes caught on Amani, who neither knelt nor spoke. Instead, Amani stood, eyes lost to the rhythm of the ocean, his gaze fixed on the great tower looming in the distance, framed by the lightning storm that raged near it.

N'Kosi's voice cut through the air like a blade. "And what say you, Bussar? Will *you* also follow me into fire and into death?"

Amani turned his eyes from the raging tempest that swirled in the distance and turned to face the king. He inhaled and chose his words with care. "May my king live forever. You are great and know of a certainty that I will give my life for you if doing so will serve Tanara. In Bussar, my people have what we call Orsee. And they are prominent men of wisdom and learning. The first was trained and given sight by the Hutari himself to receive visions. They possess the eyes of Akuma and sometimes see the future. When asked by the kings of my people if, in their visions, they see the Kifu in their lifetime, each has said no. And for centuries, none has seen the Kifu rise in their generation. And every man is set before an Orsee seer before his rite of passage to see what Akuma might show. Some have seen grand visions. To others, nothing is revealed. And when it was time for me to see what path lay before me. When my time of trial was passed. I sought the Seer of my land. And he spoke to me and gasped when he saw my path." Amani then stared at N'Kosi and frowned.

N'Kosi's gaze narrowed, sensing more beneath Amani's words, but he waited, his grip tightening on the hilt of his sword. "And what, Amani of Bussar. When you were sitting before the Seer of your people, did you see?"

Amani turned away from the king, his shoulders tense with the weight of the truth. His voice dropped, dark as the horizon, and he pointed at the towering obsidian fortress planted in the ocean leagues away. "A black tower with no storm. I saw a figure in dark robes and, with the power of Aaru, wipe clean the armies of men. Men that rose from their graves as the Kifu returned to claim them. I saw great king — the Kifu walk the earth in my generation." He continued to stare at the tower in the distance. "I saw a tower I had never seen before. I saw *that* tower."

A shadow fell over N'Kosi's face, and the sands beneath them seemed to shift in response, unsettled by the weight of Amani's words. The storm in the distance seemed to howl louder with this pronouncement, and for a moment, it felt as if the earth itself trembled in fear of what was to come.

N'Kosi eyed Amani and his mouth grew stern. He inhaled the gravity of the words spoken to him and exhaled concern. Concern because for these past months, he had grown to respect this young man...he realized that he even began to consider him like a son. He turned his gaze from the young man and looked out over the horizon to the obelisk citadel that towered in the distance.

"I know of the Seers. There are few of them in the Westlands. My report is that even the Medja do not possess such a person who can prophesy. To receive a vision from a Seer is indeed a gift from Akuma. And in your vision of the Kifu, did you see — your king?"

Amani turned his eyes from the Tower of Sight towards the Sandking and shook his head ominously.

N'Kosi nodded in understanding. "And to whom have you shared this vision?"

"None, my king. You and my fellows here are the first to ever hear me broach the subject. The thing was not even shared with my Seer, who revealed it to me."

"And yet you reveal it to us here today: we who are not your people. Why?"

Amani then looked at his peers and then his king and kneeled. "Because when *I* speak that I will serve you — that I will die to protect you. You must know, that I do not speak it because of tradition, nor merely recite from memory prepared words given to me by another. Nor does tradition drive my speech. When *I* speak. I speak from the depth of my belief of what is coming. You must know, that I will do all that I can to not face the Kifu without the power of my king to stand against it. I have seen its forthcoming in my vision. And we will need more than the power of a Sandking to stop it. And while I am loath to say it. I believe the living are running out of time. My oath to you, my king, then, is this... that my life is your life. That I will serve you without question. Tanara will need all those who possess Akuma's power to withstand what is coming. And I would see that this is done."

N'Kosi nodded. He then took his sword placed it in the palm of his hand and sliced it so that blood was drawn. He then took his blood and with it anointed the right ear lobe of all three that were before him and spoke.

"I now bind you three to never reveal what has been shared on the punishment of death. What has been said among these sands will remain here in the sand. Am I clear? None can know lest panic or unbelief rage throughout the people."

All replied as one. "Yes, my king."

"Good, now that we understand our duties. I would make camp and learn more about the men who have dedicated themselves to serve me as my ward."

But before any could move, the attack struck like a lightning bolt out of clear skies.

Without warning, a violent burst of blue light exploded in front of them, the air crackling with energy as five glowing portals tore open the fabric of reality. From the rifts emerged figures cloaked in smoke, their robes glimmering with shades of purple, black, and gold. Their eyes glinted from beneath hoods as dark as night, and obsidian daggers gleamed in their hands. They moved like shadows, swift and silent, descending upon the men with assassin-like precision.

Amani barely had time to react before the attack was underway, but N'Kosi moved as if the attack had been expected. With a single sweep of his hands, the sands obeyed their king. The ground trembled beneath his power; the grains rising in a towering wave before crashing down upon the attackers with a force that shook the very earth.

But these were no ordinary foes.

Like serpents, they slithered from beneath the heavy sands, shaking off the earth as if it were water. Their movements were unnatural, faster than any human should be. And without hesitation, they flung themselves at N'Kosi, their eyes locked onto the Sandking alone, as if nothing else mattered.

Amani's pulse thundered in his ears as he sprinted to his lord's side. The wind answered his silent command, its power focused in a straight punch as his fist collided with the sternum of an attacker. The blow sent the assassin hurtling backward into the sea, where the waves swallowed him. But Amani was not done. His fingers closed into a fist and summoned the power of his calling. He felt the air within the assassin's lungs twist, tighten, and then collapse as the oxygen was ripped away. The man's body convulsed for a brief second before falling, lifeless, into the water.

Ashar and Phatut fought to keep the King from harm, but N'Kosi was a living storm. The sands surged and shifted at his will, transforming into jagged spikes that shot up from the beach like the teeth of a beast. Impaling several of the attackers who dared come near, a deadly defense that left no room for mercy. The beach was his domain, and in his fury, it became an extension of his very being—a force that would not be tamed. On the shores against the sea as the distant black tower sentinel'd Z'otho Linithe. The Sandking showed the reason for his title.

Yet even as Amani fought to protect his king, he couldn't shake the feeling that something was wrong. The attackers' focus never wavered. They cared nothing for the other men—only N'Kosi. And despite the power of the Sandking, the assailants kept coming, as if driven by a singular purpose beyond reason or fear. When one assassin fell, another would come through the portal.

And the attackers were relentless, their dark magics created blue shields that clashed against N'Kosi's power. And the king's makeshift projectiles fell to the ground. Amani felt the air grow thick with malevolent energy. He directed a fierce wind toward a shadowed figure that had crept too close to Phatut; the gust knocking the assailant back into the sea. But it was not enough.

A sharp cry rang out, cutting through the chaos. Amani turned just in time to see—Ashar—fall to the ground, a dagger of dark metal protruding from his chest. The world seemed to slow, the sounds of battle fading into a dull roar as Amani's gaze locked onto the lifeless body of his companion. While Amani had seen men die from old age. Had witnessed N'Kosi execute criminals or traitors to Hogarth. All those were disconnected as events. Observations of no meaning. Each held no meaningful relation to him. But now, as he rushed to catch Phatut as he fell to the ground holding the dagger that was lodged in his chest. As he collapsed into the arms of Amani. He felt the hard choke of a tightened throat. The deep guttural ache of loss. Now—he knew he had lost a friend. And the pain was unbearable. A pain that became vocalized.

"Nooooo!!"

N'Kosi saw he had lost one of the men who had just sworn to give him his life and roared, the sands around him then swirled with a fury that matched the storm brewing in his heart. Sand rose from the soles of the attackers, creeping up their legs, pinning them in place. Like a living thing, the sand crawled up their torso and into their mouths until their screams were drowned by sand that filled their throats and noses until the whole of their bodies were encased in sand. The remaining attackers, sensing their doom, attempted to flee as they summoned portals to transport them to safety, but the Sandking's wrath was swift and merciless. The sand beneath them opened its mouth and swallowed them whole, leaving no trace of their existence. N'Kosi then turned to the still open portals and with a wave of his hand stalactite shaped glass was thrown into them and the sounds of screams could be heard in the air and until the portals closed as quickly as they had appeared and nothing, but the crashing of the ocean waves roared in the ears of the three men that survived the onslaught.

Amani knelt beside Phatut, his hands trembling as he reached out to close the young man's eyes. Ashar gathered around, his face pale with shock and grief. N'Kosi stood apart, his chest heaving with the remnants of his rage and fatigue. His eyes, once so calm, now blazed with a fire that Amani had never seen before darting to and fro to assess if other dangers lurked to accost th em.

The king's gaze swept the horizon once more, but this time it was not in thought—but determination. "We shall return," N'Kosi voiced, his tenor cold as the ocean breeze that now howled across the beach. "And when we do, we will find who dared to attack us."

Both Amani and Ashar nodded and heaved Phatut's body across his horse and Amani tied the stead to his reins. As they saddled to return to the city. The ride back was silent, the once joyous mood now replaced with a heavy foreboding. The weight of Phatut's corpse a reminder of the cost of defending the king against his enemies. Amani kept his eyes on the road ahead, but his thoughts were elsewhere—on the shadows that he realized lurked in every corner of their world, and on the king who he knew would stop at nothing to find those who assaulted them.

And at that moment when he ceased from thinking about the king's enemies, and when his thoughts were no longer heavy on the loss of his friend. He realized he had taken a life. That he had broken the promise he had made to M'Msee. And he wondered if his actions would give rise to the Kifu.

As they approached the city gates, N'Kosi's voice cut through his musing, a low growl that sent shivers down Amani's spine. "They think they can strike me and remain hidden. I will unearth every last one."

And as the gates closed behind them, an ominous truth settled over the group—something had changed to so brazenly attack the king openly and this may only be the beginning.

Chapter
Twenty-Seven

Zhara-Telak

The moment Amani of House Haidar had trained
for—had finally arrived. A full year of grueling instruction in swordsmanship, courtly protocol, and unyielding discipline had shaped him into a contender to serve as ward to the
King, but the weight of the final decision still pressed heavily
on his shoulders. He had risen from an outsider to a finalist, yet
doubts gnawed at his resolve. Was he truly worthy of the sacred
position of ward to King N'Kosi, a role bound by duty, loyalty,
and sacrifice? As he stood amidst the grandeur of the royal court,
every eye fixed upon him, the world seemed to hold its breath.

"Amani of House Haidar step forward." The young man
moved as he was told and stood silently at attention, facing

Guam. He stared straight ahead, his ears perked to hear the final decision after a year of training.

"For one year, the cohort of Guam has trained to determine who would be the ward of King N'Kosi. Each of you has mastered the art of protocol and has been found worthy to serve any of the high houses of Hogarth. From cup bearing to sword skill, you have learned what it means to be an amour bearer and ward of the king. While I wish all who come into my company could serve in such a role. The King only has one appointed ward that is entrusted to serve him. Only one who will surrender his life in service to our great king. And only one found who possesses the unwavering loyalty, unyielding courage, and integrity that befits one of the highest positions of trust in the land."

"I have given the king my recommendation. But in the end, it is the Lord of Hogarth who will decide in whose hands he will entrust with his life if the circumstance were to arise. He has ruminated with himself, decided, and placed his sealed determination to be read by me in the hearing of all those in his house, as is royal tradition. So that all might know and give obeisance to the ward of the king in all matters concerning the king's care."

Guam then turned to the legion of house servants that looked up where the king was seated and the array of attendants that encircled him. And continued to speak to the crowd that served the royal household and all who kept the castle grounds. "Will you accept the king's verdict and do that man honor whose name is listed on this scroll?"

All responded, even as one man. "We will."

Guam then held up the scroll for all to see, turned towards the king broke the royal clay seal, unfurled the scroll, and read the name written within. His face showed no emotion, and he bowed to his king and then turned to the two men who stood before him who were the finalists in training to be the king's ward.

Amani looked nervously at Guam, then closed his eyes inhaled, and waited for the verdict that he was sure would never come.

"Ashar, I am honored to have served as your teacher. I trust the lessons learned will serve you well with Prince J'abari. You have been selected to serve him as Zhara-Telak. Congratulations."

Ashar bowed and smiled at the honor bestowed upon him to serve the one who would undoubtedly one day become king of Hogarth. Ashar bowed and replied. "To live is to serve and to serve is to live. May the prince find my service life-giving."

Guam nodded his salutation and then turned his back to the two men and back to the king and those assembled.

"Children of Hogarth and those who serve our King N'Kosi, I present to you Amani of the House of Haidar. Prince of Bussar and now Zhara-Telak to his greatness. May his service bring all of Hogarth honor."

Amani, mistakenly thinking that Ashar had won the competition, turned to Ashar and reached out to shake his hand with congratulations. "I am honored to see you ascend to the wardship of our king. May your service to him be long and fruitful..."

Ashar laughs. "You are so thickheaded, Bussar. "YOU are the Zhara-Telak to the king," said Ashar.

Amani stood silent for a moment and realized that he had tuned out Guam when he announced his name. He quickly withdrew his hand and apologized to Ashar, who grinned at him and whispered. "You are so stupid, Bussar. May Akuma have mercy on you."

Amani then quickly turned to Guam and bowed, as was the custom. "Thank you, teacher, for your instruction."

Guam replied, "None is required, young master. I serve the king as do we all. You have been honed to serve Hogarth. And you have been elected to serve her by serving its king. Do us all honor."

The King of Hogarth stood to his feet and all of Hogarth then bowed and Amani stood before the King and, like all of Hogarth, he too bowed the knee and N'Kosi approached him and spoke. "Amani of house Haidar. Do you accept this assignment? Will you submit to my wardship and, if need be, give your life for my life? Will you surrender your destiny for my benefit and serve Hogarth by serving me?"

Amani looked up at the king and spoke aloud that all may hear. "I accept this honor and responsibility. I, who is an adopted child of Hogarth, pledge to you my loyalty. I am thine and all that I have. May the king live forever. Command me and I will obey."

The king then tapped the shoulder of Amani, "Rise child of Hogarth, and face the people. Behold Hogarth, Amani of House Haidar. Zhara-Telak to your king and servant of Hogarth. Hear you him."

Amani then turned from the Sandking and faced the great city of Hogarth. Bowed and grinning from ear to ear. All while a chorus of cheers from the city echoed within his ears.

Chapter
Twenty-Eight

Investigation and
Conspiracy

T he war chamber was heavy with tension. The walls,
adorned with banners of Hogarth's triumphs, seemed to
sag under the weight of the moment. N'Kosi sat at the head
of the table, his presence radiating strength, though his brow
furrowed as his war council gathered. Amani stood behind him
to his right, tall and poised, his face an impassive mask hiding
the storm brewing within him. J'abari and several of the king's
chief advisers sat at the table.

The remains of the beach attack lay before them: charred
cloaks, broken weapons, and the bodies of those who dared

challenge the Sandking. Among them was the body of the assassin Amani had felled, his once-vibrant eyes now dull, his hands still curled as if grasping for the wind.

"These," N'Kosi's General Dumani began, "are magic users, without question. The sand we recovered from the portals bears the unique residue of Medja magics. And yet, they wore not traditional Medja garments, nor signifiers of their people."

A ripple of discomfort ran through the chamber. The Medja had long been peacekeepers, mediators between the great nations. For them, to orchestrate a secret attack was unthinkable. Yet, the evidence whispered otherwise.

J'abari's voice cut through the silence, firm and unwavering. "The Medja are not as innocent as we would like to believe. They hide behind their towers and treaties, behind a facade of peace. We have all heard the rumors of a rogue faction of Medja. Magic users who secretly move counter to the main body. Why else would such magic be found here if they were not involved? I do not believe it is a coincidence, my king. I suggest we call them to court and account for this outrage. I would ask your leave to search out this deceit."

Amani's stomach twisted as he listened. The Medja had a history that was foreign to him—a history that had always seemed one between balance, wisdom, and fear. He had seen no real malice in them, not when he had crossed their lands, fear perhaps when their paths last crossed, but not a desire to destroy N'Kosi. He mused that they could have done that before they ever reached the Darkmouth. No, he thought, something else was at play. He kept his silence but watched J'abari closely, sensing something beneath his words—a malice that was hard to ignore.

"Perhaps," Amani began cautiously, "But I do not believe the Medja are behind this. It seems too... secretive, too underhanded. They've never acted in such a manner before. If they wanted war, wouldn't they declare it as they always have—with diplomacy first? And what would they gain by attacking a nation they helped broker peace for? They did not appear to desire war with our king when we last passed through their lands a year ago. Why now when their words before were clear in their intent?

J'abari's jaw tightened, a muscle ticking beneath the skin. "What they gain, Bussar, is our power diminished. Our focus divided. They are the snakes in the grass, waiting for the right moment to strike. You would know this if you were Hogarth."

N'Kosi raised a hand to quiet the room. His eyes moved between the two men, weighing their words with the careful precision of a man who had seen too much war and too much deceit. "Both of you will pursue your investigations. The truth must be found before any action is taken. I will not go to war lightly—especially against the Medja."

"What are you proposing, N'Kosi?" said General Dumani.

N'Kosi looked at Amani and nodded at his servant and protector. "I agree with my ward. I too do not believe the Medja is behind this attack. But neither can I discount my son's words. Only Medja use the magics we have seen. Wisdom directs his thoughts to be explored."

N'Kosi then stood and his council stood with him. "Amani." He said.

Amani stepped forward and bowed.

"It is my command that you leave to work with General Dumani to surmise the source of this attack. If it is not the Medja, then who? If the thing is, as you say, Bussar has a new enemy she must contend with. Do your king's business with haste." The king then turned to J'abari and spoke.

"As for you, my son, you are free to pursue proof of your beliefs. Show me genuine evidence—not just conjecture against the Medja. And if the trail points to the mages. I shall unleash the sands upon them until they are entombed in the pyramids of Aphis they call home. I admit I have grown tired of their veiled threats."

J'abari bowed his head, though inside, his blood boiled. He loathed Amani, an obstacle that seemed to be always in his way. A Bussari—a foreigner—meddling in Hogarthen affairs, and worse, his father heeded his counsel.

"You all have your commands," said King N'Kosi. "Do your king's business with haste." The king then turned to leave but then stopped. "Oh, and J'abari, Amani is Zhara-Telak. Selected by my hand among all those that were prepared to do so. He may have been born in Bussar. But his heart is Hogarthen and sworn to me. Do not disrespect him in my presence again." N'Kosi then left the council chamber, and Amani and General Dumani followed.

When the council was dismissed, J'abari stormed from the chamber, his steps quick and purposeful. He had a meeting to attend, one that could not be delayed. His mind fumed that he had been publicly rebuked.

***

Islu's quarters, nestled deep in the shadowed bowels of the palace, bore the weight of neglect and secrecy. The air was heavy with dampness, tinged with the acrid stench of stale water and mildew. Crumbling stone walls glistened with a sheen of moisture; their surfaces marred by the faint etchings of graffiti long since eroded. Pools of murky water clung stubbornly to the uneven floor, reflecting the dim, flickering glow of an oil lamp that seemed insufficient against the oppressive darkness. Rusted hooks and warped shelves adorned the walls, bearing relics of Islu's trade—worn brushes, clay jars of pungent oils, and cracked basins stacked precariously.

Islu himself seemed an extension of his surroundings—a gaunt figure with skin stretched taut over his hollow cheeks, his frame hunched from years of servitude. His eyes, sunken and shadowed, darted around the room like a cornered animal, betraying a deep unease. As J'abari entered, his presence casting long, sharp shadows across the damp walls, Islu stiffened. His hands wrung together with nervous energy, their knobby fingers trembling as he forced a thin smile that did little to conceal the fear flickering in his gaze.

"They failed," J'abari snarls, his voice barely above a whisper, yet sharp as a blade. "How could you allow this? My father still breathes, and now we have nothing but suspicion and evidence that leads to the Medja. You assured me success."

Islu recoiled as if struck, his face pale. "It was not supposed to be like this, my lord. The assassins were certain, but—"

"Certain?" J'abari's eyes flashed. "You forget, Islu, that your life is tied to this as well. If my father discovers what I know of your dealings... your end — and your family's end will be far more painful than theirs. I can only imagine what my father would do if he discovered that he whom he once forgave still raises up treachery against him. Would he put out your eyes for ogling my mother and pleasuring yourself? Or would he rack your sons? Perhaps he would entertain himself by allowing the guardsmen to rape your wife as you watch? I am so glad, my friend, that it was I who caught you when you violated my mother's privacy and not my father. It has proven such a wonderful thing to elicit your cooperation in my cause. between you and me, I would love to see him bury you and your family in the sands and watch each of you drown slowly as the wild birds gouge your eyes as the tide rises. In fact, perhaps I should just tell Father, perhaps you are of no more use to me?"

Islu fell to his knees, trembling. "Please, my prince. I beg you. I assure you that as a servant of the Black Medja, I will do what was left undone. I swear it. I have a poison that will eat him from the inside slowly. His cause of death will seem like it stems from natural causes. It must just be administered three times in his food or drink to take effect."

J'abari's lips curled into a cold smile. "Then make it happen. No more mistakes, Islu, or I will see to it that you suffer before the end."

Islu bowed low, his forehead nearly touching the stone floor, as J'abari took his leave and left the Bathmaster to execute his plan.

***

J'abari retreated to his quarters, the weight of the day's events heavy on his shoulders. The room was small, but richly appointed—befitting a prince of Hogarth. A single torch flickered in the corner, casting long shadows on the walls. He calmed himself and then knelt before an altar, one adorned not with the symbols of Akuma, the god his people revered, but with the twisted, dark sigil of Enkai.

He clasped his hands together, his lips moving in a quiet prayer.

"Speak to me, Lord Enkai," J'abari whispers, his voice low and fervent. "Show me how to open this world to your coming. To eliminate those who fear your power and avenge those who see through the lies told by the Hutari. For I see the truth that you would have us ascend. You have shown me the truth."

J'abari's eyes fluttered closed, his breath slowing as a chilling presence thickened the air around him. The room pulsed, not with light but with a palpable, oppressive darkness, as though reality itself bent under the weight of an unseen force. Shadows deepened, stretching unnaturally along the walls, and a faint, otherworldly hum began to resonate—a chorus of whispers that seemed to bleed through the veil of Tanara. The faint lamplight flickered violently, struggling against the encroaching void.

Then came a voice, resonant and ancient, carrying the weight of countless epochs. It was a low rumble, like thunder rolling beneath the earth, yet it pierced J'abari's mind with crystalline clarity. Each word seemed to echo endlessly, carving its meaning into his very being.

"You summon me, child of Hogarth, and I answer. You know my will." The voice grew sharper, more commanding as if it were the voice of Tanara itself rebuking its inhabitants. "The Medja weave their deceit, they are a cancer upon my design. Undermine them—strip them of their power. And the Bussar boy..." The words hung heavy, laced with malice. "He is an insult, a stain on the path I have forged for you. Remove him. Let his defiance be silenced."

J'abari's body trembled as the presence pressed closer, suffusing him with a dreadful mix of terror and elation. The voice softened, its tone shifting to one of seduction, promising rewards that shimmered just out of reach.

"Do this and ascend as Hogarth's rightful king. Make ready all kingdoms for my reign upon Tanara. Through you, my will shall be manifest. Through you, all nations shall bow. Serve me, and you shall reign as my Zhara-Telak—first among mortals, sovereign over all."

The darkness receded as suddenly as it had come, leaving the room in silence save for the ragged rhythm of J'abari's breath. The faint lamp light steadied, and the whispers vanished, but the weight of the words lingered, etching themselves into his mind.

The room shivered, its darkness retreating reluctantly as color seeped back into the walls, though a heavy stillness lingered. J'abari opened his eyes, his expression transformed by the wicked gleam of dark determination. His lips curved into a smile, cold and sharp as tempered steel.

"I will do your bidding, Lord Enkai. I will see your will done."

And as the torch flickered once more, an ominous shadow seemed to pass over the room, leaving J'abari alone in the darkness, his heart full of cold, plotting determination.

Chapter Twenty-Nine

The Pause Between Beats

Amani glided through the grand hall, a year of relentless training honing his every movement. The whispers of the court grew closer as he approached, a far cry from the jeers and hostility that had greeted his arrival. As a captured foreign prince, his days had begun in chains, but through the grueling regimen of Guam's training, he had transformed into a figure of silent power and precise etiquette. He was the king's, Zhara-Telak. He walked on his way to meet with Hogarth's sovereign and recalled his training from Guam.

"Now go and serve the king his food and those of the court," Guam's voice echoed in his mind, a constant drill from his teacher and a reminder of the path he had walked these many days since had left Bussar. And through Guam's guidance, Amani learned to become a spectral presence, an unseen attentive force ever anticipating needs without acknowledgment from those he served. His lessons were a textbook on how to serve. He smiled as he recalled several of note.

"Drinks are warmed to taste," Guam had instructed.

To serve the king a beverage lukewarm or to serve it too hot or too cold could invite death. So, Amani refined his senses, discerning the ideal temperature for each beverage. He meticulously prepared a tray, ensuring that each drink was warmed to perfection. He moved with quiet efficiency, his senses attuned to the subtleties of temperature, embodying the lesson imparted by Guam. He watched the grandmaster's hands, the way they hovered just so above a goblet to test its warmth. He mirrored his teacher's movements until his own touch was as delicate and precise.

"Remember that the beat of the drum speaks louder in its pauses. You are the pause between drumbeats. The quiet ties the rhythm together. Therefore, hear nothing, see nothing, only serve," Guam drilled this truth into all his students and above all; emphasized this cardinal rule when serving those with influence.

Thus, Amani practiced the art of blending into the background, a silent figure in the grand halls of power. His skills of immersion chameleon-like. His movements were a constant lesson and reminder from the ever-watchful Guam. *"The occupants of your room should feel as if it is empty when you are in it."* In the king's halls, he learned to glide across the polished floors, each step measured, his presence a mere whisper against the purple tapestries. He noted how the royal family and the Umdhala spoke with their eyes, a fleeting glance enough to convey displeasure or approval. And in these silent exchanges, he found a language more profound than words.

Despite the lessons of Guam and those he gleaned from being a captive in this foreign land. He yet loved his own people. Grew to understand the decision of his father as he watched rulers travel to meet the Sandking. And though the lessons of Hogarth could be those of love and terror. He would never forget the lessons imparted by his own people, and especially his father and M'Msee. A lesson he found bode well in Hogarth. *"Know your enemy."*

Over the year, Amani learned many lessons, chief was that the Hogarth were not a brutish warlike people. But they were stern, almost static in their traditions and beliefs. The last great war took such a toll that they vowed to never allow themselves or mankind to see the brink of extinction. This was a culture that trained to fight the undead. Yet respected subtly. A culture holding beliefs about Akuma, the Kifu, and Enkai that were similar if not identical to Bussar. Osumare oversaw that Amani was schooled in their ways, their culture, literature, foods, and language. Through his studies, he discovered that Bussar and Hogarth were twin brothers who fought alongside the Hutari in the Great War. Each people now ancestors to these two great generals who stood by Hutari as he battled atop Mt. Moshek to bring the Kifu and his Necrosent armies to heel. Two brothers who saw the truth of the Hutari's decision to spare the life of Hesphus. Two nations that over time had come to despise one another, war against one another, and who now held to a tenuous peace separated by the wilderness, desert, and a city of magic users. Two brothers who went their separate ways, each sharing instructions and principles to guide their people learned from Hutari. Amani marveled over the tomes he read and, over the year, immersed himself in the customs and traditions of Ho garth.

Night after night, he poured over Hogarthen poetry, relishing in the intricate verses revealing layers of meaning with each read. He traced the image-laden script, feeling the weight of history and culture in every line. The stories of ancient heroes and tragic lovers became his guides, teaching him the values and fears of the people he now served.

Amidst the whispers and dirty looks from his peers, Amani's resolve hardened. A spilled drink, a whispered insult—each slight was a lesson in restraint. His fists itched with the urge to retaliate, but he swallowed his pride, the memory of fire and the Kifu were a constant reminder of the danger should he fail in his control.

By year's end, Amani's transformation was complete. He moved through the palace as if born to it, a shadow among the pillars, his eyes speaking volumes where his tongue remained still. No longer just a captive prince, he had become an unseen force, his mastery of etiquette a shield and a weapon in the silent battles of the king's court. But beneath the veneer of his confidence, the seeds of a storm were brewing—one that would soon sweep through the palace, drawing him into the heart of a familial conflict that would test both his loyalty and his ability to survive.

And now he had attained the position of ward of the king. The Zhara-Telak. His duties to attend the King kept him busy. He figured today would be no different and entered, as was his custom, into the king's council chamber. In this room, the Umdhala met, along with important figures summoned by the king for council or to meet ambassadors from across Tanara. He set himself, as was custom, to the rear of the king's seat, ever watchful for danger and yet present to attend his master's beck and call.

The grand hall of the palace buzzed with the hum of palace life. Ornate tapestries depicting Hogarth's storied history adorned the walls, their colors vivid even in the flickering light of the chandeliers. At the head of the long, polished oak table sat King N'Kosi, his regal posture commanding respect as he surveyed the room with keen eyes. His glass and gold crown, adorned with precious gems, glittered faintly in the dim light.

Prince J'abari, his son and heir apparent, stood at the center of the room, his figure tall and imposing. The young prince's voice rang out with a force that echoed off the stone walls, each word crisp and authoritative. His dark hair, tied back in a tight, disciplined fashion, and his sharp, piercing eyes conveyed a determination born of years in the royal court.

"Father," J'abari began, his tone unwavering and filled with conviction, "we must strike hard against the Tarkan. We cannot afford to show any sign of weakness. They will see our hesitance as an invitation to challenge our might. If we do not act decisively, we risk undermining our strength and reputation."

The room fell silent as the weight of J'abari's words hung heavily in the air. Advisors and generals shifted uncomfortably in their seats, glancing between the prince and the king. The aroma of roasted meats and spiced wine, intended to mark the evening's dinner, was momentarily forgotten as the discussion turned to matters of state and strategy.

King N'Kosi, a man whose wisdom and ruthlessness were as renowned as his power to control the sands, leaned back in his chair, his expression contemplative. He had weathered many storms in his reign, his mind sharp despite his advancing years. The flicker of candlelight danced across his face, highlighting the lines that spoke of battles fought and decisions made.

The tension was palpable as King N'Kosi's gaze shifted from his son to the gathered assembly. It was clear that this was no ordinary council meeting; the course of the kingdom's future was at stake.

King N'Kosi pondered his son's words, his expression inscrutable as he weighed the gravity of the moment. The grand chamber, adorned with tapestries of ancient battles, seemed to close in around them, the air thick with the heady scent of incense. Amani stood silently in the shadows, his keen eyes observing every subtle shift in the room. The tension mounted as he performed his duties and filled the king's cup as before with practiced discretion, until both the king's gaze unexpectedly locked onto him, and his voice to his servant shattered the routine.

"What do you think, Amani? You are a prince of Bussar. Trained by your father to rule in his stead. He surely taught you the ways of kingship, statecraft, and war. Speak on this issue, as I know enough about Bussar to know that you are not without wisdom."

The request for advice was unexpected, and Prince J'abari's eyes flared with indignation. Amani stepped forward, his movements measured and respectful. He bowed slightly before speaking, choosing his words with care.

"My king," Amani began, his voice calm and even, "while military strength is important, I believe it premature to engage the Tarkan without understanding their full capabilities. I suggest that first spies be sent to gather intelligence on their strengths and weaknesses. This will allow us to undermine or destroy key military encampments if diplomacy fails. By gaining more intelligence, we can position our forces more effectively and strike with precision when the time is right. But diplomacy should not be discarded. All nations are driven by kings or rulers. We would do well to send a delegation to understand this king's motives. Before we send an army to destroy good men and lose those who could be useful to fight the undead. What are the petty temporal squabbles of the living against such a threat?"

Amani concluded, then bowed deeply to the king, and the assembled council, his heart pounding as he retreated to his usual place in the shadows. The weight of his words hung heavily in the air, and the realization struck him with chilling clarity: he had directly countermanded the advice of Prince J'abari, the king's son. The room's atmosphere shifted, a dangerous edge threading through the murmurs of the assembly, as the prince's eyes darkened with a barely concealed fury. Amani's position in the darkness now felt more precarious than ever, as he awaited the fallout from his bold words.

King N'Kosi leaned back, considering Amani's words. The silence stretched, filled only by the flickering of torches on the walls. Finally, the king nodded, a slow smile spreading across his face.

"A wise approach, Zhara-Telak," the king said, his approval clear. "Intelligence and strategy before force. We shall proceed as you have advised."

The counselors assembled also nodded in approval and echoes of "Well said!" and "Wise words indeed." Were voiced in the ears of all.

Prince J'abari's face twisted in anger, his fists clenching at his sides. Without a word, he turned on his heel and stormed out of the chamber, his departure echoing through the hall.

Amani, still standing quietly, was careful to mask the internal satisfaction he felt inside, a satisfaction that was buttressed against the weight of the moment. He had gained the king's favor, but at what cost? The shadow of Prince J'abari's resentment loomed large, promising a retribution that Amani was sure to come.

Chapter Thirty

Ambitions of Doom

J'abari stood at the edge of the beach, the sharp scent of saltwater mingling with the coppery tang of blood. Moonlight cast a ghostly shimmer across the waves, their whispers a cruel contrast to the massacre before him. His eyes narrowed as he crouched beside one of the bodies, his gaze darkening at the sight of the assassin's shattered crest plate—Medja markings unmistakable in the intricate carvings.

"Tell me, Investigator," J'abari's voice was sharp, cutting through the thick silence that hung over the crime scene. "The blue dust you found on the beach—you're positive it comes from Medja magic?"

The investigator hesitated, the weight of the truth hanging heavily between them. "Yes, my prince. While Tanara is home to many sources of magic, to our knowledge, only the Medja possess portal magic—and the residue it leaves behind is unique to the Western Lands."

J'abari rose slowly, the tension rippling through his body. His gaze swept over the sand where darkened blood pooled and assassins lay broken. "And what of Aksum, Kissum, and Elandria?" he pressed. "What of the mages within the Tower of Sight? Could they possess such knowledge?"

The investigator shook his head, voice low and steady. "Our records tell of no Medja who could port across the Great Sea. Before the Kifu, the Ephasians possessed such power, but they are long past, and the knowledge perished with them when their kingdom fell into ruin."

J'abari's brow furrowed, his thoughts turning to the tales of old. Legends of the Ephasians, their mastery over vast distances, their towers rising toward the sky like the hands of gods. "Is it possible," he murmured, almost to himself, "that this knowledge now rests in the hands of the Medja?"

"There is no way to know for certain," the investigator admitted. "If they possess such abilities, they could arrive anywhere, without warning, and lay waste to us all. But this we do know—what remains are the garments and dust of the Medja. They were here, my prince. The evidence is unmistakable."

J'abari's jaw clenched as he paced the length of the scene, his boots kicking up sand as he moved. His eyes flickered to the bodies of the assassins, then to the blackened horizon beyond the shore, where the sea seemed to stretch endlessly into nothingness. And then, an idea formed—dark and wicked.

"How many of their garments do we possess?" His voice cut through the quiet, sharp as a blade.

"Four," the investigator replied.

J'abari nodded, his mind already weaving the plan. "Take the four to the tailors. I want them restored—pristine, just as they were before their battle with my father. Then find me four men—skilled in the arts of assassination and deception. We shall return to the Medja what they sought to inflict upon us."

The investigator's brow furrowed. "You intend to send assassins to kill the Medja? Does your father condone this?"

J'abari turned slowly, his eyes gleaming with dark intent. "I will present my findings to him. And I will have my men prepared, should he command them to strike. The Medja will bleed for this. We will wear their garb, infiltrate their pyramid city, and bring those god-fearing Hesphus worshipers to ruin. Let the lovers of their dead god feel the wrath of the living."

The investigator hesitated, unease creeping into his features. "And what of Bussar?"

J'abari's lips curled into a cruel smile, dark ambition gleaming in his eyes. "Once we've seized the Medja's pyramids and unraveled the knowledge of the Medja, Bussar will fall next. We will sweep across the coast and carve our path through the interior until nothing remains of their kingdom but dust and ash."

The investigator bowed deeply, his movements tense, as if weighed down by the gravity of the prince's words, and turned to leave. J'abari noted that the wind shifted, and an unnatural stillness overtook the night. A strange sound crept in, low and guttural, like the distant growl of some slumbering beast beneath the sea.

J'abari stiffened, his eyes darting toward the horizon. The sea had grown unnervingly calm, the waves frozen mid-motion, as though something vast and unseen held them captive. His breath hitched in his throat, his pulse quickening. "Speak, Enkai," he whispered, a tremor in his voice. "Your servant listens."

And then, from far off in the distance, a single crack of thunder tore through the sky, its echo lingering in the air like the roar of a god rousing from sleep.

J'abari's heart hammered against his chest, an excitement settling over him. The winds whispered secrets he could not fully grasp, yet their ominous murmur was undeniable. Something far worse than Medja assassins had stirred. Something ancient. Something alive.

As the investigator disappeared into the shadows, J'abari's gaze remained fixed on the horizon, his thoughts swirling with a mix of dread and exhilaration. Somewhere across the endless sea, the Kifu stirred within his tomb, and the world shifted beneath the weight of the inevitable.

But J'abari smiled, the gleam of his ambition undimmed. Soon, he would set his plan in motion—to supplant his father, to crush the Medja, and rid the palace of the Bussar ward who dared linger in his father's favor. Soon, he would be king and open the gates of Tanara to Enkai, ushering in an age of darkness and power that would stretch for a thousand years, granting him the immortality he craved.

And the world would never be the same.

Chapter Thirty-One

The Veilkeep Sanctum

The Veilkeep Sanctum of the Medja pulsed with ancient magic, the air inside was thick and suffocating. Every stone, every rune carved into the walls seemed alive, humming with power, being drawn into the chamber's heart—a central dais that resided before the Bloodgate. A portal that directly accessed the tomb of Hesphus. Here, the priests of the Medja worked tirelessly to keep the ancient undead god asleep. Panic rippled through their ranks, faces pale beneath their hoods, eyes wild with fear. The Kifu stirred beneath the waters, his long-slumbering form rousing to a hunger that threatened to tear apart the fragile balance the Medja had spent centuries preserving.

At the center of the room stood Kaelthion, the high priest
of the Medja order. His voice was sharp, cutting through the
chaos with an authority born of experience, but even his calm
exterior couldn't mask the urgency that bled through his words.
"More power! Divert more power to the wards!" he barked at
the lower-ranking priests, who hastened to obey, channeling
their energy into the enchanted stones that glowed an eerie
green beneath the temple floor.

A young acolyte, barely of age, stepped forward, her voice
trembling as she spoke. "Master Kaelthion, the wards... they are
failing faster than we can sustain them. The Kifu consumes too
much. He thirsts for blood, and we have no offering to present
to satiate his hunger."

Kaelthion's eyes flickered with barely contained fury, though
his voice remained steady. "I am aware. We must endure. The
Kifu cannot wake—Tanara's very existence depends on it."

Ra'kesh second of the order and draped in red robes, whispered to his leader. "But what has caused this? Why now? We
have kept him sleeping for so long. What has changed?"

Kaelthion's jaw tightened. "An Enari has manifested power,
perhaps even spilled blood, the Kifu must sense the power of
Aaru, the power of his son. Or perhaps some power akin to
Hutari's has awakened, and it has reached across the void to
rouse the Kifu from his sleep."

The room fell silent, the weight of Kaelthion's words settled
over them like a suffocating blanket. The mention of Hutari's
power sent shivers down their spines. Hutari could not be the

source of this disturbance. He would never knowingly wake his father. There must be someone else."

"Then we are lost," one of the mages whispered, her voice barely audible.

"No," Kaelthion said sharply. "We are not lost. We must act, and we must act now." He turned his gaze to the gathered mages. "A sacrifice must be made to quench the Kifu's hunger. One of us must go to his tomb and offer ourselves—willingly—before he is fully roused from sleep and breaks his bonds."

A hushed murmur swept through the assembly. The gravity of what Kaelthion proposed was not lost on any of them. To enter the tomb of the Kifu was to face certain death—worse than death, even, for the Kifu did not merely kill. He devoured. He consumed souls, stripping them of their magic, their very essence, until nothing remained but dust.

The mages hesitated, no one daring to step forward.

Then, from the back of the chamber, a lone figure moved. His steps were slow but deliberate, his head held high. Tor'kan, one of the chief mages, old and revered among their order, approached Kaelthion. The lines of age were deep in his face, but his eyes burned with unwavering resolve.

"I will go," Tor'kan said, his voice steady despite the quiet dread that hung around him. "If my death can forestall the Kifu's awakening, then I will give myself."

Kaelthion's gaze softened, and he bowed his head in respect. "You will be remembered for your sacrifice, Tor'kan. Your name will be spoken for generations, honored among the Medja."

Tor'kan simply nodded. He turned to face the great portal that led to the Kifu's tomb, the swirling vortex of magic that would take him to his final destination. The room fell into silence as he approached the portal, his azure robes billowing softly behind him. Every step seemed to echo with finality. The mages watched; their hearts heavy knowing that they were sending one of their own to a fate worse than death.

As Tor'kan stepped into the Bloodgate, the air ignited with dark magic, swirling in chaotic currents that coiled around him like living shadows. Each step pulled him deeper into the rift between realms, and the atmosphere thickened, growing unbearably cold. The oppressive weight of the Kifu's presence descended upon him like an invisible hand squeezing the very breath from his chest and forcing his knees to nearly buckle under its intensity.

When he emerged on the other side, the world was shrouded in an unnatural gloom. Before him loomed the great sarcophagus of Hesphus, the undead god, men had named the Kifu—a monolith of carved stone etched with runes older than time itself, each symbol glowing faintly with crimson light. The air thrummed with an ancient, malevolent energy, crackling with a power so potent it made the ground beneath him tremble. The sarcophagus pulsed with the essence of death and decay, sending waves of dread through the cavern.

Every breath felt poisoned, every sound muffled, as though the universe itself recoiled from the unholy presence sealed within. Tor'kan's gaze locked onto the ancient relic, his heart pounding knowing that his life would end here—fuel for a ritual that would keep the dormant god asleep. And yet, even as terror clawed at the edges of his resolve, he stepped forward, his lips forming the incantation that would rend the veil between life and oblivion.

Tor'kan knelt before the sarcophagus of Hesphus, his trembling form dwarfed by its oppressive grandeur. The ancient words of the incantation spilled from his lips, each syllable resonating with an unnatural cadence that seemed to vibrate through the very fabric of the chamber. As the ritual unfolded, a cruel tide began to pull at his essence, siphoning the vitality from his body.

His skin cracked and withered as if aged by centuries in mere moments, the once-robust flesh now paper-thin and fragile. His bones groaned audibly under the strain of the ritual, a mournful dirge to his sacrifice. The ambient power of the Kifu grew stronger with each passing word, ravenously consuming the magic that once pulsed within him.

Tor'kan's vision swam, the room dissolving into blurred shadows as his strength waned. His limbs quivered, barely able to support his collapsing frame, but he pressed on. Each word he uttered was a defiant act of will, a final stand against the encroaching void that sought to claim him. In the suffocating stillness, his whispered invocations carried the weight of worlds, each note a tolling bell heralding his impending demise.

Finally, as the last of his strength left him, the mage crumbled into dust. The power that had wakened the Kifu began to ebb, and the ancient creature's hunger momentarily was sated. The crisis, for now, abated.

In the sanctum, the tension eased as the mages felt the power shift. Kaelthion let out a slow breath, though his face remained grim. They had bought themselves time, but only time. The Kifu would stir again, and when he did, the Medja might not be able to hold him at bay.

"What could have roused him?" a voice broke the silence.

Kaelthion turned to the mage who had spoken, his face drawn tight with worry. "There was a brief flash of aaurinte power near Hogarth several nights ago. We believe Amani—the boy we delivered into Hogarth's hands—may be responsible. Hutari would not expose himself. I can think of no other source of Aarunite save the boy."

The room fell into a tense silence. The thought of the boy's potential, of what he could unleash upon the world, hung over them like a dark cloud.

"We must act," Kaelthion said. He turned to Ra'kesh and spoke. "Go and take two of our people with you as emissaries to the King of Hogarth. While there find Master Hutari, he should be there by now. We need answers about the boy and our lord."

The mages bowed and hurried from the chamber; their faces were grim with purpose. But as Kaelthion watched them go, an icy shiver ran down his spine. Something was wrong—terribly wrong. He had seen the signs, the subtle shifts in the winds of fate.

Kaelthion feared for Tanara. Hutari had left them only days ago to travel to Hogarth to see about the boy they had left with King N'Kosi. Now, not many days since; a spike in Aaarunic power is seen, and the Kifu stirs from his slumber. Kaelthion wondered if he was sending his people into a trap.

The Black Medja had left in violation of the order to not interfere with Hogarth's leadership. A euphemism used when discussions of assassination was discussed. They had not returned. He stared out a window and looked at the stars and even they seemed darker, like piercing judgmental eyes that stared down upon Tanara with malice. He mused within himself at the dark forces that worshiped Enkai and who sought to destroy the Medja and release the Kifu once more upon the world. Kaelthion felt the suffocating constraint of invisible forces closing in on them. An intuitive knowing that something was moving in the world, some whispering dark force. Reports from the order in Elandria and the capital of Kissum showed increased unrest by the native population against the Medja, rumors of false reports that Medja were using their power to assault the local people. Allegations of mind control and stealing were making some regions increasingly suspicious of the order. A power yet revealed was stirring against them, plotting in the shadows, and soon if they were not careful, their enemies would strangle them from all sides.

How long could the Medja and Hutari prevent the Kifu's awakening? How long could Hutari forestall the inevitable and kill his father? Kaelthion wondered if Hutari's love would be the undoing of them all. For now, the Kifu had been returned to slumber, the threat of Hesphus quietly contained beneath the waters of the World Storm. Kaelthion mused over the threats that occupied the Medja order. So many threats identified among the kingdoms of men. He rubbed his forehead and tried to push back the worries of rumors from the Leaflings of the Word Tree. Reports from the Leaflings about the awakening of an Ephasian gate—a power that had the potential to break the world.

Chapter Thirty-Two

The Arrival of Hutari

The wind howled as it swept across the battlements of Hogarth, rustling the banners atop the ancient city walls. Below, the massive gates of The Maw's massive doors stood sealed, as they had for decades from outsiders, their colossal iron doors blending with the weathered stone. On either side of the gates, soldiers stood at attention, their eyes scanning the horizon. Their leather armor softly squeaked as they shifted nervously, ever watchful for danger. The Maw was not easily breached—only the Sandking himself could command it to open, and no one expected visitors today.

But then, without warning, a tremor coursed through the ground beneath them. The soldiers snapped to attention, hands on their weapons. From atop the city walls, a sharp call rang out.

"Movement at the gate!"

Eyes darted toward the Maw, where something incredible began to unfold. A deep rumble echoed across the walls, and slowly, impossibly, the great iron doors of the Maw began to creak and groan. No one stood before it, no royal command had been given, and yet the gate—ancient and mighty—was opening.

The soldiers braced, exchanging quick glances as they prepared for whatever might come through. Archers lined the battlements, arrows nocked and drawn, while the ground troops shifted into defensive formations. The air was thick with tension. Whoever had the power to open the Maw could not be ordinary.

The rumbling intensified, dust and pebbles shaking loose from the ancient stonework as the gates slowly parted. A wave of unease rippled through the soldiers, many whispering prayers to the gods under their breath. None had ever seen this before. Only the Sandking could control the Maw, and the last time it had opened without him, it was because of... him.

When the gates were fully open, silence reigned. For a long moment, nothing stirred beyond the threshold, the vast emptiness beyond a yawning void. Then, from the shadow of the Maw, a single figure emerged—a small silhouette against the bright light of the open desert beyond. The soldiers squinted, and as the figure drew closer, realization dawned.

The whispers started first, barely audible above the wind. "Hutari..."

The figure stepped forward, draped in a long indigo robe that fluttered in the wind. His staff, topped with ancient carvings, tapped rhythmically against the ground as he walked. He was not a towering giant, nor was he clad in imposing armor—yet his very presence was enough to chill the spine of even the most battle-hardened soldier.

"It's him," one guard muttered, his voice laced with reverence and fear. "The Hutari."

The archers on the battlements lowered their bows, their hands shaking slightly. Soldiers who had been ready to defend the city now stood frozen, eyes wide, as the small figure approached. Despite his unassuming stature, the weight of his presence was undeniable. The Hutari, the son of the god Hesphus, had returned.

The captain of the guard swallowed hard, stepping forward. His leather armor, adorned with protective charms, felt suddenly insufficient. He raised his arm, signaling for his troops to stand down, but his eyes remained fixed on the Hutari. Though relieved that it was not an enemy, the captain knew better than to relax in the presence of one such as him. There was a power in the air, one that demanded reverence.

As the Hutari crossed the threshold into the city, the gates behind him groaned and began to close, sealing shut with a final, echoing thud. The city bells, which had rung furiously in alarm, now tolled in a slow, deliberate cadence—a signal not of danger, but of reverence. Word spread quickly through the streets: the Hutari has returned.

The guards stepped aside as the Hutari passed, their eyes cast downward in respect, yet they dared not speak. Even the captain, a man seasoned in battle and unflinching in the face of kings, bowed deeply, unable to meet the eyes of the man who had just opened the Maw as if it were nothing more than a door to a common house.

The Hutari walked in silence, his footsteps echoing on the stone path that led toward the palace. The soldiers exchanged glances, a mixture of awe and fear written on their faces. They all knew the stories—this was the man who walked with the gods, the one whose mere presence could command the elements and twist the will of kings.

"May the Sandking have the wisdom to speak with him," one guard murmured, his voice barely above a whisper.

Another nodded. "If anyone is safe in his presence, it's the King."

The soldiers returned to their posts, but the air was thick with the lingering power of what they had just witnessed. They had seen the Maw open, a feat only one other living being could perform. And now, the Hutari—son of a god—was within their city walls, walking toward the palace.

People abandoned their market stalls and chores to flood the streets, craning their necks and murmuring in awe as the procession advanced. A figure draped in robes of deep indigo, flanked by elite guards, walked with steady purpose. His staff, carved with ancient symbols, tapped softly against the stone road. The Hutari had arrived.

"Hutari!" someone whispered, followed by gasps from the crowd. Others pressed forward; eyes wide with disbelief. Few had ever seen him, but tales of the ancient protector had long been woven into Hogarth's history.

"Is it really him?"

"Could it be?"

"The Sandking himself bows to no man, but him..."

The sea of people parted before the approaching guards, reverence and fear in equal measure, as the bells tolled a third time from the high towers. The ringing echoed across the city, cascading through every district, every ear. The Hutari's face remained a placid mask, unmoved by the commotion around h im.

At the palace gates, a squadron of royal sentinels stood waiting. Their captain, a broad-shouldered man in gilded leather armor, approached and bowed low before the Hutari, sweat beading on his forehead despite the coolness of the day.

"Master of the Sands," the captain addressed him, his voice wavering slightly, "The King awaits you in the royal hall. It is an honor... truly."

The Hutari nodded without a word. The captain motioned for the escort to proceed, and the gates to the palace creaked open, revealing the grand stairway that led to the throne room.

His pace did not falter, and with each step, the aura of his presence weighed heavier on those around him. Even the seasoned warriors guarding the palace shifted uneasily under the gaze of this ancient being.

As the procession ascended, courtiers and officials scrambled to make way, casting nervous glances at the figure whose very presence was a reminder of the old world's power. The Hutari entered the royal hall where the king, N'Kosi, sat in solemn expectation. Beside him stood his family: Queen Sala, and their children—J'abari. Jo'than, and Osumare all of whom were poised in their own regal stance. To the right of the throne and behind it stood Amani, head slightly bowed, but his eyes gleamed with anticipation.

A tense silence hung in the air as the Hutari approached the throne. The King rose and bowed his head slightly, a gesture laden with deep respect. The whispers in the hall ceased, replaced by the quiet murmur of the wind through the windows.

"Hutari," King N'Kosi began, his voice carrying the weight of formality, "It has been many years since the walls of Hogarth have welcomed one such as yourself."

The Hutari stopped a few paces from the throne, his ancient eyes scanning the room before resting on the king.

"King N'Kosi," the Hutari intoned, his voice deep and resonant, "The sands of time do not pass without purpose. I am here for my godson Prince Amani of Bussar."

At this, the court erupted into quiet murmurs. All eyes darted toward Amani, who remained still but was noticeably tense.

The weight of the words struck everyone in the hall with the force of a storm. The godson of the Hutari? The gravity of this revelation stunned even the most stoic of the royal court.

The king's gaze shifted uneasily to Amani, but before he could respond, J'abari stepped forward, his posture rigid, and his face hardened with pride. His voice cut through the growing murmur in the hall like a blade.

"Why does the Hutari worry himself over the Bussar boy? Who is he to you?"

Jo'than was taken aback by his brother's impudence and spoke of his concern aloud.

"Brother, show respect. Do you know who this is?"

J'abari responded, "I know who he claims to be. I know who others say he is. But who is he actually that any, let alone I, should show deference? What does the alleged Hutari want with a king's servant? I would have an answer. I am the Prince of Hogarth and heir to the kingdom. He will answer me."

King N'Kosi was silent and turned his eyes down at his son. His face was downcast, and he looked at M'Msee as if he was making an apology. Silence engulfed the room. And those who were present smartly dismissed themselves from the presence of the Hutari and the King's family. And M'Msee, not wanting to humiliate the royal family, waited for all to leave before speaking.

When the room cleared, M'Msee smiled at the prince while speaking aloud to his father. "He is a youth. Passion and pride flow through his veins. N'Kosi. I trust you will work with him to know the responsibilities of a king...and not just those of a prince."

N'Kosi bowed to the old man, and J'abari rose up in anger. "Who is this man that my father, the greatest general this side of the great sea, would humble himself? I think you are a ruse, old man. An aged wizard full of parlor tricks to enchant those that would question and defy..."

J'abari was held aloft in the air. Floating, as the air around him became a putrid green and toxic and the prince of Hogarth choked, gasping for air.

"N'Kosi, he thinks military power and rule are the greatest things in this world. He does not know the ancient ways of life and who walks Tanara to keep death to the world at bay. It is clear to me now that he does not know that it was I who placed your seed in his mother's womb to give him life. That without my touch, he would have been stillborn. That the power of the sands that his line possesses comes from my hand. Teach him N'Kosi. Or the next time I see the child, I will take him and transfer his life to you so that you may live long enough to sire another more worthy to protect Hogarth from the undead."

The king and queen lowered themselves to the floor, and N'Kosi interceded for their son. "Son of Hesphus and protector of Tanara, may you live forever. Forgive the insolence of my son. He knows not of what he speaks."

J'abari's hands grasped at his neck, straining to be released from the invisible grip that held him aloft. M'Msee motioned with his hand and the prince floated towards him while the

King, his children, his wife, and Amani watched helplessly. And before the boy expired, M'Msee spoke. "My business in this realm is to protect you, young one. You breathe before he who is older than the sand beneath your feet. I am from above and you are of the dirt. You live because of the love shown by your father and mother. Do not disgrace them with your foolish words ever again. Or by Akuma, I will have your mouth and eyes sewn shut by the hands of your own parents for rearing such a disrespectful child. Now away from me. I would speak to your father."

M'Msee released him, and he fell to the ground, gasping. His lungs took in great gulps of air. His eyes were red. His face flushed. He gathered his strength and for a moment considered summoning the sand to rise and overtake M'Msee. But N'Kosi, seeing the face of his son and reading his features, lifted his hand, and the earth rose around J'abari to form an earthen cage. And the great king spoke. "Do not think that we will not speak of this issue later, my son. Now go and be grateful that you still live."

The earthen jail came down and J'abari bowed to his father, glared at M'Msee, and then quickly left the room, shutting the door behind him.

"My apologies for the boy," said N'Kosi. "I have tried often to teach him humility. I fear I have failed him in this thing."

M'Msee nodded. "Perhaps. All children attempt to emulate their parents, whether they know it or not. I have seen first-hand the destruction caused by division in a family. And the pains a father would do to reconcile his children to himself."

King N'Kosi nodded, reflecting on the gravity of M'Msee's words, and understood that M'Msee could indeed emphasize based on his experience in Aaru. "I can only imagine the strife among gods. Nevertheless, wisdom. While my son lacked the tact in speaking his mind. His question bears merit."

M'Msee sighed and leaned on his staff. "As mentioned, I have come to see about my godson. His parents would know of his welfare. I see he still stands by your side. This is good."

N'Kosi turned to his ward with eyebrows raised and looked at Amani with fresh eyes as awareness dawned upon him. "Your godson? The prince of Bussar is the god..." Amani stood with his head slightly bowed and looked away from the king. N'Kosi eyed the man he had taken from the Bussar and recalled their many interactions; he remembered the boy's mannerisms. Even his speech reflected M'Msee. He gawked, caught himself, then covered his mouth in disbelief before nodding. "Many things make sense now. Your words, your demeanor. I had wondered why they were so familiar. You are blessed to have one such as the Hutari to call you family. You are ever full of surprises, young prince. Know, Hutari, that he has not been harmed beyond the fashion of training in our ways. But he is free to speak for himself. Tell him Amani of Bussar, the truth of your stay in Hogarth."

Amani raised his mouth to speak and M'Msee waved him off. He walked gingerly up towards the throne and passed the king of Hogarth. Gave his staff to the king and embraced his godson in the tightest of hugs. Shocked but pleasantly surprised, Amani smiled and spoke into his ear. "It is good to see you, old friend. I have missed you."

M'Msee's eyes watered as he grinned from ear to ear. "Not as much as these old eyes do you."

"I am well Wisdom. King N'Kosi speaks the truth. I have been well, and the king has indeed seen to my training in the ways of Hogarth." M'Msee nodded, turned to the king, and reached out to retrieve his staff. "King N'Kosi."

"Hutari?" replied The Sandking.

"I request the ward be allowed to train with me. I trust that there is a space available to us?"

N'Kosi looked at M'Msee, then at Amani. "Training Wisdom?"

M'Msee was silent and just stared at the great king and N'Kosi, not wanting to appear as if he misunderstood the request, replied. "Of course, wisdom. I will make the catacombs available to you and the boy. When would you like this training to begin and how long can I expect to be without my ward?"

"I will need an outside space, great king. My request is to take him to Moshek. After three days in the mountain, I will return with the lad, and you may continue as you have."

N'Kosi nodded, "Of course, Hutari, of course. I will provide transportation so that you may leave the city quietly."

Hutari bowed in respect to the king. "Thank you, my friend. Jo'than, and Osumare, it is good to see you. I trust you still mind your father and mother."

The two children present bowed their heads and replied as one. "We do"

M'Msee smiles. "Good. You will both make wise and great rulers to protect against the darkness. Now if you would permit N'Kosi. The boy and I will take our leave."

N'Kosi bowed and spoke to Amani. "I give you one command to follow while you are away. Do not waste his time. Absorb what he would say and teach you. Let not his words fall to the ground of deaf ears."

Amani bowed and replied. "I believe those are three commands, my king."

N'Kosi looked at M'Msee. "Take him, Hutari, and see if you can do something about his mouth while you are at it."

M'Msee looked at Amani, who gave them both a feigned look of offense and replied. "There are some things not even the son of Hesphus can do."

M'Msee motioned for Amani to follow, and the two men left to trek to Moshek.

Chapter
Thirty-Three

The Truth

Many circles had passed since Amani last was outside the boundaries of Hogarth. His duties as ward to the King meant he was always at his ruler's beck and call. If the King left the land, Amani would also leave. But the Sandking chose to stay safely within the boundaries of his nation. Cautious to treat with other nations in person ever since the recent attempt on his life. Amani knew that although Hogarth was powerful, it was not invincible. And N'Kosi was wise not to venture from his domain.

And now, as Amani left the borders of Hogarth and trekked close to the borders of his homeland, he could not help but think of his home. To wonder about the state of his nation and of his parents.

"M'Msee. How fares my father and mother?"

M'Msee was quick to reply. "Haidar cannot, of course, publicly speak of you. But your banishment has left a rift between your parents. Your mother mourns her son as though he were dead. And blames your father for his choice to be a king before a father. However, she cannot bring herself to accept that if Haidar were not king, you might not have even been given the choice to live. He is king and your father. Finding a path that would assuage both claims would test any ruler. Your banishment was a choice you and I know would weigh on any ruler. When all is said and done, they both sorely miss their son."

Amani sighed. He understood the choice of his father. It was a king's choice. A choice other men of lesser stature are privileged to not make."

Amani listened and, though he was loath to agree with M'Msee, he neither could dismiss his words. Kings were not like other men. Their decisions are beyond the thought of those they rule. He remembered watching N'Kosi rule. Watched as the Hogarth king sentenced people to die for their crimes. No one was exempt from his judgment whether they be men or in rare cases, women. In private, N'Kosi had expressed that he enjoyed the company of some he was forced to punish. He never took pleasure in the deed. And despite his personal feelings, their decisions forced his hand to enforce the laws he had helped create. Thus, when such people were discovered of crimes, he could not keep them in his presence lest his competence and integrity be impugned. Watching his father and now N'Kosi taught him a simple principle. A ruler who will not rule fairly will not rule long. He allowed himself to move from the thoughts of how he might have acted if he had a son and mediated on the duo's journey ahead. He thought of his trek with his father to Moshek. And now a second time he traveled to the mountain with someone he cared for and someone who cared for him. Moshek and its magics was where he first envisioned the Kifu. Where he knew that the creature's existence was not a myth. Moshek was where he learned M'Msee was the one to dispatch the Kifu to the deep. And it was at Moshek where he learned the Ephasians had erected one of their portal gates. And with such, he could walk from one end of Tanara to another. And now he wondered what other mysteries he would learn at the mount, and he expressed his wonder aloud.

"So why Moshek? What is it about the mountain that we travel there?"

M'Msee looked forward as his horse swayed under him and replied. "It is one of the few places where the power of Aaru can be exercised without risk. The mountain blocks the Nephty's ability to sense this power. In the mount, our abilities are invisible to the Kifu. Hesphus, even asleep, can sense the power of Aaru, if your use changes elements, moves oceans, or changes the patterns of the weather, he can sense you enough to wake from his sleep.

Amani strained to understand. "Then Moshek is a shield of some sort?"

"Of a sort. Know, young prince, that there are ley lines of great power that run throughout Tanara. Several of these lines run through Moshek. The power of Tanara itself masks Aarunite power. We go to train. I must see what you can do without concern that our actions will give notice to the creature."

Amani eyes narrowed in suspicion. "Exactly want is it you desire to teach me?"

"To understand the power that life has over death." The aged man replied.

Amani knew Moshek was seven suns by horseback from Hogarth and they had just left the shadowed maw of the Dark-mouth, venturing now into the lands of the Medja. As they passed, Amani's thoughts wandered back to his last journey this way. It felt like a lifetime past, yet he knew there were only two routes from Hogarth to Moshek: past the pyramids of the Medja or along a path that skirted near his homeland, tracing the outskirts of their lands. A question, long-simmering, finally broke free, and he voiced it to his godfather.

"M'Msee? In all my studies and your recounting of your travels about Tanara, I noticed you have never mentioned the Medja to me. Father himself rarely, if ever, mentioned them. But their home towers in the sky, visible from a distance from both Bussar and Hogarth. I know we could cut through their lands, or ride near home. You appear that you will not travel directly through their lands. Before my captivity to the Sandking, I had never encountered them before. Father commanded me from traveling near their border during my rite of passage. But now I am a man and servant to another king. Will you now tell me about them? For upon my last time upon this way, they happened upon us and a dreadful fog lifted from the ground. I note that no such thing occurs now. Why and what can you tell me of them?"

M'Msee chuckled. "I was told by the Medja that you threatened them."

Amani then snapped the reins of his horse and galloped and placed the animal barring his mentor's path, preventing M'Msee from moving further. "Wait, they speak to you?"

M'Msee's jerked back, surprised by the interrogative nature and action of his godson, and replied. "And what, my son? Would you threaten me as well? Is this not the way of Enkai?"

Amani's face grimaced in anger. "M'Msee do not toy with me. No riddles within riddles. No puzzles that lead to more questions. Please answer me. Do I not deserve to know the truth? Who are you? Really?"

M'Msee sighed and spoke. "It will be night soon, and the wilderness will get cold. Come, and I will answer any question to me. But beware, my son, some truths kept from you when you were a child are horrors when known as adults."

Amani moved his horse, and the two continued their ride as the looming pyramids, which towered over the Medja's trench, loomed in the distance. M'Msee could feel the eyes of his godson impatiently pressing for answers and spoke. "Understand, Amani, that I am older than you might understand. When you look into the sky and see the sun rise and fall, you call it a day. And when the seasons change, and Tanara travels its full journey around the sun, you call it a circle. I have lived in Tanara for over five hundred of these circles. I have seen history turn over and over, and I have turned with it. But you have surmised this by now, have you not?"

"Amani nodded. "I had once asked father if he knew how old you were. But he said he did not know. Only that you walked with his grandfather and father."

"Yes, my son, and his grandfather before him. I have viewed Tanara from the stars above and am almost as old as Tanara itself."

Amani seemed shocked at this answer but wanted to learn more. "How is such a thing possible?"

M'Msee continues. I am from above. You are from below. I am from Aaru. And Aaru sits higher than even the stars you see above you. In Tanara, you look up and see stars. From Aaru, I once looked down and saw them."

Amani marveled at how such a thing could be but continued in his inquiry. "And the Medja?" Amani asked.

"The Medja are from a race of men once called the Medjani. They were one of the few races that escaped the Age of Light and survived to see the Second Age. Most of the Medjani were destroyed during the Endwar fighting against the Kifu. But most of those that survived pledged themselves to me. Pledged themselves to the work I have dedicated my life to. The Medja order watch for those that have the Karash'Enu the God taint."

"What is it?" asked Amani.

"The Karash'Enu is the Kifu's influence, the power or Aaru that has manifested to become contaminated, dangerous, and darkly powerful. The Kifu's march during the war contaminated the land. Spreading contagion. Akuma's power resident and seeded in Tanara to bring ascension is sometimes given to one. But because of the Kifu, that power sometimes becomes corrupted. All those born in Tanara and who hold the power of Aaru are susceptible to it. These men and women are rare. But Akuma's life is in Tanara, and occasionally it sprouts within a person or a creature to create a godling. In the common tongue of Zaratu, it is called *Enari*. It sprouts in someone like you. And when an Enari is found, they must be trained. But most times they are killed."

Amani looked troubled. "Killed? Am I then being led to my death?"

M'Msee chuckled. "No, I saw long ago that you were an obedient youth of wisdom. You would not use your power recklessly. You would not endanger Tanara by releasing the Kifu. Or by becoming a minion of Enkai. Enari are sometimes unstable in the mind. If they are allowed to live or not controlled, they could dominate men and unleash havoc. The Medja help to maintain the garden of Tanara. They prune the weeds so that the grass may grow unfettered. Enkai can speak to his own. And the Enari are of his work. Not Akuma. An Enari cannot be allowed to live lest they give room for Enkai to enter the world."

"Wait, so you have killed Enari...others like me before?" said Amani.

"I have. And will again if the need were to arise. When I tell you that nothing can be before keeping the Kifu asleep to stop Enkai from entering this world. I do not lie. If Hesphus were to awake and be loosed from his bonds, there is little on Tanara that could stop him this time."

"But if you are Hutari, can't you defeat him a second time?"

"Perhaps, but I am old...my strength I have given to keep Hesphus asleep. And much of my power I have spent on this cause. I knew long ago that there must be another trained who can, if needed, battle the Kifu. I believe I have found such a one in you, Amani of Bussar."

Amani was quiet, attempting to digest what had been told to him. And assessing what responsibility M'Msee might expect from him. Or what duty he thought Amani was suited for. He turned over thoughts in his mind and noted out of the corner of his eye that M'Msee looked at him as if waiting for him to articulate more of these thoughts. Amani instead looked at the dusk sky and took in the fresh desert air as they rode peacefully through the Medja's trench. He stared at the jagged surroundings and remembered the promise he had made to the mages who tested him in the trench.

"No Death Cloud is descending upon us, Wisdom. I see no undead that walk here. Why?"

M'Msee chuckled. "The undead have not strode the world in mass since the defeat of the Kifu. Be grateful that this is so. What you have seen are but tricks of the mind. What the Medjani call *Kujisa*. It means "living reflection or mirror of fear". They can conjure from the mind the fears of those they encounter. Few are powerful enough to resist their magic. But the images you and the men of Hogarth saw were not real. Nothing more than a group phantasm. A ruse to keep the Medja safe from kings and wicked men who would seek to enslave them and use their power for selfish ends. The Medjani are not who you think they are. They are scholars, counselors, and advisers to kings with delegations across Tanara. They are Halamari "ones who speak peace" and broker peace between nations and factions of men. They are but some of those who serve me that peace may rule in Tanara and warn me if the need arises. It is they who, on my behalf, brokered peace between Bussar and Hogarth, and who stand between the two nations as a surety that none cross with intent for war."

Amani looked at M'Msee with concern. "Wait, warn you of what?"

"If signs are shown that my father has awakened. On the day that this is so, know that we will enter the fourth age of Tanara, and the world will once more be plunged into darkness. If that day ever comes, I must gather the races of men once more to combat the walking death."

Amani's face soured, "You said earlier that *most* of the Medjani serve you — not all?"

M'Msee sighed "No, not all. There is a faction of Medja, who serve Enkai. Those who would seek to see the Kifu rise and destroy me and open the door for Enkai to ravage Tanara. They are called the *Medja Shakuro,* the Black Medja. They have been known to shelter the Enari."

Amani looked at M'Msee, concerned. "But why? What possible gain could come from such a thing?"

M'Msee stopped his horse, and Amani did the same. "Know, boy, that Enkai is very real. He is greater than even I. And holds the power to create worlds. A power given to him by Akuma himself. But Tanara is a mockery to Enkai as it is the living testament to Hesphus's power to bring true life into the stars and its existence stands as a living testament to Enkai's failure. *My* existence and escape from his capture grates at him from afar. My life is a taunt to his children's deformity. For the Nephthys are a misshapen people, they are *Zithurani* bound by death. And never forget that, just one... one Amani. One Nephthys controlled by my uncle from Aaru almost destroyed Tanara. And in Aaru there are thousands, times tens of thousands, that he controls with his magics. A horde so thirsty for life, they at one time threatened even his existence. I have sought counsel to find a way to return to Aaru to destroy Enkai or the Nephthys. And we have determined with the help of the Medjani that the Nephthys cannot be destroyed without destroying Enkai. Nor can they feast upon him, for he is the source of what insignificant life they possess; lest they die. They are *Nashara,* each having the essence of the other. Each sharing each other's life: strengthening one another. Enkai seeks to break this union. Understand that he believes that taking my life and that of Tanara will not just feed his children, but make them whole. And he will stop at nothing to make this happen. He will promise to give men whatever they desire. If they help him breach the magics Akuma has placed around you all. And know that of a certainty that if Akuma's standard to protect Tanara ever fails. You, me, all that you know and love. Know of a certainty that we will all be destroyed."

M'Msee turned his stead towards the boundary of Bussar and the two rode in somberness.

Amani ceased his questions for a time. They were still several days' ride to Moshek, and he knew his godfather enough to know that he would not appreciate being continuously pelted with questions the entire ride there. Especially those that required him to relive the tragedies of his father's defeat at the hands of Enkai.

***

The two men sauntered upon their horses to the mouth of the cave, the jagged entry was a dark maw opening into the bowels of Mt. Moshek. Dismounting, Amani gathered their gear, his movements purposeful yet tinged with an unspoken reverence for what lay ahead. M'Msee, leaning upon his cane with deceptive frailty, took a step forward, casting a sidelong glance at Amani. The old man's weathered face was shadowed, and unreadable, but his eyes glinted with a strange light.

"Come, boy," M'Msee said, his voice resonating with both gentleness and command. The title was one he'd never abandoned, though Amani was far from a child.

Together, they crossed the threshold, swallowed by the cool darkness that pressed in as they wound deeper and deeper into the mountain. For a time, silence wrapped around them, broken only by the rhythmic crunch of boots on stone and the occasional murmur of water dripping somewhere in the depths. Amani blinked, eyes straining to adjust to the dim, but he could sense M'Msee moving confidently beside him, each step sure and precise. He knew this place, Amani realized, every nook, every hidden fissure of stone. It was as though the dark belonged to M'Msee, and he, in turn, belonged to it.

They came to a bluish-lit cavern where a faint, eerie glow spilled down the walls, illuminating strange symbols etched into the stone—markings that seemed to twist and shimmer like ghostly firelight. Amani dropped his pack and straightened, glancing around the cavern with fascination mingled with apprehension.

M'Msee walked to the center of the cavern, his cane clacking once against the floor, and turned to face him. His gaze, sharp as the point of a dagger, settled on Amani.

"Show me," M'Msee said quietly, his words carrying a weight that made Amani stand taller. "Show me what I taught you all those years ago if you remember it. You haven't grown soft, I hope."

Amani met M'Msee's eyes and nodded. "I remember, old man," he replied, a slight smirk playing on his lips.

Without another word, Amani shifted into a fighting stance, legs braced wide, body poised and taut. M'Msee's stance remained deceptively relaxed, one hand resting atop his cane. But Amani knew better than to be fooled by that ease.

He sprang forward, faster than any mortal eye could track, his fist slicing toward M'Msee's shoulder. In a blink, M'Msee dodged with supernatural grace, sidestepping and swiping his cane up to block Amani's arm, deflecting the blow with the sound of wood cracking against knuckles. The jolt shot up Amani's arm, but he didn't pause. Instead, he pivoted on his heel and lunged again, this time aiming lower.

They danced back and forth across the cavern, their bodies moving with an elegance honed by years of practice and training. Amani threw punches and kicks in rapid succession, each move blending into the next, but M'Msee parried every strike effortlessly, eyes glinting with something close to pride. He let Amani push, let him test his strength against him, almost as if he was holding back.

But M'Msee's restraint only lasted so long. With a sudden shift, M'Msee ducked beneath Amani's punch, abandoning his cane to lunge forward. He seized Amani's wrist, twisted it behind him with a ferocity that belied his age, and swept Amani's legs out from under him in one swift motion. Amani landed hard; the wind knocked from his chest as M'Msee pinned him with an iron grip.

"You're faster," M'Msee muttered approvingly, his face close to Amani's, "but not enough."

Amani gritted his teeth, muscles straining, and pushed back against the old man's hold. His strength was formidable, honed by years of rigorous training and now enhanced by an uncanny power he still didn't fully understand. M'Msee held him firm for a heartbeat longer, but then, with a final surge of will, Amani forced himself up, breaking free.

They squared off again, breaths heavy, and this time, Amani's gaze was fierce, almost defiant. He'd waited for this moment, trained for it—trained to be the man who could stand against even M'Msee. The tension in the air thickened as he shifted his stance, summoning every ounce of strength he possessed. He lunged forward, twisting to deliver a blow that was precise and devastating, aimed not to harm but to kill.

The blow struck home, landing directly at M'Msee's side with a force that echoed through the cavern. Yet, as swiftly as it came, M'Msee's hand intercepted the strike, catching Amani's wrist in a grip that felt like iron. He held it there, eyes boring into Amani's with a mixture of pride and something else—something darker, edged with caution.

M'Msee nodded slowly, his grip loosening at last, though his hand remained steady. He lifted his hands to signal the discontinuance of their sparring, and the old man reached sat upon a rock and leaned upon his cane.

"You would have killed a lesser man," he mumbled, his voice barely more than a murmur in the cavern's eerie stillness. "But do not think that such might brings power. It does not. It only brings enslavement to the want of more. And so now you must be ever mindful that you do not follow the path of Enkai. To truly follow Akuma, to learn the lessons he tried to teach his sons, is to know that the power of creation is what grants true power. To create and to give life — not to take it. For it takes nothing to destroy. The power of Akuma is to create life. To bring something from nothing into existence. This is the inheritance of the sons of god, a passing of wisdom I now give to you. Remember that Enkai failed in his bid to bring life into the world. Master the power of life, not death, and you will achieve something not even a god can do. Behold."

M'Msee held out his hand took a knife, and sliced his palm. He squeezed his hand, and blood fell to the volcanic dirt floor of Mt. Moshek. He grabbed some of the bloodstained mud molded it into a ball and held it into his hands and the viscous glob turned into a small mountain hare. M'Msee then placed the small creature on the ground, and it darted into the darkness of the caves.

"This, my son, is power." M'Msee's voice thrummed with a depth that seemed to echo from the earth itself. "To create life. Death is not the domain of Akuma. Death is the domain of men. To create life. That is the domain of gods. Do life young man and leave death when possible to lesser men." He paused and stretched out his hands for Amani to see. "Know that it was these hands that cut the umbilical between you and your mother." He flexed his fingers and held his hands aloft. "It was these hands that were used when N'Kosi's wife lay barren and allowed her flesh to bring forth a child." M'Msee leaned close, his gaze fierce yet tender. "And it is this heart that stands between the Kifu and the obliteration of the world of men. Always remember, my son, that it is life that withstands the shadows of oblivion. Not power, nor wealth. But the fierce love of life and those that protect it that guard against the darkness. Know this and know peace. Betray this lesson and the path you tread will, in time, lead you into the grip of Enkai."

Amani looked at M'Msee, attempting to absorb all that was said to him. "M'Msee, you just made a rabbit out of mud. Are you suggesting that *I* can create life?"

M'Msee inclined his head, his eyes dark with a knowing that stretched beyond mortal years. "You and I possess the power to resurrect, transfer, and, yes, create life itself. And if you can abide in time, you might be the key to saving even Aaru itself. I have traveled the breadth and width of Tanara, and I say that the power of Akuma flows through you in a way I have only seen once in my travels. Rarely has a mortal held the power of Aaru as you do... except me." He paused, a ghost of a smile tugging at his lips. "But by now we both know you know I am no mere man." He looked away as if peering through the veil of centuries past. "I don't fully understand how or why," he continued, his voice low. "Yet my father, before he was turned into this vile abomination of life, shared a truth—that Akuma's essence was buried like a seed, waiting. I know not exactly for what purpose, I can only guess. But after a thousand silent years, it seems his seed has finally borne fruit... in you."

"But you taught us that Hesphus shaped this world," the young one questions, a glint of defiance mingling with curiosity in his gaze. "Does that mean we share this power?"

M'Msee's gaze grew distant, shadows of memory clouding his eyes. "Once, I wielded the power of Aaru to strike down my own father, all to keep his vision of Tanara alive. That day, my strength tore through the very bones of this world." He took a slow breath, his voice dropping to a murmur edged with reverence and fear. "I dread to use such power again while my feet still tread the soil of Tanara. To use the world force once more. The very power to create a world here, with that force... it would shatter this one into ruin."

He fixed his gaze on Amani, his tone a quiet warning. "Yes, you, too, hold the power to create life. But whether it matches the scale of my father's or his father before him, I cannot say. Attempting to birth a new world on Tanara would be a death sentence for it. Remember this well—you must never summon such power here." His voice softened, a rare hint of hope shining through. "But perhaps, one day, from the distant reaches of Aaru... perhaps there, you may yet shape worlds."

Amani looked at his mentor puzzled and M'Msee smirked and continued with his lesson.

The old man raised his hand to the sky, fingers curling as if grasping something unseen, something sacred. His voice softened, reverberating like the last echoes of a storm. "The power of Akuma is to reach forth with one's hand and gather the very threads of existence and weave them to create. His eyes darkened, haunted by memory. "These threads are fearsome. With them, you can pull at the oceans and tear asunder the land. During the End War against my father, I summoned all my might towards one purpose... to defeat Hesphus. And in doing so, that one act leveled entire civilizations and drowned lands never to be seen again. Zar'atal, Drakhar, Tarkan, all nations swallowed by the earth, destroyed by great storms, or drowned by the sea."

M'Msee stared at his raised hand as if observing a thing of disgust. "All destroyed by this reckless hand. Wiped clean from Tanara by the power needed to defeat the Kifu." His hand clenched, his voice carrying the weight of a thousand shattered lives. "I have vowed a vow to never wield the power of Aaru in that manner again. The risk is far too great. And so, I have traveled the length and breadth of Tanara to escape the eyes of wayward men who would seek to use me and this power that they might consume it for their lusts. To subjugate one another to feed their lust.

He looked away, his gaze falling on the murals depicted on the cavern's walls, murals archived in stone the great battle of men against the undead. M'Msee closed his eyes. His thoughts were heavy with the burden of years "In all my travels have I made Bussar home, because your people, Amani, bear a love for

Akuma and his ways that is pure. The Bussarim do not seek to rule over the lives of other men."

M'Msee pointed his staff at the mural on the cavern wall. "I have walked the earth until those that have known me are dead. Trekked until the knowledge of my power has become myth, all that my presence would no more entice kings and mages and the common man from worshiping me as a God. But to a few have I revealed myself so that those who can shape the course of this world might know that should the Kifu once more rise. I and they upon my calling must once more assemble to battle the threat. I have done this to protect you and to keep the Kifu...my father asleep lest his waking once more rends the world."

Amani nodded with an awareness and understanding. He had watched how alone King N'Kosi was as the ruler of Hogarth. He could only imagine how alone M'Msee must have felt. Perhaps wondering who truly cared for him. To always wonder if those who surrounded him only saw him as a means to an end. He gradually understood the wisdom of M'Msee to remain hidden. His curiosity got the better of him and he queried his godfather once more. "The scrolls tell that many thousands died in the great war."

M'Msee face grew downcast as he reminisced of things past. "Thousands upon ten thousands."

Amani looked at his mentor and said. "And of those who have died. Can we bring them back?"

M'Msee looked away and grimaced. He paused, as if unsure whether or not to answer.

He turned away.

"Wisdom?" said Amani.

M'Msee looked up and into the eyes of his godson. "Yes, the power to return the living to this life is possible. But know this. It is not a joy to return the dead to life, my son. For the dead know nothing of what came before. To use the power of Akuma this way is akin to the wickedness of Enkai. It is to hold hostage the life spark of a person's soul. To prevent them from crossing the river of life, to return that spark of life to another. This refusal to release, which must be returned to the ground, causes the plague of Hesphus when he walks. What is the saying that your people say? *'Return to the wilderness that which belongs to the wilderness.'* To hold hostage life that must be returned to Akuma is what steals the life from the soil itself and turns the land black such that even plants cannot grow. You must never use Akuma's power in this way. Lest *you* could become Kifu. For the use of such power is a consumption. I have learned this...to my hurt. And now I too am a prisoner bound to Hesphus, who in my foolishness thought my father could be freed."

M'Msee reached out with his hand for Amani to support him. Amani grabbed the old man, and they walked to a stone bench and sat down.

"I could have killed him then, Amani. I could have rid the world of the Kifu. But for a moment I saw him." M'Msee was almost tearful.

"Saw who, Wisdom?"

He looked at Amani as if he released a great burden of regret. "My father...Hesphus. For the power of Aaru had burned him so that he could not heal as before. The creature within him was injured and for the moment severed from the influence of its master. And when it no longer controlled Hesphus' mind. My father ceased from being the creature men call the Kifu. And Hesphus was alive once more and able to speak."

"And what did he say?" said Amani.

"Kill me," said M'Msee. His voice was a mixture of regret and sorrow.

Amani gasped. He surmised the rest from the look on M'Msee's face and what he knew of history. "And of course this you did not do. But kept him alive...to what, to free him?"

"Enkai would not let my father die. He would use his body to house one of his children...and raise the corpse of Hesphus. Holding his spark prisoner locked within his own body, unable to return to Akuma. Watching from Aaru as the Nephty's made my father destroy the very world he had created. Puppeteering from afar the burning of the creation he could not make. A jealous god was Enkai. In his envy, he would see Tanara burned to ash. A seared and lifeless orb floating among the stars. And all in his rage to find me. And free his children from their accursed thirst for life."

"How can your uncle be so rabid as to seek to kill his nephew?" wondered Amani.

M'Msee guffawed. "You think Enkai is such a monster that he knows not love? To me, he is evil incarnate. A being resolute in destroying anything that stands in his way. I have witnessed with my own eyes the battle between him and Hesphus. Witnessed my father falling at his hand and being turned into the horror men call the Kifu. But even I know that the dark one loves. He too has children. Even the Nephthys are hostage to the impatience and the foolishness of their father. For Enkai did not follow the dictates of Akuma and never learned the properties needed to sustain life and now they are unfinished, broken. A tumor of creation that does nothing but consume. Enkai hunts me because he believes that my life will allow his offspring to thrive and restore his children to a life of normalcy and in doing so release he and they from the chains that he, in his foolishness, have created. I have learned from the Nephty's in my father. Its secrets over centuries have been revealed. In the same way, I have kept the Kifu asleep. Enkai keeps his children under control. From his creation, with the help of the Medja have I learned this. He is as much a prisoner as I...more so. He would stop at nothing to loose himself from the *Gathuri* of his own making. For in the same way, if I were to relent, the Kifu would run amok, so too would he be overwhelmed by his own. Aaru is not just the birthplace of creation, my son. It has become his prison. One that he desperately seeks escape."

Amani looked at his Master of Studies and spoke. "He would kill you just to take your life and give it to them to finish the work he started? To free himself? Incredible."

M'Msee nodded. "Not just me, boy. But all life on Tanara. The stars are dung to him if he believes a solution exists to complete this task. He is fixated on nothing else and has destroyed his family and broken creation to obtain what he seeks. He believes that my power added to the Nephty's would sustain them forever. He needed a god like him. Like his father to complete his work. I am all that remains of the family of Aaru. Only two exist, from what men call Heaven. But I am cast out. Hunted. And like my father, captive in a world never meant for me." A tear welled up in the old man's eye. And Amani having heard the tale of the Hutari his whole life. Never considered that this world was not M'Msee's home. Never thought that he might yearn to return. Or that he was an exile on the run. A fugitive hiding and ever moving to escape the clutches of the god Enkai. Fleeing from his own uncle. And it was at that moment Amani sorrowed for his godfather. But pity turned to a hardened resolve.

"What can I do to help Wisdom?"

M'Msee smiled, knowing he had chosen well. "You have shown me your combat training. Now show me the power of Aaru."

Amani stood and looked through the cavern and found a cropping of stone. He lifted his hand, and a ball of electricity crackled in his palm. He then, with his other hand, summoned another orb and he rolled the sparking spheres together until they merged and grew larger. The heat in the chamber increased, and it grew hazy, and the clothing of both M'Msee and Amani began to smoke. Amani then flicked his wrists and released a bolt at the stone column, and it split in two and shards flew toward them both and simply bounced off the two men. The mountain echoed as thunder and a tremor could be felt in the earthen floor.

M'Msee nodded. "You have learned control...good, good. And your strength?"

Amani looked at M'Msee, puzzled. "Strength Wisdom?"

M'Msee rose and walked gingerly to a boulder and threw his walking stick to the ground and extended his arms around the boulder and his fingers dug into the stone and he lifted the rock and squeezed, and it shattered in his arms."

Amani stood wide-eyed, and his hands instinctively lifted to cover his face to protect himself. He had never seen M'Msee display his power. But he always sensed that he was a threat if he chose to be. His presence somehow projected an unspoken message to anyone who might dare attack him. Tread at your own risk. There was an aura to him, a presence unspoken yet felt. Invisible yet seen. And now Amani saw for himself why kings, Medja, and warriors bowed to M'Msee. He was his god-father, a grumpy but beloved mentor he had known all his life. But here in the depths of Moshek. In the twilight of a cavern created during the last great war, when the Kifu was defeated. Amani understood M'Msee was more than a man. He was the son of Hesphus. A child of Aaru and the fabled Hutari.

"Why do you stand amazed? You gawk at the feet of strength that you have seen me display with a rock. But look here." M'Msee pointed to a small stream that wound its way through the cavern. "This water has cut a path through the stone. Not by sheer force, but by consistency. By repeated movement across the stone's surface. This repetitiveness has worn a path such that the stone has given way to the water. This also is strength, my son. Know which strength is needed at any given time and you will be strong on all occasions. And if you forget this lesson, remember this one."

"And what is that?" asked Amani.

"Always remember that a flea can trouble a lion more than the lion can trouble the flea."

"Meaning?" Asked Amani. "Meaning, my son, never underestimate the power of small things. Now this last piece of wisdom I leave you, for your father and mother have arrived."

Amani turned in shock and the flood of emotions draped over him as joy coupled with grief overwhelmed him as he beheld for the first time in three years, the faces of his parents. The stoic but gentle outline of his father's kingly face and the soft nurturing smile of his mother gleamed in the cave light. And Mudiwa ran to him and the two opened their arms and embraced in tears and sobs of joy.

Haidar was slower in approaching. The last he saw his son, he had sentenced him to kill or be killed. A decision that ached at him as his duty as king of his people took precedence over his love as a father. But before him now was not a citizen of Bussar but his grown flesh, his beloved son. Haidar was a proud man, but the weight of the years of regret of his decision and the wonder of the wellbeing of his son who now stood before him and the memories were too much to bear and his eyes also began to well, he struggled in a pathetic attempt to speak. To apologize and explain himself. But as he searched for words and strove to bypass his pride to utter them, he was engulfed in the embrace of his only son. Emotions flooded him and the wellspring of guilt and turmoil was released with the simplest words of a son to his father. "I forgive you."

And when Haidar heard the words of his son, he allowed himself the joy or the receipt of love and responded by embracing his son and the two men sobbed as the years of separation rained from their eyes.

M'Msee looked back on the family, once broken, now restored. He smiled, knowing that for the moment, they would have peace. He looked at his hand which was withering, he could feel the numbness that increasingly made itself evident in his body. A small pustule of blood revealed itself on his hand. A sore wound he knew would not heal. A tale tell sign that the Kifu was feeding upon his life.

M'Msee sighed, knowing that he must hurry to prepare Amani before it was too late. Time was running out.

To Be Continued...

Appendix

Timeline of Hutari and the World of Tanara

The Dawning before Time and Tanara

   Duration: Unknown (Shrouded in Myth: Time of the Ather)

- Akuma creates Aaru

- Akuma creates Hesphus and Enkai and commissions them to study to create a world.

- Enkai creates The Duat and the Nephtys

- Hesphus creates Tanara **(This period after Tanara's creation and before Hutari falls is the Age of First Light: 0 A.)**

- Hesphus creates a son named Hutari **(5500 A.)**

- Akuma anticipates Enkai's actions and seeds himself in Tanara. His essence provides a protective shell over the planet, preventing Enkai's direct incursion.

- Enkai and Hesphus battle over Hutari and the Nephthys are unleashed in Aaru.

- Hutari escapes Aaru and falls to Tanara **(6000 A.)**

- **(This event ends the Time of the Ather and begins the Second Age of Tanara: 0 A.C.) Hutari is 500 years old.)**

- Enkai places a Nephtys within the defeated Hesphus and raises him as the Kifu, an entropic force of nature to capture Hutari and destroy all life on Tanara.

- The Kifu falls from Aaru to Tanara in pursuit of Hutari **(40 A.C.)** destroying everything in its wake and making undead life.

1. The Age of First Light (Before Hutari's Fall)
Duration: Unknown (Shrouded in Myth)
Calendar: The period before the fall of Hutari is speculative, but scholars estimate it spans thousands of Tanarian circles (years). This era is divided into the First Age, with its great civilizations flourishing, especially the Ephasians and their ley-line mastery. Time was less formally measured by many cultures during this age, except for the most advanced, like the Ephasians.
Key Events: A (Time of the Ather)

- **0 A.** – The beginning of known civilization: ancient kingdoms such as Ephasia, Medja, and Tarkan rise. The Ephasians harness leyline magic and construct their Teleportation Gates.

- **6000 A.** – The height of Ephasia's power: The Ephasians expanded their gates and constructed the Walking Guardians, gaining control over vast territories.

2. The Fall of Hutari (Creation of the Navel) "When the stars blinked" The Second Age.

Calendar Reset: This event reset the calendar, marking Year **0 A.C.** (After Creation). The Creation of the Navel of the World, formed by Hutari's fall, becomes the new baseline for Tanara's history. All records after this point are based on this cataclysmic event.

Key Events:

- **0 A.C.** – **The Fall of Hutari**: Hutari (M'Msee) falls from the celestial realm, creating the **Navel of the World**. This marks the beginning of the **Second Age**.

- The disruption of the world's leylines begins, throwing magical currents out of balance. This causes natural disasters, leyline distortions, and the malfunctioning of Ephasian gates.

- **10-20 A.C.** – **The Leyline Crisis**: The instability of leylines grows worse, affecting many civilizations. The

Ephasians, dependent on leylines for transportation and power, begin to experience catastrophic failures in their teleportation gates. Whole cities were said to have vanished. King Donovan in a desperate bid to keep the Kifu from using the gates of Ephasia sacrificed himself and his kingdom to prevent the evil god Enkai from breaching the realm of Tanara and stayed Tanara's destruction.

3. The Age of Dread or Night (The March of the Kifu) aka The Reaping.

Calendar: The time after Hutari's fall is divided into two **Eras**: the **Era of Hutari's Fall** and the **Era of the Kifu's March**. The **Era of the Kifu's March** begins forty years after the fall of Hutari when the Kifu arrives. The most catastrophic events are marked in **Great Circles** and **Years**. This 40-year time period is where men fought to survive and is also known as the End War.

Key Events:

- **40 A.C. – The Arrival of the Kifu: The Reaping of Life aka "the Reaping", and "The End War."**

- The Kifu falls to Tanara seeking Hutari. This begins the Era of the Kifu's March. Its impact crater is called "Hesphu Akar." Meaning "The Abyss of Shadows" it is a desolate place where no life dwells.

The Kifu, the undead God Hesphus, descended during this time from the stars. He is an embodiment of chaos, death, and corruption. Unlike later generations, the people of the Age of Legends had no knowledge or warning of the Kifu's power.

- The Kifu corrupted entire regions, twisting the land into wastelands and creating undead of entire peoples. It devastated early human civilizations.

- The Kifu's Nature: Hesphus was more than just a creature of destruction; he embodied the primal force of entropy. Wherever the Kifu walked, life withered, time seemed to distort, and reality itself frayed.

- The Kifu marches across the world, laying waste to all he encounters. The Kifu's armies cross even the ocean floor, spreading death to civilizations untouched by the mainland's chaos. Entire cultures, such as the Ephasians and the Tarkan, are annihilated.

- In the end, the civilizations of the Age of Legends were overwhelmed by the Kifu's relentless advance. Entire cities were razed, and kingdoms fell into ruin. Many of the most powerful magics and technologies of the ancient world were lost during this time.

- The Kassuran Empire crumbled into dust; their great strongholds swallowed by the earth. The Medjani, in their final act of defiance, sealed away their greatest knowledge in hidden vaults, hoping future generations might reclaim it.

- The Lokohi were driven beneath the waves, and their once-great empire became a legend whispered by coastal peoples.

- Only a few remnants of these civilizations survived, scattered across the world in small, isolated tribes and settlements. They retained fragments of their ancient knowledge but had largely forgotten the true scope of their former greatness.

- **40-80 A.C. – The Destruction of Ephasia**: The Kifu's armies sweep across Ephasia, destroying their cities. Their advanced technology is no match for the relentless tide of undead. The malfunctioning Teleportation Gates cause more havoc, transporting some cities to unknown dimensions and trapping others in perpetual loops of time. The Ephasian Walking Guardians are unable to defend against the Kifu's magic, and the empire collapses.

- **80 A.C. – The Battle of the Seas**: The Kifu crosses the oceans to reach the lands where Hutari now resides. This event is chronicled in both myth and history, as survivors recall the dead walking beneath the waves, creating whirlpools and dragging entire ships down into the depths.

- **80 A.C. – The Final Battle**: After forty years of terror, Hutari and the remaining allied forces of Tanara confront the Kifu in the far western lands. Hutari uses the leylines to trap or destroy the Kifu, but the victory is bittersweet. The destruction wrought by the Kifu and the power Hutari had to use to stop the Kifu leaves Tanara in ruins.

4. The Age of Rebirth (500 Years After the Kifu's Defeat) The Third Age.

Calendar: This age is measured from **0 R.B.** (Rebirth), marking the defeat of the Kifu. The **Era of Rebirth** starts after the Kifu is defeated. This new era is characterized by slow recovery, a return to civilization, and attempts to rebuild a shattered world. This marks the beginning of the third age.

Key Events:

- **0 R.B. – The Defeat of the Kifu**: The undead menace of the Kifu is vanquished, marking the end of the **Age of Dread**. Hutari, now a weary and guilt-ridden figure, helps guide the remaining peoples of Tanara toward rebuilding.

- **50 R.B. – The Wandering of Hutari**: Hutari, having lived for 1000 **circles** (years), spends the next several centuries wandering the world, witnessing the rebuilding efforts and helping where needed, but remaining distant from leadership or direct power. In some places he is revered, others despise him for not completing the destruction of the Kifu.

- **200-500 R.B. – Resurgence of New Kingdoms**: New kingdoms arise, but they are wary of tapping into leyline magic after witnessing the extinction of the Ephasians. Some rulers, however, begin secret explorations of ancient Ephasian ruins, hoping to uncover lost technology and power.

- **500 R.B. (Present Day)** – Five hundred years after the Kifu's defeat, Tanara remains scarred but has healed. The Navel of the World still serves as a reminder of Hutari's fall, and the ruins of **Ephasia** are a forbidden zone where leyline anomalies, malfunctioning Walking Guardians, and strange time warps keep adventurers at bay.

Epochs and Calendar Structure

The Great Ages of Tanara are divided into notable Epochs based on key historical events. The timeline also incorporates the celestial cycles of the world, measured in circles (years) and seasons.

Units of Time:

- **1 Circle** = 1 Tanarian Year (the time it takes for the planet to orbit its sun, similar to Earth's year).

- **10 Circles** = 1 **Decade**.

- **100 Circles** = 1 **Great Circle**.

- **500 Circles** = Half a Millennium, the significant unit for marking larger epochs of history.

Recorded History at a Glance:

1. **Age of First Light: aka The Age of Legends (The First Age)**

- Early civilizations, pre-Hutari.

- Marked by the Ephasians' rise and the construction of the leyline network and teleportation gates.

1. **Age of Hutari's Fall: (The Second Age)**

- The fall of Hutari and the subsequent leyline disruptions, leading to the collapse of great civilizations like the Ephasians.

1. **Age of Dread (The Kifu's March): aka The Reaping.**

- The Kifu's arrival, destruction of ancient civilizations, and the final battle with Hutari.

1. **Age of Rebirth: (The Third Age)**

- The world is recovering from the devastation of the Endwar, with new kingdoms rising and Hutari wandering the land in the background.

The Era of the Amani (500 R.B. to Present)

- Amani's birth **500 R.B.**

- Amani's taken to Hogarth **518 R.B.**

- Amani made ward to the Sandking King **519 R.B.**

Zaratu Descriptions for Various Shades of Skin Color

1. White Complexion – *Ndalu (Silver-Skinned)*
- **Zaratu Word:** *Ndalu*

- **Literal Translation:** "Silver-skinned"

- **Description:** This term refers to those with pale or white complexions, likened to the reflective and pure sheen of silver. In Zaratu culture, *Ndalu* represents clarity and the cold brilliance of the moon.

- **Example:** *Sura yake ilikuwa ya Ndalu, nyororo kama jua likimulika milima ya mbali.*("His face was of silver, smooth like the sun shining upon distant mount ains.")

2. Black Complexion – *Nyati (Onyx-Skinned)*
- **Zaratu Word:** *Nyati*

- **Literal Translation:** "Onyx-skinned"

- **Description:** Those with deep black complexions are honored as *Nyati*, reflecting the powerful and mysterious onyx stone. Onyx is valued for its strength and deep, unwavering presence.

- **Example:** *Ngozi ya mlinzi ilikuwa ya Nyati, nyeusi na yenye kung'aa kama usiku wa giza tupu.*("The guard's skin was of onyx, black and gleaming like the deepest night.")

3. Brown Complexion – *Shaba (Bronze-Skinned)*
- **Zaratu Word:** *Shaba*

- **Literal Translation:** "Bronze-skinned"

- **Description:** This term describes those with brown skin, akin to the warm, rich hue of bronze. *Shaba* is seen as representing the earth, warmth, and the endurance of metalwork.

- **Example:** *Mfalme alisimama mbele yao, ngozi yake ya Shaba iking'ara kama jua la jioni.*("The king stood before them, his bronze skin shining like the evening sun.")

4. Light Brown Complexion – *Tumbaga (Copper-Skinned)*
- **Zaratu Word:** *Tumbaga*

- **Literal Translation:** "Copper-skinned"

- **Description:** For those with a lighter brown complexion, *Tumbaga* compares their skin to the bright reddish gleam of copper. In Zaratu culture, copper symbolizes vitality, malleability, and beauty.

- **Example:** *Alikuwa Tumbaga, uso wake uking'ara kama nyota za usiku wa majira ya kiangazi.*("She was copper-skinned, her face glowing like stars on a summer night.")

5. Dark Brown Complexion – *Dhahabu Nyeusi (Black Gold-Skinned)*

- **Zaratu Word:** *Dhahabu Nyeusi*

- **Literal Translation:** "Black Gold-skinned"

- **Description:** For those with a deep, dark brown complexion, *Dhahabu Nyeusi* evokes the rare and prized nature of black gold. This term conveys a sense of wealth, prestige, and the fusion of power and elegance.

- **Example:** *Ngozi ya askari ilikuwa ya Dhahabu Nyeusi, yenye nguvu na ya kung'aa kama mchanganyiko wa usiku na mchanga wa jangwa.*("The soldier's skin was of black gold, strong and shining like a mix of night and desert sand.")

6. Yellowish/Olive Complexion – *Madini (Gold-Skinned)*

- **Zaratu Word:** *Madini*

- **Literal Translation:** "Gold-skinned"

- **Description:** For individuals with a yellowish or olive skin tone, *Madini* compares them to the radiant and valuable qualities of gold. Gold is seen as a symbol of prosperity, balance, and harmony in Zaratu culture.

- **Example:** *Ngozi yake ya Madini ilikuwa kama jua, yenye mng'ao wa utulivu na baraka.*("Her gold skin was like the sun, with a calm and blessed radiance.")

7. Pale Complexion with Reddish Undertones – *Fahari (Rose Gold-Skinned)*

- **Zaratu Word:** *Fahari*

- **Literal Translation:** "Rose gold-skinned"

- **Description:** Those with pale complexions tinged with a reddish or rosy hue are described as *Fahari*, the prized and beautiful rose gold. It conveys elegance and a soft inner strength.

- **Example:** *Uso wake wa Fahari ulikuwa kama mapambazuko, nyororo na wenye uzuri wa utulivu.*("Her rose gold skin was like the dawn, soft and serene in its beauty.")

8. Red or Reddish-Brown Complexion – *Shamsi (Red Iron-Skinned)*

- **Zaratu Word:** *Shamsi*

- **Literal Translation:** "Red iron-skinned"

- **Description:** For those with a reddish-brown complexion, *Shamsi* reflects the vibrant hue of iron heated in the forge, representing strength, resilience, and fiery determination.

- **Example:** *Ngozi yake ya Shamsi ilikuwa yenye nguvu, kama moto mkali wa chuma kinapofyonzwa kutoka tanurini.*("His red iron skin was strong, like the fierce fire of iron drawn from the forge.")

Linguistic and Cultural Context

In the *Zaratu* language and culture, metal is highly revered for its qualities of durability, beauty, and transformative power—just as each skin tone is seen as a reflection of an individual's inner strength, resilience, and spirit. The association with metals is not merely about color but the virtues these metals represent within Zaratu society. These descriptors are often used in a poetic or respectful way, recognizing both the physical and the metaphysical traits of individuals.

This system of classification serves as a source of pride and identity, reinforcing the cultural significance of the diverse people within this world. Just as metals have unique properties but all contribute to creating tools, weapons, and adornments, so too do individuals of various skin tones contribute to the strength and unity of their society.

Thank You

T hank you for sharing the first book of this new fantasy series with me. More books are coming and I hope you will continue to follow my journey. If you loved the book and would like to be informed of other books, please make sure you sign up for my mailing list you can be notified of new releases, giveaways, and pre-release specials at donovanmneal.com

Feel free to leave a review! Your help in spreading the word is appreciated and reviews make an enormous difference in helping new readers find the series.

God bless you and I hope to see you within the pages of the next book!

Remember...there will be more stories so sign up for the mailing list!

About the Author

D onovan M. Neal is the Amazon best-selling independently published author of the Third Heaven Series: a speculative Christian fantasy four-book series that explores the captivating story of the fall of Lucifer. The book takes readers on an epic journey through the celestial realms, offering a unique perspective on the events surrounding Lucifer's rebellion and his descent into darkness.

In this imaginative tale, Donovan weaves together elements of Christian theology, angelic mythology, and fantastical world-building. The story delves into the cosmic conflict between good and evil, painting a vivid picture of the spiritual warfare that unfolded in the heavens.

Donovan has published fifteen books. His books have reached thirteen countries including India, Japan, the Philippines, Mexico, Brazil, and across Europe, Canada, and the U.S.. He has sold over thirty thousand units of his books and generated over a quarter million in gross sales part-time and without an agent. Donovan has produced fiction; non-fiction and most recently published a graphic novel. His genre of preference is fantasy and he has been named among such notable authors as Frank Perretti, Brian Godawa, and the late Dr. Michael S. Heis er.

When he's not writing or working, Donovan can be found gaming or enjoying various forms of media. He holds an undergraduate degree from the University of Michigan (Ann Arbor) and a graduate degree in Non-profit Management from Walden University. Prior to his current career, Donovan served in ordained ministry from 1993-2011 and has extensive experience teaching the Bible.

His favorite movie is The Lord of the Rings Trilogy. He also enjoys gaming and can be found on the PlayStation 5 deep in Destiny 2, He's owned most gaming systems all the way back from Atari and Pong! and has made several friends from his beloved days on World of Warcraft. A lover of such classics as chess and backgammon he loves most games and the strategy behind them.

When he is not imagining comic conflicts between good and evil he is helping to secure employment for housing insecure women as the Executive Director of a non-profit in the city of

Detroit and serves in the prayer and discipleship ministry of his local church.

www.ingramcontent.com/pod-product-compliance
Lightning Source LLC
Chambersburg PA
CBHW031417240626
47154CB00001B/73